Praise for Mark

'*The Pirate Devlin* is top quality hist[...] knows his period inside-out and his stylish prose and devilish plot fold it into a gripping read. This is the start of something big.'

Harry Sidebottom, author of *Warrior of Rome*

'A superbly imagined, vividly written debut. Devlin is set to become the Sharpe of the high seas.'

Saul David, author of *Zulu Hart*

'Keating's latest novel continues his insight into the pirate life with technical seafaring detail, bloody sea battles, treasure hunts and exotic settings. High adventure does not get much better than this.'

Sunday Canberra Times

'Devlin is an anti-hero to savour . . . fearless and flawed, ruthless and roguish but with all the endearing honour that traditionally flourishes among fictional thieves.'

Lancashire Evening Post

'A swashbuckling 18th Century adventure . . . sure to delight both fans of Sharpe and Hornblower.'

Peterborough Evening Telegraph

Mark Keating was born in North London and has spent most of his life working in the South East selling everything from comic books to champagne. He now lives and works in Windsor, Berkshire, with his partner and son.

HUNT
FOR
WHITE
GOLD

MARK KEATING

HODDER

First published in Great Britain in 2010 by Hodder & Stoughton
An Hachette UK company

First published in paperback in 2011

1

A CIP catalogue record for this title is available from the British Library

ISBN 978 0 340 99271 5

Typeset in Simoncini Garamond by Ellipsis Digital Limited, Glasgow

Printed and bound by Clays Ltd, St Ives plc

Hodder & Stoughton policy is to use papers that are natural, renewable
and recyclable products and made from wood grown in sustainable forests.
The logging and manufacturing processes are expected to conform to
the environmental regulations of the country of origin.

Hodder & Stoughton Ltd
338 Euston Road
London nw1 3bh

www.hodder.co.uk

For my sons

Life is neither good nor evil,
but only a place for good and evil.

Marcus Aurelius

Prologue

Charles Town, South Carolina, September 1717

*T*he young black boy did not cook for his master although he was the only servant in the house. The desire for privacy outweighed his need for slaves to attend him, so the boy's trusted daily task was to fetch his master's meals from a different inn or coach-house each day – his master had stressed that point – and from what he had gleant of his master's work in the past year this habit was not just an eccentric quirk.

It was always simple suppers: smoked fish and potatoes, a steak or loin of pork, but his master would prepare his own breakfasts, a honey or nettle porridge, depending on his mood; and he would graze on hard-boiled eggs throughout the day to sustain him. The boy would watch his master examine the eggs with a jeweller's loupe, searching for pinpricks before coddling them in the water, but never queried his odd compulsions. Despite his solitary position of power within the household he was still his master's possession. Silence was his prime attribute.

The lamps had started to be lit along the walls of the street and a curfew against unescorted slaves was one of the colony's strictest edicts. The boy began to hurry with his silver charger of Scotch Bonnet peppered steak. He crossed the street, his eyes on the dish warming his arms through his scarlet coat, the concentration on his balance too intense to see the black velvet fist as it almost plucked him off his feet.

He gasped. The strong hand held him tightly and the boy stared wide-eyed into the face of the man who had seized him. He was fifteen but not tall for his age and had to look upwards into the pale face and its elegant beard shaved to a knife-edge.

The piped purple doublet, black cloak and long blue-black hair gave the man an almost medieval appearance, like a figure from a stained-glass window. Despite the violent arrest his voice was sable soft, his eyes darting, alert for witnesses.

'Take me to Ignatius.' There was something foreign in the voice. 'I will not harm you, boy,' he promised, but the golden basket hilt at his side suggested other possibilities.

'My master has no visitors,' the boy said bravely, daring the malice in the tall man's eyes.

The gloved fist shook him roughly. 'He will see me!' He pushed the boy forward along the street, the right hand crossing his body to rest on the pommel of the sword. The boy obeyed.

The man in the suit of black sat at his desk of Office in the rented home in Charles Town. It was a fine building, as fine as that of Lt Col Rhett, champion of Charles Town, but indrawn, without the friendliness and swagger that the presence of the soldier and famed Indian fighter seemed to bestow on his own residence.

The town knew nothing about the stranger in black who had settled among them. He had rented the house from Governor Johnson himself over a year ago but still did not stroll the summer streets or attend any of the churches, French or English, that the town had already grown famous for.

Lamps flickered in the windows of the stranger's house all through the night and the children of Charles Town had already begun to whisper that the house was haunted.

His oak desk was buried under a heap of papers and ledgers, the dark-suited man further darkened by their shadow. His lithe frame was hunched over paper and pen and he scribbled like a frustrated widow embroidering her past. The room too was dark, its corners hidden from the single candle that burned low on his desk. He did not notice that the time to eat had arrived, and his silver Dassier watch, open, ticked unheeded. It was only the knock upon the study's door that made him drop his pen and slide open the drawer that held the pistol.

The knock was not the prescribed three-tone rap but rather a single tap against the door. His boy was not alone. The man in black calmly pulled the hammer to half-cock and let the pistol lie in the open drawer. He glanced at his watch. Seven o'clock and his supper due. That could wait for now.

'Enter,' he called, his right hand beneath the desk.

The door swung open and the servant was pushed inward, scrabbling with his tray. The man in the purple doublet bowed his way into the room which was briefly lit by the light from the passage. The radiance behind the intruder framed him dramatically. It made him the perfect target.

'I have come, Ignatius,' said the man and swept his cloak behind him. 'Please forgive my coarse introduction. I wished my announcement into your town to be as discreet as possible. I hope I have not offended.'

Ignatius closed the drawer. 'Not at all. I value discretion above all the other virtues.'

His visitor bowed again and indicated the terrified servant. 'Please, do not allow me to interrupt your meal.'

Ignatius dismissed the boy who bowed meekly, grateful to close the door behind him and careful not to upset his tray. The room sank into darkness once more.

'It is of no matter. It is more important that you are here at last, Governor Mendes.'

The visitor approached, curiosity on his face, and took the proffered seat. Ignatius had never seen Mendes to know his face and the expression of curiosity was not lost on him.

'I know everyone I need to know, Governor. But I pay special attention to those whose letters intrigue me most.'

'Intrigue?' The word amused Valentim Mendes. 'A fine choice of phrase indeed.' He slapped some dust the long voyage from Sao Nicolau had ground into the expensive cloth of his doublet. His island home in the Portuguese Verdes was the seat of his governorship and the birthplace of his revenge. One night, several months past, had been enough to change his life. Enough to have him enlist a man on the other side of the world yet known throughout the courts of Europe – even if only by whispers behind princely hands.

A drink was offered and declined. Ignatius's world being too large for small talk, he picked up the letter penned by Valentim's own hand.

'Your correspondence informs me that you know where the letters of the priest lie? The arcanum I believed lost with the pirate ship they went down on. Letters I paid a young captain a considerable sum to bring to me from China. You should be congratulated that you could establish that which I could not. This is valuable information, and not just to me.'

Valentim's black eyes narrowed with a nobleman's hauteur. 'I am not interested in their *price*, Ignatius. Let baser men deal with the devil, if you wish the porcelain that is your concern. Since my . . . *disgrace* . . . I pursue higher ideals.'

'Disgrace? My understanding is that you lost a frigate to pirates. In April was it not? The same time I lost my letters with Bellamy's ship. An expensive loss for both of us as far as we have let pirates into our world, but hardly your own disgrace, Governor?'

Valentim leant forward, carefully enunciating his words for the ignorant. 'You Englishmen do not understand the meaning of disgrace.'

Ignatius nodded. 'Or perhaps we simply have too little experience of it, Governor.' He steepled his fingers beneath his chin. 'And what is my side of our bargain? What do you require of me that is beyond your worldly reach?'

Valentim looked to the ceiling, gathering himself for words he had long desired to speak. 'I do not have the measure of your trade or your fine thread of connections, Ignatius. Your abilities, so favoured, outshine my reach or power. especially in this "New World". And I am sure in the underbelly of this New World also.' Ignatius inclined his head at the near-compliment. 'It is therefore to you I come. My information and my purse are at your disposal. *If* you can find me the man whom I seek.' Valentim stabbed a gloved finger towards Ignatius. 'And it is *he* who must be sent to retrieve your precious letters. He who must be brought before me to pay. He whom I must *kill*. That is my price, Ignatius.'

Ignatius studied Valentim's face. The overarching intricacies of hate had ever been the manifesto of the noble. He had learnt that early. He had profited by little else. 'And who is this man you wish me to find, Governor? What is this "underbelly" you wish me to scratch?'

Valentim sprang to his feet and stepped around his chair. Ignatius heard Valentim's left gloved hand strike an odd chiming sound against the back of the chair as he did so. His eyes followed it as Valentim began to pace the room. Something unwholesome lurked in its size and limpness.

'Do not mark me as a petty man, Ignatius! I seek personal redress against one who has robbed me of more than coin!'

'I apologise, Governor. My manners sometimes elude me when I am so long removed from company. Inform me of this villain you wish me to locate and bring to you. Who is it that you seek?'

Valentim spun back to the desk, his refined English reverting in his passion to that of the struggling foreigner. 'He is a *pirate*! A filthy, stinking, *pirate* dog! His name is Devlin. As the *pirate* Patrick Devlin he is known. You have heard of him, no?'

Ignatius straightened his white silk cravat. Cleared his throat against Valentim's vehemence.

'I will do, I'm sure.' He picked up a stylus. Pulled some vellum towards him. Valentim continued, seething, willing his hate into Ignatius's pen.

'He stole my *ship*! Killed my *friend*! My *men*! You write this!' His left hand struck the oak desk with each outburst, and Ignatius's eyes watched its unnatural movement at every emphasis.

Valentim tore the glove from his hand. 'And with *this* he has affronted me even more so!'

The glove fell to the floor. Valentim held out the cold porcelain mould of a hand that protruded from his sleeve, its elegance mutilated by the rough leather straps and nails that clamped it to his arm. He rolled up his cuff to show the white scars like spilled wax that crawled up his forearm.

'This he has done to me! For this you write his name, Ignatius! For this you bring him to me! And for this you may have your letters!'

Ignatius scratched on the paper beneath his hand. Valentim watched the ink spell the name. 'It is written, Governor, it is done,' said Ignatius, his voice reassuringly cold. 'It will take time. One man takes up such little space in the world.' He placed the pen back on the desk.

Valentim studied his china hand with its fingers permanently set half open as if about to grasp at an object of desire. 'And when you find him, my friend, then I will tell you of where the letters lie. But not until that day.'

Ignatius smiled wearily. 'You Iberians. Every page of you a threat always. How very dull.' He pushed himself back in his chair and stretched. 'I am a man unaccustomed to paying attention to those who threaten me. Most unaccustomed.'

His left hand gestured to the darkest side of the room. 'Allow me to introduce to you my adjutant, Governor.'

Valentim turned his head. He saw the wall itself move. A shape formed in the gloom, too tall and wide to be human. It stepped into the circle of light and the study shrank as Valentim looked up into the wide-set dead eyes above the creature's massive broken nose that made of its breathing a low growl. Its muscles pulsed and rippled beneath a thin shirt like a straining horse, as if the beast would explode if Valentim looked at it for too long.

'This is Mister Hib Gow, Governor.' Ignatius spoke quietly beneath the breathing. 'Formally an executioner. Now my assurer.'

Valentim's hand felt for his sword's golden pommel while his eyes remained fixed on the giant. His voice sounded almost numb. '*Assurer?*'

'He will assure me that the man you seek will be found. And he also assures me that I do not have to listen to idle threats from those who wish to be my partners.'

Valentim resumed his graceful demeanour, his hand clear

of his weapon. 'I understand. I intended no insult, Ignatius. Only a bargain. For which, remember, I promise to fund whatever price you demand. That funding, naturally, would no longer occur should anything . . .' he shrugged away the rest of his words.

'Naturally,' Ignatius concurred and pointed Hib Gow back to his corner. 'As long as we understand each other, Governor,' he picked up his pen again, 'we shall begin.'

Chapter One

*I*t was said that the secret was in the clay. It had to be.
Either that or it was something arcane, magical, like the
mystery of silk centuries before. Yet that mystery had turned
out to be something mundane, something natural. Stolen silk-
worm eggs smuggled out by two priests in their hollow canes
had brought it to the world.

The Chinese ware would turn out to be the same. It had
to be. And if one man could make it, as with the silk, as with
the miracle of gunpowder even before that, so another man
could steal it.

La Société de Jésus had embedded itself comfortably within
Chinese society under the Qing. Emperor Kangxi in his wisdom
had welcomed the trade vessels of the West with open arms.
In a few short years Chinese goods had become the elite
fashion throughout Europe and, almost in exchange, the Jesuits
insinuated themselves as premiere ambassadors for the Western
world.

A decade hence and they had become trusted astronomers
and mathematicians within the Qing court, allowed to trans-
late even sacred Confucian texts and to present in Europe
that comparatively naïve faith as a credible religion, despite
the Jesuits' initial abhorrence of the Chinese worship of ances-
tors and evidently idolatrous ways.

One of these Jesuits, adorned in Chinese robes, a custom

his fellow priests had adapted to over the years, bowed his way into the heartland of Kangxi porcelain, Jingdezhen, and thus became the first European to witness in action the last great Chinese mystery: the production and art of the *true* hard-paste porcelain, the exquisite tableware that had since become the 'White Gold' of Europe.

And he noted it all.

The nations of Europe – rich Europe, peaceful Europe – had in the blink of history's eye become infatuated with the luxuries offered by the New World.

Chocolate, once the heavenly delight only of Royal Spain, now poured, albeit still expensively, alongside coffee and tea in the new trade of gentlemen's clubs springing up all over London.

Whether a Tory or a Whig, depending on how far one walked up St James there would be a chocolate shop where, it was noted, '*the disaffected met, and spread scandalous reports concerning the conduct of His Majesty and his Ministers,*' or conspired to wheedle some advantage from the king's extended absence from the country.

And, once all of Europe had developed its taste for the hot beverages of the New World, the demand for cool elegant 'chinaware' spread from the drawing rooms of royalty along the cobbled streets of Europe's cities to the coffee and chocolate houses.

In 1710, through science, effort and luck, the Margravate of Meissen in Germany began to produce its own miracle hard-paste porcelain. Although inferior to the Chinese, the clamour for it rang around the world like the porcelain bells of its Frauenkirche, the chime of Saxony's cups and serving pots mocking the French and English attempts to mimic the cool chinaware that had captivated the world.

Hot beverages had become the mark of civilisation. Chocolate prolonged life and raised virility; coffee stimulated the brain and heart and was exotic beyond diamonds as if it had come from another universe. These new commodities were traded far and above the old-hat of hops and cloth, and so fortunes were made and companies born that would outlast empires.

But these glorious luxuries all suffered from the same drawback. To savour and appreciate them fully they must be hot – too hot to be served in silver or pewter or gold. The table-services of kings were now simply an embarrassment to their guests and no matter how determined English and French potters became, the chinaware could be but poorly imitated.

One English potter affirmed that the clay that held the secret to the coolness of porcelain could be obtained in the Americas for he had discovered native wares that possessed the same properties. The South Seas Company declined his offer to invest in further explorations.

In 1712, Father d'Entrecolles wrote his first letter to Father Orry in Paris describing the full process, the firing and mixing of both soft-paste and hard-paste Chinese porcelain. The letter failed to make it out of China, but rumours abounded that the secret had been broached. The first letter soon became more valuable than the product whose manufacture it described. Father d'Entrecolles disappeared back into his missionary order and did not write again to his ministry for eight years. Any country or individual that could rediscover the first letter of Father d'Entrecolles would hold the secret of the first great industrialised product of the eighteenth century.

*

Captain William Guinneys successfully purchased the first letter of Father d'Entrecolles from Wu Qua of the Foreign Trade Hongs for sale to a man, known only as Ignatius, in the American colonies. The transaction completed, Guinneys began an ocean voyage as wide as his bumptious smirk.

Whilst Guinneys' creditors in London mopped their brows in relief, the general hunt for the letter forced Ignatius to spirit it away to a secret location for safekeeping. He entrusted pirates with this task, believing they must surely have no interest in the ways of men beyond the lining of their purses

He charged a pirate captain, one Black Sam Bellamy named for his flowing mane of black hair, to carry the letters north, sealed in a greying, bronze Chinese cannon wisely chosen by Guinneys as fitting concealment.

But the device was not enough to hide the letters from the vengeful Chinese gods.

A storm off the Cape Cod coast – a maelstrom from nowhere – drowned Bellamy and sank his ship, the *Whydah Galley*. It was April 1717 and the letters were lost again, the Gods satisfied. For a time.

William Guinneys, his task completed, his pockets sufficiently full to banish worry about his peacetime deduct or the black-coated and black-hearted men in Leadenhall Street ruling the waves with their vellum and ink, continued his waltz back and forth from the Chinese and Indian factories and awaited war to speed him from the doldrums of the Company ledgers.

Two years later, his first and last experience of action was ended with cutlass and powder. Not by Spaniards or Frenchmen, as his heart would have wished, but by a jumped-up boot-wipe turned pirate captain. The pirate Devlin was his executioner.

Guinneys told no-one of the letter. There was no need; the letter spoke for itself.

But first it had to become known again.

Chapter Two

✗

Madagascar, June 1718

One year since the letters disappeared.
One year since Patrick Devlin became a pirate.

*I*t was the onset of a storm that had brought Albany
Holmes and George Lee ashore on Madagascar to escape
the dark skies and the rising whitecaps, and to dry their
Parisian shoes in the winding streets of the port of St Augustine. Their captain had decided that a day or two in safe
soundings would diminish any risk of a squall's edge becoming a wallowing grave in wider waters. And as long as one kept
to the towns the island's notorious reputation for pirates
should remain only that.

They had been told that the land was ten times the size of
their great United Kingdom and that although it boasted
kingdoms and princes you could hardly count, there was barely
enough tin to feed the coffee-coloured children that swarmed
around the docks and shores.

The two had travelled beyond the normal perimeters of
the Grand Tour that occupied many unmarried gentlemen of
a certain status, and were now stretching their horizons to
sample the almond eyes and jet-black hair that encapsulated
all the promise of the Orient Sea.

They had ignored the pleas and warnings of their captain to not stray from the Dutch and French taverns and brothels that littered the bay of St Augustine. Instead they climbed the shingle roads that meandered into the hills until they became but dust tracks and the civilised sounds of cart and hoof were replaced by the bad-tempered clucking of the brooding hens around their feet and the dull bleating of the goat by the roadside.

They walked through the homesteads and inhaled the smell of spit-roasting boar on wood fires outside the shacks. Cautious white eyes followed the path of the two colourful peacocks strutting through their midst.

Albany and George found the hot smoky township and the drawn, dark people unsettling and felt the silent stares that lay cold upon their backs. They had perhaps trod too far inland.

It came as a relief to hear the sound of English voices singing from within the stone-built tavern that dominated the hill-side. Their pace increased as the heady aroma of tobacco and ale-soaked sawdust pulled them over the threshold.

They swung into the heat of the room, the sudden silence wafting over them as strongly as the pipe smoke, while heads swivelled sullenly to take them in.

The patrons judged them gravely, then turned back to their games and blackjack mugs, the murmur and songs slowly brewing up again: just a couple of silks. Not worth the first look let alone a second.

'Perhaps we should return to the port, Albany,' George whispered. 'I'm not so convinced this is a wise venture.'

Albany Holmes had never backed out of a room in his life. 'Come, George. This is the real tour is it not? I'll wager some of these damned souls know the finest quim this island has to offer, and do you not want to scribe something in that tome of yours?' He cocked an eyebrow at a bearded sot heaving into his own mug. 'George, I thirst.'

They strode to the bar across the sawdust floor, Albany's ebony cane tapping his way like a blind man's, and elbowed a space.

'Keep!' Albany piped to the leather-aproned bear behind the nailed decking that made up the bar. 'A noggin of rum and a carafe for my friend and I.' He slapped down a Dutch dollar and pushed it to the bear's side. 'I will hold for pewter mugs rather than this leather you favour for your fellows, if it is not too bold, sir.'

The bear rolled himself in front of them, his half-lidded eyes never straying from the silver. He slapped down the pewter goblets with the green bottle of wine and wearily began to pour from a barrel atop the bar a spurt of brown treacle into wooden cups. He slammed them down and scraped the dollar away in the same movement.

'I am indebted, sir.' Albany winced a smile and swept the wine into the goblets, pushing one into George's nervous hand. He turned to face the room, taking in all the dirty unshaven faces and broad backs at the tables engrossed in their games and drink. No women, Albany sighed. No matter. A day or two yet. 'Come, George, let us find a seat.'

'I fear we may be wanting on that matter, Albany,' George noted, sipping his wine with distaste. 'The place is full with bodies.'

'Nonsense,' Albany almost shouted, his raised voice sucking a glance from a scarred face along the bar. 'There is a fellow sleeping over there,' he lifted his cane to point to a cushioned bench beside the door where a small-paned yellow window gave pitiful light into the den. 'He will not mind to move up a notch to let two Englishmen sit.'

George followed the cane to the bench and table.

Sure enough some vagrant had secured himself a rather resplendent portion of the tavern. He lay in shirt and waist-coat only, a black three-cornered hat pulled over his sleeping brow, brown leather boots resting, crossed, upon the rough tabletop.

'He looks awful peaceful, Albany,' George attested. 'Perhaps we should let him be.'

Albany had already begun to move, carrying the carafe, leaving George to fumble with the mugs and goblets.

Albany slammed down the green bottle, spilling a spittle's worth, hoping to startle the man from his drunken slumber, but the hat remained drawn down, the boots planted.

He took the goblets and mugs from George and crashed them down likewise at several points on the tabletop to re-affirm his intentions, but thought it wise not to disturb the crock bottle that stood close to the occupant's legs.

Albany took in the man. He was tall, grimy with work or time but dressed in strong Dutch linen with a black Damask waistcoat worth a year's wages to a common man. His boots however were older than Albany. They were perhaps Spanish or French judging by the fine cut and quality of stitch that still left English bootmakers slapping their heads, but the leather was limp and cracked. Stolen most probably, Albany surmised.

He lifted his black cane and rapped upon the man's ankles. '*Sir*!' he voiced. 'Kindly afford some space for two gentlemen who wish to sit for a while, if you would be so inclined!'

Silence. The hat never stirred. Albany pursed his lips, exchanged a glance with George and began again.

'You there,' he prodded with the cane's silver tip. 'You will make way for two gentlemen who wish to be seated. I do not feel it a tremendous inconvenience to accommodate two others at this sitting! Move now!'

George swallowed his cup of rum, his eyes roving around the room, the free hand behind his back as far away from his pistol and sword as he could demonstrate it to be.

The black hat stirred slightly. 'I am tired, sir.' A soft Irish accent drifted out from beneath the brim. 'Leave me be.'

Albany looked again at the length of the man. He could see no pistol. No hilt. His eyes travelled to the door where a hook held a black twill coat and crossbelt with hanging sword.

'I would be of a mind to advise you, sir,' Albany's hand drew out, with the faintest scrape, the etched portion of the London and Birmingham pride of his sword-cane, 'that it would be unwise for an unarmed man to question the actions of one such as I.'

Albany tasted the salt sweat from his upper lip. This is why he had travelled. This was London and all of Paris in a cup. His sword-cane, partially committed, the fervent sting of battle in the turgid air. A drunken, unarmed vagabond defying him.

How easy to cut him slightly, to just nick him and watch the fellow skulk away with all eyes on him, warily shrinking from Albany's steely glare.

The vagrant dragged his feet from the table, only to fill the bench more fully with his languid form, his eyes never rising from under the shadow of his hat. The voice was unaltered from the drowsy tones of his first utterance.

'I am of a mind to believe that of late I do not need to be armed so often.' He pulled his hat tighter down as a hundred clicks and rattles of flintlocks and scabbards filled the air behind the two gentlemen. 'I finds I sleep better that way.'

'Albany, old boy?' George nervously tapped the silk shoulder of his tall companion, who had already turned his face to the sound. He stared, rigid, hand upon cane, at a room full of black pistols answering his gaze. The faces of the men behind the weapons appeared minuscule compared to the gaping black barrels aimed at every inch of his body.

Albany tightened his grip on his half-drawn swordstick, then discreetly and silently pushed home the glinting steel.

'Of no offence, gentlemen.' He painfully executed a bow. 'We will stand. Not wishing to deprive a working man of his rest.'

'You should say goodbye to the sun, gents,' sighed the sleepy fellow who now tipped up his hat and swung his feet to the floor. 'You have not done well here.'

He sat up straight. Albany and George looked into his tanned face and mess of black hair straggling out beneath his cocked tricorne.

Albany was surprised at the cold cynical stare, more gentlemanly and solemn than he had supposed. The soft voice continued.

'What brings such colourful stripes to the realms of the Malagasay? Only pirates and fools stop along these shores. Or lost souls. And only ghosts come into the hills. I myself have strayed too far. Captain Avery's inbred fools haunt these paths.' He swallowed from his crock bottle and counted with one eye the guns of his brethren still hovering in the gloom.

He slammed down the bottle and waved a gentle hand for all to lower their pistols. A moment later, the two stranded coxcombs saw only backs as the patrons returned to their murmurs and bottle mouths.

Albany found his voice again.

'We are mired here, sir. To ride out a storm soon to be.' Then gallantly he broached, 'And who might I be addressing, if I may address you, sir?'

'I am the one who has kept you alive, sir. That is all.'

'In that case, prudently observed,' Albany continued. 'I am Albany Holmes, and this is George Lee. Gentlemen abroad and devoid of experience.' He affected a grin. 'If you may gather my meaning, sir.' Albany hoped still to fish from the fellow some whereabouts of iniquity despite the ill opening of their conversation.

The pirate enjoyed the exchange. A sloping rakish grin lightened his face, but only for a moment.

'Then in spirit I return the address,' he touched his hat. 'I am Patrick Devlin. Captain Devlin. Of the frigate *Shadow*.' His gaze passed between the two, enjoying the recognition of his name and the nature of their fate dawning on their pinched faces.

Albany, as pale as his shirt, whispered the name into the air like escaping steam, 'The *pirate* Devlin?' His hands winged to the sides of his coat, away from his weapons. 'Well, I'll be damned!' A rough cackling broke out amongst the patrons. Devlin bowed slightly.

'You may well be.' The lightened look had gone.

Albany stiffened and reached for his bottle. 'May I?' he asked.

Devlin opened his palm towards the bottle and sat back. George caught his eye and swiftly lowered his gaze to his shoe buckles, feeling the weight of his pistol and sword dragging his eyes lower.

Albany poured, the sound of the gulping carafe settling his nerve. He swigged a goblet full and wiped the red line, mixed with beads of perspiration, from his lips.

The wine encouraged him. Here he was: having sailed over oceans of colour, and witnessed the crossing of tides that before his eyes marked out boundaries of nations along the hull of the ship they patronised. Albany had breathed in the scent of olive and ebony limbs draped around his neck. He had lapped at their feminine sweat and marvelled at the whiteness of their teeth and the depth of their almond scented tresses. But now he felt a beat within him he had never known.

'I am honoured, sir,' he spoke at last. 'Your fame has become great back in England. I would never have thought that I would come so far as to be standing before you yourself.' The subtle hint for a stool was ignored.

Devlin cocked his chin, 'How so my fame, Albany?' He riffled through his waistcoat for his pipe, the sudden movement of his hands causing George to shuffle uncomfortably.

'Why, Captain,' Albany bowed. 'You are well known as a Jacobite terror this past year! Month after month your pamphlets are posted upon every guildhall in the land!' He swigged his wine again. 'The tale of the island and the gold is sold wherever a noggin can be purchased! You are an infamous soul, sir, to be sure and found!'

'Aye,' Devlin said quietly. 'The island and the gold.'

Had his mould been cast already, shaped and poured to fit forever? Better than the servant he was before, to be sure, but to have these fops – who would happily sit in the stands at Tyburn and watch him swing – tip glasses to him seemed too strange.

If Devlin had never fled London for St Malo, learning Breton French from coarse fishermen and therefore understanding the words of a dying sailor of the Marine Royale telling of the gold and bequeathing him the map, he would be smoking lice out of Captain John Coxon's waistcoats even now.

Such a time ago, yet not much time at all. For some, one

year passes much as any other. For others a single year can roll by and yet a new dice is thrown and a new life begun.

Patrick Devlin. Butcher's boy. Servant. Captain. Pirate.

'And it is a pleasing moment to meet you, sir,' George proffered. 'And we have no need of any reward to announce your presence by and by, sir.'

Devlin's face shone. 'I have a reward do I? A wanted man?'

A voice came howling from the crowd, 'Reckon you be right popular, Cap'n!'

Devlin struck a light from striker and flint; let an age pass as he drew his pipe into life. A lowered head showed only the crown of his hat to the uneasy gentlemen before him. Eventually his face upturned, hidden in blue smoke, and he blew a wraith of it into the waistcoats of the two men.

'Tell me more about this ship you came in on, Albany,' he squinted and grinned through the haze, his eyes smarting from his own smoke. 'What be its name?'

Chapter Three

✗

*D*andon's eyes blinked open painfully. He closed them
again as sunlight stabbed into his skull then resigned
himself to his awakened state and rolled himself upwards, his
boots ringing against empty bottles as they gingerly settled to
the floor.

His hands cradled his head. He rubbed his temples and
raised his eyes to the shafts of dusty light fingering their way
through the slatted walls of the den.

He breathed deeply, feeling a rustling in his lungs from
poor tobacco, a wretchedness about him that had been well
paid for.

How many days did he have left now? How many more
times would his withering body drag him awake to regret the
sinking of another tavern? He looked absently at the back of
his hand. Barely thirty and counting brown spots like domino
pips.

Sure enough he had been a drunk of some measure upon
Providence Island, vaguely performing medical favours to the
whores and pirates in exchange for a straw bed and his own
leather mug rarely empty, but now? With these men? Another
class of drinking ensued.

This past year with the pirate Devlin, a man he considered
his friend, had been dangerous and rewarding. Dandon now
had golden coin where before only bits of silver occasionally

dusted his pockets. They had stolen a gold treasure, although from their own viewpoint they had certainly earned it, and the apothecary's assistant from colonial Bath Town had never looked back.

At times, after a couple of bottles and in the glow of a guttering early morning candle, he would spout that he would return to his original schemes now that he had coin aplenty. He would set up a saltern in the Bahama islands, a string of them, and manufacture his own salt pills and healing potions and join the multitude of quacks growing fat on the desperate gout-laden rich who refused to believe it was their own greed that perpetuated their ill-health.

He would slap the table and bid them all farewell on the morrow. And then he would awake, as now, and not remember a word he had said.

Now he hazily recalled joining the *Shadow's* giant quarter-master Peter Sam and Hugh Harris, another pirate rogue who had become a friend, in a tour last night of some of the more rancorous and mysterious holes of the town. The windowless pits where the opiates wisped and where the women – and the men that looked like women – snaked and writhed and ran your coin through their fingers like water.

Peter Sam had disappeared off to the darkest alleys leaving Hugh and Dandon to avail themselves of the long pipes and clay-like powders that made you feel born anew, light of conscience, beloved and eternally free. Until the next day.

Dandon looked up and saw that part of the wall of the den was Hugh himself, sitting angled against it and staring straight at him, an evil grin spread across his jowls.

Last night, or the night before, or the week before, Dandon's cot had been a duck down delight of comfort. He looked at the straw and burlap mattress with a terrible disdain and brushed his shirt free of invisible vermin. He coughed, swallowed something foul.

Hugh responded to the cough with a crack of his throat. 'How's the morning to you, Dandon there?' He raised a brandy bottle to pass along but Dandon waved back a sorrowful hand.

'Nay, old boy,' he heaved. 'I need an egg and some bread if I can find some.' He looked about the smoky room. 'Where are we, Hugh? Apart from hell.'

Hugh laughed coldly. 'No matter, Dandon. We be safe as long as we have tin. What a day or two, eh mate?' He stretched himself and clasped the bottle to his lips.

'To my own mind, Mister Harris, I recall very little. I will take your familiarity with the events for truth therefore.'

He rubbed the mess of his narrow beard and reeled at the smell of his own hand. 'Where is Peter Sam? What became of him? I seem to recall his back drifting away to some other abode a time ago.'

'Aye,' Hugh hacked. 'He be wandering back along his own path soon enough. We'd best make our way back to the Cap'n.' He slapped his head to waken his senses. 'This time be done.'

Dandon stood and straightened his clothes, his eyes wandering to his yellow silk coat, golden waistcoat, weary plumed yellow hat and white necktie all slung down in a dank corner. He had, however, chosen to sleep in his buckled shoes, much to his regret.

'We best find him though, Hugh. The big man's weaknesses can be his undoing I have noticed.'

'That be true.' Hugh struggled up and lifted a note from the broken table that stood in the centre of the room. 'He left us a scribbling I reckon. I sees it last night but paid it no mind. Your eyes be better for reading, Dandon, mate.' He gave the paper across to Dandon and picked up his cross-belt and sword.

Dandon stretched the paper in his hands, sniffed and pulled his head back to focus on the rather official-looking handwriting before his aching eyes.

The first pass made little sense, so Dandon read it again more slowly. He found himself sitting again on the fragile cot. By the third reading his heart had begun to race, and his head was clearer.

He stood up, folded the paper with care and reached for his coat. 'We must grab ourselves coffee and get to Devlin with great haste and flight, friend Hugh. Some strange act is afoot.'

'What says it? Is it not from Peter?' Hugh's voice leapt like a boy's.

'It is *about* Peter, at least,' Dandon flapped his silk justacorps about his scrawny body. 'But it is not from our quartermaster.'

Feeling Dandon's anxiety fill the room, Hugh checked his pistols.

'Rather it is from some deluded soul who has taken it upon himself to free us from his company under pain of good Peter's death.'

'Eh?' Dandon's utterances were puzzling to Hugh at the best of times.

Dandon yanked the door and let in the dazzling late morning sunshine and crash of the sea.

'He has been "kidnapped" from us Hugh, a terrible term from my less eloquent cousins in the colonies. I may have a better phrase for it after a dose of hot brown when my head is better. Make haste man! I hunger but may not eat until this note be in our captain's hand!'

Hugh missed the last several words as Dandon was already striding ahead through the crowds that hung around the port. He observed Dandon's wake, calling for the yellow back to slow down, while he ducked back into the hut for his bottle.

Dandon had spied one of the Chinese shanties selling hot brews and bowls of rice along the winding paths. He veered away to stand before the bent old man in the red skullcap who bowed and cracked his face at the emergence of Dandon's purse. Although he was obviously busy, he took the time to ladle steaming black coffee into a small porcelain bowl for which Dandon passed a broken quarter of a reale into the soft small hand.

Dandon sidestepped to let another customer take his place and inhaled deeply the powerful vapours which cleared his passages almost instantly. He sipped carefully at the scalding liquid and suddenly craved his tobacco pouch.

Hugh stumbled up to his side, every corner of him bristling with weaponry, the brandy bottle peeping out of his coat like another gun. He waited while Dandon drank his coffee, his eyes darting back and forth, reading every passing face for conspiracy.

Dandon passed back the cup with a bow. The stick-like hand took it with a swipe and laid it next to a fresh pile rattling beside other towers of bowls, cups and ladles. The old man gave the bowls no thought. He had known them all his life, as his father had known them. Cold to the touch, translucent in the sun. They never chipped or ran with cracks even after a thousand uses. A portion of them had faint green paintwork that told their own stories, but most were plain, bone white.

The Chinaman grabbed another bowl and poured boiling green tea for a Dutch whaler who had lost his way. The whaler gave no thought to the cold cup in his shovel-like fist either, and Dandon and Hugh moved on.

They made their haphazard way up to the top of the town and to the inn on the hill, pausing for a breath to look back and down over the smoking wood-fires billowing from the ragged chimney pots like an avenue of tornadoes curling to the sea; then to the cobweb riggings of the ships huddling in the harbour, seemingly stringed together as one mass of rope and masts.

Beyond this in the sky above, a dark smudge was growing and swelling, whilst on the horizon a foreboding curtain of grey swept ever closer.

'Dandon!' A cry from the tavern steps swung them around. It was Sam Fletcher, the wretch from London, a gallows dancer of a deserter and *Shadow* pirate. 'Where have you been, mate? Come see the sport Devlin has a-going!'

Dandon pulled at Hugh, the note tight in his hands.

George and Albany's eyes lit up at the apparent sight of a fine fellow crossing the threshold, then dropped again at the tripping of the scarecrow that followed him.

Dandon cultivated the illusion of being a gentleman, but his once fine golden justacorps was now damp and worn, his yellow silk waistcoat frayed at the shoulders, its buttons loose and dangling. He had found himself of late new shoes, stockings and breeches, but had not found any store equal to replacing his favoured coat or limp, dandelion-hued, broad-brimmed hat.

Dandon only differed from his brethren in that he carried no weapon, unless absolutely necessary. Otherwise he joined them in every curse and vice of their clandestine existence. Besides, he had often found that going unarmed could open doors that would otherwise remained locked and barred.

Dandon took in the party seated at the long table dragged to the centre of the tavern. George and Albany faced him, their coats removed to the backs of their chairs, a line of cups in the centre of the table, six in all.

Their heads swayed with drunken concentration, the pirates crowded round them, crowing and jeering at each success and failure.

The game was simple: two teams, and each player had his own coin, as close to equal value in weight as could be estimated from the myriad of currencies that jangled through Madagascar. With dexterity and skill the players would bounce a coin upon the table to ring into a cup. On the cheer following a successful attempt they would drink from the cup, to the very dregs, and keep their coin to play again.

If the coin landed elsewhere or glanced off the cup, it was forfeit to the opposing side who added it to their account to play again. Devlin and Sam Morwell were unlucky this day to play against against the skilled eyes and better blood of the two gentlemen, who were winning hard-earned gold and silver from the two ruffians, and steadily adding to their pile.

With each victory the gentlemen proved their better birth and with every gulp and slap of their backs their confidence grew. They were beating this vile group at their own game, showing their worth and even drawing respectful cheers from the dark hearts that surrounded them.

Perhaps they would deign to toss a coin or two to some of the more pitiful eyes that stared at them, red-rimmed and deferential to their betters. Poor misguided wretches. Perhaps, for one of the more sorrowful ones, Albany could find a role aboard their ship. He himself might have need of a valet if a good clean man could be found.

The pirate Devlin was particularly bad at the game, he slapped the table with a curse as he gave up another reale to Albany, then excused himself and even tipped his hat when the man in the yellow coat bent to whisper in his ear.

George won again, amid a song to his luck, and he let the rum trickle over his face and down his neck and called with a bang of his empty cup for more and for the pirate opposite him to try again, damn him, for George would not be beaten, despite the swaying of the room.

Dandon spoke low, lest others cocked an ear to his message, 'I have been gone, Patrick, but now am found again. Yet I bring strange, possibly grave news that I do not understand but am sorry to impart, I fear.'

Devlin, too, sometimes grew impatient with Dandon's flowery phrases. 'Speak Dandon,' he snapped. 'You're pale with Turkish pipe no doubt.'

'I am a capricious *capote,* Captain, true,' he ushered Devlin to the door. 'But I know not who lies within this tavern that can be trusted.'

'Speak, I said. I'm working on these silks here and it's costing me a sum to get them under. I intend to add their ship to ours. Peacefully if possible.'

'Peter is gone. I have this paper here for you,' he said, and passed the vellum to Devlin. 'Tis not my fault, Captain. You know full well Peter's want to travel dark.'

Devlin pulled the paper taut. He read swiftly, growing paler with each word. The print was gracious, clearly dry by weeks for it had become a paler blue.

The paper was unsigned. Just a name, printed proud and tall, was embossed at the foot of the page.

'*Ignatius.*'

Then the address: *Charles Town*. South of the Carolinas. A trade colony of great fortune and civility, the fifth largest in America. A harbour town often plagued by pirates. Devlin's eyes fixed on the final portion of script:

'*I will know the hour this letter reaches your hand. Attend alone and without force. Announce at the House. There will be no harm brought if no member of your crew enters the streets of the town.*'

'When did you last see Peter Sam?'

'A day ago, Captain. Maybe two. You understand I was not counting his absence for fear of such a happening. Who after all could hope to drag away such a fellow as Peter?'

This was true, perhaps the most disturbing aspect. Peter Sam was a brute of a man. He laughed off bullets, broke cutlasses for toothpicks and took gunpowder with his eggs.

Devlin himself had seen him sling two men over the gunwale, like bags of straw, one in each hand. That had been aboard the *Noble*, Devlin's old frigate where he had lived as servant to Captain John Coxon. Over a year ago now and a world away. A lifetime away.

What manner of man or men could spirit away the mammoth in brown leather who had become Devlin's mainstay amongst the crew? The quartermaster that the men held their breath by and lowered their eyes at his passing. The old stander that had sailed with Seth Toombs, Black Bill and Will Magnes. The man who had sailed to The Island, the French island of the gold, and rescued them all. Came back for them all. Came back for his captain and defeated Coxon's frigate.

'It would take a fair plan, to be sure, to bring him down. A trap, I'll lay to that.' Devlin read through the epistle again. 'And this script is not fresh.' He folded the paper with care, placed it inside his shirt. He swore a silent promise, to give it back to the man who wrote it.

'And what do we do, dear Captain?'

'They have two days you reckon at most? Two days ahead of us?'

'Aye. Maybe only one, but that's two hundred miles with a good wind and a fast ship. And *Shadow* ain't so fast.'

Devlin turned to the game at the table where the two gentlemen now sat drunk and laughing like lords. 'Do you have some laudanum about you, Dandon?'

'I could not sleep otherwise, Patrick.'

'Then I will have a fast ship,' Devlin turned back and winked at the grinning Hugh Harris.

'There is one more thing, Captain,' Dandon leant on the threshold and beckoned Devlin to follow him outside.

They stepped out into the bright noon where Devlin could see in the offing the black clouds forming and sky meeting horizon in an endless blanket of grey.

'We could not make it past the Cape of Africa amid *that*, Captain,' Dandon sighed. 'Even *I* know that much.'

Devlin looked to the whitecaps swelling on the sea, the bucking of the ships in the harbour far below, their masts swaying like reeds. He placed a foot upon the low wall that skirted the hostelry's vegetable garden and thought on.

Luck was obviously with the fellow in Charles Town who commanded Devlin from afar. A gentleman's luck. The luck that comes from having a large enough purse to tip the world to your bidding. Devlin had known no *good* gentleman, and the irony of that form of address was not lost on him.

The first he had encountered had been back home in Kilkenny, a fuming English magistrate sentencing him to death for poaching. The gentleman had not objected to buying the poached bird, only to the damage some embedded shot had wrought upon the teeth in his wife's rotting jaw.

Like the child that is bitten by a dog and is wary of even the smallest yap for the rest of his life, Devlin would keep the ruling class a long berth away from him. Now was different of course. Now his class was measured with steel and lead. The white faces of the two young coxcombs inside the tavern reminded him that he had jumped from his allotted peg-hole. Jumped ship, as it were, from the constraints of his former master, Captain John Coxon, and every other sniffing ponce that had handed him their shoes to clean or empty cup to fill.

He wore their clothes, though sullied and old, drank their wine, though stolen and without salute to their king, and spent their coin that they had stolen themselves from the backs of others.

Aye, like a child bitten by a dog and then wary of even the smallest yap all his life. The only resolution for the child in a world of such dogs: resolve to become a wolf.

'I'm back to the ship. I need Bill's conference.'

Black Bill Vernon, the old Scot, sailing master from the *Lucy*, Seth Toombs's old ship that had started Devlin's path. The only man they had who could plot and divine the latitudes as well as Devlin, more from experience than learning.

'I want you to sort for those men. It's been a while since we had a consort and we could do with the hands.'

Dandon looked back to the open door. 'A consort yes, another ship to be sure, but you want those fops for hands?'

'I want the men they rode in with.' Devlin stood, his face in shade from the brim of his hat. 'The ship is a brig called *Talefan*. Thirty hands. Captain Moss commands. Bristol man.' He came to stand at Dandon's shoulder. 'I've got those fools drunk for a reason. Use your talents to ensure they do not wake. If we give chase it'll be best in a ship that none will know. Get the ship without blood.'

'And how am I supposed to achieve such peaceful reversal of ownership?'

Devlin walked back inside to grab his coat and weapons before winding his way back to the harbour and the *Shadow*. He turned. His expression appeared almost insulted.

'If I have to tell you, Dandon, I have sorely overestimated our acquaintance.' He took one more glance over Dandon's shoulder to the blackening sky. 'Send someone to me by six to tell me it's done.'

Devlin emerged a moment later, shrugging on his black, calf-length double-twill coat. His favoured left-locked pistol with its eleven-inch barrel was shoved into his belt and his sword pushed up the tail of his coat as he swept past Dandon with a tip of his hat.

Dandon watched him meander away. He stroked his narrow beard and tapped his thumbnail against his gold front teeth.

The sounds of another triumphant play by George and Albany drew him back to the comfort of the tavern. His hand darted from his chin to feel in his outer pocket where his fingers fell upon the cold vial of laudanum. He smiled softly and walked slowly back into the dim hole.

Chapter Four

Charles Town, South Carolina. Undated.

The letter.

For the intimate concern of the pyrate hitherto familiar as Patrick Devlin.

Allow it to be known that on receipt of this communication it have passed that the member of crew known as Peter Sam, afforded the position of quartermaster amongst, has been removed from company at my request to be brought to the body of my Office.

Your presence is demanded to attend at the address marked at the finality of correspondence. Your attendance will secure the freedom of your fellow.

Your failure in attendance will result in the forfeit of his life after the necessary act of securing the names of formal officers to be passed to the appropriate Offices of Governments most active in the acquisition of your ignoble crew.

In my possession Warrants of Execution signed by three Councils are to be issued to the Navy Board should you also be in failure of attendance.

I will know the hour this letter reaches your hand.

Attend alone and without force. Announce at the House. There will be no harm brought if no member of your crew enters the streets of the town.

Magnolia House. New Church. Charles Town. Southern Carolina Colony of Charles II.

IGNATIUS

Hands *were* needed. There were plenty of hunched rat-like fiends hanging around the heaving shores of Madagascar to pick and choose from. Men with dark and soiled histories that had found themselves hiding or lost among the silent palms and secret alleyways.

But these could be dangerous men, men that needed watching. Devlin preferred, and a year of the preference had paid well, to find good men who could be swayed, be shown the benefit of having pockets weighted down with coin instead of troubles. And his success had brought fame and admiration.

Why, was it not barely a year ago that the pirate Devlin had stolen a King's fortune that enabled some of his crew to retire like lords themselves amongst the islands?

Was there not a couple of Portuguese hands, pressed from the Verde islands where the pirate Devlin had stolen his great frigate, *Shadow*, now living it up on Providence with Jennings, Hornigold and the rest?

And those Dutch fellows. Broad, tall trees of men who had signed up after the pirate Devlin attacked their Dutch slaver. One of those now lived in Spain, married to a lady of the Court no less, did he not?

True or not, the tales brought whispers to his back and respectful nods to his face wherever Devlin strode out.

He always seemed in a hurry, eyes down, brushing through the crowds like a guilty man walking away from the hanging of an innocent one, or simply like one who knew that crowds always walked in the wrong direction.

Rumours abounded: He had buried the money like Kidd. He had spent it on whores and a hundred ships. He was funding the restoration of the Stuarts. He was building an army against the Spanish enemy now France was at war again. He was king of the country he had discovered in the unknown lands of the South Seas. All of these speculations and more circulated along the trade routes of the world and hung in the air behind him. Always behind him, following in his footprints.

Devlin was closing on thirty, old for a pirate to be sure but young for a man of his wealth. The pirate Devlin. Patrick Devlin. Sold by his father, servant to his master, chosen by his men.

Like a hand of cards he had gambled with the easy fortune of youth and won. Now he was a pirate captain of a hundred souls and the richest man in a Gomorrah of his own making. He had weaved his own tapestry by stealing a cache of gold from under the noses of the English and French navies and the omniscience of the Trading Companies that filled their governments' coffers.

Devlin had bucked them all, ducked the shots against him, and him an Irishman at that. He left them coughing and spluttering over their ledgers whilst he and his men splashed brandy over their curses. And now he had seen his name in print. He had been marked. To be hunted. To be hanged.

For infamy has a price.

He pulled a whole gold Louis from his waistcoat to silence the man who rowed him to the *Shadow*'s anchor, far out in the bay where she could turn and run if need be. The old fellow had been reluctant to ferry him across the rising waves but the profile of the dead King of France had settled his stomach.

The squall was just getting into its stride, the wherryman's oars barely skimming along, and he cursed his greed that set him about in such weather. The sea was as grey as the sky; the rain sprayed up from the water as well as down from above.

Devlin did not appear to notice. He sat forward and looked over the old man's cloaked shoulder to the ship beyond, anchored fore and aft yet still dancing against the swell as if pleased at the sight of him returning.

Shadow was a small light-frigate, ably suited to the narrow channels of the Mediterranean but too weak for a ship of the line and thus classed a fifth rater in the Fighting Instructions of 1653.

She was French by birth and had been commissioned by Valentim Mendes, the governor of the small Verdes island of Sao Nicolau, in 1715. She had begun her pirate life two years later when Devlin plucked her from the pocket of said Valentim, and the *Sombra* became the *Shadow*.

Nine nine-pounders stood on the weatherdeck, and another three beneath the quarterdeck and part of the Great Cabin. Two more were on the quarterdeck and one at the fo'c'sle and still two more to chase in the bow, a distinction of Mediterranean ships where the low winds hindered turning to broadside. Her final complement was a brace of niners at the stern waiting to poke out of the Great Cabin, and two breech-loading half-pound swivels along the quarterdeck rail – but the pirates had added yokes to mount more.

Shadow was a fine ship, chipped here and there but her

black and red paint still bright. New strakes had been nailed over old where she had been holed once or twice, and some furniture was missing along her rails and gunwales where misguided fools had attempted to defend themselves with shot and grape. To be fair the Atlantic treated her narrow beam unkindly but she was still here, and the pirates, whose normal way had been to trade up or even down when a ship became worn or in need of repair, had kept her and careened and caulked her with care. They painted that which wanted painting and took from others whatever fresh sail or rigging she had need of.

Perhaps if she had not been so young when they had found her, or perhaps if she had known other crews and seas years before, she would not have sat so well for so long. Aye, perhaps.

A short time later Devlin climbed up the *Shadow*'s ladder as waves ran up her freeboard, soaking his boots while the wind tugged at his billowing coat and tried to pull him from the ropes as he hauled himself through the entry port.

His boots clamped on the deck as it yawed against the rising wind. Black Bill had already set the storm shrouds and sheets. Good. She was secure, anchored at every quarter to roll merrily against the waves.

Men tugged at their forelocks as Devlin made the short walk to his Great Cabin. He passed through his coach into the room, the sea through the stern windows already appearing to climb against them. Spray streamed off the panes, crept in through the brass catches and pooled along the sill like tiny islands.

Black Bill sat at the table, rounded and complacent after a lunch of Solomon Gundy and port, with the peppery smell of his dish thick in the air. A Virginian cornpipe dangled from his mouth and smouldered in his long deep beard, hazing the cabin with blue tobacco smoke.

'Cap'n,' he belched. Dog-Leg, ship's cook, shuffled forward and slapped a cup of peaberry coffee into Devlin's fist.

Devlin patted the shoulder of the one-handed man who had once been Seth Toombs's cook. He put the cup down and drew out the Mercator map of the world from its becket, rolled off the ribbon, and spread it on the table. Bill pulled his pewter plate away from the map to rest against the fiddle rope around the table's edge, designed to stop plates and glasses sliding off during rough seas.

'What goes on, lad?' Bill asked, ruffled by the black look of a man he generally knew to be as calm as waving wheat. Devlin weighted down the corners of the map as he relayed that which he knew.

Peter Sam had been removed from their account. Some deviant Whig who had signed himself to be called 'Ignatius' had bid them to Charles Town to assure Peter's safety or risk his death and the death warrants of them all.

'How would one make off with Peter?' was all Bill asked. Devlin said nothing as he opened a baize-lined drawer under the tabletop and picked out his dividers, compass card and hinged rule. Aye, it seemed unlikely – unholy, even. Peter Sam, all six foot two of him, feared for his terrible look along all the *Shadow*'s decks despite his predilection for delicate young men that would otherwise have marked him for scorn.

The great Peter Sam, who had even tried to kill Devlin when the chance came after his part in the death of Seth Toombs, their former captain.

Peter Sam, who thought to leave Devlin on The Island before the gold had become theirs. Aye, it would have to be a prodigious foe that could lift Sam out of the world.

Both men hunched over the chart as they plotted between them. Peter had been vanished away maybe for two days and Devlin marked with two crosses the limits to where a ship could be now, be it one day, be it two.

The wind whined through the windows and the doors of the coach rattled against the coming storm as they staked out a route to Charles Town, that most successful Carolinas colony, whose rice plantations fed much of England's poor and whose deerskins warmed many an English Lady's hands.

Shadow might make the journey in forty-seven days if she drew the greatest and noblest following wind.

The *Talefan*, a brig with bluffer lines, the ship Devlin had set Dandon to take, could maybe cut no more than ten days from that tally.

Bill drew calmly on his pipe, seeing the frustration rising in Devlin as they both came to the same conclusion.

'Steady, Cap'n,' he advised. 'Can't be helped. We'll get there when we get there. Can't make the world turn any faster. We could still catch 'em.'

Devlin threw down his divider, turning away to the stern windows and the storm being born outside. Seeing his own faint reflection in the glass mocking him, he banged a fist against the pane.

'I have given this letter not enough thought, Bill. I have treated the man who wrote it like some kind of magician.' His voice was bitter, his breath steaming in gasps against the glass.

Bill exhaled a plume of blue smoke. 'Cap'n?'

Devlin spun round. 'Look at it! Look at the letter, Bill!'

Bill ran his eyes clumsily over the script. 'I'm at a loss to know your mind, Devlin.'

Devlin strode across the cabin, his forehead furrowed in thought.

'It says he will know the day, the hour I receive the note, as if he has plotted my path with me. Knows my every hour, by damn!' he cursed. Devlin waited for a response from his sailing master, but Bill was still running his troubled gaze down the page.

Devlin's rant went on. 'A bluffen brag! He could not know that! He does not know that! If he truly knew where we were he would know we could not get to him in thirty days! I reckon that note has been sent to every town from Maracaibo to Trepassey. Yet I read it and believed it true. I read the fancy hand, the noble address and was swayed to believe that some soul has watched us all! I have grown flabby this past year, Bill. This storm I believed a malcontent on the side of this villain, but it has stayed my hand and given me thought.'

He stamped, rattling the lamps in their chains. 'He knows me well enough to be sure. He has plied me with blood to come to him. Not gold or jewels. Blood.'

His voice dropped to a mutter as he paced the room. 'Takes a man from me. A trusted man. Aye, he knows me well enough. That will draw me out to be sure.'

He grabbed a bottle from his desk, an amber liquid within. 'We have been followed. Watched. For Peter is gone, but gone where?' He drank, tipping the bottle high, releasing it seconds later with a gasp.

'Hah!' he snapped at Bill. 'Did not you and I and Dandon all voice the same thought?'

Bill shook his head and shrugged.

'Who could take Peter Sam? Did you not say such a thing?'

'Aye, but . . .'

'But nothing. It would take you and me both to make him kneel on Judgement Day!'

'That's as may be. So what do you say, Cap'n?'

'I say that I was expected to weigh anchor the hour I got this note. To sail at all speed after some phantom ship and plot my course for the Americas without a glance behind me.' He drank again. 'I'll wager you half my gold that Peter Sam is still here. Easier to chain him in some prison than drag him to a ship through a town where I have a hundred men at any time to get past.' He swigged again, feeling the warmth of the rum mixing with the glow of his thoughts.

Bill watched his captain take a long draught. 'Aye, that could be it to be sure. We'd have been chasing after nothing but our own wind. All the while Peter Sam would be behind us, safe from our rescue.' Bill damped down his pipe. 'Fools to be sure. So then, we should stay? Find him?'

'No,' Devlin's dark look was returning. 'We sail. I need to see this man who goads me.' He drank again. 'Pick ten choice men to stay here and scour for Peter. Will Magnes to lead them. Spread some coin about. With luck their guard will drop when they see *Shadow* sailing. They will think us all gone.'

'Aye, we could all stay too. If Peter Sam is here we could find him that much the quicker to be sure.'

Devlin looked hard at Bill. 'He *goads* me, Bill. This soul pulls me to him like a rope is wrapped about me. Are you not yet tired of fine gentlemen beckoning you like a dog?' He chinked the bottle back on the desk. 'And Peter Sam? He means perhaps more to the men than I. How would they feel if I let their man be taken? What kind of lord would I be to them then? Aye, it's a trap of sorts no doubt. Dragging me,' he stabbed the bottle at Bill, 'dragging us back.'

'Yet you will go? Sail into a trap?'

Devlin did not reply. His face showed warmth and his eyes sparkled. Bill understood: Madagascar had no game. No glory. No craic for a pirate.

Devlin stepped back to the map. 'I need you, Bill, to sail the *Shadow*. Show them we are leaving whilst the others look for Peter here.'

'And what of you, Cap'n. Where'll you be?' Bill asked, one eye to the storm now broiling the air in the cabin.

Devlin scraped the 'waggoner' from beneath the table. It was the *Shadow*'s manifesto of maps. Soundings and charts pilfered from other ships. Some lay between oilskin wallets, others were secured with genteel ribbons. It was the pirate's record of the world on paper, written in different voices, each with their own longitude depending on the nation from whose pocket they had been wrenched. It would be a long time yet before Greenwich set the meridian for the world.

Devlin flipped through the maps and stopped at a dog-eared French chart of the Greater Antilles. He waved Bill over and pointed at a dot almost hidden in a fold.

'You and the *Shadow*, once past Ascension, are to make for one of the Deadman's. I'll go to Charles Town.'

Bill looked down at the unnamed spot and nodded. Several islands carried the name, desolate sands where souls could be marooned and night-sailors have their keels ripped out by invisible reefs. Bill knew this one fair enough.

'If it is a trap, set for fools, I don't want to gift our girl to the dogs as well. We'll keep some of our cards under the table. Once I leave Charles Town, *if* I leave Charles Town, we'll meet there. If you don't find me . . . come and get me.'

'Leave a sign at Deadman if you has to leave before us. No

44

telling how late this girl will run, Cap'n. I don't wants to charge Charles Town if I can choose not to.'

'Aye. A bottle under a sword-stroked tree. Agreed.'

Devlin still admired the old ways of these strange men he had become a part of. The sign was a simple thing yet baffling to the Navy hounds that hunted them.

Letters flowed back to all the courts of Europe from the myriad of governors that commanded the pearls of the Caribbean expressing wonder at how it was possible their merchants could be attacked by fleets of pirates under the same flag yet their navies seemed unable to stumble across six or even seven outlaw ships boldly cruising the waters beneath their bows. The answer lay in the islands themselves.

A naval squadron would sail within topsails' sight of each other. Their messages to each other were flags and cannon fire. The pirates sailed out of sight, alone for the most part – the good ones anyway.

They used the thousands of smaller spits of land to careen, smoke and caulk. Then a bottle with a note inside it would be left behind, buried, its location marked by perhaps a volcanic rock that should not be there, a cross carved on a tree, a fresh-cut branch or any number of contrivances agreed upon in advance.

It told of a date, or the next destination, all left for their brothers to find. It meant a chain of command stretching hundreds of miles and the navy scratching their heads.

Devlin slapped his hat down. 'I'll get Dog-Leg to feed me, then sleep out this storm. We'll make sail together. Make our enemies lax with our departure. By six a man will be here to welcome me to my new consort. Four hours from now this squall be over I'll wager.'

Bill cocked an ear, certain he had missed something important.

'What consort be that, Cap'n?'

Devlin smiled. 'I'm going below. I'll talk to them before I leave.'

Like half the outer hull, the inner heart of *Shadow* was painted red, although it could hardly be seen in the murk, especially now the main hatch had been sheeted for the storm. More than fifty men sat below, and all turned their eyes to the brown boots of their captain as he climbed down the companion.

Devlin closed the hatch behind him as he came and turned to face them, all sat afore him, stretching all the way past the fore companion to the manger beneath the fo'c'sle where even the goats twisted their glowing yellow eyes to him.

The pirates sat on blankets or lay on Indian cushions, chewing or drinking their way through the squall. No benches or tables, the furniture of the ship having been long since ripped out along with the bulkheads to make more space. More space for hammocks, more space for lading, more space to fight when it came to it.

They ate and drank together, not in watches, or according to position, no vanity amongst them, just in groups of favoured company for gaming and respite. Most of the time they would eat or drink above, the dry heat below too uncomfortable. But the weather kept them below at this hour. They held their cards and dice and waited for their captain to speak.

Devlin ducked under the lanthorn hanging at the bottom of the stair. The amber light from its panes of polished shell swung over the young faces as the ship rolled. Men younger than him who a year ago did not know him. And a year ago he was less than them.

They had at least been free.

'Lads,' he nodded to the faces he knew well, keeping his head low beneath the overhead. 'A lot's happened. And a lot's about to happen.' He moved amongst them, the rain pounding on the deck above the only sound. 'I know the rest of you are due to go ashore, but we have a change of plan. It seems someone has taken it upon himself to steal Peter Sam from us. And this man now bids us to come and get him.'

Faces in the weak light turned to one another. The man nearest Devlin, Andrew Morris, spoke out. 'Who could take Peter Sam, Cap'n? Why?'

Other voices echoed his questions. Tempers were rising as the pounding above grew more furious.

Devlin pitched his voice over theirs. 'Me and Bill said the same. But it's a ponce in the Americas who has taken him. And if he's managed that, he has some means at his hand that he thinks makes himself greater than you or I. Like all of them, save for the dead ones.'

'What's to be done, Cap'n?' Will Magnes stood, the oldest, one of the originals of Seth Toombs's old crew.

'You to talk to Bill. And to stay here. There's a chance Peter might still be on the island. That we should sail off in chase whilst they hold him here. We don't get fooled like that.'

Others began to stand, shaking the cramp from their limbs and putting away the tools of leisure, replacing them with steel and iron.

'As for the most of you, you're to stay with Bill. Back to the Caribbean with you all. To wait for me. If it's a trap, they'll be looking for the *Shadow.*' There were rumbles of agreement. 'I'll come at them under a different coat.'

The word of going back to the Indies lit up the gloom. Fat merchants lingered there, begging to be fleeced. Civilised towns waited for the pirates to trade and spend their spoils. There were a thousand islands to call home. Only Will Magnes had caught Devlin's departing words.

'You not be with us, Cap'n?'

Devlin put his hand to the companion stair. 'I'm to go faster to the Americas. Taking us a new ship. Short handed and weak but you all just a horizon behind me. This sod calls for me alone.'

Now the protests began. This was not the way. We split company when in danger, not before. And was not Peter Sam all of ours? All to have a hand in cutting the throat of the beggar that took him?

Devlin waved down their cries. 'This is not for coin, lads. It's much to ask you to sail for no profit, but none of you have questioned, and for that I am proud. And as to that, know I would come for any one of you taken from us. This man threatens us with warrants against us all, from all of George's bedfellows. Threatens torture to Peter Sam to drag all your names from him.' He leapt up the stair, hanging a few feet above their heads. 'I'm going alone, aye. But I'm taking all of you with me.'

They cheered, and *Shadow* lurched as if in agreement.

'And what do we say to those against us?' Devlin yelled over their clamour.

Dan Teague hollered back – a pirate as good for blood as Hugh Harris. 'Give us the name of the man first to be killed!'

Devlin grinned. That was it. That was enough to leave them. He would carry them in his pockets now. 'I'll come and give you the name of the last!'

He pulled his pistol and fired a ball square into the main-mast in the centre of them all, their cheers drowning the shot. 'That's me, lads! Leave it there 'til I return!' The hatch slammed shut behind him. Now it remained only for the other ship to be got. Only for Dandon to play his part. Devlin had done his.

Chapter Five

'*View halloo!*' came the cry from St Augustine's quayside. It was the largest bay on Madagascar, and the safest, for the pirates favoured the northern jungles and hills. A sixteenth-century Spanish castle loomed over the bay, its guns still watching all those arriving from Africa's cape. Enough iron showed to keep the pirates shy.

The watchman of the *Talefan*, his storm cape wound tightly around his face, turned to the hunting yell. Instinctively he raised his lamp to the sound.

Thomas Adams, bosun's mate, stood by the foremast, reasonably well sheltered under the storm sheets and the furled sails, and was reluctant to move away.

Another call came, the more familiar 'Ahoy there!', still undoubtedly from a lubber, judging from its high effeminate pitch. He cursed and slopped his way across the deck to the fo'c'sle to improve his view of the quay.

It was still the noon watch. Another bell and Thomas would be relieved. The squall was spitting hard, the blue sky of an hour ago now an eerie purple and gold. Had Thomas been more poetic – and warm – he would have appreciated it. Instead it had been dark enough to light the mast lamps and he had shared emanations of woe with the French watch on the smart hoy beside the *Talefan* as the skies opened.

He slammed his lamp on the bowsprit and looked below to see who summoned him. He was sorry to have bothered.

Standing on the quayside, sheltered by a white *ombrelia*, stood a dandy of a gentleman in yellow silks, which would have been bad enough had he not also brought with him the unconscious forms of the two English gentlemen passengers that had disembarked that very morning.

They were clearly drunk and probably newly poxed as well. So drunk in fact that they had to be carried by three men apiece – no doubt rumpots that had taken a ducat or two to hoist the pair down to the quay.

Thomas Adams' face could only be seen above the nose for his eyes were hooded by the brim of his hat, his mouth by his cloak's collar. Even so his enthusiasm for the scene before him could be read from what sliver of his features remained visible.

On seeing Thomas, the yellow-coated fool waved a glove and raised his umbrella.

'Hoy hoy, there, man!' Dandon cried. 'I believe these two belong to this vessel? Are you the *Talefan*?'

'Aye,' Thomas replied stoutly. 'Who goes there?'

'I bring you Albany Holmes and George Lee. Two fellows with whom I have had the pleasure of taking an early lunch. I fear they may not be used to some of the flavours we enjoy amongst the islands of the East!'

Thomas pulled himself up by a sheet to see the better and set his foot on the gunwale. 'Drunk are they? They usually are. Let them sleep it off ashore. I've no time to watch over them.'

Dandon lowered his shade to appeal with both hands. 'In truth, as well you know my good man, St Augustine is not a place for those who cannot hold their drink. I have sworn on my honour to take them to the safety of their quarters.'

Thomas gave the matter brief contemplation. He looked back at the belfry, to the glass of sand and the man standing beside it. Another turn of the glass and the drunks would be some other soul's problem. His watch done, he could take a meal and put his head down for a few hours. It really made no odds to him to take them aboard. He looked back down to the quay.

'Aye. Bring them on.' He swung down and moved to the larboard gangway. The rain was easing and its sluicing through the cocks of his hat and down the back of his cloak had stopped, which brightened his mood almost as much as watching the party struggle awkwardly across the gangplank.

He cast a cautious eye to the bedraggled brace of men that carried George and Albany aboard. They met his eye with a jolly wink.

They were, however, armed with cutlasses and pistols. He thought of asking them to remove this surplus weight and swept aside his cloak to display his own steel. Then George began to spew like a hose through his tiny mouth, dashing the woodwork around the deck. With that, Thomas ushered them to carry the pair down the companion, out of his watch.

The men chuckled and shook their heads at the foolishness of gentlemen as they lowered the drunkards down the steep ladder like a pair of rolled-up rugs.

Dandon stepped from the gangplank to stand beside the shorter Thomas, who was looking at the trail of vomit now smearing his deck. Dandon tipped his wide hat.

'Much gratitude, my good man. Tell me, is Captain Moss aboard?'

Now Thomas showed a marked interest in the man whose eyes were nearly as yellow as his coat when seen at closer quarters. This one at least was not armed.

'Aye, sir. Cap'n Moss be in his cabin aft. Why?'

Dandon looked with curiosity at the young watchman. 'Are you normally of a manner to ask a gentleman his attitudes, sailor?'

Thomas could have said a dozen things to counter such an affront. He was bosun's mate and master of the watch, after all. Yet none came to mind and he merely felt his ears redden beneath his wet hair.

'Beg pardon, sir,' he said, the phrase that issued forth whenever a gentleman's horse trod on his foot, or a silk coat barged past him in a town square.

Dandon asked the young man his name, seemed to record it mentally, then continued.

'Now, Thomas, I have George's winnings from our gaming this morning. I need to assure myself that they will make their way to George when he wakes.'

He pulled from his coat a silk bag that chinked heavily as only coin can do. Dandon weighted it in his hand twice then dropped it into Thomas's alertly-open palm.

'Would you deposit this sum with Captain Moss for me, Thomas, for safekeeping?'

Thomas held the bag as if a star had grown out of his palm. The coin within tumbled satisfyingly as he hefted it in his hand.

He mouthed something then began to tread slowly along the gangway to the low-roofed cabin aft of the mizzen. He had forgotten about Dandon. He had forgotten the six roughs that seemed to be employed a long time below. He thought only of the heaviness of the bag that rolled in his hand.

He rapped twice on the single arched door, then pushed it open at the sound of Moss's voice. Thomas briefly glanced back to Dandon still standing by the entry port then stepped inside.

Before the door had clicked shut Dandon was three steps down the companion ladder. He ducked beneath the deck and swept his eyes down the dark interior of the ship.

There he saw his six pirates with two pistols apiece at different quarters covering the fifteen men who had been eating below. George and Albany lay sprawled on a table, the tender expression of sleeping children shining from their faces.

Sam Fletcher saluted to Dandon with a pistol, which Dandon returned with a gloved hand, then vanished back above where he met the other sailor, the sentry at the sand glass by the belfry. He had been watching Dandon jump below just as ten more pirates came bouncing across the gangplank with pistols drawn and aimed at him.

His hand had begun to crawl to the bell but then drew back wisely if not bravely. Dandon greeted him, gratefully, for not forcing his men to kill him.

The next minute was frantic. In the cabin, Captain Moss and Thomas were seated at table, entranced by the silk bag of gold coin, which signified more than three years' wages to them both. It would be worth silencing – doing in – the two gentlemen for such a purse and dispatching that pompous yellow fool outside would be a bonus.

At that very moment the yellow fool outside was sending men down the *Talefan*'s starboard side with a line to one of her boats to warp her out of the harbour. He passed an axe to another to cut her cable and loose them from the quay.

Meanwhile some Frenchmen from the hoy alongside began to notice the activity aboard the *Talefan*. Like good Frenchmen they minded their own work and shrugged their shoulders. All Englishmen were *forban* anyway: pirates born.

One minute: the tiniest trickle of sand in an hourglass, less time than it takes to count a bag of gold coin. Dandon smoothed himself down outside the cabin door and swallowed a breath at about the same time Captain Moss became horrified at Thomas's admission that he had let six men vanish below. He had begun to rise, looking round for his pistols and cursing the bosun's mate for a fool, when the narrow door flew aside and James Moss froze.

The captain had always dreaded this moment. He was sure it would happen one day and had resigned himself to it, playing the scene over and over in his head, and was in a small manner ashamed of the relief he felt now the nightmare had finally become reality.

Dandon stepped into the room, followed by a murder of crows with black pistols and wide grins, whose ragged clothes steamed from the rain as if they had just climbed out of hell.

'I see you have accepted my offer, Captain Moss,' Dandon trilled as he swept off his hat.

Moss was still rising from his chair, his right hand resting on the edge of the table. His voice quavered. 'Who are you? Get out of my cabin! *Get out*!'

Dandon took a further step into the room so that he stood a mere hand-swipe's distance from Thomas. 'Come now, that is surely my purse you have there before you? A fair price would you not say for such an aged brig?'

Moss took in the pistol mouths staring at him and his words tumbled as if he were dreaming. 'What do you want of me, *pirate*? Who are you?'

'Make your choice, Captain Moss,' Dandon's eyes were cold. 'Take your coin. Say to no man that you came to harm. Captain Patrick Devlin would hold no quarter if you did.'

Thomas looked between Moss and Dandon as the name

Devlin danced merrily across the face of one and fell like a hanged man down the face of the other. The corners of Dandon's moustache pointed jauntily upwards as he bowed his head while Moss's mouth turned dry and his eyes widened. The table trembled beneath his right hand.

'We have an accord?' Dandon asked, politely enough. 'Find the rest of your crew ashore. Take what you want of your own,' he tossed his hat onto the small cot between the bulkheads. 'Then get off my ship, sir.' He bowed again, slowly, his eyes more deadly than the pistols' promise.

At five o'clock Dog-Leg woke Devlin with coffee. He had napped in his cabin for a few hours, peaceful in the tight comfort of his cot. He spent the next hour lying on his side leafing through a book. Outside the squall rumbled on its path northwards and the stamp of feet above his head signalled the readying of the ship, its pace becoming more urgent with the improving weather.

As the hour drew near to six he heard his coach door open. For a moment he forgot the business of the morning and looked to the door expecting the red-bearded face of Peter Sam to be there. Instead it was Hugh Harris's dirty grin.

'Ship's all ready for you, Cap'n,' he said, entering the room. Harris had rowed over from the *Talefan* to bring Devlin back with him. There were no congratulations or even thanks from his captain for capturing the ship or braving the dying squall to fetch him.

Devlin went back to his book to ingest a few more colourful words that he did not fully understand.

'Grab my bag for me, Hugh,' he asked. 'The storm's gone I take it?'

'Aye,' Hugh looked around for the bag, seeing it at once

beside the table. 'Lucky too. She'd have held us up for a few days otherwise.' He picked up the sack of clothes and books. 'But now we can get after the bastards that have it with Peter. She's a fair ship. Fast I reckon. Faster than this old girl.'

'How many guns?' Devlin closed his book and rolled out of the bed.

'Eight. Six-pounders. I'll be glad *Shadow* be behind us should any wood start flying about.' He indicated the closed book in Devlin's hand, 'What you reading there, Cap'n. Instruction is it?'

Devlin stood, then crossed the cabin to pick up his weapons and coat. He placed the small book softly upon the table.

'No. Something by a fellow named Cervantes. Spanish. Poems. Songs.' He dragged on his coat, holding the cuffs of his shirt not to have them carried up by the sleeves.

Hugh gave an admiring and thoughtful hum.

'Oh, I don't understand it, mate.' Devlin checked his belt and silver capped powder flask. 'But it's pretty to read it. And I can gather some of the words from our own. Don't know which was first, mind, ours or theirs. What say you, Hugh Harris?'

Hugh opened his mouth but was pushed through the door by Devlin before he could offer his opinion.

'Never mind, Hugh. Takes me to me new ship. If Will Magnes and the boys can't find Peter ashore we'll find him at sea. Chase those bastards down then on to Charles Town and kill the bastard that summons me.'

They moved out onto the main deck and into a rushing world of calls and ropes. The air from the storm seemed to sharpen the edges of every corner of wood. The crew's eyes glistened with every lowering of sail and crank of the capstan.

A fiddle broke out in a wail and a Welsh voice began to sing. It was a song of cuttlefish combs and Cape Cod girls of questionable virtue that pulled the *Shadow* to life. The flukes dragged free from the seabed, stirring a cloud of sand that spread through the waters. *Shadow* began to breathe awake and she shrugged the storm from her yards like a dog shaking itself dry.

Devlin looked about him to the men and the ship he had known for a year now. Her wounds from the battle at the island, now scars, gave him pause. To step aboard another – to captain the *Talefan*, to cheat on *Shadow* – brought the guilt of betrayal to a part of him. He was thankful to see the welcome bulk of Black Bill lumbering towards him, to pull him from his brief melancholy.

'Bill!' Devlin's voice sang. 'What goes on?'

The mariner's boots clumped to his captain's side. 'All's well, Cap'n.' He looked down to his empty pipe and began to fumble through his outer pocket. 'We have food enough for six weeks. With good eating.'

'But it wouldn't hurt to pick up a little fresh timber on the way.' Devlin elbowed his sailing master's side as they walked to the entry port. Hugh Harris was already clambering down to the boat.

'We'll keep behind. Eyes to your masts,' Bill affirmed. 'They'll be looking for *Shadow* not a wee brig.'

Devlin rested on the gunwale, looked out to the *Talefan* laying to the North. 'That's the game of it. If eyes are upon us at Charles Town they'll look for our black and red girl. She'll be fast, Bill. We'll make a half-sail. Give you a chance to keep up until we reach Ascension.'

'Aye.' Bill lit his pipe slowly, ignoring the world as he drew the bowl into glowing life. 'Patrick,' he said at last. 'There be something you should know. I been of a mind to bring it up for a time now.' He looked hard to his captain. 'About Peter.'

Devlin had grown to know Bill well over the past year. A serious man. Drank less than most. Walked the decks at night alone, smoking his pipe over the taffrail watching *Shadow*'s wake crawl behind them. His confidence was rarely bestowed.

'What about Peter?'

Bill stared out to the mountains of Madagascar as he spoke. 'That time. At The Island. With the land in sight. Peter Sam . . . and I to confess true,' he lowered his head, drawing deeply on his pipe. 'We changed sail, Cap'n. Headed South. Leaving you to yourself.' He sighed out a cloud of blue smoke.

'I believe you may have known that, Cap'n,' his usually growling voice was smooth and tinged with shame. 'But I wanted to be sure you knew. Before you went after Peter and all. Before you gave me the *Shadow* to command.'

Devlin took Bill's left forearm in both his hands. He shook it once then backed himself through the port, his feet already upon the ladder. The hours on The Island flashed through his mind. He looked up into Bill's round face.

'But you came back, Bill.' He minded his footing as he descended, looking up once more before the final drop to the jolly boat. 'You came back, and you would again.'

Devlin sat down with Hugh at the sheets. Slipping off his coat and hat he welcomed the two crewmen at the oars, men he had never seen before and who eyed him warily.

'Take me to America, boys!' he cried. 'There be a man waiting for me to end his days!'

Bill watched the boat fight through the waves until he could no longer hear the slap of the oars. Since the month they had been shored in the east he had not seen Devlin so charged. Idleness did not suit him. Horses have need to run.

He came away from the gunwale and made his way up to the helm, barged through the men too slow to jump out of his path.

'Make sail!' he bellowed. 'Move your arses! Your cap'n is waiting! We're going to the Caribbee! Put your hearts away you sons of bitches! We're back to the Indies!'

On the cliffs above the town of St Augustine, to the north of the bay, a man with a telescope watched the *Shadow* begin to turn south-west, her grey sails full.

The man lowered the brass tube. He had sat with the scope resting on his knees, watching the ship for the past hour. Occasionally he stretched his back and dipped into his canvas satchel for some goat's cheese and the flat salty bread that he had endured at first and then grown ravenously fond of.

He pulled the cork from his leather flask of Arrack, making a note to refill it at one of the taverns on the way back to the guardhouse.

He drank some of the spicy sweet wine, rewarding himself for his vigilance. He replaced the flask and the scope in the satchel then heaved himself up, flashing the departing ship a final horrible grin before turning to see two boys with butcher's knives who stood blocking his path.

They were natives. Wiry black fellows with bare bony chests. Young men. Too young to be anything else but hungry. Too young to know how to kill properly.

The watcher rose to his full towering height, seven foot in his buskins, his breeches tucked in the knee–length boots.

The two youths quaked somewhat at the sight of his frame,

as broad as them both together. A glance passed between them and then they began their chatter.

The watcher did not understand the words but he knew the sentiment. The boys laughed between themselves, their white teeth glowing behind their wide brown mouths. The watcher had known the laugh all his life.

He kept his eyes on the rusty blades wrapped in twine and balanced in the boys' hands as they finished their chortling and their deadly look returned.

Hib Gow, for that was the watcher's Scottish name, had fought all his days over that laugh, was used to it very well. His great slab of a head was uncommonly blessed with a proboscis – more monstrous horn than nose – that grew aquiline out of his huge square face. Hib was ugly, to be sure, but that had not mattered in his previous life, when his days had been spent with his head covered by a black hood.

The cruelty his large nose provoked had led to a more scarred and mis-shapen visage than he might have grown up with, but the streets of Greenock had not allowed him to pass by without some punishment for being blessed with such a beak. A lifetime of beatings had not served to improve his looks. Broken face. Sunken eyes. A never-ending fury scarred across his face.

He watched the two boys as they mouthed their strange language and rubbed their fingers together gesturing for coin.

Hib would gladly have given them his flat bread and cheese if empty bellies were their only problem. He reckoned they had loftier plans for themselves that only his coin could realise for them.

He pitied them for their greed and grasping hands. Their laughter had brought him back to Wapping and Tyburn, back to before the Hanoverian had wedged himself into the throne.

All the way back to when Hib in his black hood was the crowd's favourite.

The hood was a pointless subterfuge, for his nose lifted the black cloth out of shape and the scaffold of his frame announced him more grandly than fife and drum ever could.

'*It's Hib*!' the crones would cackle. '*Hib's doing it*!' the crowds would hum, knowing that he would give them a show, with a rope too short that would make the villain dance for twenty minutes rather than ten. And he would thrust aside any misguided tear-eyed fool who tried to pull the man's legs to snap his neck.

Hib gave them a choking, a hempen jig, a proper hanging. But then there had been the Jacobite rebellions. Damned politics had ruined the chances of a Scotsman to be good at an English job. They had taken away the killing, then blamed *him*, imprisoned *him* in the same cells he used to march past when he had needed to bleed his moods.

It was neither his fault nor his doing. The man Ignatius had rescued him from his own noose when other bodies led to Hib's doorstep. He had new life now, a foreign life. And a worthy letting of blood.

His hand moved slowly to his belt and eased free the Estilete dagger. The two youths chattered even more at the sight of it. They rocked on their heels and began to wave their wretched blades at him, beckoning again for his coin.

His dagger was worth more than the small purse he carried. They should appreciate that fact and sample it for themselves. Its Spanish blade was older than all of them, dark and tapered to infinity. How proud they should be to taste it.

He checked them both, playing the blade in his palm. One boy had sharp, panicked eyes. He talked the fastest. He would not move first. The other had the wide eyes of the damned, the brilliant whites making of his pupils just black spots in a desperate face.

Hib's next thought was how to clean his shirt in such a parched land. The mad stare had ended with the popping of a wind-pipe. A rush of air like a bellows flew out of the boy as he tumbled backwards. He would die slowly now.

The second was already dead when Hib cursed the blood that gushed over his clothes. In a single twist he had pulled his dagger from the throat of the first and whipped it straight through the silk wrap of the second boy. A hard punch of steel to the gut. The boy had gripped Hib's arm, imploring, begging as Hib damned him for the arterial spurt that soaked his waistcoat right through to his shirt.

He let the body drop then wiped his Spanish dagger on the skirt. A noise made him look up at the rustling branches of a bush. There had been another, perhaps a girl who had urged them to it, now running home to her brothers. There was always a girl involved in such a waste of life. London had been the same. It had been easy to please himself at night in London's inns when women were around. Always someone who asked for the blade if you looked too long at his girl. It was so easy to bleed his mood back then.

It had been a while since Hib Gow had felt the pain in the base of his skull. The old pressure back as blood pumped at the sight of death. He twisted his broad thigh of a neck, trying to stretch the pain away, and rubbed a bloody palm to the throb. No good. The blood still slammed hard at the very bone of his head like a hammer blow.

Get back to the guardhouse. Kick that pirate scum some more. That would calm the blood. That would scarify his mood.

'*It's Hib!*' they used to scream. Those old toothless hags. '*Hib's to do it! It's Hib I tells you! Look at his beak for God's sakes!*'

He loped away, snapping some more of the flat bread with a powerful bite, forgetting about his bloodied clothes already drying.

Aye, scarify his mood with another's pain. That always helped. For a time.

Chapter Six

✗

Providence Island

*Petition of merchants trading to different parts of
H.M. Dominions in America to the King, 1716. (Extract)*

Sir
*Complain of severe losses occasioned by pirates sheltering
in the Bahamas, so neglected by the Proprietors that they
have been often plundered and ruin'd in times of peace,
and during the late war four and several times taken and
destroy'd by the enemy.*

*Urge the securing of Providence under H.M. immediate
government.*

*These Islands are so advantageously situated that
whoever is well settled and securely fortified there, may
in time of war command the Gulf of Florida, and from
thence be capable to annoy or obstruct the trade of other
Nations to most parts of America.*

Fifty-five signatures follow.

The flotsam and waveson had started the day before sighting
the island. Captain John Coxon had been called to the fo'c'sle
of the *Milford*, summoned respectfully by the bosun to attend

to the spectacle of the dozens of barrels and hundreds of bottles merrily bobbing along beside them.

The crew had shared whispers and winks at the tide of waste that grew with each passing hour. Their mutterings were silenced by the cold stare of the captain who tried hard not to contemplate the significance of these unofficial buoys marking the way to Providence.

Providence Island. *New* Providence, now designated. A pirate kingdom. The filibusters and buccaneers of old had Tortuga. This new breed of ex-privateers and unemployed peacetime mercenaries had the Bahamas for their throne. And a fairer throne at that.

Sixty miles square and sitting in the twenty-fourth parallel, it gave swift access to the Florida coast and with the trade winds running northwards a crew could reach the snaking inlets and fat ports of the Carolinas in five days or less.

It had been almost a decade since the law's writ had last run on the island, Whitehall being quite content to leave matters to a succession of Lords Proprietor who seemed ever more content to let the island fester.

Said island, in absence of proper government, had thereby found its own 'law'.

British captains, whose letters of marque had promised them freedom to plunder as long as they fleeced only the Spanish sheep, found that the peace after Utrecht – the almighty treaty that ended the Spanish war – was a little too becalming and light of coin. Their country had been grateful in spirit but was at a loss what to do with them now. The privateers thus busied themselves in their own employment.

Men such as Henry Jennings and Benjamin Hornigold became lords of their own creation once the crown had no further use for them. And who could blame them for naming an island called Providence their realm?

But enough was enough for the Crown. With Spain fortifying in Florida the strategic placing of the island had made it attractive again and the strangulation of trade by the rovers that dwelt there would have to cease. But who to send? Who but a madman or a fool would undertake the task to rid the Bahamas of a two-thousand-strong pirate brotherhood?

The Lords Proprietor and the Privy Council had found such a man. Half broken in spirit, fully broken in purse, this sailor had girdled the earth and fought in every war he had been pitched into. He had captured treasure galleons, sacked Spanish towns in the name of the Crown and suffered to have the entirety wrested from him through a *danse macabre* of lawyers and taxes. He had been perhaps as much a pirate as any of them if not for the letters of marque in his name that had been sealed by the king.

Captain Woodes Rogers. He had actually petitioned for the duty.

He had been the only one.

As day broke and the horizon undulated with the haunches of the island herself, Captain John Coxon paced the deck, unable to avoid watching the clothes, the chests and hogsheads that bounced off the lines of the *Milford* as she swept towards the aptly named Providence.

Captain John Coxon. Post Captain. Veteran of two wars, wars for which every civilised nation had redrawn their maps. Now he was Captain John Coxon of the Company of Woodes Rogers, assailing Providence under the King's Act of Proclamation against the pirates of the Bahamas.

His father was a Norfolk parson. His elder brother had been given a bible but Coxon had been sent to sea at nine years of age with a bag of clothes and a commission. He had never been home again and was now forty-two, his father dead, John's brother preaching in his stead.

It was in the spring of 1712 that he had liberated an Irish sailor of a French sloop of war. He had smiled that first day when the Irishman stepped forward out of the line of captives to offer their services to the King's officers rather than have them slaughtered for their lack of English. Coxon had subsequently received his Post-Captaincy for the level of intelligence he was able to provide his admiral whilst still at sea. The Irishman had saved many lives that day. Coxon had rewarded the man by making him his steward. More than that, Coxon, a stranger to the ballroom culture of his officer peers, found companionship in the young man who was not only literate but could also divine the mathematical intricacies of navigation as if they were psalms to be recited. Coxon had seen something of himself in the Irishman. For years he had felt his father had turfed him out to sea, to be rid of him whilst coddling his elder brother to follow along the path of righteousness. It had taken a decade for him to understand that his father, who had sensed the approaching wars, had sent the brightest of his sons to sea. God would be best served by good hearts and knowledge in the struggle against the Catholics. He had never seen him again, but Coxon had been grateful to his father when the wars had ended and he contemplated how he had slashed his own way through. Coxon had written his name on the world by dint of his victories at sea.

Then it had ended. A few years working for the South Seas and India companies on peacetime half-pay followed. Then an illness, the African curse of dysentery, had almost carried him to the grave.

Bedridden for a month, he had sent his steward and his

ship home to England without him. It was a month of dying for Coxon in Cape Coast castle on Africa's Guinea coast, from which he awoke to find that his trusted servant had turned into a pirate – and a captain no less – and his beloved ship was lost. The Irishman whom John Coxon had taught to sail, taught to compare watch to map, peg to board, star to brass, was picking the pockets of the world and laughing at him the while.

Now this scatter of breadcrumbs from a pirate island was leading them deeper into an unknown forest. *Turn away*, the waves whispered. *Turn your tiller home, Captain. For your own sake and the sake of your unborn.*

See this debris, the tons of it upon the waves? This is us. We are legion. And this is our kingdom. We burnt your King's ships the last time they came. We tore up his Proclamation of Peace. What can you do against us?

Coxon climbed to the quarterdeck and looked to his ship's wake. He gave a small nod to the helmsman who was also trying not to look at the spent goods ornamenting the sea.

Coxon looked back to the ships of his fleet. *This* was the difference. *This* is what he could do.

There, majestically cutting the waves, was *Delicia*, an East Indiaman of forty guns. The new Governor of Providence, Woodes Rogers himself, was her captain. That diving bow galloping through the sea belonged to the frigate *Rose*. Shadowing her on either side, a cable length away, skipped the sloops *Shark* and *Buck*.

Altogether the Company mustered over three hundred able men and officers. Thrown in for good measure, by King George himself, were one hundred redcoats to establish a garrison on the island.

Lastly, confidently, two hundred and fifty colonists had signed on, refugees and hopefuls from the final pages of the wars.

They were Huguenots, Swiss farmers and German Palatinates who treated London as their second home and now went looking for ripe land in the Antilles.

Whole shops lay in the hold waiting to be nailed up and trading by dawn of their disembarkation. The missionaries of the Society for Promoting Christian Knowledge shuddered at the sorrowful sight of ladies' torn clothing that floated by the head of the ship as they took their morning ablutions.

This is what I have, thought John Coxon, and steeled himself as the black forest of masts began to fill his spyglass and the green and blue hills rose up from the sea.

The flotilla approached from the south-east following the shore of Andros to the west and crawled past the treacherous coral reefs of the southern shore to make for the north and Nassau. Already they could see the sandbar that would prevent the *Delicia* from sailing inshore. This hazard was one of the island's strengths, a natural barrier that halted any ship above three hundred tons.

To the north-east lay a smaller island, a long flat spit that created the great shallow harbour of Nassau. Hog Island.

Coxon took a moment to check his officers' faces as he gave up counting the ships in the harbour. To his left and his right his lieutenants swept their spyglasses across the bay.

They saw a solid mile of nothing but sloops, brigs and hulks. He saw them gulp and observed their foreheads break into a sweat that trickled onto the brasses clamped to their eyes.

He slapped his three-draw scope closed, loud enough to

break each officer from his study. They turned to the captain, glad to stop counting.

'Gentlemen,' Coxon looked at each in turn. 'Two pistols apiece. Five chosen men to your sides.' He pulled his hat down at the brim and walked to the stair. There he turned and looked back – not at his officers but over the taffrail to the *Delicia* close behind.

'I know each and every man on that island, lads. And so do you. They cleant your boots and touched their forelocks to you.' He clumped down the stair, 'Remember that, lads. Hands and backs, that's all they were. And they fear your coming, mark me.'

At the foot of the stair he met the young man with the coarse blond hair and cracked tan who had come aboard in Bristol, the one who had worn a burgundy three-cornered hat tied with leather cocks, far too gentlemanly for a sailor, that Coxon had forced him to remove. The man had winked at Coxon as he came through the entry port that day, and the captain had noticed the scarred and bony jaw of battle. Toombs, Seth Toombs, that was it. Something seditious about that one. Something in his eye. Or perhaps it was just the yellowing wound that marked him as a wrong'un.

The man glanced up at him, tugged his forelock beneath his straw hat and returned to swabbing the deck around Coxon's feet.

Coxon lowered his chin in a snap and ducked aft to his cabin to record his morning watch. Soon he would take the gig across to Woodes Rogers, and try hard not to stare at a wound similar to Toombs's, inflicted by a musket ball that had blown off half his jaw and now caused Rogers to suck saliva down his throat every finished sentence.

Rogers was a privateer, a chartered pirate of war chosen

like Harry Morgan before him to sweep his former brethren from the Caribbean. Yet he was a good man nonetheless, Bristol born and of solid Dorset stock, a sailor like Coxon and also like him no highborn gentleman. Rogers' hands and face were cracked with salt and sun. He could pilot merely by the colour of the sea, using only sun and stars to confirm and satisfy his sailing master. His sword was worn and his pistols blackened.

Coxon wrote briefly in his log: The island sighted. The appointment made with Rogers to plan their assault and proclamation of amnesty to the pirates that ruled Providence.

His pen hovered above the page for a moment then he wiped the swan quill and replaced it in the crock holder, dusting his ledger and blowing it dry.

The sailing master knocked and entered the cabin. Coxon ordered the shortening of sail so to come about and point the prow towards the island; and also to bring his gig from beneath the counter.

He had not observed a black ship with a red-striped free-board and grey sails. It was pointless to record its absence, however significant in his own eyes. The *Shadow* was not there but then who could say that Devlin still kept the frigate?

He armed himself with pistol and cutlass and swathed himself in his boatcloak to meet his Commander.

He had not sighted the ship. He would give no further thought to his former servant, not even recall his name.

Coxon winced slightly as he pulled open his coach door. The pain he felt was from the tell-tale, star-shaped soft scar hidden beneath his sleeve. It was his souvenir from his last meeting with Devlin.

He saw again the white flash of gunfire in his mind and felt the clashing of blades, the racing pulse and heaving breath of combat. His arm twinged again as Coxon stepped out onto his deck head down and walked impatiently to the entry port to see if his gig had appeared.

An hour later and Woodes Rogers stood with his captains in his state room preparing the order of the day. A month they had waited for this dawn, weeks of expectation on the high seas that would culminate in the next few hours.

On the table encircled by the four captains Rogers had laid the King's Proclamation. Beside it were some tracts from the Society for Promoting Christian Knowledge. The small books, typeset in an octavo format, were to be handed out to each pirate who took the King's pardon. The society had even brought along a printing press, should they require more copies.

Rogers stood in a fawn-coloured great coat with a long elegant waistcoat to match but a simple calico shirt beneath, which was cooling in the close warmth of the cabin. His captains wore dark heavy wool coats and waistcoats, garments too heavy for the Mediterranean let alone the Indies.

The new Captain General and Governor-in-Chief over the Bahama Islands in America poured a glass of port for his gallant commanders.

'Gentlemen,' he raised his glass. 'To our endeavours.'

They sipped in silence, broken only by the scuffling of feet above their heads. Rogers put down his glass beside the Proclamation. He began to speak as if he was already half-way through his forthcoming address.

'Last year the Proclamation Act came to Providence. A pardon for all Englishmen who had turned to piracy. You may know that the pirates burnt the ship it came in on. Her captain and crew were never heard of again,' he paused to allow his audience to dwell on the fact. 'We therefore are delivering it once again. Personally. And with a bit more iron to back it up, eh? Our aim is to colonise this hole. Turn these scoundrels into farmers. Build two more forts to protect against the Spanish mongrel. I know some of you, probably all of you, would rather be at the war, out in Sicily or wherever, but *this* has metal too!' He banged the table, dragged a fingernail along the map secured there, from Bermuda to Providence and up to the Carolinas. Spanish Florida lay just a couple of inches away.

'This island must be taken! It sits precisely at the point where one enters the Caribbean or leaves it to reach the Americas. Bermuda and Providence are like watch-towers for the provinces and they will be held! They will remain English!'

No-one spoke. No huzzahs or rapping of knuckles against wood commenced, only some sniffing of port and nods of approval. Rogers went back to the map.

'The *Shark* and the *Rose* will sail into the harbour as soon as practicable, gentlemen. Let our colonists know that we are here in force. Meet any party who comes out with grace. I will row in with Captain Coxon, the keels of *Milford* and *Delicia* being too deep for these sands. The *Buck* will stay as a rear guard.'

Cawford, the *Shark*'s young commander, nodded confidently to them all and drained his glass. 'I'm sure we will find some good men still abroad.'

Whitney, captain of the *Rose* and a seasoned sailor, eyed Cawford with raised brows. 'I hear there may be as many as two thousand pirates, Cawford. Where do good men hide from such a force?'

'As I understand it,' Cawford returned, 'there be the shopkeepers, the tavern owners and such.'

Whitney sniffed and finished his port. Rogers continued.

'These are the ringleaders we must seek out, my lads.' He passed out a note to each, in his own hand, hardly pausing to let them read as he reeled out the names himself from memory: Barrow, Burgess, Jennings, Hornigold, Vane, Teach, Martel, Fife and a dozen more. As he spoke Rogers sucked at the saliva draining from his ruined mouth.

'These are the ones who must take the pardon. If they fold, their crews will follow. I will offer the principals, Barrow, Burgess, Jennings and Hornigold a place within us. As privateers. I will flatter them that I need their service. And in truth perhaps I do.'

Coxon was no longer listening. He had reached the bottom of the list.

'Governor Rogers?' he spoke for the first time since he had entered the cabin. Rogers swallowed some more saliva and lifted his head. 'Yes, John?'

Coxon drew a breath and held out the waxy paper. 'I do not see the pirate Devlin's name here, Governor.' He looked at the eyes watching him. 'I assumed he would be among such a band. His name is not here, Sir.'

Rogers looked at the list, 'Quite right, Captain. There is no Devlin listed. Were you expecting him to be?'

Coxon looked over Rogers' shoulder to the lapping sea outside the stern windows. 'I had thought that after all . . . after his notoriety, he would be one of the main. That is all.' He dropped his eyes back to the paper.

'I see,' Rogers said quietly. 'My intelligence does not deliver me any knowledge of Devlin being on the island. Although I agree he would be a bird to bag, Captain Coxon.' He smiled politely. 'Perhaps we will be fortunate, eh?'

'Aye, sir,' Coxon folded the paper and slipped it into his coat. 'Fortunate we may hope.'

Whitney elbowed Coxon. 'Perhaps he will join you again, eh, John? Perhaps he misses starching your breeches!'

The others grinned and showed their white teeth. All except Rogers, who now could only ever leer.

'He might at that,' Coxon acknowledged. 'I'm sure he's missed such pleasures.'

'Perhaps he can wash all our breeches, lads.' Rogers dabbed at the drool on his chin with a shirt cuff. 'Now. Back to the fox at hand. We have a door to knock on this day. And no doubt we shall not be welcome.'

Chapter Seven

✗

*T*he post-noon watch saw the sloop *Shark* and the fifth-rate frigate *Rose* approach the bay of Providence. Cawford raised his linen to his nose at the milky spume of bubbling effluence that floated out on the tide to pollute once sparkling waters.

His First Lieutenant's voice issued profanities as he looked along the beach to see the tents of whores, carcasses of hogs and discarded horseflesh strewn along the white sands, a putrefying red and yellow morgue piling upon the beach already decorated with bottles and human waste.

The waves made an effort to drag away the junk of the hell the pirates had created, and the flotsam bumped against the *Shark*'s hull, as if begging for a new home.

Smoke drifted from beyond the beach. Pillars of grey, dozens of them, signalling the presence of camps and shanties littering the woods. Cawford had seen engravings of Nassau, a pretty English town set amongst palms and springs with smiling farmers and milk maids. He wondered what it looked like now.

The commotion of brigs and sloops that bobbed in the bay showed no colours. Amongst them were the hulks of stolen ships, now dark and lifeless. Nearly all these were mastless and devoid of sail. Others seemed to have chunks of their bulwarks bitten out of them by some mythical nightmare colossus that fed on decks and cannon, prowling the shores and discarding the hulks like chicken bones to rot upon the shoreline.

'Good God!' Cawford exclaimed. 'What manner of life is this?'

His lieutenant stood closer to him and raised his hand toward a sail slipping free from the general litter.

Cawford drew up a little at the sight of the French flag of the sloop that had broken away from the other ships.

'An ally, boys!' he cried. 'Some souls come to join us!' He raised his scope for a fairer look.

'And a brigantine too, sir,' his lieutenant pointed to a white ship also casting loose of the line of cruisers under a British pennant.

'Good men. Always good men,' Cawford stated and studied the French ship. 'All will be well, lads.'

Through the silence of his glass he watched the bowsprit of the brigantine streak ahead of the French sloop. Her shrouds were hung with armed men. Her deck alive with bodies.

The brigantine veered away, leaning to larboard. Cawford swallowed at the shouting mouths too far to hear and the fists full of weapons pumping the air in derision directed at him.

Standing on the gunwale was a man in a white frock coat and black hat with white trim. He fired two pistols into the air and a hundred men did the same. Captain Charles Vane, one of Providence's former pirate lords, was welcoming his new masters.

'What the devil?' Cawford lowered his scope. He glanced back to the frigate on his starboard quarter. The *Rose* had pulled in all sail and sat high and patient. He could see the scopes along the fo'c'sle observing the display calmly.

If the *Rose* was not bothered, Whitney keeping his ports closed, then Cawford would stay also. After all, the brigantine was sailing away, its stern already turning to escape the bay. Only the French sloop at full sail and hard to starboard, yards braced to a hard angle, flew to join the *Shark*'s quarter. She was bearing on them fast.

'Odd,' spoke Stanford, his First Lieutenant, squinting through his spyglass. 'The deck is empty, sir.' He swept left to right across the whole ship. 'Not a man. Not a man at all. Yet she is hard to braces.'

Cawford raised his scope again. The shrouds, ratlines and yards were indeed free of hands. The bowsprit crossed his scope's narrow eye and powered straight for him, her jibs suddenly obscuring his view of her deck.

'Aye, Lieutenant. Not a man on deck. Perhaps hiding from the pirates? We'll wait and see.'

John Coxon almost broke his spyglass on the quarterdeck rail as he slammed it down. His officers jumped at the sound and lowered their scopes.

'Sir?' Rosher, his First, started.

'It's a fire-ship! Heading straight at them!' He jumped to the stair then swayed powerless, holding on to the rails. He was too distant to be of any help and could only holler to his own officers.

'That's Charles Vane on that brigantine! That's a fire-ship he's set against them!' He shouted in vain to the ship, 'Hard to, you *fools*!'

The young gentlemen on Coxon's quarterdeck looked between each other, then raised their spyglasses again to watch the drama unfolding a mile ahead of them.

A fire-ship, a 'smoker', that old pirate standby. Drake and Raleigh had used it against the overpowering wood of the

Armada generations before. The lower decks would be loaded with powder kegs and ball, then a fire set and the tiller lashed. Put on as much sail as she can muster and set her running.

Captain Charles Vane was indeed warmly welcoming his new masters.

Woodes Rogers stood on the *Delicia*'s fo'c'sle, his fingers whitened along the gunwale then braced against it as he watched the French sloop explode in a ball of fire and cataclysm of splinters spearing across the water and making every man aboard the *Shark* and the *Rose* duck for cover. The roar quaked the waters of the bay and jostled the warships that had dared upon her.

The sloop had in fact gone up too soon, but the smoke and the fire on the water had served Charles Vane's purpose. He could sail out of the other end of the harbour unhindered, sail north and out to the Carolinas with his *Ranger* intact. To the men of the *Shark* and the *Rose* it did not bear to consider the consequences if Vane's timing had been five more minutes in his favour.

Teach had sailed the day before, broken free from Hornigold and the coming justice that the others were willing to bow to.

Those others, the lords, had held a court and eagerly rubbed their hands together at the thought of a King's pardon to avoid a choking whilst still retaining their coin.

Vane and Teach would not pick up a hoe for the Hanoverian King's sanctimony. They would never take an acre of land and the freedom to pay taxes for the peace of going with the grain; to their minds a pardon was merely the first chain-link of slavery. As privateers, abandoned when peace descended, they remembered how weak paper could be and how shallow ink ran.

*

Woodes Rogers paced his quarterdeck, looking up to the rising black smoke, the small fires carried on the tide. 'Damn his eyes!' he spat at his officers. 'That man has cost me a day!'

'We could still row you ashore, Captain?' his First offered. 'When the smoke clears.'

Rogers ignored him. 'Get my gig round. Take me to the *Milford*. I will confer with Coxon.' He ceased his pacing and looked to the shrinking stern of the *Ranger* already clearing the bay. 'Cost me a day! Cost me my sleep. On the morrow then. So be it! Damn his eyes! Damn him!' He slammed the rail and wiped his mouth. 'Damn him!'

The burning French ship crackled on through the afternoon and early evening as Venus and then Mars winked into life. The slumber of the darkening sky was disturbed only by the blackened mainmast eventually yawing over into the sea with a drawn-out death throe.

The man by the belfry on the *Milford* watched the end solemnly. He tapped the last grains free from the sandglass and tugged on his bell-rope four times.

The four other ships echoed the same song across a mile of sea. One by one the side-lights and lamps were lit until the line from the *Buck* to the *Delicia* resembled a small village settling down for the night.

'One could get used to this almost perpetual twilight don't you think, John?' Rogers drew on his ivory pipe of Virginian tobacco, growing light-headed as the blue smoke twisted through his shoulder-length wig. 'Here it is. Ten of the clock and I could still fish in this light.'

'It does get darker, sir. I'm sure I do not need to tell you that,' Coxon stated flatly, pulling a silver fork though his rice seeking more titbits of chicken.

Rogers had joined him for dinner and to empty a few bottles of Coxon's wine. They sat in Coxon's Great Cabin, alone. Rogers' furious humour abated after the first carafe and both men had burnt Vane's ears in condemnation then appeased their anger with another bottle. At length, they had even laughed at the boldness of the stratagem.

Rogers straightened in his seat, the pipe hanging from his wet mouth, and began again as if he was already halfway through his speech. 'This will be a good match for me, John. To be backed by such a consortium of businessmen after coming back to England with the bones of my arse showing through my breeches. And with the King reposing especial trust in my prudence, courage and loyalty. I have the smell of knighthood in my nostrils if I can turn this.' He tipped his glass to Coxon. 'Mark me, John, we shall all do well of this.'

'We had better, sir, not being paid and all.' Coxon gave up on his fork and lifted his glass of Oporto's cheapest offering.

Rogers craned forward, almost choking on his drooping pipe. 'Profit, John! Profit for us all! Better than wages! A colony! An income of taxes! I could build a nation here!'

'Aye,' Coxon agreed. 'If we live so long.'

'Oh come, John! Were we not chosen for our swords! Our habit for blood! We don't shine chairs with our britches! We fight, man! We sail! Necessity has frequently set men on noble undertakings.'

Coxon held his chin and looked at his plate. Rogers' enthusiasm was inspiring but not infectious. New Providence had only been leased to him, despite all the noble titles bestowed, his badge of office was nothing more than a decorative rental agreement signed by a king. But Rogers could not easily afford the rent and had turned to financiers to loan him the necessary fifty pounds per annum. Seven years' worth. Even Thomas 'Diamond' Pitt had put his hand in his pocket. Coxon had only known such men to open their purses at the hint of coffee, sugar, or slaves. It would not be for the pirates alone, as Rogers' first petition – to clear Madagascar – had fallen on deaf ears. So why now? Why Providence?

'Would you not wonder, sir, how it was that a string of London purses gladly sent us here? To capture a small lost colony already raped by Spaniards and impregnated by pirates. What wealth is left here to be gained?'

Rogers leant back in his chair, his teeth clicking on his pipe stem. A rivulet of spittle seeped from the crooked corner of his mouth. 'Four thousand pounds of expenses has helped us, John, and it's not my own ships this time. No, this is important, John. This is special. The pirates seize almost one third of the trade from the colonies and another third of that which comes back. Bad enough the damn natives war with the towns constantly never mind suffering pirates to boot. I feel that some, back in Whitehall, believe the Americas to be a lost world rather than a new one.' He watched Coxon not listening. 'What ails thee, John? Is it more of this pirate of yours?'

'No pirate of mine, sir. He was my steward, as you know, as all your captains know.' Coxon coughed on his port. 'I have become a laughing stock, Governor, because of the man. I have fought in two wars, been posted captain, yet I shall be remembered for the man of mine that became a pirate under me.'

Woodes Rogers leant forward. 'And what of me?' he chortled with his cheeks now port red. 'Thanks to old man Dampier's damned book I will be remembered as the man who rescued that simpleton Selkirk. I believe some scribbler is writing a novella of it now. An English novella! Leave that to the French and Spanish for God's sakes! Plays and poetry for Englishmen!'

The coach door slipped open and Oscar Hodge, Coxon's valet, hobbled in with a hand cupped over a tallow light. The two men paid him no mind as he gently lit the lamps. Coxon poured more port for his guest.

'What ails me, Governor, is that I returned to the board in shame,' he filled his own glass, with a chime from the bottle kissing the rim of his goblet. 'I was sent to protect a fortune in gold. Trust me on that: I saw it with my own eyes.' He drained his glass in two gulps. 'But I lost it. Forget the men that were with me. *I* lost it.'

'Is that so?' Rogers rubbed his aching jaw.

'I take it as so.' Coxon breathed quietly, turning his empty glass in circles on the table. 'But that is not all.' He looked Rogers in the eye, testing to see how much he knew about events.

'I have never told this to another soul, sir.' He lowered his voice to barely a whisper.

'That gold was not for protecting. Far from it. My First Lieutenant had other plans. Other orders.' He checked Rogers' eyes, but they were only glazed with wine.

'Other orders?'

'Aye. I was not supposed to return from that place. The gold was not . . .' he hesitated, and changed his line of conversation slightly. Just in case. 'Something else was to happen. Maybe Providence is part of it. I have become an embarrassment to my rank and do not have the backing of wealth to clear my name except by this man's death. Or my own.'

He filled his glass again and grinned in defiance. 'Or maybe I have just drunk too much of late.'

'A dark thought indeed, John. I hope your darkest suspicions do not cause you to question your loyalties?'

Coxon shook his head thoughtfully. 'I trust in those who trust in me, Governor.'

Rogers saluted him with his glass. 'But let us talk of the morning,' he said, attempting to cauterise Coxon's brooding, which had dampened his mood.

'Now tell me: I need, I think, a dozen nooses. What say you? To make a point. Who do you have to avail me of such?'

Chapter Eight

✗

Charles Town, South Carolina.

*E*dward Teach regretted nothing. Privateering had taught him so. All coin was milled in blood and he had watched captains like Hornigold and Jennings, good captains fighting for their country against the French and Spanish dogs, be dis-avowed and denied as soon as treaty had replaced touchpaper.

He had gone from Bristol to Jamaica for his country and little profit and, after the crowns of Europe had signed their names at Utrecht, it was natural to follow Hornigold on the account rather than break his back for a living. Besides, he cut too tall a figure to be below decks. He felt tall enough even for the stars to be within his reach.

Two years had now passed since he had been given his own sloop from Hornigold's hand and grown the long, matted beard that won him his devil's name. He wore a triple brace of pistols holstered across his chest, a broad black hat with twists of match set around the brim – and in his beard – to light and add a mythical quality to his battle face. Teach was a fearsome towering sight to see in a blood-red coat swinging aboard his prey, all wreathed in smoke as if he had ascended from the bowels of hell.

Blackbeard.

And so, success after success and on to the *Concorde*, a

French slaver of three hundred tons, square-rigged with poop, quarter and fo'c'sle decks. Massive for a pirate and likely to run aground if she even saw a sandbar, but to Teach she was equal to his stature.

He re-christened her the *Queen Anne's Revenge*, a typical pirate gesture for in their eyes their only crimes were loyalty to the late Queen and a Stuart sentimentality. They were political exiles awaiting the day when Hanover fell and they could return home to a righteous welcome. Their profession had nothing to do with criminality at all. Piracy was how they ate, for what choice did men have whose country had been stolen from them?

Aye, and you can swallow as much shit as you like but it won't feed you.

Gold, drink, freedom and adventure were justification enough to keep men from the capstan and the field. And Captain Teach had ambition beyond the ken of most.

He had bought land in the Americas, at Bath Town, married a plantation owner's daughter to add to his many other port-wives and had even shared his nuptials with some chosen men of his now four-hundred-plus crew whilst he sat in a wicker chair by her bedside in the dark, watching and smoking without a word.

Teach now associated with Governor Charles Eden of young Bath Town and Tobias Knight, his secretary. After Providence grew too hot, he ensured the relationship grew closer. Edward Teach planned to make the leap from pirate to New World gentry and Governor Eden offered him a proverbial apple. One final great cruise. One last act before taking the King's grace and hanging up his cutlass and becoming a citizen of the regular world.

Go to Charles Town, said Eden. Take your great and terrible

ship and hold to ransom the largest and most profitable settle-
ment in the whole Carolinas. It was not a royal province so
there was no garrison to deal with, just whatever drunken
militia the Lords Proprietor provided. Do this for me, said
Eden, and I will grant you clemency.

Approach but do not attack. Demand but do not harm.
Halt its trade but do not plunder. It possesses one thing that
I want and there is only one man who can give it to you.

Ignatius's life had grown immune to the notion of surprise,
his face even more so, but he raised his eyebrows at the brash-
ness of the pirate who had come to his home.

First there was a note for Governor Johnson delivered by
Teach's captains Marks and Richards, then the same to another
address given him by Eden. The note demanded a ransom
for their burgeoning city, price to be paid in full. Ignatius's
rare sensation of novelty on receipt of the demand had
produced an invitation for Teach to attend him.

'You wish my chest of medicines, Captain?' Ignatius, clad
in black velvet with white Holland linen shirt and cravat, held
his hands calmly in his lap, leant back in his chair and observed
the beast before him. Ignatius himself was lean in compar-
ison, older, narrow as a hat-stand, and Teach could have
snapped him like a wishbone if he chose. But Ignatius, his
real name almost forgotten after nine years of anonymity,
feared villains as the wind fears the sea. The years of peace
had necessitated the use of the lower species of the human
world.

Blackbeard drank, standing, unconvinced that the elegant
elm-wood chairs the room afforded could survive him. 'Aye.
My intentions be but that,' his voice was Bristol-rich. 'Though
whatever silver finds its way to me in negotiations I'll not

return.' He pushed his glass forward for more liquor. Ignatius waved him to the commode to help himself.

'Do you know where I acquired this chest, Captain Teach?' His voice was gently testing.

Teach's back rose in humour as he poured. 'I might. More important to me is that it comes out of here and away.' He turned back with his brimming glass. 'Else it will not be my will that besets this town . . . but the fault of yours.' He raised his glass to the man behind the desk.

'But of course, Captain.' Ignatius smiled. 'You would have no blame in the matter.' He spun his chair to look onto his garden, his back to Teach. The garden remained cool within its high walls despite the spring season, with a sundial in the centre that caught no sun. 'Whoever your benefactor is, his knowledge of the origins of the chest is perfectly correct. Therefore his summary of its contents is a shrewd assumption. But still erroneous, as I discovered myself when I purchased it last year. It's certainly not worth the risk of blockading a whole town.'

Ignatius stood up and Teach shifted instinctively at the sudden movement.

'Very well. You may have your chest, Captain,' he said, crossing the room to Teach and keeping his hands in view. 'I would certainly not wish to be held responsible for the consequences if you did not.' He sampled a measure of his own rum, mindful first to top up Teach's glass. 'However, you may be able to assist me in an endeavour of my own, entirely related to yours. You see, I have knowledge of the *correct* location of your benefactor's interest.' He touched goblets with the pirate, flinching a little at the grimy hand holding his crystal. 'And there will be an incentive for yourself as encouragement.'

Teach swallowed his rum and bid for another. 'I have my loyalties to contend with. I will be owed privateering rights for my troubles here,' he paused as he watched his glass fill. 'I be nearly forty now. Too old to be a pirate. Too slow to rule over pups. I wish to rule on land. I have my eyes set to be a man of *land*.' The word 'land' he spoke with a smirk and a West-country drawl, as if the thought were ridiculous even to him.

Ignatius betrayed no reaction and returned to his desk, where he sipped at his glass thoughtfully. 'Then I may have aptitudes beyond the powers of your present partner, Captain.' He picked up several sheets of vellum and flourished them at the pirate. 'My services are not just limited to these provinces. Almost every crown and faction in Europe is at my ear. Why limit your ambitions to these climes, Captain, when I could grant you rights to France, to Holland, to anywhere? Perhaps you may fancy a castle in Portugal? An Earldom in Ireland even?'

Teach, his eyes fixed on the vellum, moved closer and snatched them from Ignatius. He spread them in his hands like cards, spilling drops of his drink as he did so. The scripts were in a number of languages, each one sealed and signed with noble boldness, each one more elaborate than the last. He passed them back respectfully. 'I look upon you differently, sir.'

Ignatius replaced the sheets on his desktop. 'Naturally I do not wish to interfere with your present loyalties, but merely to extend your horizons and guide you on the correct path, Captain.'

Blackbeard straightened his back, and the pistols holstered across his chest rustled under his long beard. 'What is it you would have me do?'

Ignatius sat, his desk of Office once more between them. 'I am used to having more than one iron in the fire so to speak, Captain. I am currently seeking to return to my possession the item your partner believes to be in the chest. However, I am waiting on my chosen party to begin his quest for it. He has yet to arrive here to take his instructions. He will be your competitor, but I am sure not your equal, and two of you working on the task independently would prove to be of the highest utility to me.'

Teach closed one eye, inclining his head as if he had misheard Ignatius. '*Two* of us? What does that imply? Speak careful now.'

'Another pirate, naturally. Are you aware of the one known as Devlin? A Captain Patrick Devlin?'

Blackbeard's open eye widened. He breathed deeply and drew himself up even taller so that he seemed to almost reach the ceiling beams. 'Aye. I know a man named Devlin. Know a man who betrayed his good pirate captain. Who took his ship and his men and left him to die. Aye, I know such a man.'

Ignatius watched Teach undergo a sea-change before his very eyes. Even beneath his customary filth he could see the pirate's skin flush at some raw, livid thought as he drained his glass.

It had been back on Providence, before the days of *Queen Anne's Revenge*, when Teach had commanded one of Hornigold's sloops and had but eighty men to call his own.

He had come ashore early, fancying himself a little dalliance in town at The Porker's End, and had left his quartermaster, Israel Hands, in charge of the ship.

Seth Toombs's men had been there, only now they were Devlin's. It turned out that the man ridiculed as 'Dandelion' needed his spleen vented. Teach had aimed to provide but Devlin had intervened. He had raised a pistol to Teach. Devlin had dared to point a gun at Blackbeard.

Teach pulled out the stump of candle he kept under his coat and close to his heart, but Ignatius's quizzical expression passed unnoticed by the pirate in his reverence. The odds at the time against him, Blackbeard had backed down from the young upstart. But not for long. Teach had cut the candle right there in front of Devlin, cut it for the last hours of Devlin's life. The candle was to damn him for his pride against one such as Blackbeard. The small spermicetti stump was to be lit once Devlin had received his mortal wound. Then it would burn away the final hours of his life. It was one of the old ways. The Tortuga ways.

Teach's eyes seemed to focus again and his ill humour evaporated as the candle went once again beneath the folds of his clothes. He looked directly at Ignatius.

'Aye, Ignatius,' he said. 'You have your man to do your bidding.'

Chapter Nine

✖

*B*y the time four bells rang out for the fourth time Coxon was crouched with Rogers in the *Milford*'s longboat. Ten sailors sat at the oars, their backs to the island, their eyes to the cutlasses lying at their feet. Two young lieutenants sat side by side at the tiller, eyes sharp to the beach pulling ever closer and their fifty-guinea swords clamped between their knees.

Coxon looked over to the other boat drawing slightly ahead of them, crammed with scarlet men whose muskets pointed skyward like a dozen masts. He examined Rogers' granite face. His governor's chin was held high. His eyes were fixed on the crowd gathering on the beach.

Coxon pulled his pistol from his belt. He checked the screws with his thumbnail and the tightness of the leather-wrapped flint. He tipped the pistol down sharply to satisfy himself that the patch was loaded and packed well. Coxon regretted not polishing the brass plate or waxing the whole and stuffed the gun through his belt on his left hip to prevent the lock digging into his side. He sniffed, raising his head to assess the size of the assembly shuffling down to the beach, now less than a hundred yards away.

Coxon looked to his right, past proud Rogers' puffed-out chest, to the third boat crawling its way to shore. Six hands sat huddled in the jolly boat, rolling their backs with the oars, trying not to disturb the three main pieces of the gibbet lying amongst them in case its bad luck should afflict them. A box of bolts rested between the sheets, wrapped in coils of hemp rope.

They were into the last of the murky breakers now. Rogers said nothing. He wiped neither the spittle from the side of his ragged lip nor the streaks of sweat seeping from beneath his wig. He simply held his head high as he took in the band of three hundred souls that had come to meet him. Three hundred armed pirates.

They formed a colourful and undulating line, an assortment of unshaven figures glittering with sheathed weapons and among them a motley selection of fine fashions as well as filthy coats and hats. Unkempt hair tumbled down their faces like straw or was restrained in head-scarves. They would be pitiful were it not for their wealth of warlike steel. A large proportion was arrayed as tattered gentlemen above but with no shoes or boots on their black feet.

Two men stood separately, in advance of the line, whose clothes appeared recently brushed and crossbelts newly polished. Their hair looked wet from some swift attempt at cleanliness.

Coxon guessed one would be Benjamin Hornigold. And the other? Maybe Burgess or Barrows. Jennings? Was he still alive? News travelled so slowly, but no matter. It was just some illiterate who fancied himself Governor of his own kingdom. Some drunken footpad that had eaten his last breakfast.

The company leapt from the boats, shattering in the breakers the tension of the sombre row to shore. Then there was the slight awkwardness of Rogers and Coxon being carried to the beach on planks as if they were boy kings.

Coxon was at first grateful to feel the sand under his boots after a month at sea, only to realise that he now stood before a crowd of heavily armed reprobates who, without question, despise his very bones.

His head swayed as the steady ground beneath his feet felt like it was falling away. He focused on the crowd, to pass off the sensation.

Coxon's eyes met those of any that dared to stare him down, and then he moved to join the troops to his left, a quarter of the mob stepping further back as he did so.

Rogers looked hard into the face of Hornigold. They stood fewer than than ten yards apart but an abyss yawned between them.

Benjamin Hornigold gracefully raised his left arm and swept off his limp black hat as he bowed. The swift movement alarmed the soldiers and their muskets rattled along with their nerves.

Hornigold held up his hat, turning to the crowd. 'Three cheers for Governor Rogers, lads!' he cried. 'And for good King George come to save us!'

Rogers blinked once as a primeval roar erupted, accompanied by the intense staccato of hundreds of pistols and muskets going off, which drowned out the second and third cheers – cheers that would have made even the Palace of Westminster tremble to her rafters if she had seen the throats from which they came.

The marines' fingers twitched in their trigger guards as the volley carried on and on above their heads. The young lieutenants resisted closing their hands over their ears and instead smiled nervously, watching Rogers' straight, steady back.

A light breeze dispersed the dense cloud of cordite over the camber of the beach to redden and water the eyes of the visitors, then sent the echo of the tirade over the bay to the deck of the *Milford*.

The midshipmen stood with the crew, almost biting the gunwales in anticipation. The weapons lockers had been flung open and shot garlands brought onto deck. Just in case.

A tar with bold black sideburns but a shiny red bald pate nudged Seth Toombs.

Seth seemed even more mesmerised than most by the events taking place on the distant shore. During the morning watch he had spent the time pointing out any ship in the pirate bay that he had a recollection of to anyone who would listen. Seth had grown ever more eloquent below deck over the past few days.

The men had come to hang on his nightly tales. It only took an extra wet from a cup to make his eyes turn wistful and bring out the stories. By the strum of a Spanish guitar and the mellow amber of the lanterns Seth regaled them with legends of a darker life, never quite admitting which episodes involved him.

Most of the crew eagerly awaited details about food, the endless rivers of drink, the rustle of a virgin's petticoats. They dreamed of the African beasts with armour plate and necks taller than the mizzen, of the tribes with no heads but faces in their chests and of the sweet taste of crocodile that could send you mad for human flesh.

The sweet trade. Going on the account. Terms describing the life were given with a wink. And Seth, without a word about himself, had become an authority on the pirate way.

Now the seamen flocked to him, keeping him in the centre of a circle, as if by his closeness he could protect them if the day went the other way.

He looked down at the man who had elbowed him and cocked his head. 'Aye, Tom?'

'What goes on, Seth? The firing and all?'

Seth's wound made of any grin a painful grimace but he had learnt to bear it. 'Oh don't you be worrying about that, Tom,' he nudged him back. 'That just means we should be all a-visiting those there tents along the beach tonight. If you're lucky there may be some of that Chinese I be telling you about,' he winked.

Tom looked harder toward the shore and the soft dreamy look on his face quickly changed to one of tighter, lustful concentration.

One of the young midshipmen glanced over disapprovingly, and Toombs knuckled his forehead and took a step back. The midshipman turned back to the shore. Toombs turned to his entourage and raised his eyes to heaven with a kiss of his lips, drawing smirks from his followers. Then he too looked back to the shore, his eyes narrower. His time was coming and his thoughts tumbled back to that night. The night in the Verdes, on Sao Nicolau, where Seth, *Captain* Seth Toombs no less, had been betrayed by the man he had made his trusted sea-artist. The night he had been left for dead by Patrick Devlin, left to suffer the vengeance of Valentim Mendes alone.

He stroked his cold ugly wound. His time was coming.

The way Rogers sucked in his scarred left cheek brought a cynical smirk to his leathery face. The rounds of shooting had died away, and in the silence he stepped forward against Hornigold so that it was now too close for either man to draw steel. Likewise their pistol barrels would clap together if pulled. Rogers could smell wood-smoke in every fibre of Hornigold's clothes.

'Benjamin Hornigold,' Rogers raised his voice for the crowd and withheld the 'Captain' from his address. 'I come to deliver the Proclamation granted by King George. The Proclamation sent forth last September to these very shores. I am delivering it in person. By order of His Majesty.'

He moved his eyes along the line at every word, looking for movement, waiting for some foul exclamation. None was uttered.

Last year the Proclamation came in on a sloop and the trembling captain that delivered it had been erased from the earth. The sloop's timbers kept many a 'boucan' burning through a lively night.

This time the inhabitants of Providence looked upon five men-of-war stretching out over miles to the south of them. The furthest one, the forty-gun *Delicia*, was just a shimmering grey ghost. Whole forests of wood, hundreds of miles of sail and thousands of pounds of iron. All were ranged against them.

Hornigold held out his hand, expecting to receive the Proclamation, then lowered it to rest on his belt when Rogers looked at his hand in disgust.

'Is Jennings still abroad here?' Rogers asked.

Hornigold thought for a moment, touching his lips softly. 'No, Governor. I'm afraid he not be amongst us at present. On account of him volunteering himself to the Governor of Bermuda. To take the Proclamation in your absence. So to say, Governor.'

'Very well.' Rogers cast a raised brow to the dark rover standing at Hornigold's shoulder. 'Who be this? Will he second you?'

Hornigold looked back to the young man in black and grey with a sharp black tricorne tight on his head. 'This be Thomas

Burgess. He will count in my stead, Governor, aye. And follow my hand, Governor.' Hornigold had determined to repeat the word 'governor' as much as possible, in order to remove the idea from his own ambition.

'Good,' Rogers looked away from the pair. 'I take it,' he spoke louder, for all to hear, 'that you, stood here now, will take the Proclamation. And its promises. For law. And that you will accept myself and my garrison as representatives of the King. So say you all?'

Hornigold's eyes widened. 'Aye.' It was the promises that he wanted to hear. He had scratched his head with the rest of them when they had convened a council to discuss their options. It all hung on the promises. He bit on his thumbnail, waiting for Rogers' next words. Then a man stepped out of the line.

'*No!*' came his cry. 'Not, *aye!*' The bony form launched a bottle upwards that arced through the air to thud into the sand by Rogers' buckled shoes. Rogers never moved. Hornigold's nail flicked on his teeth at the transgression. Before he could channel his fury the rebel continued his tirade.

'Who is *he* who comes amongst us? What have I done to bow to *him*? Bow to his King? His King. Not mine. Not mine!' Half turning, he pleaded with open arms to his fellows. 'Not yours, lads!'

'Silence, you *dog*!' Hornigold bellowed. 'Back in line!' He moved closer to Rogers, confirming his allegiance. The soldier's muskets rattled some more. Coxon rested his hand on the butt of his pistol.

'What?' the pirate sauntered away from the crowd. 'Are we all to speak bloody German now, eh? Is that to be the manner of it? I say we should have gone with Teach and

Vane. We'll take the whole bloody Americas so we should! Stuff that paper up this ponce's arse!'

Rogers shifted away from Hornigold. His sword scraped out of its sheath and flashed blindingly in the sun. The pirate span round at the metallic sound. He was drunk and was surprised to see a gentleman act so bold. But Rogers only wore the clothes of a gentleman. He had almost itched for such a moment to present itself, so that he could make a point.

'*Marines!*' he called behind him. He raised his left hand to the drunken pirate. Pointed his sword down to touch the sand. 'Hang that man and the seven nearest to him. By my order. Raise that gibbet!'

Hornigold quaked more than most at the finality of the statement, but not more than the rapidly counting pirates standing behind their bemused brother, challenging each other as to where seven ended and eight began. The matter was quickly settled by the spade-like hands of the marines who dragged them out of the line.

Coxon stiffened at the flight of the marines from his side, but left his weapons be.

This will tell it, he thought. *Spent their shot. But enough steel to pound us to flour. This will be the hour it goes up.* Rogers had inspected each noose himself that morning. Coxon wondered how it would have happened if the pirate had not tripped out of the line. He felt his heart thump against his ribs as he watched the crowd.

The condemned and struggling eight, wrapped with scarlet arms and hidden by scarlet backs, pleaded to Hornigold as they were dragged to the shoreline. The sailors were clumsily trying to make sense of the three parts of the gibbet they had rapidly pulled from the boat. Each piece twice as tall as them.

Hornigold felt the eyes of the crowd on him. He looked to Burgess, whose hand had already strayed to the hilt of his cutlass, and who was waiting for a sign from his hallowed pirate lord. Hornigold was their protector, a privateer captain of the war, like Jennings, who had left them. But Hornigold had stayed. Hornigold was for them. Bad enough they had all agreed to surrender, to take the pardon, but to be hanged for it?

The frame of the gibbet had already been laid flat on the sand and now the rattling of bolts and tools filled Hornigold's hearing. Before he realised it he had laid a hand on Rogers' shoulder and pulled him round face to face.

'This is wrong, Governor. I cannot see the good of it.' He tried to contain his temper and make his anger sound like reason. 'I cannot allow it.'

Rogers shrugged the hand from his coat and examined the fawn shoulder as if it had been stained. He left his sword-point where it was, touching the sand. 'You cannot allow what, Captain Hornigold?' He disdained the title but acknowledged the local standing of the man confronting him. 'Justice? Order? What do you propose to deny your King?'

Hornigold swallowed. He opened his hands. '*This*. Hanging of these men for some drunken slurs. We wish only peace.'

'Good,' Rogers said. 'We are agreed. I too wish only peace. The difference between us is that I am well aware of how to ensure it, Captain.' He touched the arm of Hornigold's coat almost tenderly. 'And mark me, Ben, you will do well as a privateer in my service. I have come here for profit. Backed by wealth in London. I will remember your help to them all.'

Hornigold raised his eyebrows. He now found the banging of hammers on the shore merely irritating. He swallowed once more and wiped the sweat from his lip.

'I only wish peace, Governor. Whatever else comes . . . well, I won't suppose to consider. Let me address them all, Governor. It will be better coming from me.'

'Of course, Captain. Whatever you wish to deliver I will grant.' He stepped back and ran his sword home into its scabbard in one swift move, just as his silhouette was framed by the raising of the gibbet behind him.

It was a simple gallows, an oblong frame of fresh oak nine feet high and not enough of a drop to snap a man's neck. Kicking away the barrel the condemned man stood on would only ensure a choking, swinging dance. Men shivered at the slow hammering into place of the gallows' feet in the sand and the whores tied up the mouths of their tents and crossed themselves within.

Hornigold turned away from the sight, from the struggling of the eight men having their wrists and feet tied.

He lifted his arms to his brethren, stepping along the sand in front of the line that had slowly begun to form into a huddle. Crews gathered and looked to their individual captains and quartermasters.

Burgess remained still, his eyes on Rogers, his left hand caressing the hilt of his sword. He had not fired a shot. Three pistols rested snugly at his waist. He would stand firm behind Hornigold but only up to a point. His sloop remained crewed and ready, awaiting nightfall. He had long given up on the word of gentlemen and the imminent hangings confirmed his distrust. As much as he approved being recognised and pardoned, and sailing legitimately under letters of marque, he knew the beatings and privations allotted by society to those of his birth. His guns would abide, aye. To a point.

'Brothers!' Hornigold cried. 'We should not let those who choose to sow discord amongst us sully our decision finally to grow into the community we have longed for. For years we have wandered, seeking our own liberty on the seas. Justly our King has seen to know us as kin. To grant us boons beyond our grasp. To form his colonies for him!' He began to appeal to the captains, who had separated from the crowd and were waving down the protests of their crews, to listen.

'You, Martel.' Hornigold pointed to a fat greasy fellow in ancient coat and black wig. 'Did you not dream of "Libertalia"? The fabled land promised to all of us by Captain Avery? And you, Captain Fife. Would you not allow your King to show you gratitude for the years you've spent slicing the Spanish dog?'

Fife shrugged and listened on. Hornigold spied the tall form of Oliver La Bouche, singled him out with gusto.

'And Captain La Bouche. Can it not be of worth to have your slate wiped clean? To be a captain in service to a new kingdom?'

La Bouche ran a dark finger along his moustache. His eyes told Hornigold to move on. La Bouche had fed men their own lips and it was rumoured he had acquired a taste for the 'long pork' after being lost at sea for months. His eyes still bulged from weeks of thirst several months previously. He always said little and was uncommonly still. Hornigold looked away and continued with his speech.

'Would we not all benefit from this day? I tell you, brothers, this is the day we have dreamt of!'

His words were punctuated by the slap of the noose being cast over the bar of the gallows.

'Aye,' a voice rang out. 'This is the day I dreamt of, Ben!'

Hornigold threw a glance at the gallows, then turned to hand over to Rogers. He dipped a weak bow to the governor who nodded in recognition of a job fairly attempted.

'Captain Hornigold speaks the truth, gentlemen,' he announced. He strode to the centre of the beach.

'Return to the town. We have hundreds of colonists who will help you in your new lives. Your King recognises your loyalty. I have a garrison of soldiers to guarantee your protection and social order. Each of you will be granted an acre of fertile land and a year to build a home for yourselves. Leave now.' He paused to look along the line of shaggy men. 'This act of justice will continue in your absence in respect of your allegiance to one another.'

He looked to Hornigold to carry out his wishes, and the pirate captain began to usher his own men to rally the crowd, which duly turned its back to the eight pale-faced men who contemplated the noose swinging lazily before them. Their names had already been forgotten by their brethren.

John Coxon had taken fifteen steps up the beach, leaving behind the gallows and the rest of the marines. As Hornigold and then Rogers had spoken, he had begun to move along the line looking for a familiar face, but had found none.

Hornigold's speech wafted insipidly to his ears as he walked down the line, hands clasped behind his back, his weapons proudly apparent. The pirates all watched him. They recognised something in the worn shoulders of his coat, the cracked leather of his belt and the salt stains on his hat. Something about him was different from the shiny lieutenants and even the gentlemanly, noble look of Rogers. This was a hunter. A seaman. An enemy. He looked into their eyes and spoke to them individually.

'Devlin,' he asked them. 'Patrick Devlin. Who knows him? Where is his ship? The *Shadow*?' He walked slowly. He varied his questions with each face, and received nothing but looks of hatred in return. 'A black- and red-painted frigate. Who knows it?'

Some spat on the ground. Others looked past him and laughed. The crowd began to shuffle away back to their town-ships, turning their hides to him.

Rogers appeared beside him. 'John,' he said, 'I want you to remove those whores from the beach. Get them to gather their tents and return to the towns. Take five marines and make it so.' He looked to the gibbet. 'I will stay and carry out my duty.'

Coxon nodded. 'Aye, Sir.' He began to move but was stayed by Rogers.

'And John,' Rogers' face lightened affectionately, 'I heard you. Don't be too bothered about Devlin.'

Coxon blinked at the mild words. He sniffed and ducked from Rogers' eyes. He moved further away and looked at his feet rather than the tents along the crest. He had gone five paces when a small voice stopped him.

'Señor?'

Coxon looked up at the young brown face and blue eyes of the man summoning him. He appeared to be under twenty and wore loose cotton cloth and linen without a hat or shoes. His shirt was open to the chest, revealing a taut skeletal frame.

'Capitao?' he continued and put up his hand. He did not know Coxon but he had been one of the original sailors of the *Shadow* when it had been taken, along with his hand, from Valentim Mendes, Portuguese governor of Sao Nicolau, of the Verdes. The young man had been there when Devlin's story had begun.

He had decided, after watching the gallows go up, that he should make any attempt he could to gain favour with the new administration in the interests of his own neck. He grinned wildly at Coxon.

'I know pirata Devlin, Capitao. Si. I know of where he has gone. Where he is. Si, Capitao.' His smile broadened at Coxon's interest. 'I can take you to a woman who knows more, Señor.'

Coxon grabbed the startled young man and heaved him, legs flailing, up the beach. It was perhaps not the reward the Portuguese was expecting.

'Take me to her,' Coxon demanded hoarsely, his heart beating violently as he struggled to carry the man, sand flying from his feet.

Chapter Ten

Peter Sam awoke much the same as he had done every day for the best part of a month. His hands were shackled in irons behind his back so he had become accustomed to sleeping on his front.

The stone cell had only one barred window, close to the ceiling. From the moss on the walls and the waving tufts of grass by the narrow vent of light he guessed that most of his confinement was below ground.

He had never seen the sun through the bars and was sure that the opening faced north, the knowledge of which gave him some sense of power.

I know that is north. I now know south, east and west. Little good whilst chained in iron but something to hope for.

He rolled up from the straw-packed sack. A grill in the slabs afforded him his morning relief. His leather breeches and jerkin had been replaced by a linen smock and he crouched over the grating to urinate over the centipedes and beetles that scurried through his faeces.

Once a week the Scotsman came in and threw a cask of water through the grating. Peter looked forward to that day but had cursed himself after he had offered thanks for it on the third occasion. The Scotsman with the enormous nose had paused at the door and smiled down at Peter Sam. Then he had slammed the door behind him and laughed his way up the stairs. On that day Peter began to hate himself.

He had woken in the cell for the first time seemingly months ago now. He had left Dandon and Hugh Harris to follow the white smile and black locks of a fair-skinned boy to a shack that was more curtain than wood. He remembered softness. He remembered dark drink. He remembered nothing more until he awoke with a rough sack over his head upon this same mattress.

And then the Scotsman had entered Peter's world. For the first two days the sack, tied with leather to the shackles at his wrists behind his back, had remained over his head. Those first days were spent still in his own clothes. He was still Peter Sam, quartermaster to a hundred men who shrank from his dark glare.

Then he had knelt before the Scotsman with the sack pulled back from his face while he was spoon-fed the green soup that had become his only sustenance.

At that time he had thought only of death to the tall man with the hanging hair and bony face. He thought of grabbing the spoon with his clenched teeth, of springing up and ramming the end into his captor's eyes.

Somehow the Scotsman could read his thoughts and always took away the wooden spoon and bowl before the perfect moment arrived.

Then there came the week of nakedness when the soup had contained something different and Peter Sam had fallen into a drugged sleep to awaken in his own flesh and shame.

That week was when the beatings began.

The Scotsman would come to the door whistling. Peter could hear the feet pad down stone steps from some hole above and the tune would begin. Not a sailing tune. Some disjointed theme from childhood, so merry and simple.

The door would swing open and the Scotsman would put the bowl down with a resonant rattle. Peter had come to hate the sound of that bowl, and found some solace when it sometimes failed to arrive.

When it did come the Scotsman would continue his whistling for a moment and then stop, looking at Sam with something like pity, his stupendous brow furrowed. The first few times Peter had met his gaoler's eyes with hate and thought of steel and lead, of cutting flesh and breaking bones.

Two weeks further on and he looked at his knees while waiting for the kicks and elbows to his back to stop. The Scotsman never touched his face, nor anywhere he would bleed. Open wounds would require care and might fester. So just the back and haunches.

And after that the food. The soothing words. Always the reassurance that this would all end. That this was his duty to others. No malice was meant towards Peter. He was only doing what he was told. They were much the same as one another. Together they would get through this.

And after all, had he not brought him the smock to wear? Made the soup himself? Even smuggled some meat into it just for him?

Aye, Peter thought. When he did not beat him the Scotsman was not a bad man.

The bolt of the door rattled. A rush of cool air chilled the cell. Peter lifted his head to see Hib Gow standing in the doorway, wooden bowl in hand. No whistled tune had signalled his approach.

Worry was etched on Hib's face. He had the look of a begging dog in his eyes and his chest was heaving beneath his shirt – his blood-caked shirt. Many times the Scotsman had returned with the same sorrowful aspect and Peter again noticed how the Estilete blade, sheathed naked in his belt, was always polished to a cold shine. Hib closed the door slowly, never taking his eyes from the kneeling figure of Peter.

Peter lowered his head as he heard the wooden bowl rap upon the floor. He hungered. His gratitude for the food would take the sting from the kick of Hib's buskins.

Chapter Eleven

✗

*T*he *Talefan* lay becalmed somewhere north of the 8th parallel just before noon. Devlin would await the zenith of the sun to take his latitude. By his own reckoning, after passing St Helena three days ago he would spy the island of Ascension by tomorrow's noon.

This close to the equator, the minutes of the degrees stretched as the Earth spread her waist. A globe was perfectly round, the world not quite so. Sometimes line of sight replaced Davis quadrant and demi-cross. Only the stepping stones of small volcanic islands that God in His wisdom had dropped in the sea could certify the location of the fragile ship of wood.

She was as vulnerable as an infant amongst the majesty of the sea which laughed at the foolishness of the twigs that dared cast themselves upon her surface. The sea reminded them with every catspaw lick that she could crush them like eggshells if she had a mind to.

The man aloft seventy feet on the mainmast, a patch of white linen tied over his head to shield him from the evil of the sun, was solidly sure he could see the curve of the earth itself.

And nothing else.

It seemed as if the sea had engulfed all the land. Claimed it back. Perhaps there had never been any land, and the only souls alive belonged to the voices echoing from the deck way below his bare feet. They might be the last voices he would hear all his life.

He swung around the mast that rolled with the buck of the sea to look abaft over the endless waves. South, somewhere in their past, the *Shadow* was heaving along with one of his brothers hanging by a manrope off its main mast. He strained to glimpse the white fleck on the horizon that would tell him *Shadow* was still behind the *Talefan*.

Devlin and Black Bill shared between them a spiritual chain of invisible lines and finite equations so that, alone every night with their dabs of ink and pencil scrapes, they still nodded to each other silently across the leagues.

The topman's privacy was interrupted by a round of cackling from the deck below. He adjusted his hold and looked down, twisting his head away from the hot wind to try and decipher the jovial noises beneath the sails.

Devlin rang his sword off a fairlead hanging around the mast, silencing the laughter. He cut through the air as if it was the throat of a giant bearing upon him, admiring the gleam from the blade.

His simple shirt, the cuffs tucked into his wrists, was open to his chest and his ebony-hilted poniard stuck behind a sash around his waist.

'Come, Dandon,' he let the sword, carried by its own beautiful weight, fall back through the air in front of him. 'I promise I will not cause any offence or affront.'

Dandon stood by the mizzen, similarly attired in white linen, resting on the pommel of a sword as if it were a cane. 'Oh, I am sure my captain, that it is only my honour that will take a beating, by your honour, *naturellement*.' He bowed elegantly.

Devlin turned to the crowd languishing in the shade of a

sailcloth tent raised above the fo'c'sle. The crew reposed like Bedouin gipsies complete with dates and pombe, a grain and fruit spirit favoured by Africans – and also pirates.

'What say you, lads? Is it not time this popinjay learnt something of the ways of the sword?'

'Aye Cap'n,' some chorused, though most just chuckled into their cups.

Hugh Harris chirped, 'I think I've carried the harlequin through enough, Cap'n!'

Devlin walked forward. 'Then it's settled, Dandon. *En garde, mon ami.*'

Dandon lifted the sword as if holding a snake. 'Some code of combatants surely, my picaroon commander? Perhaps there is some anthology on the matter I could study *a fortiori.*'

'I don't know your meaning, Dandon, therefore I shall ignore it. Now raise your blade.' Devlin's stance grew wider. He began to step forward with his left shoulder facing, his sword hanging low like a faithful dog by his side.

A hollow laugh rose from the fo'c'sle as Dandon bent his back and brought up his sword like a poker. The weight surprised him and the tip began to sink back down as a pain grew in his forearm.

Devlin turned without looking at his friend and paced away again.

'First, my man, your choice of weapon: a good hanger. A fair face-cutter, but no bone-breaker. A good short cutlass can make a periagua canoe from a single tree and won't get caught in the rigging as you hack your way along a deck.'

Dandon looked at his hanger. For the first time he noticed the etched wolf issuing out of the guard and running up the blade.

Devlin had spun again, faster now. 'That's a horse blade

you have there, which I favour myself, and it's a gentleman's sword even if he does not know how to use it,' he bowed and continued. 'Your movements must be small on deck. Lest you find your blade snagged on a sheet before you strike.' He had reached the larboard shrouds and played the point of his sword along them like a harp. He faced Dandon again.

'When you board, once you get past the pikes, go for an officer.'

Dandon nodded intently, his blade trembling.

'The officer would have been trained to fight whilst still at school. He'll be holding his sword in one hand even after his pistol shot. That's the officer to go for. Thus you go at him so . . .'

Devlin rushed at Dandon with a double grip on his sword, raising it and swinging at Dandon's face like a scythe.

Dandon leapt away, slamming his back against the mizzen. He dropped his hanger rattling to the deck, raising his hands in defence.

Devlin pulled his swing before the edge sliced Dandon's fingers and buckled over in joyous convulsion, his laughter drawing sympathetic howls from the tent.

'Aye,' Devlin raised himself. 'I reckon that is what he'll do and all, eh, lads!'

He winked at Dandon and put his left palm out to him. 'Come mate,' he brought his cheek close to Dandon's. 'That'll do for today, eh?'

'Aye, Patrick,' Dandon, tremulous of voice, welcomed the sudden end. 'That'll do for the New Year I feel, Captain.'

Devlin relished the laughs and slaps he witnessed beneath the tent. The weeks of sail had been easy but long and bland.

There were the young silks below, Albany and George, that complained every day. He would let them off at Ascension.

There were some of the hands of the *Talefan*'s original crew who were uncomfortable to be pirates, but at only thirty men he needed them all.

And the food store had dwindled to rice, durum, peas, garlic, onions and a hogshead of pork more vegetable than flesh. The wine and rum was all gone which just left beer, casks of brandy, the punch, and the pombe.

It was barely enough for even a small house of priests let alone the pirates' thirst.

The entertainment today and the luncheon beneath the tent had been a godsend. And the mark of a good captain. He would have an hour of swordplay for them all. He would parry with them until his sweat swabbed the deck. Such folly was needed today for there would be no time to spare to celebrate the crossing of the equator soon to come.

He raised his sword and they crowed back, the tent billowing with raised mugs and cheers.

Devlin recalled a day in St Malo. He was back again in Brittany for a moment. René Duguay-Trouin paraded through the streets, promoted from pirate to admiral of the Marine Royale. Women pulled open their chemises baring their breasts and calling the young man's name like cats in heat. Devlin watched from the steps of the guildhall smoking Brazilian tobacco through a terracotta pipe. He had wanted to be that man instead of stinking of fish and living on bread mashed with onions and cod bones. Devlin was running from England for fear of a choking and running from Ireland for fear of the same.

He ran no more. He thought of Peter Sam. Be he in America or back in Madagascar Devlin had covered both badger holes but still the loss of his quartermaster had riled the crew.

They were the *Shadow*. Now they were the *Talefan*, the weak *Talefan* sailing into Charles Town. But he was strong. This was all it took. This is what they loved. Soon they would reach the Dutch and Spanish trade routes to South America. A slaver would rise up from the horizon and good victuals would come.

Keep them hot. Keep them up. It would take but one sail to sate their appetites. And it would come. He looked to the sky and the orb that marked the passage of his day.

He sent Dandon away to find a drink and called for John Watson, the cooper, who had become a temporary quartermaster based on his popularity and sober head.

Watson was an old hand from Seth Toombs's lot, a great teller of rumbustious tales and a fine musician of pipe who had slotted in tidily as a rough quartermaster.

Devlin called for the backstaff and Watson brought it aft. Together they walked to the quarterdeck where Devlin took a moment to assess their lot under the guise of the magic of the latitude he was to perform.

Watson, in his refined Kent ictus that somewhat mystified his origins, relayed the stores. The need for fresh meat was paramount. The brig had no manger but they could find space for a couple of hogs and they had a coop to fill afore the mainmast. It was a fortnight still to reach Charles Town.

'We could do some hunting at Ascension,' Devlin suggested. 'Leave those fops there.' He checked the compass in the binnacle, reset the sighting vane to the five degrees he estimated from yesterday and raised the backstaff, a good English one of brass scales, oak handles and vanes belonging to his new ship. He put his back to the sun just as Albany Holmes, one of the gentlemen carried aboard in Madagascar ascended to the deck, shielding his eyes with his shirt sleeves.

'Speak of the devil . . .' Watson nudged Devlin and stood away to inspect the tiller.

Albany, without invitation, stepped closer. 'Captain Devlin,' his salutation issued forth as if passing Devlin in Piccadilly.

Devlin looked up, pulling out his watch at the same time. 'Aye, Albany, how may I be of service to you this day?'

Albany gave another brief nod. 'I have been in consultation with my fellow, George, this morning, Captain. There is a matter which I feel we have been avoiding these past weeks.' He looked up to the spanker above them as he spoke, avoiding Devlin's eye.

'What matter is that, Albany?' Devlin took a small pleasure in the familiarity as he loosened the wooden screws of the backstaff's shadow vane.

'The matter of your intentions towards George and myself, Captain Devlin.' He met Devlin's querying look.

'Besides a brief conversation the first morning we have not addressed our . . .' he hesitated over the word, withdrawing whatever it was completely, and simply waited for Devlin to pick his own.

'Future?' Devlin playfully proposed.

Albany jumped on the word. 'I am more concerned with our ransom. We are heading to the Americas for such purpose I presume. All of our belongings have been stolen. I should like to know, sir, what I may be worth to you. That is all.' He looked around the narrow beam of the ship disdainfully, the more so now it was a pirate vessel.

Devlin looked at the watch nestling in his palm – George's watch in fact. He would indulge Albany. After all, he could play a fair guitar on a Sunday when he had a mind to.

'You are of the mind we are heading to Charles Town to

ransom *you*?' He spoke loud enough to provoke a cough from Watson aft leaning on the tiller.

Albany was indignant. 'Well, why else, sir? Are we not your prize?'

Devlin sallied to the rail swinging the backstaff idly. He called across the deck, 'Hoy, Fletcher!'

Sam Fletcher jumped from the tent on the fo'c'sle. 'Aye, Cap'n?' he answered, his hand cupped to his mouth.

'Tell me Sam, how might you hazard a latitude, if you cared to?'

Sam swayed along the gangway scratching his chin. 'Well, Cap'n. Without your proper skill and mechanicals. Roughly like,' he had reached the hatch and stood upon it in his bare feet rather than the hot deck. 'I reckon I holds out my arm thus,' he stuck out his left arm to the horizon aft of the ship. 'Then I points my other to the sun. When she be at her highest, mind,' he squinted at the sudden glare as his eye followed his salute.

'And then what, Sam?' Devlin called back.

'I scales the angle betwixt, Cap'n. And there I may be.'

'And what do you make it now, Sam Fletcher?'

Sam's lips counted visibly as he inclined his head to the gap between his arms. Albany watched, bemused.

'Reckon it to be about just over ten, Cap'n?'

Devlin had already begun his own reading, his left hand moving the shadow vane slowly, 'Back to your drink, Sam. Good man.'

Sam tapped his forehead with a thumb and skipped back to his mug. Devlin turned to Albany, slamming the backstaff to his chest.

'I make it ten forty-two or thereabouts. What make you, Albany?'

Albany cradled the backstaff awkwardly as Devlin walked away, down to the deck. His final words to the gentleman were spat over his shoulder.

'Just *what* are you worth to me? That man can't even read and is worth more. You're lucky I feed you, you dog!'

Albany heard Devlin's boots stomping about the cabin beneath the deck. He listened to Watson's mocking laugh, bit his lip and turned to the stair. Dandon saluted him from across the way with a leather mug and then their joint laughter followed him down the companionway to the gloom and George's expectant face.

'What did he say, Albany old boy?' George looked up from his hammock just in time to catch the backstaff in his lap as Albany tossed it to him.

Chapter Twelve

✖

*T*hree weeks had passed. The bamboo scaffolding surrounding the ramshackle fort on the eastern cliffs rising above Nassau appeared like a skeleton re-growing its own skin. A yellowing British flag showing the Union colours, still new to some of the eyes that looked upward at it, flapped limply in the early summer breeze.

It was now mid August on New Providence. The two main taverns-cum-brothels, The Porkers End and The Cat and Fiddle, both owned by Mrs Haggins (Mr Haggins having long since whispered himself away), swelled with soldiers and 'citizens' now friends under the petticoat.

Then there was the old widow, who slept her nights under a blanket of brandy after sewing calico skulls and hour glasses onto black cloth. She had even made Devlin's flag, the simple skull above crossed pistols set in a compass rose. She had died suddenly the day Woodes Rogers nailed the Proclamation to the walls of her shack.

As she died, in a foul sweat, others began to feel a bubbling within their chests, their eyes raw and weeping. They attributed the illness not to the saddles of horseflesh rotting on the beach or the effluence that failed to sluice down the dusty streets, now swelled by the immigration of hundreds of Europeans unused to the broiling dry heat. Instead they linked it to the redcoats and wigs that used Roman numerals to list the things they could not do and what they should be forced to pay if they dared do them.

The island stores now sold cloth, Protestant pamphlets and tilling tools instead of French powder, rum and Spanish grape wine.

Children appeared, like goblins, running amok. Scarred faces shook their heads above the rims of their cups at the proliferation of the tiny foreigners and whispered of the inlets of the Carolinas, of Ocracock and Bath Town, where Teach and Vane were holding mile-long gatherings on the beaches – whole parties of pirates carousing fearlessly and trading freely, for Lion Dollars and guineas not reales or maravedi – under more welcoming governors.

New Providence. And so it was. So Rogers claimed it to be. He sat sweating beneath his wig of Office copying his Latin from a Protestant-proffered tome. Boldly he raised his letter above Whitehall and Secretary Popple who received all governors' addresses. He penned to King George himself and scratched his quill across the vellum with relish.

Expulsis Piratis. Restituta Commercia. Pirates expelled. Commerce restored.

Hornigold sat opposite, his nails bitten down to the nub. He wore a French suit, five years out of fashion, impregnated with a week's worth of sleep-creases and sweat.

Rogers dusted the paper, brushed it with the feather of his quill for one stroke then slipped the pen back in its pewter well. Finally he raised his eyes to Hornigold.

'Ben,' he voiced gently. Hornigold straightened. 'I have need of you.'

Hornigold sprang up from his ancient Spanish velvet chair and approached the governor's broad desk, cut from a single oak.

The office stood in the old Spanish fort where the English governors had made their home before the Spanish returned to burn them out almost two decades before.

It was sparse and unrefined but some furniture from the ships had made it officious and comfortable enough.

Two cathedral-like windows stretched and arched to the high ceiling, most of their lead work shot out and hanging grimly to the glass panes swinging loosely in the breeze.

The windows looked out over the whole winding slum that Nassau had become under the pirate regime and Rogers spent an hour every morning counting the bodies dragging their way to church at ten each day by order. He clenched his painful jaw at the volume of trade still disappearing within the doors of the taverns.

He looked up at Hornigold standing unsteadily before him. He spoke as he ever did, as if halfway through a speech.

'We have the redoubt at the harbour built and work goes well on the new western fort. However, Ben, to date only six hundred of your fellows have taken the pardon,' he adjusted his summer wig like tipping back a hat. 'I need more.'

Hornigold pinched at his nose, muffling his mouth and apologetic words. 'Ah well, Governor. It be early days yet. I think a lot of the English boys here be a bit at odds with the Dutch and German throats setting up here.'

'They be the colonists, Ben. Like it or loathe it. There are few English hearts willing to come. We should all welcome good Protestant stock from wherever it comes.'

'Aye, Governor,' Hornigold sighed.

'I also have become aware that some of the principals have slipped cable and have gone a-roving again.' He observed Hornigold's renewed perspiration.

'None of my doing, Governor, I assures you. Burgess and I have taken up our privateering stations with honour.'

'Oh yes,' Rogers picked up one of his garrison's reports. 'Your militia company is often drunk on watch, if on watch at all. I fine more of them than any other soldier, and have more of them confined than I do prisoners.'

'As I say, sir: early days.' Hornigold lowered his head and fingered his sword hilt.

'Indeed,' Rogers placed the paper down again. 'The matter, to be blunt, is that a good deal of the pirate captains have gone "off". That leaves our province open to attack. Leaves the trade routes vulnerable again. I cannot allow that. I will *not* allow that.' He checked Hornigold's eyes. They were rheumy and wide, but faithful.

'I will take my duties honourably, Governor. Even if I have to hunts them down myself.'

'I am glad to hear you say it, Ben,' Rogers' eyes lightened. 'It will come to that I am sure.'

A rap on the door startled Hornigold and set the collection of pistols and blades he wore clinking like a bridled horse.

Rogers waved him down, 'Just in time. I wished Coxon to be present this morning.' He called for Coxon to enter and they both looked to the door across the room, the path to it suddenly emblazoned in golden cobwebs of sunlight patterned through the windows.

The door swung open and in stepped Coxon, accompanied by an emaciated black tomcat weaving amid his ankles and looking hopefully at all the men one by one.

'You sent for me, Governor?' Coxon glanced at Hornigold whilst sweeping away the cat with a foot.

'Indeed John, come hither,' Rogers opened a hand to

Hornigold. 'You know Captain Benjamin Hornigold of course?'

Coxon bade good-day as he crossed the room. He removed his dusty hat, holding it behind his back. The cat trotted after, then became mesmerised by the warm shafts of sun and sat down in the glare, sniffing the light contently.

'How can I be of service, Governor?' Coxon asked.

Rogers pushed himself away from the desk, scraping the floor with his chair and affording himself a view of both captains at once.

'Benjamin here offers himself and Burgess completely to our cause, John,' Rogers wiped his shirt sleeve across his jaw as he spoke.

Coxon leant forward to listen more closely. 'What cause is that, sir?'

Hornigold leant in also.

'Let me tell you a little about Ben,' he stifled a rise of bile in his throat and coughed. 'Benjamin has been captain to no less esteemed patroons as Edward Teach and Samuel Bellamy. Teach of course has become the brigand known as Blackbeard. I feel Ben will be invaluable in netting such a rogue.'

'He left some time ago, Governor,' Hornigold interjected. 'We went our separate ways a long summer since. And Bellamy of course, God forgive his young soul, went down with his ship last year.'

Hornigold crossed himself in a clumsy twitch at the memory of the young pirate. Rogers carried on undeterred.

'La Boche has gone. Also Williams, Penner, Fife, Martel, Cocklyn and Sample. All slipped away in the last weeks with most of their crews. Jennings and Barrow have taken the pardon abroad and Charles Vane roams free from under our very bows.' He looked at both men, his eyes swivelling between them. 'We are close to failure, and now *this*!' His fist suddenly slammed down on the oak, sending a stylus jumping from the desk. The cat started, flicked his tail twice, then nestled himself back in the sun.

Rogers wiped his mouth again. '*Disease*!' he hissed the word sibilantly. 'Thirteen cases this week alone. And it is only August! By September we shall all be dead if this continues unabated!'

'I can report that the garrison is without blemish, sir,' Coxon proffered. 'It is the town that is infested.' As he spoke he cast an eye to Hornigold who shifted uncomfortably.

'I can only say, Governor, that it is due to the pirates and the townsfolk leaving their cattle heads where they fall, and their desire to gather together around the town rather than spread out amongst the hills.' Hornigold stroked his hat-matted hair forward and distracted himself by watching the cat stretch and writhe in the sun.

'Exactly. Ben, I want you to man two ships to the brim and go a-hunting. Take some of these idlers out of the town before we are all dead. We share too much foul air. It will help the newcomers to settle down with a couple a hundred of you gone.'

Hornigold's ears burned as he looked back to Rogers. 'A-hunting, Governor?'

'Aye, lad,' Rogers slapped the desk. 'You are a Privateer to his Majesty. As you were in the war, again. It is your duty to bring these brigands to bear is it not? You spoke the same yourself did you not?' He tested Hornigold's mettle with his own.

'And, naturally, any prize you find of yourself, you may keep two thirds.' He pulled some parchment from a leather wallet, preparing to pen the thought. 'The final third for your King, naturally.'

'Oh, aye. Naturally,' Hornigold agreed.

Coxon sniffed and plucked at his vest. So that was it then. The old game afoot to be sure. Rogers had played it well enough. Privateers – but pirates with a few extra strokes of ink. And it would not hurt if some Spanish ships sailed a few leagues too near. Maybe one on its way back from Potosi, lying low in the water with a ballast of silver.

Coxon cast a warm look at the cat that had sidled up and begun rubbing against his calves. Wild cats. The town was full of them. Thankfully rats could not be blamed for the fever.

'John,' Rogers addressed, 'I wanted you to witness the order I am giving to Captain Hornigold. My sanction to go abroad from New Providence.'

Coxon bucked up. 'Aye, Governor.'

'And something for yourself, my good man.'

Coxon stepped forward, flicking the cat away again, watching Rogers inscribe the order on the vellum sheet.

'We are short on supplies. I underestimated the provision of goat, cattle and crop required on this island. The colonists will farm, but we are in a desperate fix which I do not wish to be known. In another month it will be common knowledge.'

'And I am to go north to Virginia for supplies I take it?' Coxon surmised.

'There is no time. And the price will not be as good.'

Coxon breathed in. Breathed in dread. As good as what?

'I want you to tally what we can trade. Sailcloth and rope. Comandeer the salterns. Iron and weapons. That we have plenty of. Man the *Buck* and another sloop and sail to Hispaniola. Trade there for fresh victals so we may stock ourselves without applying to England.'

Coxon looked to Hornigold as the only other compatriot in the room. Rogers' head furrowed to his writing, paying as little mind to the words he had uttered as if he had merely asked Coxon to clean out a cupboard for him.

Trading with Hispaniola meant trading with the Spanish. An illegal act for a King's ship.

Intolerable for an English captain to entertain the thought.

Coxon cleared his throat. 'You want me to sail to Hispaniola, Governor Rogers?'

'My God, man, no!' Rogers glared up from blotting his ink. 'I want you to send some pirates thus! Not a King's man!' He laughed at the possibility.

The cat, encouraged by the laugh, jumped up on the desk and nudged himself against Rogers' sleeve.

'Take some time to gather a couple of good crews, that's all. I want you to find some good pirates to sally forth. There must not be a single Royal man aboard.' He pushed the cat away, only succeeding in urging more ardour from the feline. 'How goes the word for your former servant, John? This pirate, Devlin.'

'I chanced on a man who had served with him.' Coxon winced from a sharp pain that came on cue from the star shaped scar beneath his sleeve. 'He led me to one of the whores that had served his purpose a year ago. She has the fever. She tells me the pirates sailed to the east. To leave the Antilles. He is gone, apparently.'

'Ah, left for safer climes. If we could all do the same, eh?'

Coxon could still sniff an air of illegality about the room, mixed with the aroma of the streets wafting in through the broken windows.

It was at that moment that something red sparkled beyond Rogers' shoulder and glinted to Coxon.

He noticed then the pile of chattels and goods piled in the dark corner of the room. His brow twitched curiously and Rogers followed his eye.

'Oh, you note my waveson, John.' He stroked the cat playfully then blew on the paper before him, causing the cat to flinch, and handed it to a bowing Hornigold. 'Your orders, Ben.'

'I thank you, sir.' Hornigold took the parchment and squinted a watery eye to read it over, slavering at the prospect of adventure ahead.

Rogers shifted his chair to face the collection in the corner. The cat struck out a paw towards him as he moved.

'I have tidied all the junk from the fort and kept it here. There may be some value in it. I should like it assessed. But I have more at hand for the moment.'

Coxon moved around the desk, his eye drawn to the red glare that had now vanished. Only a dull heap remained. A heap of black sacks and barrels. Clothes and broken weapons or weapons too old to care about.

He identified a few ornate harquebuses and matchlocks from Spanish ships and a small pile of astrolabes and cross-staffs. Iron ballast, in sheets and lumps, lay there crude and shiny. It was a collection with as much heart as a child's broken toys from yesteryear. Partially forgotten, but potentially too precious to throw away.

Coxon found the source of the red spark: a small-bore cannon. It lay under a wealth of sacks, having been dropped at the earliest convenience for its weight and then everything piled atop it.

It was green and thick with age. Its barrel was sealed with some mixture of crustacean and barnacle. It had one redeeming if slightly gruesome feature, for gripping the barrel was a coiled dragon, its jaws panting and the tongue lolling over its teeth. The dragon was grey and green like the rest of the gun, save for its glowering red eye that appeared to be watching Coxon intently.

'Oh that?' Rogers anticipated the question. 'Damn thing's all sealed up. No use at all. I may put it in my garden. When I get one. Don't get too excited, John. I am sure enough that its eyes are only glass.'

Coxon studied the dragon. He thought of Guinneys on The Island. A year ago, Coxon had come aboard Guinneys' ship, *Starling*, on its way back from the Indian factories. He had been weak then. Weak from dysentery, the fate of many stationed in the castles along Africa's slave-coast, but Coxon had not been stationed there. He had been struck down whilst his ship waited for resupply and favourable winds. It had been the wrong decision to send his ship home without him rather than escort a blackbirder, a slaver of the South Sea Company to the Americas.

His ship had been taken by pirates on her way home, burnt and sunk. *His* ship. The ship he had captained in the war, gone forever. His servant taken along with her.

But his man had not been so burnt.

He had gone with the pirates. He had become their leader somehow. Coxon's ravening for revenge was matched only by his shame.

Before he stepped ashore in England he and Guinneys were sent to take the pirates who had destroyed his ship. He was to sail to The Island, to protect the French gold, but Guinneys had a different agenda. Blood had flowed following a fight on sand and in shallow waters. Hence a star-shaped scar on Coxon's arm – and another ship almost lost by the man he had taught. And more shame to be paid.

There was something unsettling about the Chinese gun. Coxon thought of the dead Guinneys and his years spent voyaging from China. And then this dragon, staring at him this very morning, here on an island worthless to his mind, riddled with disease and pirates.

A Chinese gun. Here. Now. And himself sent to this island to sieve the seas of pirates. And a Chinese cannon winking from the corner of this very room. And Devlin not here.

A warmth spread over him that had nothing to do with the day's heat, the same sort of warmth he used to feel just before a line of French frigates appeared on the horizon.

A muffled guttural howl from the desk followed by a soft snapping sound and Hornigold's belly laugh brought him out of his daze.

Coxon turned to see Rogers' fist around the cat's neck, a satisfied leer on his face. He tossed the corpse away and it spun along the floor back into the sun.

'Bloody cats are driving me to lunacy, John. Do something about them, eh?' Rogers mopped his brow.

'We need something to keep the rats at bay, Governor.' Coxon replaced his hat and bowed an exit without waiting for his orders, sidestepping around the cat, now peacefully reposed in the sun.

Chapter Thirteen

Extract from the journal of George Lee on his Grand Tour.
Notes specific to the Islands of Ascension.
July 1718.

> *As of this month, myself and my companion the venerable*
> *Albany Holmes have been abandoned on this forsaken rock*
> *by the hand of the famed pyrate Devlin. We are assured we*
> *will be rescued inevitably within the month, the island being*
> *a favoured point for passing ships to pick up fresh meat and*
> *turtles that come to lay their eggs in the May month.*
>
> *The pyrate Devlin, our notorious Captain, tells how*
> *Dampier survived for sixty days on this black land with*
> *thanks to the Portuguese who chose to land goats in the*
> *hills two hundred years before to provide a continuous*
> *larder for mariners using the island as a bearing point.*
>
> *We believe, as our captor enlightens, that the island sits*
> *almost central between Africa and the Southern Americas*
> *and is oft visited by all nations for the purpose.*
>
> *We have been given musket, cutlass, and sailcloth for*
> *shelter and have a plentiful supply of fresh water from the*
> *springs on the island. There is no population save for the*
> *birds which I believe to be terns, petrels and boobies which*
> *I have spent much of my days depicting with charcoal,*
> *which is in abundance.*

The pyrates spent two days hunting goat and tipping turtles. I understand that one turtle feeds fifty men with meat and soup. I am reluctant to partake as the creatures look and smell most unpleasant but I gather are a delicacy to the sailor and his ilk.

There is much Norfolk pine planted on the island as well as whole forests of bamboo which I gather was introduced as spare wood for the mariners, and for us also if our time here necessitates the construction of a more permanent abode.

As to the pyrates, my journal may act as a record that they left this place to continue to the Americas. There the pyrate Devlin, I gather, is on some misadventure to secure the safety of one of his brethren. I wish it to be known should I not return to England that I with whole malice and aforethought wish the Governments of whomever shall find my journal to pursue the ending of this rogue and his brood and concur with the proclamation of our parliament that these men surely be hostis humanis generis *with whom neither Faith nor Oath is to be kept.*

George Lee. Ascension Island, July 1718.

August. The bells of the steeples chimed for nine o'clock as the *Talefan* crept into Charles Town by main course and spanker sail. Under the moon the wharf along Bay Street reflected grey and silent in the still water. Small slatted-wood warehouses stood along the quay, coldly still after the day's work, whilst the ropes of the stevedore's cranes swayed restfully in the warm updraught of air from the sea, as if gathering their strength for the morn. It was a walled town. A redbrick front surrounded the whole with bastions anchored at every corner like an English castle. Those that faced the land had a trench dug around, further increasing the castle-like aspect, and a seven-foot barricade of cypress trunks lay beyond this. The Indian wars had turned the town into a fortress.

The ship regarded the fortress before it, almost a mile long with two jetties acting as bridges into the town. Three triangular points acted as redoubts, guns included, facing seaward. A half-moon-shaped guard tower complete with minions stood between the two bridges. Charles Town seemed as much a fort as the one they had passed coming up from the south, and not to protect against native invasion. These were defences against the Spanish, for this was the King's most southerly colony, his most precarious line of defence against the forces in the Florida Gulf. But this was a Lords Proprietor's town not a king's. Protection came out of their own pockets. And battlements are just walls if there are no soldiers standing at them. Never mind Spain: pirates were Charles Town's greatest nightmare.

As the little brig turned her tiller to draw her larboard side and her puny guns to bear, the lamps along the wharf began to light one by one as some unseen soul moved his ladder along.

Wave by lapping wave the *Talefan* drew closer with each light until, after finishing his evening's duty, the lamp-lighter turned to see the brig a stone's throw from him. The drop of the anchor satisfied him that the hulking black shape had not been there when he had started his chores.

The harbour sheltered a fleet of sloops and pinks twinkling and bobbing sleepily beneath their sidelights and mast lamps. But the brig had come in dark, almost on the swell, and now sat tugging defiantly on its tether.

The lamp-lighter shouldered his ladder and turned his back on the brig. He had heard of black ships before and it was best to be some place else when you saw one.

Then there came the slap of the gig hitting the slate-like water. The *Talefan*'s arrival after forty days' hard sailing from Madagascar was announced by the triumphant setting down of the boat. The *Shadow* perhaps still lay four days behind, perhaps ten. Perhaps she was not there at all.

Two figures rowed to the stone steps. Once there, one of them scampered up with a rope and tied the gig whilst his companion trudged up the steps and looked about at the tumbledown warehouses and custom-house shacks that made up the East Bay wharf.

This was how Patrick Devlin first set foot in America. It was fitting therefore, especially to him, that his first sight and sound was as familiar as the reeking alleyways of Wapping and the Pelican Stairs of his briefly adopted London:

A scream. And the rush of a chase across cobbled stone.

He took ten fast steps across the flagstones of the wharf, the lick of the sea already leaving his ears and his legs wavering at the feel of land, and cocked his ear to the sound of the footsteps. Dandon too inclined his head to the tip-tap trot of a woman's feet echoing around the harbour as he joined him.

She appeared from around a crooked corner of wood in front of Devlin, surprisingly closer than the echo of her buttoned boots had indicated.

Her head was down, black curls and black shawl flapping, and as Devlin opened his arms and stepped into her path, she ran into him like a startled crow.

He had her arms and swung her around as she struggled against his grip.

'Easy there, Miss,' he happily greeted his first local acquaintance. 'What goes on?'

She pushed herself away from him, her heels kicking the stone, gin and tobacco wafting from her hair. Dandon merely flashed his gold-capped grin at her pale face and held her fast. Gasping, she looked from Devlin to Dandon and then clasped herself to them as two male figures hurtled around the corner baying like hounds, their howls ceasing the instant they caught sight of the two seamen.

Devlin turned to the dark newcomers silhouetted by the trail of lamps lining the street. They skidded to a halt, almost sparking the cobbles. Two sloping devils they were, rubbing their chins in dark thought, with scabbards for tails. They split apart, sidestepping across the path.

Devlin needed no comment, no tale. The story was in the air. The girl's shrill voice split the night open.

'Them is after me! They be grabbing me off the street! Help me, sirs! I done nothing.'

The two continued their crab steps, stalking now, outflanking, then moving inward to pincer Devlin. He stood still. Waiting.

The taller of the two, on the right, broke his silence with a consumptive rasp.

'Let her go, gents. It's no mind of yours. Just a little game that's all.'

'I may mind that the lady does not want your game.' Devlin kept his eye on the one to his left. The one not talking. The movement stopped. The three of them now two sword lengths apart.

'Know how it is, mate,' the talker reasoned with a sociable laugh. 'We're here a month gone now. Cap'n Teach leaves us here for courting and wedlock. Don't you know that, sailor?'

The other dragged out his hanger with a chuckle, stepping into the range of everything bar teeth.

'Ain't worth dying for a piece of quim, mate,' he spat.

Devlin stepped away and drew back his coat to show the butt of his pistol and the hilt of his hanger. He pulled his hat tighter on his head and grinned at them both.

'A noble sentiment, lads.' He gave them one moment to drink him in. 'I'll shoot the youngest first. I'll make my guess. The other will lose his face.' He stepped slowly to his left, blocking Dandon and the girl, framed by the sea and the masts behind. The moon would have helped but the lamp-lighter's work gave him enough to work with.

Unfortunately for their mothers the assailants were too drunk for dancing.

They swept forward, confident enough, with a roar that never fully rose.

The one with the drawn sword pulled it back to strike, only to have his face explode in black and red the instant a snap of powder slammed a bolt of lead through his nose. His sword sang on the stone as he dropped to the ground.

Given the sudden smoke now masking his opponent the other believed his dagger was the way to go.

He dived in, then felt himself lifted off the floor. Something cold punched through him and out again as he followed through to the cobbles.

He coughed at the ground and his own blood jumped back into his eyes. He pushed up weakly only to feel an icy spike pressing him back down. He belched blood and sank into its warmth.

'Welcome to America, Patrick,' Dandon said, letting the girl go.

She ran from Dandon, kicked the man twitching in his

bloody puddle and fell into Devlin's arms as his blade scraped back into its sheath with a wet sigh. She smelt saltpetre and dampness as she breathed into his chest.

'Oh thank you, sir,' she cried. 'Thank you for my honour.'

Devlin was unsure of her honour and her closeness for that matter. He wheeled her away by her wrist, blood still ringing in his ears. He moved forwards and away, dragging her behind him until his panting ceased and the night became darker again.

They moved into the street to their right. He saw English three-storey houses; the heady scent of Dogwood and Red Anise.

Dandon caught up and took her from him without a word. She rubbed her wrist where Devlin had held her. Devlin kept moving, his back heaving as he lumbered up the street.

Dandon took in the girl's distress, more than his friend and captain could. She had witnessed something rare.

'Where do you reside, young lady?' Dandon said sooth-ingly.

She looked, startled, into his calm eyes. 'New Church. An inn.'

'Then I will take you home,' he promised. 'And speak of nothing of what you have seen. And speak less of what you have not seen and on that point I mean that my dangerous friend and I do not exist. Would that be clear to your young ears?'

'For heavens, sir. You and your . . .' she looked at the black figure still stamping up the street, '. . . friend have done me a service untoward. I will hold with my voice, I swear it.'

'Good girl,' Dandon smoothed his moustache. He looked to Devlin pacing in circles, reloading his pistol. 'Now, my child, I am a Bath Town resident myself, but know nothing of Charles Town, and we have a house we need to visit. Please understand that we have just arrived and this address is the only place we have to stay. If you would be so kind.'

Her face lightened. 'Oh, by all means, sir. Wherever you wish to go. I owe you that much.'

'Thank you, *mademoiselle*. I am looking for such an abode.' He opened the bottom part of the letter to her, shielding the rest of its contents from her.

Her eyes gleamed. 'My way home. I can take you there in moments. We cut through Union and the alley.'

Dandon called to Devlin who spun around, twisted from his mire. He again screwed his hat on tighter and flapped his coat about him as if shaking it dry. He fumbled for his pipe as he came across. The captain again.

'All's well, Captain?' Dandon queried as gently as he thought appropriate, for he knew that although Devlin had developed a natural talent for death something of an old conscience hovered within him.

Most of the men Dandon now knew had buried thoughts of virtue and sin in drink and new shores that wiped their souls clean with each sunrise. But Devlin was not naturally cut out for that life. He lived it but was yet to own it. He enjoyed his talent for killing and such realisation did not always hang well with him. Dandon brushed away the notion that he should be wary of Devlin when it did.

Devlin looked about. The tall spiked gates of the colourful homes contradicting the welcome of their hanging baskets and pastel paintwork. The spikes were a last defence against a slave uprising, their numbers far exceeding the gentle towns-folk. He put the pipe back into his waistcoat, telling himself that it would only serve to slow him down.

'Aye, Dandon,' he said. 'All's well. But those men spoke of

Teach.' He looked down at the girl. 'By Teach do they mean the Blackbeard Captain Teach?'

The girl, Lucy as she revealed – a name close to both their hearts, for *Lucy* had been Seth Toombs's old ship – screwed up her features at the ignorance of her two saviours.

She walked with them and told of the terrible May just gone, the month when Charles Town almost bled at the hands of Blackbeard.

Lucy blushed at her culpability that, pardon her, she did take a drink every now and then, but mostly, and upon her soul, it was due only to the circumstance of the summer that had driven her to it.

They walked north along deserted Queen Street. Oil lamps lined the walls of the three-storey shops and light also shone from within the rooms above. The notes of a clavichord playing high above them drifted on the air. They turned into narrow Union Street as Lucy told of her town's recent history.

The pirate Edward Teach – Blackbeard – had blockaded Charles Town in a week of terror. Nothing came in. Nobody dared venture out. The harbour became a cemetery of wooden hulks, and this only a month after Charles Vane had visited their waters and harried them with all his boldness.

Lucy stammered as she told them how the pirates walked the streets, immune to threat, ignorant of decency or law.

Teach arranged the kidnapping of a councillor and his four-year-old son and offered Governor Johnson their heads if his unholy terms were not met.

'What terms, Lucy?' Devlin touched her arm.

Lucy caught her breath. The talk had made her parched, the men's ignorance more so, and she expressed the same.

Devlin repeated his request as softly as he could.

'The strangest thing. The very strangest. Of all he could have had. Of all he could have wanted.' She rolled her eyes and pulled her shawl tighter.

'What?' Devlin asked as she turned right into an alley and they followed single file as the street closed in on them.

'A chest of medicines. That's all. Even gave the address of where it was to be found. Can you believe it, sirs? A chest of bloody mercury things and whatnot. The devil of it.'

Devlin and Dandon instantly became hen-house foxes. The events meant nothing to them but their whiskers twitched. So here they were, summoned to Charles Town with elaborate intrigue, only a few reevings shy of Teach himself.

'He left when he had the chest, Lucy?' Devlin asked as their pace slowed.

'Aye, sir. The very night. A night as black as when he came.'

They had come out of the alley into New Church. The inn, which stood opposite, was actually a wealthy-looking carriage house with stables attached and glowing windows in the upper storeys. Lucy led them across the wide road with Devlin looking left and right along what must have been the town's main thoroughfare. To his right he could make out a high red-brick wall at the end of the road: the end of Charles Town. To his left the road stretched away, pricked by yellow light all along its length.

Dandon peered through the tobacco-stained window panes of the inn. 'I would have the firmest imagination that pirates would be most unwelcome in your town after such a defilement.'

'Aye,' Lucy agreed. 'Though those sods back there be of such a kind. Lawlessness abounds and the King pays us no help.'

Devlin looked behind, suddenly aware that morning would dawn on two corpses by the wharf.

'Lucy, those men will be discovered soon enough. I would hate to inconvenience our acquaintance with scandal.'

Lucy took his arm, her head leaning towards the inn. She winked and said that rats often had a time with drunks by the water and the pair were but pirates after all.

Now, she went on with a smile, wasn't it too late to be visiting your friend in the big house? Wouldn't a little rum be just the thing on so mild a night?

Devlin bowed, pulling away gently, explaining that they were not too late but must make haste. Dandon tipped his hat to the girl, joined Devlin's side and asked her again for directions to the house.

Lucy, disappointed that her handsome rescuer had declined her nubile charms, consoled herself that she at least knew exactly where he would be.

'It's over there,' she pointed across the road behind Devlin and Dandon. 'That blue house. That's where a fellow never comes out. Just his boy. And the light burns all night long.'

They turned to look and true enough lamplight from the four tall windows, upstairs and down, shone brightly. The white shutters were flung wide open.

The house was gated like all the rest. It had a paved garden in which two fine Magnolia trees would offer privacy and shade during the day.

The only solemnity about their destination, the only point of darkness, was the austere black door. Above it, panes of red glass stared out in a horseshoe arch, shivering from the light of the hall.

Lucy offered some parting words before she was swallowed up by the inn. 'That's also the home where Blackbeard's chest came out of, sirs. From my room I saw it carried up the street.' She kissed her lips and bustled through the door, her entrance generating a roar of approval from deep inside the inn.

Dandon opened his mouth to speak but Devlin was already striding to the black door. Dandon followed, whistling to Devlin's back to slow up, whilst they perhaps took time to contemplate the situation over a roasted bird and some wine.

Devlin announced his arrival by shoving open the gate, slamming it against the railings like a gaol door. But despite his temperament, he paused as the black door crept open at his approach to reveal the red hall beyond.

Chapter Fourteen

✗

*T*he young black boy in the white bob wig, attired in a scarlet coat as finely embellished as that of any Saxony footman, led them along the red-flocked walls of the hall. He did not speak. He did not ask for weapons to be discarded.

The pirates followed him to the end of the narrow hall where the boy tapped a silver-topped cane against a door on their right.

Silence; then the sound of a chair scraping accompanied by the boom of command.

The door opened and the boy gently tugged on Devlin's arm to enter before stepping back into the hall and closing the door of their escape.

Before them was a fine study, a gentleman's repository of books and ornaments, clocks and silver. Two glass doors leading to the garden faced them. Standing beside one, a black-clothed stick of a man looked away into the night outside.

He turned his head to look at Devlin, then Dandon. When he spoke his tone was sharp with the patronising resonance of the licensed and appointed.

'You were to come alone.'

Devlin wondered whether this man remained in the room for weeks waiting for the rap on the door, counting the leaves on his trees.

'You are Ignatius?' he asked flatly. 'The man who summons me?'

The ebony figure turned fully, his taffeta-bag wig flapping on his shoulder, his white stock collar drawing his face to a bony point.

'I am.' His eyes took in Devlin's considerable stature. 'I imagined you shorter, Captain. Like a sailor. No matter.' He sat, at his oak office, pulling a stylus and parchment from a drawer. 'No matter,' he repeated. 'However, due to your lateness it is quite possible that your quartermaster may already be dead.'

Ignatius raised his head at the sound of the trinity passage of the lock and trigger engaging on Devlin's pistol.

'You had best clarify that statement, sir.' Devlin held the pistol at his side. Not a threat. A tiger yawning; showing his teeth.

Dandon chewed on a thumbnail, happy to be ignored. Ignatius put down the stylus and leant back in his chair.

'I do not scare, Captain. And I know my game well. If I am dead you will never find your ridiculous quartermaster and your ship would not make it out of the harbour I assure you.'

'I would not kill you. I would *hurt* you.'

Ignatius picked up his stylus again. 'Captain, I have had Blackbeard himself in this very room, and barely tolerated his idle threats. A lesser pirate such as yourself will more quickly exhaust my patience if you persist with this *mélodrame*.'

Dandon began to fade away from the conversation, taking in more of the noble room. Convinced Ignatius probably had a pistol lying in an open drawer of the desk, he twisted his heel away a little, opening a space between himself and his captain whilst he looked innocently about.

The door they had come in was the only one. To his right, against the wall, glowed a display of pottery upon a long tombstone commode. An impressive collection, Dandon noted, as it seemed to span several styles.

His wandering eye was attracted to the floor. There were wet footprints by the curtained window where Ignatius had been standing; more around the desk. He could not be sure why it bothered him, then he had no more time to dwell upon it as he jumped at the sound of his own name.

'Dandon, is it not?' Ignatius prepared to write the name down.

'Aye, sir,' Dandon tugged his hat-brim. 'I have been known to be called such. By serpents and lambs.'

'Then I take it that Captain Devlin does not know your real name?' Ignatius looked for a conspirator's reaction. Devlin did not move his eyes from Ignatius; he never even blinked.

'No, sir,' Dandon concurred, heat suffusing his face at the thought that this stranger had such a deep knowledge of him. 'It has scarcely come up in our conversations.'

Devlin interceded, 'I know the real names of but a few of my men. Pirates mostly adopt new handles when they go on the account.'

Ignatius scribbled as he spoke. 'That is good to know. Until now I would happily have penned Dandon here as innocent. He will be noted pirate along with the rest of your crew. Now,' he slapped the pen down and sprang up, moving from the desk to the maple orange commode against the wall. 'To the business at hand.'

He drew their attention to the cabinet, loaded with trinkets of extravagance – cups, teapots, fluted vases and fat terrines – all of the finest white and blue-glazed porcelain. Thousands of pounds' worth.

'Before I begin, Captain,' as he spoke, the corners of Ignatius's mouth rose above the stock collar. 'Do not concern yourself with your quartermaster's well-being. He should already be on his way to join us. But it was important for me to know, if I am to be convinced at all that you are a potential champion for my cause, whether you truly cared about his welfare. Your violent introduction gives me some encouragement, but your suitability and usefulness depends on more than just that.'

Devlin put his pistol back in his belt, the dog-head half-cocked for a speedy draw if necessary. The two pirates stepped from the heavy weft rug in the centre of the room to join Ignatius at the commode.

Ignatius picked up some small intricate pieces, snuff boxes and thimbles, lowering his voice as if quoting a psalm.

'This is faïence. From Saint-Cloud,' he looked at them both pitifully, 'in *France*. It is the finest attempt the French have made at replicating the true porcelain.' He tossed a thimble in the shape of an embryonic elephant to Devlin.

Devlin rolled the glazed oddity around his palm with as much interest he afforded any thimble.

Ignatius regarded him scornfully. 'It is an expensive failed attempt, an educated guess. Baubles for the wealthy who know no better. A man would be laughed out of court if he succumbed to collecting it.'

He moved along to a clearly European coffee service, more ornate and vulgar than the refined Chinese sets of which Devlin himself possessed two.

'This is Meissen,' he spoke admiringly, picking up a softly tapering and floral cup. 'For the past six years it has become *the* object of desire in Europe.'

Even in the lamp-light Devlin could see the cold shimmer, the skin-thin translucency of the mouth of the cup.

'The world has changed much since the end of the war,' Ignatius's voice swung down to a resentful baritone. 'Ten years ago the most important things that transpired in this world were objects of blood: iron, steel, gold, silver, slaves and guns.' He put down the cup with a melancholy eye.

'Now all the allied Kings and gentlemen ever talk of is wig-powder, tea, chocolate, coffee and porcelain. The most fashionable, the most charming corner of any debate? Tea, coffee and chocolate. The celebrated beverages of the New World. All medicinal. All prohibitively expensive. All the young fops care about. That and how joyous it is that one can obtain French linen again.'

At that moment Devlin saw Ignatius clearly. In his voice was the spite and indefatigable appetite of a warmonger. His face was old enough to have witnessed the passage of two wars and new monarchies and lords with weaker and weaker values who wanted only to hunt on their horses, not ride them into battle.

This man spoke now with pirates. He probably spoke with Spanish admirals, ambitious princes, dukes, assassins and torturers. He was known only by a single name. There was no title and no reverence or courtesy – not even the wetting of a windpipe for his guests.

Ignatius twisted his face away from the coat of Dandon who had sidled up to the commode to pluck up some of the faïence.

'My God, sir! You smell of atrocity and fat. It is quite pungent, you are aware?'

Dandon sniffed his shoulder. 'I have been at sea for six weeks, sir. You should try it some time. It has a very liberating way of relaxing one's sense of dignity.'

Ignatius lifted his eyebrows and continued his speech.

'I need you, Captain, to understand the importance of my preparations. I have gone to the trouble of bringing you here under great expense. I had agents across all the known pirate shores looking for you. Each one with the same letter. You have reason to hate me, Captain: I am threatening the life of your brother and the liberty of all your crew. And yours, naturally.'

'My liberty?' Devlin stood back.

'I have letters of arrest signed by the Dutch, the United Kingdom, and the French. All excluding you from pardon. If you refuse to aid me I will have them distributed throughout the hemisphere. And as I torture your quartermaster I will add the names of your officers to the hunt.'

Devlin turned his shoulder to the man, his head lowered. His voice was tight, almost trying not to laugh.

'Why do you rile me so? Surely you must have some sense? Some tale of me?'

'I knew I would not be able to bring you here with a bribe or a reward, Captain. But a threat? A challenge perhaps? That might task you.'

'Might *kill* you,' Devlin walked to the desk.

Ignatius sighed, 'Again with the *mélodrame.*'

Dandon had picked up a Chinese cup. The blue glaze, part of the shell-like surface, seemed naturally ingrained, painted by heaven more than man.

'From the Italian, *porcelana*,' Dandon feigned an elaborate accent. 'For its shine and opacity is akin to the lustrous down on a sow's back. Only the Italians could whittle such an allusion.' He placed the cup back while noticing an appreciative look from Ignatius, and he winked at him.

Devlin flicked a finger at the ream of papers upon the desk, musing on how many referred to him. 'Enough. Tell me now what this has to do with me? And Blackbeard's part of it.'

Ignatius showed a marked pleasure in Devlin's bark. His eye brightened. The pirate had known him not one chime of the clock and yet he could feel the chill of enmity.

This was exactly the response he had hoped for. Hate was a better motivator, an impulse that might drive one beyond ordinary ability with enough will to force open even the most sturdily-bolted doors. Hatred was an energy that all great generals had learnt to harness.

Ignatius leant back upon the commode and took a deep breath as if about to break into song.

'Several years ago, a Jesuit priest and missionary began a ministry in the Jingdezhen province of China. In truth he was an industrial spy. His studies centred around learning the secrets of the production of the Jingde hard-paste porcelain. And being a man of God he was foolishly trusted to be privy to the process itself.'

Ignatius looked hard at Devlin. 'Understand, Captain: this is a product of royal value and the East India companies have been smuggling porcelain for years. They disguise it as parcels of tea. Straw wrapped bundles. Customs count four hundred jars of tea, not four hundred porcelain vases. Over the years the Dutch alone have "imported" over three million pieces in such a manner.'

He lifted himself up and moved along the cabinet to the Chinese set Dandon was still admiring.

'The priest observed and recorded all that he saw. He wrote down the entire process from start to finish, for both the soft-paste porcelain and the superior hard-paste formula. Unfortunately his complete letters never made it out of China.

'In Europe, just a few years before the priest wrote his

account, a certain alchemist fled from Prussia. He escaped from one tower only to be imprisoned in another. In Prussia he had been forced to the method of transmutation of metal into gold. Now the Elector of Saxony imprisoned the unlucky man until he could discover the secret of the "White Gold" instead. After many years of research he succeeded, perhaps not only by his own hand.' Ignatius paused to pick up a small delicate white cup, a rueful look appearing briefly on his face and vanishing as the cup went down again. 'But he succeeded nonetheless. That young alchemist had achieved what the world's greatest craftsmen and experimenters had been trying to discover for centuries, since the first pieces began to trickle back to Europe during the crusades.

'As is common with those who discover things of great interest to more powerful men, the alchemist soon died mysteriously, leaving his secret to the pottery at Meissen. The Meissen manufactory began to produce Europe's first, Europe's *only*, hard-paste porcelain. Many in Europe believe it is unfair for one power to have the monopoly. For many years others have only been able to produce the lesser form, the faïence, the inferior flux and frit that chips, stains, breaks and burns.' He gently cradled in both hands a blue-dragon serving pot and held it before him like the Baptist's head.

'Pai-Tzu. *True* porcelain. The Japanese have armour made of it. The Chinese have gilded royal homes with it. And a King can drink chocolate from it without burning his fingers.'

Devlin tipped his hat. 'Aye. It's of a price. I know that. Baubles for the rich have many prices. Saxony alone has this secret?'

Ignatius breathed out heavily and put back the pot. 'They have as close as an approximation as one can hope for without possessing the actual formula. It is the same clay that Saxony is fortunate to have beneath its earth. I believe the Americas also contain this same clay. Certainly some of the savages use pottery wares akin to it. And the priest's notes contain the precise mix, the firing, even the design of the kiln in which the clay must be fired. The country that owns those letters owns the largest secret in a world at peace. More than a secret: an *arcanum*! The most valuable man-made substance on Earth, gentlemen. A product as profitable as war and even more capable of starting one.' He held up a schoolmaster's finger. 'Think on that! What if a country as young as *this* one could manufacture such a product? Imagine the wealth that could bring to the Americas!' He lowered his voice, drawing them in. 'Why would you want such a secret to fall into King George's lap, Captain, if you could take it from him? Imagine the discord when it is discovered that it is *you* that has denied England such a prize.'

Devlin looked back into Ignatius's now gentle face. 'Aye. I'm sure you'll be wanting to enrich the Americas with such a gift.'

'And I owe it all to you, Captain.' He opened his arms and smiled.

Devlin looked once to the bemused Dandon then back again. 'How so?'

Ignatius's soft smile did not fade. 'Three long years ago, three years that have aged me terribly, the letters resurfaced. Oddly enough from a young officer of your own acquaintance.'

Devlin's ears pricked up. Dandon had almost stopped listening. He removed his hat and dragged a cuff across his brow. The study of cups and all the talk of drinks had brought a great thirst upon him.

'Captain William Guinneys,' revealed Ignatius, and took pleasure in the obvious recognition of that name.

Dandon fanned himself with his hat and glanced wide-eyed with surprise at Devlin, 'The little filth is reaching to us from beyond the grave. Fancy.'

Guinneys had been the young captain with Coxon on The Island. He had turned. He had betrayed. He was dead.

Ignatius pattered on, hoping he had baited them enough with intrigue. The final hammer blow might be too much. All might yet be lost.

'The arcanum was sealed inside a Chinese bronze cannon. A clever hiding place of Captain Guinneys'. This gun made its way to the Americas. Unfortunately the word had already begun to spread. Intellectual property is a commodity more blood-stained than gold. I needed to get the gun hidden again. That is when I discovered how useful pirates can be amongst these inlets.'

He pulled his silver Dassier pair-case watch, a nervous act for he seemed to pay no attention to it. Devlin could sense anxiety encroaching on Ignatius like flies to meat. He was now a fisherman trying hard not to lose his catch.

'The Chinese had lost the secret of silk, and of gunpowder. I began to feel that their Gods did not want their last mystery revealed. I arranged for the pirate, Sam Bellamy, to sail the gun north on the *Whydah Galley*. I desired to get it out of the Carolinas and away from those who were showing most interest before I myself was able capitalise on its promise. Unfortunately . . .' he looked between the two pirates and had to explain no further, '. . . I believed the gun lost forever. But she has come back to me. Providing you, Captain, can bring her here.'

'And why am *I* so privileged as to be chosen for such a task? What have *I* done to be singled out so?' He stepped within a foot of the bony face, his interest waning as his anger percolated. 'What is so *special* about me?'

'Ah, yes,' Ignatius brushed past him and creaked across the floor to stand behind his desk, Dandon watching his footsteps with focussed curiosity.

'There is indeed a reason as to why you were absolutely necessary for this mission. Why I had no choice but to bait you here, Captain.'

He pulled from a drawer, not a bottle as Dandon had been hoping, but a black-edged envelope of darkest vellum. He walked back to Devlin and held out the packet.

'The nobleman who has funded my enterprise, the same man who informed me that the gun was not lost, and of the place where it now rests. It was he who insisted that I appoint you for the task.' Ignatius handed over the envelope.

'And once I had separated you from your quartermaster – him in particular, mind – I was to give you this.'

Devlin tossed the thimble to the desk and took the envelope. Even without opening it the thin bone-like form and the crackle within gave him a clue.

Dandon looked over Devlin's shoulder as he broke the purple wax seal and withdrew a single, white, almost transparent feather, plucked from the wing of a crow-like bird.

Devlin rolled it between his fingers. The sight of the white fletch brought back the memory of a weighty downpour, of staring through a straggling forelock, running in his drenched coat from men on horseback. The feather spoke to his memory of the spark of swords, of the taking of the *Shadow*, and of Valentim Mendes, governor of the Verdes whom Devlin had tied to a tree. He had wrapped a grenadoe in the man's hand and lit the fuse. It had been such a long way to come only to see in his mind's eye that bird again; for Valentim's pet had been a startling white raven.

'What is it, what does it mean?' Dandon asked. He had not been there. Had not seen the albino bird. He had only heard tell of Valentim Mendes, who bequeathed them their fine frigate.

'A white raven's feather.' Devlin dropped the envelope and the feather to the desk. His eyes glazed momentarily.

'Have you seen the man himself?' Devlin asked quietly.

Ignatius smiled just enough.

'Hate is not the word for it, Captain. Not even the manner of the word.'

'What am I to do for you? For Valentim?' Devlin looked at the feather and felt a calmness emanating from him. Suddenly his fate was back in his hands and the impersonal world was his once more.

Ignatius clasped his hands behind him. He moved back to his desk, picked up his stylus and opened a ledger, furiously scratching away as he spoke.

'You are to sail to Providence. For the cannon is there. Time is not with you however, Captain, for Teach is after the same. His involvement is not for you to know. You are to bring it here to me, to secure the freedom of your quarter-master. And the continuance of your own liberty of course. I have here a description of the gun for you.'

Devlin's derisive laugh stayed his writing hand.

'You are amused by my proposal?'

Devlin had half-expected the letters to be hanging around King George's neck. That at least would have required some effort – a second load of pistol perhaps. He smirked in disbe-lief at the man behind the desk.

'You want me to sail to a pirate island? As a pirate? There is some difficulty in this that I am unaware of I take it? Or do you always use a hammer to clean your windows, sir?'

Devlin doffed his hat theatrically. 'Goodnight to you. Dandon and I will abscond to the tavern opposite. We'll try not to over-plan our assault. As for Teach, if he is my only concern, we'll be back in two weeks. I have stared him down before. And with an empty gun. I hope, for your sake, Peter Sam be here awaiting me, fat and found.' He plucked Dandon's sleeve and made for the door.

Ignatius's words halted them at the threshold. 'Oh, of course: you've been away haven't you?'

They turned. Animosity had returned to Devlin's eyes.

Ignatius continued: 'You've spent some time out of these seas. News travels so very slow, does it not?'

'What word am I unaware of?' Devlin rested his palm upon his pistol.

Ignatius leant back, his hands tapping in his lap.

'The *good* word is the word you are unaware of, Captain. Peace has come to the Bahamas. I want you to sail to the island of *New* Providence. The island is now under the control of the infamous Woodes Rogers and seconded by your own Captain John Coxon. You remember him? Doubtless he remembers you. New Providence is now a colony of England, piracy wiped from its face. A garrison of one hundred soldiers and three hundred Navy fellows is there. Five men-of-war are anchored in its harbour making sure it never returns.'

He watched Devlin's cold look swim across the room towards him and rocked back in his chair. It had been worth the wait.

'*That* is the island I want you to sail to. Not this piratical paradise you assumed. Oh, and the cannon? I'm afraid it is in Governor Rogers' fort. The one he has made his home along with the garrison and militia of citizens. Your former brethren, by the way.'

Devlin and Dandon looked at each other. Devlin felt along his belt, running his fingers from pistol to sword.

'When? When did this happen? There is nothing on Providence to warrant a colony.'

'Fifty years ago I would have agreed,' Ignatius chimed. 'But fifty years ago this town did not exist either. Even your colleague's town of Bath,' he lifted a hand to Dandon, 'barely existed when he left Mobile with his master ten years ago.'

Dandon shivered. The memory of his past-life had become a mystery even to him, so much had his world changed. Now he was back. Just a thieving apothecary's assistant poring over medical dictionaries, who believed he could become a learned man without a purse to back him. Just a boy playing doctor. The shivering did not go unnoticed by Ignatius. He held out the description of the gun.

'Take this order and instruction, Captain. Or should I simply kill your quartermaster when he arrives?'

Devlin did not move. His fingernail tapped against his pistol flint.

Dandon tip-toed forward and took the paper, succentor to his holy captain. He tapped it against his forehead, backing away.

Devlin snatched the door open, then looked back to the desk. 'Tell Valentim I am sorry about the hand. It was required at the time. It was . . . democratic.'

'I'm sure you can tell him yourself. Success or not, he will be waiting for you. However, if you die in the pursuit I'm sure he will not weep.'

Devlin paused beneath the lintel. Dandon edged past him, making his way to the front door.

'I expect Peter Sam to be here. A fortnight from now. I'll have your letters. And by the time I do I'm sure one more death will not make much odds.'

Ignatius said nothing. He pulled himself back up in his seat, lowering his eyes to his page, and began to write again the notes that would exalt him, the notes that would exempt him, depending on the reader, until he heard the door click shut behind the pirate. It had been worth the wait.

Still writing, he spoke aloud to the empty room. 'I trust you have heard enough, gentlemen?'

A pause ensued lengthy enough for the two men that waited in the garden to ready themselves, open the glazed double doors and step into the room. They had indeed heard enough. A hidden vent in the wall had carried the entire conversation.

He waited for the two to sit down on uninvited chairs at opposite sides of the study, their full-length black cloaks sweeping the floor. Prudently Ignatius finished his work, placed his stylus down and lifted his head to them.

Hiding his amusement he addressed them both. 'Still the pretence of your masks, gentlemen? How very droll.' In each dark corner his guests wore white clay Bauta masks and full tabarro lace that covered their heads and necks and ran beneath their tricornes.

The almost glowing Venetian masks stared back coldly with blank eyes. One of them spoke, the beak of the mask hanging over and away from the mouth, thus perfectly distorting the direction and identity of the voice.

'Our anonymity preserves some dignity amongst ourselves, Ignatius. It is no deceit against your person.'

'Quite,' Ignatius noticed their canes impatiently trying to twist their way through the floorboards, while their dead faces betrayed nothing. The frustration of trying to engage with statues detached Ignatius even more from the emotions that his enterprises often provoked in him. 'You have listened;

you thus understood the full control that I enjoy over our situation. In a month, perhaps less, the secret of the porcelain will be here in this very study. Yours for the taking.'

'For the purchasing, Ignatius,' one of them snapped back. Ignatius bowed to the adroit observation.

'Indeed. Now, as I understand, one of you,' he waved a hand to them both, 'owns a considerable iron refinery which might easily be turned to the production of the porcelain.'

A mask nodded back, the unseen and sweating face behind it quickly grimacing in regret at giving away the knowledge to Ignatius's quick eye.

Ignatius spoke directly to the other mask. 'And therefore I assume you, sir, would be the gentleman most able to purchase native lands that supposedly hold deposits of the appropriate clay?'

No nod or word was returned, but the ebony cane tried to screw itself through the elm-wood floor. Ignatius resisted the impulse to put ink to paper. The masks twitched and a muffled voice was heard.

'You imply that our motives spring purely from profit, Ignatius. I say you are mistaken, sir.'

Ignatius rested an elbow on his desk and leant his chin on his hand in a pose eloquent of opening his mind to enlightenment. The mask continued. 'You have spoken yourself to the very pirate now on his quest, of the importance of the porcelain to our country.'

Ignatius raised an eyebrow. '*Your* country?'

'*This* country, these colonies, provide the most valuable commodities in the world. In less than a generation you may add cotton to the tally. Yet we are compelled and restrained only to sell our goods to the motherland, my pig-iron included, at a price set by men I have never seen. A third of the kingdom's income is generated by the colonies yet we are taxed for the privilege and our countrymen may send no representative to our King's parliament. If I wish to breed a horse I must write to a secretary in Whitehall. Yet if I need a garrison of soldiers to protect against the pirates and the Indians I must pay them from my own purse at a penny a day.' Even muffled by the mask Ignatius could sense the bitter tone of personal grievance in the man's voice.

'I have lived here for almost a year, gentlemen. You bleat long but you have government and legislature enough of your own. Many of you grow wealthier than your fathers despite king and crown. And I've read nothing in your pamphlets of complaint except for the somewhat thwarted desire to grow richer still. The porcelain you seek is only for your fortune. Do not pretend or plead to me otherwise. I will bring it. But do not think that I am guided to give you some leverage against the motherland. This is business, gentlemen. Nothing more.'

'Yet you spoke to the pirate of "ideals"? His task was decorated by you as a noble endeavour.'

Ignatius could tell which mask the voice came from and he watched it tremble as the voice behind it grated hoarsely. 'Do you betray yourself so often Ignatius, that you are unable to tell the difference between cause and trade?'

Ignatius glared back with his own effortless mask of indifference. 'Devlin needed those words. Tomorrow he could sail from here and be richer than either you or I. Perhaps he is so even now. I can make a starving man do anything, and a man born rich only aspires to get richer. But a man who steals wealth, even his very food, needs other motives. I know this well. I have taken a man from him and he now hates the living bones of me. I have threatened his liberty and he hates the blood of me. I have set myself his master and he would drag my corpse in the street if he gets but the breath of a chance. This is my game, gentlemen. I know how to play it and you will pay me to play it well.'

The masks shifted in their seats. Ignatius bit down on them with his final words.

'He is better than you, this *pirate*. I know men. I know you. You wish to gain. You wish to gather more riches and gain some hold over your king. He merely wishes to save the life of his friend. You should be hopeful to live so long to understand him.'

Ignatius stood, his head down, folded away his ledger and straightened his inkwells, showing more interest in the order of his desk for the morning than in the two uncomfortable masked men. 'You may leave the way you came, gentlemen. My servant will assist you. I hope this evening has assured you that our plan will be a success for all our . . . causes.' He did not suffer their protests. He crossed the room to the door, opened it to let his black servant boy enter and then vanished beyond it. The white masks exchanged silent glares; they removed their hats but not their masks as Ignatius's servant rolled back the rug in the centre of the study, keeping his head lowered from the lifeless faces as they gathered near him.

Chapter Fifteen

✗

*D*andon slapped down the description of the gun upon the small round table, shaking the jug and pewter mugs. 'Nine feet long and bronze!' he jeered. 'It will take three men to lift it. It is our curse that everything grand we liberate weighs more than we do!' His voice was almost a bellow to make himself heard over the rolling din of the hostelry. Their table and stools sat in the middle of the floor, surrounded by more small tables not much larger than the brim of Dandon's hat.

They did not lower their voices, did not care if the whole town – all of which seemed present with them that night – heard them.

Apart from the girl, Lucy, now rosy of face and glassy of eye, who rested her buttocks pertly upon Dandon's knee and nibbled at blackened chicken like a squirrel, the inn heaved with sailors. Some partook of a nefarious history judging by their proliferation of weaponry, noted by Dandon and Devlin as too great in value for any honest mariner.

Also present, and the loudest, were one or two overseers from the rice plantations which produced Charles Town's richest trading good. They had no songs about Cape Cod girls, unlike the seamen in their rolled shirts and head-scarves. Their loud tirades were concerned with the weakness of the slaves coming in from Sullivan's island and the prevalence of lice that seemed to outwit their latest powders.

Amongst such society Devlin and Dandon felt no need to be subtle. Besides, they would be gone before anyone there could remember they had seen the two dank and miserable-looking fellows.

Devlin sat tall, drawing hard on his pipe as it threatened to go out. 'Never mind the weight of the gun. It is only the letters inside the gun that we need,' he reminded Dandon. 'Now, what do we know?'

'I do not know anything,' Dandon slurred. The tensions of the day and the lure of the comforts of an American town had seduced him into drunkenness. His thoughts still lingered on what a stranger knew about him and something else he could not quite put his finger on. Something faint but intrinsic and just out of reach. More rum would help. 'Perhaps, Captain, you could enlighten me more on this Valentim Mendes and his part in all of this. If I am to die for your past, that is.'

Devlin bit his pipe and touched his mug as if some comfort could be found by it. 'There is not much to tell that I suspect you have not already heard, Dandon.'

'I have heard little of the matter from yourself, Patrick. And that would be the most important word to me.'

Suitably the inn grew momentarily quiet as Devlin lowered his voice and Dandon and the girl Lucy leant in.

'Valentim Mendes was the governor of St Nick, a good pirate stop in the Verdes. As are all the Verdes.' He lifted his cup as if saluting ghosts around the table. 'Seth Toombs had a mind to take him for ransom,' recalled Devlin, and drank as if swallowing the qualms he had felt as he had run from the house that night, leaving dead brothers behind. 'Valentim had better plans. Seth was killed. I took his place. Took his ship and his men. Took Valentim's ship. His *Shadow*, not mine. Only left him shame.' Pouring another measure, he gave out his next words carefully, not wishing to offend the delicate nature of their female company. 'In revenge for killing Seth and some of the other lads we staked him to a tree. Wrapped a grenadoe in his fist. Gave him an axe to free himself or be blown to chum. I would guess that he cut the grenadoe free.'

Lucy pursed her lips, a puzzled eye half closed. '*Cut* the grenadoe free?'

Devlin drained his mug with a sigh. 'Aye. One arm free. One arm strapped. If he has survived, as now I know he has, it is not as a whole man.' He poured again, including a drink for Dandon this time.

'I suppose that gentleman would not be too enamoured by your continued presence in this world.' Dandon rang his mug against his friend's.

Devlin cast an eye around the crowd. 'I am wondering exactly who is enamoured of me of late.'

Dandon leant back, '*Company, villainous company, hath been the spoil of me.*' He sunk his rum. Somewhere in the bottom of the chased and pitted pewter something leapt to him as if an angel had briefly touched his shoulder before moving on to worthier causes. His cup slammed down on the table. 'I have it!' he snapped his fingers. 'That's the rub of it, Patrick!'

The girl jumped at his cry, adjusted herself again on his lap and went for her mug to calm her nerves. Devlin had seen Dandon's wild exclamations often enough to remain composed. 'What is the rub of it?'

'It was there all the time!'

Devlin sat back. 'What do you jaw about now, Dandon?'

Dandon, trying to break Devlin's melancholy with a higher pitch of his voice, pulled Lucy closer to his lap. 'Now tell me, Lucy, did Blackbeard actually step abroad in your fair town?'

Lucy confirmed, as far as she could, that the rogue had not tramped up and down their streets. His men had, but the man himself had stayed on board the Jacobite-sounding *Queen Anne's Revenge* – three hundred tons of French Guineaman, bastardised to the teeth to wallow under the weight of forty guns. Lucy whispered that the harbour fell into shadow when the *Revenge* rolled in.

Dandon nodded, ruminating on a chicken leg. The knuckle snapped satisfyingly in his mouth, but that brief pleasure was eclipsed by the dark face of Devlin looking to the bottom of his black rum.

'Did you hear that, Patrick?' Dandon tossed the bone to the table. 'The *Queen Anne's Revenge* he calls it! Forty guns and probably more in fowlers and falconets. And Lucy says he never came ashore. What do you make of that?' Dandon, now much familiar with the black moods that his captain presented of late, ever since Peter Sam had vanished, felt that a levity of conversation brought more relief than the sinking of liquor.

Devlin raised his eyes, 'What do I care if Teach never came ashore?' His rumbling voice was almost challenging.

'Now, Patrick,' Dandon ignored the ill-humour. 'Did not that there fellow, Ignatius, take pride in informing us that he had Teach in his very company? In that same room?'

'So he lies. They all lie. Else the girl is wrong.' Devlin sank his drink while his eyes roved the room for prying faces over the rim of his mug. He caught a few surveying him between puffs of tobacco or the filling of mugs. Discovered, they turned away from him, finding more to interest them in a lamp or the sawdust floor. Devlin slopped more rum into his mug, four fingers' worth. 'Who cares? What differs anyways?'

Dandon leant towards him, lowering his voice. 'What ails thee, Patrick? Do we not have an adventure afore us after months of idling in Madagascar? Peter Sam to rescue. Capture awaiting us in Providence. What more could men ask for?'

Devlin swirled the liquid in his cup, absorbed in its depths. 'I should have held him to the wall,' he murmured. 'Stuck a blade to his throat and told him his future. Not bow and tip my hat.'

'I don't follow?' Dandon sat back, stroking Lucy's hip.

Devlin curled a lip and continued, 'I have come so far to be free, only to find there is no such thing. I am still commanded by those that were born in better beds.' He clasped a fist to his chest. 'Even those I thought bested pull at me from the shadows.'

Dandon took a small drink, choosing his words with care. 'You could still do nothing,' he sighed. 'We could sail away, meet up with the *Shadow* and Bill and forget it all. Even go back into that house and slit that *cochon*'s throat. You can do anything you want, Patrick, that is the difference. But a man of your world has been taken into theirs. His well-fought-for freedom taken from him. What would become of you if you did nothing to bring him back to the path? And, at this point, whoever is involved in our conspiracy, we know more than they *think* we do.' Dandon drank tall, letting his cryptic words ferment in Devlin's ears.

'What do we know, Dandon?' Devlin's left hand was beneath the table, his fist opening and closing on the antler hilt of his hanger.

'We are now aware that Peter Sam is not here: Ignatius informed us that Peter is on his way. Ergo, he is not in our presence.' Dandon tugged on his goatee. 'He sent agents to find us, so there is, probably, only one or two men holding

Peter. And we have Will Magnes and a stout band to find him on Madagascar. In all fact he is most likely drunk with them as we sup here.'

'Aye,' Devlin leant in. 'That may be. Peter could be with Will by now. Ignatius would know no more than us.'

Devlin's eyes narrowed, the rakish grin returning. Dandon saw the change, almost heard the capstan turning with the prospect of cannon fire and pistol shot in the days ahead.

'There is more, and this you shall like,' he winked at Devlin's curiosity then brought the bleary Lucy back into the conversation.

'Confirm for me Lucy, if you will my girl,' he squeezed her closer. 'You said that the man in that house yonder never goes out. Is that common knowledge? Is that solemnly true?'

Lucy dipped her head slowly several times, 'Aye sir. He been here a year now, renting the house from the governor his-self. Only ever see his boy and the trade coming and going. Asks anybody. And the lights are on all through the night.'

Devlin shifted himself on his stool, eyeing the room again, now looking for trouble from any eye that might meet his and waiting for Dandon's expatiation to conclude. 'And what of it, Dandon? What difference if Ignatius goes out or not?'

Devlin's patience was exhausted. 'We leave. Back to the ship.' He scraped back his stool. 'We sail in the morning.' He dropped some silver upon the pewter charger, paying for the hen and the rum, the clatter drawing glances from every dark corner of the room, not least from behind the bar where the aproned host counted the rattling coins as they fell.

Dandon looked up quite crestfallen to his mate then began to slide himself up from under Lucy, expertly managing to slip her onto his stool in his place with her barely aware of it. He plucked his captain's shoulder, drawing his cheek close to his mouth.

'I merely wished to allude to the fact, Patrick – and your failure to observe such tells often concerns me – that for a man who never goes out Ignatius makes a fine mess of puddles in his home.'

Devlin paused. He tapped out his pipe upon the table and listened to his friend.

'His feet were *wet*, Captain. Every step he took. The only damp I have seen around is by the wharf is it not? And Blackbeard never came ashore, but sat in that same room?' Dandon's eyes gleamed ochre as his liver tightened its grip on him, almost stifling the joy of his revelation. 'And such a beautiful rug upon the floor did you not think?'

'I'll take your word on the water. I did not notice. Agreed, if you are suggesting that he has a tunnel to his home from the harbour. I'm sure in a town where a slave revolt and Indian attacks are an everyday concern such contrivances are common. Now let's go. Say goodbye to the girl.' Devlin turned and snaked his way through the mess of tables to the door.

He did not need to hear any more. There was a time for posturing – Devlin enjoyed it as much as any man – but bile had begun to rise in him. He stood outside on the street and looked across to the glowing red arch above the black door opposite, the four windows still flickering from oil lamps within. Those lamps would burn the place up well if one should fall, perhaps knocked by a bold and inquisitive rat. Aye maybe that would do it. Show this Ignatius what a pirate affronted can do. Burn him in his bed for his arrogance. See how smug he is charred.

But what of Peter if he did such a thing? What then for his quartermaster? All told, it was just the rum steaming his anger and Devlin shook the thought away. How would his men look upon him if he abandoned their oldest hand? And how better their regard if he rescued him?

A captain's choice should never be his own.

He looked down the street as Dandon stumbled out behind him. It was maybe a quarter of a mile down to the wharf. Not a long walk, nor either a tedious creep down a tunnel.

He smacked Dandon's chest with the back of his hand, 'Come. We'll talk of this aboard. I think you may be right, mate. Knowing that Ignatius has a hidden passage from the house to the wharf could give us a sure advantage.'

'I am glad you agree,' Dandon hiccoughed at the suddenness of the cool air.

'But remember, he seems to know us well. Knows more about you than I do.'

Dandon tutted his disapproval. 'Ah, no. He knows the history of us. He does not *know* us. He looked down at us about ourselves. Patronised us about France and faïence. He is like all the well-born and wealthy, believing ignorance to be the common man's contribution to the world.'

'Aye. But now the measure of it . . .' Devlin looked about the broad street taking in the warm night, the laughter and glow from the inn, the quiet dark houses. The murderous chill in his bones was at odds with it all. 'Providence will be our destination, as cold to us now as England, and Coxon there to boot. Blackbeard has been set to the same task and Valentim Mendes, hate-filled enough to traverse the ocean, seeks to find me. My page is marked, and all for the recipe for cups and saucers for Sodomites.

'And the rescue of dear Peter Sam of course. Our lost companion.'

'Aye and that and all. That's all I came for. To save him who came back for me.'

He began to walk away, back towards the wharf, his grin briefly returning. 'All I need now is for Seth Toombs to return from the dead.'

Chapter Sixteen

✖

Valentim Mendes, Madagascar

Six weeks had passed since the *Shadow* left. There had been no hint of Peter Sam. Not a footprint. Not a glimpse. Devlin's remaining crew had given up the chase and waited for their brethren to return, convinced of the notion that Peter Sam had indeed been carried from the island and it would be their captain that would find him.

The ten left to scour for their quartermaster had pooled their coin, Will Magnes acting as purser, but six weeks of tavern living had still taken their toll on their silver in addition to their spirit and morale, for gambling and whoring were the black trades of Madagascar.

After a fortnight, six had sold their pistols and drunk an anker of brandy between them. By the month's end four were living and pimping with young women they had fallen for, bouncing someone else's nipper on their knees and teaching them songs perfectly inclined to the understanding of their mothers' trade.

Three others had sailed, desperate and worn by the heat. Madagascar had, almost within a week of their captain's departure, become swollen with pirates all telling the same terrible tale. Providence had fallen, reclaimed by the King. The last friendly port in the Caribbee was no more. Now the Americas, the crooked inlets and the swamps, or the East Indies and her belly of wealth waiting to be pierced would be their ports. Devlin's men had sailed with Captain England, late of Providence, and paid Devlin no more mind.

Of the others, one had been shot dead, not for want of speed or due to drunken sloth, but the failure of his 'snap' – the diligence to check the effectiveness of his flint, which was forgotten with the fat living he'd had on Madagascar.

Only Andrew Morris and Will Magnes remained. They shared a room in one of the Dutch taverns in St Augustine. Their loyalty had come from their brotherhood. They had been true mates ever since the *Lucy*, Magnes had taken young Andrew Morris under his wing. Magnes, now in his late forties, was old for a pirate and Morris made good kin for an old man's hands.

The 'mate' for a pirate was as close to a partnership as he might ever come. A man to eat with, to share with, to reload for, to fight alongside watching the back of the other.

The most successful ships of the sweet life generated crews of such men. Hence, Magnes and Morris hung together awaiting their captain's return.

Late noon found Morris creaking out of the inn to stretch and welcome the day. He stood beneath the sailcloth awning that shaded the old men lounging on the porch and began to sweep his eye over the masts languishing in the bay, seeking a familiar shape.

The streets were already crowded with traders at their stalls, teeming with new lumbering sailors trudging up the hill, keeping their heads low and their histories lower. Madagascar was the cornerstone of the edge of the world and wandering mariners were drawn to it like a shrine.

Morris scratched his beard and clumped down the steps

of the porch to watch the local folk at their best. He had abandoned his waistcoat for a loose shirt and breeches. He wore no stockings, just straw shoes and a straw hat, his headscarf tied limply around his neck for the wiping of sweat.

He had a dagger tucked behind him and a freshly beeswaxed pistol – a foot-long French arm – boldly sticking out of his belt front and shining like a diamond necklace on a pig. A pirate might have black feet, lice on his head and groin and fingernails like a dog's claws but you could mark him by the sharpness and shine of his weapons.

His attention was snagged by the approach of a cedar-wood sedan chair struggling up the slope of the street. Such an emblem of wealth was unusual in St Augustine and the sight drew urchins like ants to sugar. Whoever sat behind the closed purple curtains of the carriage was doing little to dissuade the small brown hands from poking through as the bearers trudged along.

Morris found pleasure in the scene. A rich ponce had no smarts if he entered a poor town in such manner.

His face dropped however when the chair's progress was halted by the growing crowd of children and the front curtain was swept aside as the passenger leant forward to encourage his bearers with the prodding of his cane.

Morris had seen that snarling face before and recalled the black shoulder length hair almost blue in the white sunlight. Then the face was gone, sunk back behind the velvet curtain, and the sedan plodded on.

Morris stepped forward, dreamlike in remembrance, unsure of his recollection. He watched the back of the chair as if he expected the occupant to lean out and wave back at him and found himself perplexed as he struggled to curl his tongue around a name just out of memory's reach. Then it came back to him.

'That's Valentim Mendes,' he mouthed as if waiting for applause. 'That's the man we took the *Shadow* from. He ain't dead.'

Peter Sam, Valentim, Devlin – and Andrew Morris – had been there that night. Had taken the *Shadow* with Devlin and Peter. Killed, with Devlin and Peter.

Perhaps unwisely, with hindsight, the Devil's own view of the world, he chased after the sedan, weaving amongst what little shadow the parched street provided, leaving Will Magnes sleeping in his bed.

After half an hour the town shrank into the distance leaving only the chirrups and howls of the forest. Morris swapped barrels and doorways for trunks and ferns as he crept behind the sedan unnoticed. He repeated in his head that he had his cartouche of fifteen cartridges for his fine pistol and a dagger and a belly full of breakfast timber to see him home.

He was not so stupid as to connect so large a world with what little coincidence the Lord provided. Yet this meant something, and he knew it would mean nothing to no-one if he was seen.

The sedan chair stopped at the baying of a black horse hushed with a pat on its jowls by a giant of a man who almost dwarfed the animal. Morris could see, even beneath the shadow of the large straw brim of the giant's hat, a horn of a nose shining red like a five shilling ham drying in the sun.

He saw the back of Mendes, a purple doublet plumed by his black hair, climb carefully from the chair and confer with the giant. His hair appeared temporarily like a ridiculous beard for the giant as he stood before him. Then Mendes turned to command his chair-bearers and Morris quickly ducked to the ground, slowly lifting his eyes up in time to see Mendes mount and then pull the horse away into a trot. The giant ambled dutifully behind.

The chair-bearers padded away back down the path as horse and rider were swallowed by the jungle. Morris watched the chair pass his tree. He strained his eyes looking into the jungle after Mendes and switched his gaze between both paths. He considered running back to town to fetch Will. That would be a wiser judgement. But judgement was for judges. Like a gun-dog bounding after a stricken bird, helpless against instinct over brains, Morris loped after Mendes and the giant.

Chapter Seventeen

*P*eter Sam poked at the hollows of his cheekbones. For some time now, how long he was unsure, his hands had been free of shackles. He wondered what he looked like now. His beard had stopped growing. His once powerful arms, his slabs of fists, now hung flaccid and weak. His cotton smock was black and reeking. He marked his days by the bowl and the bowel. He could spend hours muttering to himself in the dark, marking his errors, berating the years. Always his sentences trailed off into a beating down by the other Peter Sam, a younger, more handsome Peter Sam, who had a pipe and a good head of red hair, who stood for an hour or so within his shell and paced up and down stabbing indiscriminately, mostly at Spaniards, magistrates or Newfoundland codmen haunting his cell.

The conversations would dwindle until he sat rocking on his haunches as his stomach signalled the approach of the bowl and he craned his ear for the whistle of the Scotsman.

That was now. Late afternoon. His arms were wrapped around his knees, and Peter could feel his stomach feeding on itself, sucking at him for some bread and meat with his cabbage soup, which Hib always promised if he could steal it for him or swipe it from his own plate for his friend.

A different day. A new sound. Peter Sam stopped rocking. Down the steps came *two* pairs of footsteps. The soft patter of the Scotsman and the stomp of hard boots mingled with the unmistakable rattle of a scabbard scraping along the stairwell.

The cell became brighter with the prospect of a new voice. Peter stood up, shakily so, then backed away shyly as the footsteps approached the door. He cringed as the key turned and the bolt dragged back, and Peter sought the shadows.

The torchlight from the passage beyond burst into the cell as two men filled the door. The familiar frame of Hib Gow melted into the room and folded back the door for his companion to enter.

Peter Sam held his face in his hands and lifted it slowly to the newcomer. His eyes were drawn straight to the sword. The only steel he had seen was the Spanish knife of his guardian. He had missed the sight of a true blade – and one of such sophistication, whose filigree hilt and double-knuckle bow now filled his sight. A thought passed in him that he would have mocked such fancy not so long ago. Peter would have snapped the artful rapier like a twig. He had tossed lockers'-worths of them overboard as useless pins in his time. What a fool he had been.

Then he looked at the man himself. A purple suit, white lace collar, razor sharp moustache and beard. Black gloved hands. A beneficent countenance framed by a glorious black helmet of hair. The stranger cocked his head at Peter then raised a kerchief to his face as the grating in the floor introduced itself.

Peter lowered his hands as a dim recollection of the stranger began to stir within him. He looked at Hib for reassurance.

Hib sympathised, his vast nostrils flaring, 'I have brought

a friend for you, Peter. This man will take you home. We may have to say goodbye after some supper.'

The stranger moved closer to Peter, keeping himself a sword strike distant, then lowered his kerchief to speak.

'Such pleasure to see you again . . . Peter. Do you remember me?' He spoke as if to a child, his voice softly sinister with a foreign accent stabbing every staccato syllable.

Peter Sam looked into the black eyes. Then his own grew wide as he remembered the island of Sao Nicolau in the Verdes. The signpost for the Indies. The night of Seth Toombs's passing and Devlin's rise.

The tree. A man had been tied to a tree. A grenadoe was wrapped in his fist and a fuse lit.

Peter's eye fell to the left hand of the stranger, its black glove larger than the right.

The stranger followed his eye and lifted his left hand in response. 'So, you remember? I am so glad. It means much to me that you do.'

Peter Sam's eyes narrowed. Hib lay his fingers on his dagger hilt as a glint sparked from across the dank room and the weeks melted away as the old scowl returned to Peter's face.

'*Valentim*?' Peter croaked through his beard. 'You're dead. Toombs is dead. Thomas. Dead.'

'I do not know anyone called Thomas,' Mendes sighed. 'I know of Toombs. Seth Toombs I know very well.' He began to tug and peel the glove from his ungainly left hand, slowly revealing a white wrist. 'You will come with me, Peter. I will protect you. I will protect you from Devlin and those who cause you harm. It is, after all, because of him that this terrible situation has arisen.' He paused to watch the face of the quartermaster sink again. 'He has done much to harm both of us.'

With his final words and a flourish carrying off the glove, Mendes revealed the cold, startling white and blue of his exquisite porcelain appendage.

He waved it in front of Peter, its unmoving fingers crafted to appear pleading, like Adam begging for the apple.

He appreciated the horror his lifeless hand brought to Peter's eyes then looked down to the stump of his wrist, still scarred white, with the leather stitching sewn to his skin stuffed crudely into the base of the hand. Iron clasps nailed into his wrist bone also bolted him to the porcelain hand.

Mendes pulled his shirt cuff back over the wrist and moved away. 'We have much to thank *Capitao* Devlin for, you and I.'

He joined Hib by the door. 'He is good, yes? He can sail?'

Hib looked at Peter's huddled form. 'He is healthy enough, aye.'

Valentim looked back. 'He is a different man. I almost failed to recognise him. Why the need to change him so?'

Hib bent to Valentim's ear. 'You do not know the joy of it. I can make a man knot his own rope and thank me for hanging him. Besides, he was a big one, aye. And me on my own.'

'He infests the air,' Mendes grimaced. 'Wash him some. Then bring him to the ship.'

Hib glowered. 'I am to be accounted for at some time?'

Mendes snorted. 'You will be paid, executioner. I employ your employer. It is written. It is marked. Do not worry. Or would you rather go back to hanging the stinking English? Ah, but perhaps that is not a threat? Perhaps you would enjoy that very much, no?'

The slap of feet landing from the stairs spun them both in the direction of the stairwell, and Mendes' good hand flew to his sword.

'*Enough!*' Andrew Morris yelled, pistol steady, its mouth gaping at both of them. 'You should both worry now!'

His soft sandals had afforded him a silent entrance and now he stood before them, a vagabond swashbuckler in straw hat and matted beard. 'Get back! I would see my mate, Peter. Alive, you'd better be hoping. I have one clean pistol. Swan load on top. Enough to warm both of you, I swear.'

Slowly, Hib and Mendes preceded the gun back into the cell.

Andrew Morris stepped forward, his left hand fumbling behind him for the dagger in his belt. He felt suddenly unsettled by the ghostly white, oversized hand of the Porto.

Neither of his opponents were carrying firearms, just Mendes' deadly *espada* and Hib's long-bladed dagger in his waistband. Good, but not that good, for Andrew Morris was but one man and could add no more teeth to himself. No matter, he would have Peter Sam in a moment sure enough.

Keep your head. Take what they have.

'Drop your weapons, ladies.' He eyed the giant up close then and saw breast bones like a barrel. Morris had doubts that lead could stop him. A thought came to drop him anyway. Just for looking so dangerous. He was an awkward one to be sure.

He crossed the threshold as the weapons rang on the flagstones and were both kicked to the left wall under the wave of his pistol.

He edged towards Peter Sam, sparing a look at him for one heartbeat. His heart gulped at the sight.

Once Peter Sam's shoulder had been as large as Andrew Morris's head and his ruddy arms like other men's legs. Now there was this pale thing that shrank from Morris's stare in the weak square of light let in by the narrow window high above, like the grating of a ship's hold.

The cringing, ragged form and the heavy tainted air reminded Morris of the first sight of a slaver's lower decks and the fearful shadows rattling in the dark. He had done nothing then. Could do nothing then.

'*Peter*?' His eyes darted back to the two men by the wall as he spoke, his pistol steady. 'Tis me, Peter. Andrew Morris. I'm here with Will Magnes. He's top-side with the others. Come to get you out of here. Back to Devlin. Back to *Lucy*, remember? Remember *Lucy*? And Will?'

'*Lucy*?' Peter's cracked voice sparked like a fuse at the name. '*Lucy*'s gone. Thomas has gone . . . Andrew Morris?'

'Aye, Peter. It's me,' his voice began to rise softly like he remembered how Thomas used to lilt. Tenderly coaxing Peter from the corner. '*Lucy* ain't *gone*! We went and got her back. That's where we been all this time. Getting her back for you. Won't Seth be pleased? And Thomas is waiting for you,' Andrew hoping that the memory of the moon-faced lad that Peter Sam had favoured could drag him from his stupor. 'I'll call Will down and we'll get going.'

The pale face with the grey and copper beard stepped out and looked to the terrible Scotsman against the wall, his blade gone and his merry whistle silenced under the stare of a pistol.

'Here, Peter,' Andrew passed his blade across the square of light and thin fingers lingered over the blade before grasping the bony handle.

Good. Andrew breathed better now. All the teeth were his. His eye never left the huge Scotsman, now raising himself to his full height, almost scraping his head upon the ceiling.

'Now, Peter Sam. I'll have my orders. What'll it be for Andrew Morris, Quartermaster? I'll take the big man, aye?'

Hib had only to whisper.

'Drop it, my boy.' And Andrew heard the chime of the knife against the stone as Peter let it go.

'Shoot me, Andrew,' Peter's crumbling throat begged. 'Shoot me, I orders.'

Andrew's gun-arm sank. His quartermaster now pleading with him to shoot and finish him off, his body trembling. The once great and terrible Peter Sam.

It was all Hib needed.

With one stride he crossed the stones to sweep up his blade. A hand clamped onto Andrew's pistol lock.

Andrew pulled back, kicking at the big man.

The pistol came greasily free, miraculously back under Andrew's power, the beeswax applied the night before paying its due. They shared a look of surprise for one moment as Andrew held the upper hand. Then the moment had gone as Hib smothered him with his arms and they danced in the square of sun. Somehow Andrew's thumb cocked the pistol's lock.

Mendes dived for his sword and sampled the fray before him, looking for a gap to make his mark.

Andrew Morris's time was short, he could feel it. He was never the best at the game. With Peter by him he had a chance. As it was he knew the saints never paid him much mind so he chose the action that would affect the world most.

As Hib's blade sunk under his ribs and twisted up into his heart, as the huge left hand pushed down on his shoulder sinking it deeper, and he clasped the giant closer like a lover, Andrew fired his pistol at Valentim Mendes.

The crack of the shot thunder-clapped around the cell. Pellets of swan-grain. Andrew Morris had not lied about that.

Mendes was close enough to die. Instinctively he held out his porcelain hand to the barrel as it swept up at him.

*

The last thing Andrew Morris saw was Valentim Mendes wiping the powder burns off his hand with the kerchief he tore from the dying pirate's neck.

'We will go now.' Mendes looked down at the corpse, checked himself for wounds.

'He said there were others?' Hib wiped his blade.

Mendes scoffed. 'A pirate lie. They always lie. You will learn this, executioner. Bring the oaf.'

William Magnes sat on the shaded porch of the tumbledown tavern. One eye was on the *Jeu Force* board that he played with one of the local sots, who never smiled or even spoke, the other nervously cast up and down the dust road seeking his mate. But both men looked up at the carnival rolling down the road to the harbour.

Magnes looked hard at the big man at the head of the horse. A glint of danger about him in his shifting eyes pricked at Magnes's neck. On the horse, a black-gloved gentleman fanned the flies from his pale noble face and preceded a curtained sedan chair borne by four regretful locals struggling down the hill.

He snorted at the folly of the wealthy and said as much to his silent opponent who ignored or did not understand and simply took two more of Magnes's pieces from under his nose. William Magnes cursed the toothless old man and fell back to the game, paying no more mind to the colourful display.

Magnes had never seen Valentim Mendes before that day. There was no fault but only pity, as his long restless nights ahead would remind him endlessly, that he chose that moment to concentrate on his two counters snatched from the board by the leathery drunk rather than to question the curious sight trailing down to the ships.

Chapter Eighteen

✖

*J*ohn Coxon did not normally frequent the lascivious upstairs quarters of The Porker's End. He had passed only once before under its swinging sign depicting the startling sight of a Great White flinging himself at a mutton-chopped sailor stoutly fending off the fish with a marlin spike.

Backs turned from him as he cut through the benches, his path guided by the smiling young Portuguese who had led him there weeks previously, only to be disappointed by the confirmation that Devlin was most probably on the other side of the world.

Upstairs was intolerably warm, dubious justification for the swift removal of clothes from most of the usual patrons.

Coxon removed only his hat as he ducked into the room where Sarah Wood made her billet. The Porto sailor stayed on the landing.

The room was cloudy and dark. Petticoats draped loosely about the tiny window kept the white light out but not the dancing flies that welcomed the stranger.

Coxon looked down at the girl on the giant bed that reached up to his waist. She was a broken doll within it, slipping away from life now, the fever outside her as well as in. She was falling into whatever grace she was destined for.

Her jaundiced skin glowed with a greasy layer of almost

effervescent sweat. Her open eyes were as dry and surprised as yesterday's smoked fish.

Still, she made the strained effort to rise when she heard the captain's voice.

'Sarah,' Coxon said impatiently. 'You called for me?'

Her voice lilted weakly through white flecked lips. 'Captain John. You came!'

'I cannot stay long. The boy said you had some word for me?' He wanted to keep the appointment brief. Sweat had already begun to bead around his necktie.

'So good for you to come, Captain John.' She dragged herself up to the headboard, swallowing hard. Her breast shivering. 'Patrick slept in this very bed you know? Seems so long ago, don't it?' Her voice faintly carried some of her Carolina origins.

Coxon ran his tricorne through his hands, feeling a fool that some delirious whore had pricked his wound craftily enough with the damnable name to drag him up here just for companionship.

On his arrival on New Providence, as the ropes were thrown over the gibbet, the young Porto had approached him with the name. Devlin's name. 'Captain' Devlin. And Coxon had dragged the Porto into Nassau to take him to the woman who knew its whereabouts.

They had sailed east she had said. East to spend their coin and seek sanctuary. Gone from the Bahamas. The certainty of her belief that Devlin had flown brought some small measure of absolution to Coxon. He could focus on the colony as Rogers dictated, on his duty of assuring that the pineapple trees took hold and flourished.

Now she had called him back. Only by now the creep of the putrescent fever had found her.

'What do you want, Sarah? You have already told me that Devlin sailed. Is there something else I need to know?'

Sarah sank inches down, too weak to hold herself up for long. Her eyes looked through Coxon, trying to recall something from beyond him, long ago, before she knew of his name.

'Yes,' she breathed. 'There was something, Captain John. Something about them both . . .'

'Both? Who?'

An angry knock shuddered the thin door, then it was pushed open, ushering Mrs Haggins' white powdered face into the chamber.

Haggins looked down at Sarah who pulled the sheet to her neck. Then she twisted her gaze to Coxon.

'What goes on here, Cap'n Coxon?' Haggins demanded, her vexation causing Sarah to clasp a hand to her head. 'Guv'nor Woodes don't allow no officers in my rooms! I'd be thrown out! You must leave at once. I insist on it I do, Cap'n! Out, I insist!'

Coxon pulled back his shoulders. 'Mrs Haggins! I will insist that you await me downstairs or *I* will insist that Governor Rogers permits *me* to throw you off this colony!' He paused for her outrage to recede. '*Now* Madam! *Now!*'

Haggins gasped, almost properly shocked, although she no longer knew the sense of the word, and bundled out of the room with fuming recriminations smothered by her bulk. The Porto sailor tugged his hair to Coxon as he leant in and pulled the door to again.

Sarah shifted beneath the grubby bedclothes, her breath coming in shallow drafts. Coxon looked around for some water. Finding none he pressed her regardless.

'Who were you going to tell about, Sarah? Go on, my girl. I won't let her bother you again.'

She looked up at him softly, smiled at some kindness that hundreds of others did not see, that no other woman had ever seen.

'I recall it, Captain John. I recall it now. I have a mind to tell you that Patrick and Dandelion will be back. Back real soon.'

Coxon sighed, lowered his head. The risk of fever had not been worth the revelation that at some point, some day months from now, Devlin might possibly decide to set his course to Providence. Hallelujah.

'Is that it? Devlin is coming back? He fumbled with his hat, finding it difficult to locate the front-cock as he squared it on his head again.

Sarah looked hurt, dismayed, as if she had imparted a mighty secret upon the officer and he had not heard.

'Why, he'll have to come back. He'll be back for *this,* won't he? He asked me to hold it for him. I'm the only girl that stayed, see.'

Coxon looked up as Sarah tried to lean over her bed, her delicate hands reaching beneath the frame, but failing as a rasping cough sent her flat.

'Is under there. I can't gets it no more,' she hacked.

Coxon knelt to the bed, prostrating himself as if praying in a mosque to see what the girl could no longer grasp, and then he saw it.

From out of nowhere, amongst the old dolls and half-finished sketches in a whore's bedroom in a fever-ridden pox-hole at the rat-end of Christendom, there it lay: the black chest. *The* chest.

It lay innocently beneath Sarah Wood's bed and winked at him. *Why, hullo there, John. Very pleased to see you again. How you doing this fine day?*

His forearm ached. Just his leaning on it stressed the weakened bone. He pushed himself back up, somewhat in awe of Sarah Wood as she lay retching on the bed.

'That's the gold. That's the chest from The Island. He left it here? With you?' His voice sounded incredulous, but then again why sail with your gold? There was always the risk of capture and defeat at sea. And why carry the evidence of your crimes with you to be taken by the first lucky soul that chances across you? Pirates usually buried their troves on spits of land. The whole world knew that. Every small boy in England knew that. It lit their dreams. So, contrarily, why not leave it on a pirate fortress with a bruised little girl who believed she loved you?

'They were always so nice to me,' she coughed. 'I told you they'd be back you see? Oh, it ain't all there. Just the might of it.'

Coxon felt oddly cold. His legs had turned weak. 'Why have you told me this, Sarah?'

'They won't be back before I die,' Sarah smiled, 'I know that. I didn't want *her* to have a hand on it, Captain John. No one knows, save you.'

'Sarah, why would you entrust me with this?' He tapped the box lightly with his foot, confirming its reality to his disbelieving senses.

Again she looked hurt that the officer did not understand her reasons.

'You were nice to me too, Captain John. Gentlemanly. I remember it. And I needed someone to have it who was there. Who'd know it. Who even bled a little for it. Don't that make sense?'

Coxon took his hat off again. Loosened his necktie.

'Yes, Sarah.' He noticed the goose-pimples on his wrist

despite the heat. 'Now that you say it. And I thank you. You have done your King a great service.'

'Oh, I hope not, Captain John.' She sank lower. 'I hope not. Don't let *him* hate me for giving it up. I'm sure it ain't lost with you.'

He met Haggins again at the top of the stair. Her own syrupy aroma mingled with the stale beer from the tavern below. Her bosom halted his descent. Followed by the Porto sailor, he offered his disrespect by not doffing his hat as he delivered his orders.

'Bring her some water and brandy. I will fetch a doctor. And a guard.'

'A guard? What guard? What for? What doctor? There's been no doctor here since Dandelion left on the account.'

'I will send for my surgeon. No one is to enter that room. She has the fever. I want it contained.' He barged past. The Porto grinned at her and followed.

'I can't have a soldier cluttering up my stairs. Putting good folks off. I shall lose me business!' Haggins screeched.

Coxon turned back to her, 'Perhaps you'd prefer it if I closed the whole place? Just in case. Would that suffice?'

He did not wait for a reply. He had already spied Seth Toombs idling his arm on the final baluster and sneering up at him.

Seth managed the extraordinary facial feat of beginning to wink then freezing it as he remembered Coxon had an intense dislike of such familiarity. He knuckled his burgundy hat instead.

'I hadn't favoured you as the visiting type, Cap'n.'

Coxon ignored Seth's jibe. 'Do you want my attention, sailor?' he snapped as he walked to the door. Seth pursued him, shadowed by the Porto sailor.

'Aye, Cap'n,' Seth chirped as the door swung open to a different, colourful world outside. 'I was of a mind to enquire about the sloop-trading? I gather we be going to market somewhere south of here. Via and vis the *Buck* and the *Mumvil Trader*?'

'I am on my way to Governor Rogers, Toombs. Speak your mind.' Coxon's pace increased as his mind raced ahead. A cacophony of questions spun his sensibility into a gyre.

'I was only wishing to make an annotation of the matter, Cap'n, that I have sailed with the *Mumvil* afore. And I would be much inclined to offer my capable knowledge on her manners, Cap'n. If it might be of use.'

Coxon wheeled round to face him. 'When did you sail on her?' He squinted in the sun at the lank and dirty sailor. Seth's scarred cheek was not the only aspect of the man that unsettled Coxon. There was something of a mask about him wholly, as if he was a reflection of someone else. There seemed to be pretence even in his salutes and leers.

Seth scratched his eyebrow evasively. 'Oh, time ago, time ago. Labrador. Cod to Bristol. Captain Snow – *good man*. Hard days.'

Coxon nodded. 'No doubt.' He looked at his Porto entourage, contemplating how much English the man might know. What inkling he had of the scene that had transpired in Sarah's room? Perhaps minimising the ranks of avarice would be a sound action. And Toombs with his gallows countenance, the itch of the sea-rover all over him. A mistake waiting to happen.

'A man familiar would be of use. Sign yourself up with the master. She sails to Hispaniola. And take this good man with you. He has taken the Act of Grace, being formerly acquainted with the pirate Devlin.'

Seth rolled his head to the diminutive Porto. 'Oh is that so? Devlin is it now?' He touched the boy's shoulder. 'What tales you must have, young man!'

The boy's chin bounced eagerly.

Coxon sniffed. 'He knows little English I feel, Toombs.' He moved on.

Toombs hailed after him, 'Thank you kindly, Cap'n. I'll lade myself with his well-being.'

Coxon turned. 'One provision, Toombs: there are to be no personal arms aboard the ships so stow any you have with the master. Each man will be only permitted a gully to eat with.'

Seth dipped his head. 'No concern, Cap'n. A gully will do me just fine. Good day to you now, Sir!'

Coxon watched him bow, but he turned and left before Seth rose again, attempting to erase the scarred sneer from his mind's eye.

He came to the staggered path that led to the old Spanish fort, Woodes Rogers' residence. It overlooked the east of the harbour and most of the old town, and was a reminder of better days. The guns that had kept even Morgan's tiller hard to larboard; thirty-two pounders of Spanish bronze sat on the cliff-top parapet staring out of their embrasures as if waiting for glory to come again.

Coxon was standing stock still. Without noticing he had been looking up at the yawning windows of Rogers' rooms long enough for some children to begin a game around his statue.

He could not hear their rhymes as they skipped at his feet. The only sound in his head was his own voice stumbling through a report before the board. He was again listening to the grey wigs cough uncomfortably as he listed the miseries of his failure a year ago.

By rights, by duty, he should break the circle of hands that whirled around him. He should immediately inform Rogers about Sarah Woods and her silent bed partner.

But Rogers had commissioned two sloops to trade with the Spanish. Had hung pirates like clothes pegs. Had been a privateer in the war. Had drowned natives reluctant to kneel. Stripped Spanish Ladies for their secreted jewels. Coxon politely lifted apart the chain of arms around him and turned away.

No, Rogers could remain oblivious for a moment. It was better Coxon summoned his surgeon for Sarah Woods, and a guard for her door. The fever would suffice as validation. He would enjoy dwelling on consequences yet to come.

He had found the chest. And Devlin would find him holding it.

Chapter Nineteen

✖

Bath Town, North Carolina

Governor Eden's mansion.

*G*overnor Eden had not welcomed Teach when the pirate had first come to his attention. Eden was loath to associate with such a notorious brigand and enemy of mankind.

On the other hand a privateer enjoyed a certain degree of formality and Eden might lower himself to the occasional social engagement.

So it was that Edward Teach came calling again at the governor's acres in Bath Town, in a carriage no less, and gave notice that he had come to take up the Act of Grace so recently appointed by the King and offered Eden his loyalties as privateer in lieu of which he presented Eden a sack full of coin in good faith. After that, Eden courteously listened to the crimson-coated sea-dog and let his secretary count the coin.

They enjoyed a fair companionship. Eden had granted Teach his Grace, and Teach gave tribute with his own hand from whatever happened to chance across his bows.

Teach had sniffed the Proclamation a year past and knew its meaning to his trade. Granted the French Guineaman, *Concorde*, by Ben Hornigold, his former captain, he took the three-hundred ton square-rig and re-christened her the *Queen Anne's Revenge*; he then proceeded to haunt the colonial coast. His resolution was to remain several steps ahead of his British would-be enslavers and gain legitimacy and position with the frustrated governors of the Carolinas.

He raided those who refused to let him trade in the towns and he courted those that let him in to savour their daughters and unload his tenders.

To the governors it was an opportunity for free trade, a tax-exempt boon to their coffers and, as the nod to the pirate began, other sloops crept up the inlets and the pirates found a new and willing home.

This day was different. A new covenant had come for Eden and Teach. The trust between the two had been split by Eden's sudden change of humour when the smashed medicine chest lay strewn across the oak floor of his drawing room.

'Where are they, Teach? Where are the *letters*?' Eden stood with an axe heavy in his hands, breathless and sweating in the dry August heat. Although his bob wig had been cast aside after the third heavy swing, he was still the gentlemen in silk waistcoat and stockings.

Teach sat behind Eden's desk in full garb, crimson coat, black hat and boots, seemingly immune to the heat. Pistols representing every nation stuck out of his every nook like voodoo pins from a 'poppet'. Their unlikely cabal lay before them as broken as the shattered chest.

'What letters, Charles?' Teach spoke softly as he sucked on a long-pipe, his scowl as black as his matted mane. 'You sent me for a chest from that man. And I brought you a chest. I know nothing of any letters. Save the ones you promised to *me*, Charles.'

Eden let the axe fall, chipping the floor, and stepped towards the desk.

'I sent you to Ignatius. I sent you for a chest. That chest came off the *Whydah*, Sam Bellamy's *Whydah*, with Palgrave Williams over a year ago.'

Teach plucked the pipe from his teeth, 'Who?'

Eden wiped his brow. 'Palgrave was Bellamy's partner. He left the ship to visit his mother on Block Island. The only thing he took off the boat with him was *that* chest!' He stabbed his thumb over his shoulder at the pitiful splinters.

'Perhaps she was sick,' Teach speculated, replacing his pipe. Then he lifted his feet to the desk and leant back.

'Edward,' Eden cooed. 'Two men survived the *Whydah*. I paid fifteen hundred pounds to one of them for that information and spared him the noose.'

'Well, Governor, you were fair robbed, so you were. That there chest ain't ever worth more than three. Course, worth even less now, mind.' He pulled his bracken beard out of his linen shirt, allowing it to cascade down his chest. 'Now, I have fulfilled my part. And I want my letters. The Admiralty pardon, promised to me, that says every ship is mine by law. A fair price I would say for what I have done.'

'*Done*?' Eden swept Teach's boots from his desk. 'Done? You have done *nothing* except cost me money and wasted a year of my life hunting for that chest! I swear, Teach, if you do not give me what you have betrayed you have slept your last peaceful night!'

The black eyes fired at Eden's words like pistol balls shooting across the desk. Teach's knuckles turned white as he gripped the desk's edge. Then just as suddenly the coals went dull and lifeless, wide and placid as a doll's. Eden stepped back as Blackbeard rose up, covering him in shadow.

'Done?' he whispered. 'What I have *done*? I will tell you what I have done, Governor.' He stepped around the desk. The three brace of pistols slung around his neck seemed to jiggle in anticipation as he moved.

'I have damned myself for your will by holding a whole town to ransom! I have run aground the finest ship I ever owned. Grounded the *Revenge* to maroon my own men with the promise that I'll be back. Sailed here on a sloop with just a few trusted brethren all because *you* wanted that there chest a secret.'

He growled his way to Eden's cabinet of glass, picked the finest dark carafe and drained half of it, the great back to Eden stretching taller with each swallow.

'All because you wanted that chest,' he swallowed his rising bile. 'What I have done . . .' His voice trailed away.

Eden watched the carafe go back in the cabinet as Teach's head sunk down beyond his shoulders. He looked at the axe on the floor, then back to the crimson figure as it spoke again.

'I have a house here at Bath. Another wife. And land.' Teach turned round, wiping his mouth with the back of his hand.

'I have plans, Governor. A future beyond the sea,' enunciated Teach as he took in the red face and then the tight waistcoat straining across Eden's paunch. 'Where you be standing, there stand I, Governor. Mark me.' He reached back for the carafe. His first draught had slaked his temper. The second would steady the furious trembling of his limbs that normally preceded someone else's pain.

Eden looked at the splinters of the chest and stroked the grey pelt of his hair, kept close-cut for under his bob wig. He was grey as a rabbit at forty-five and governor for the last five years. The letters were not in the chest. *Think again.*

He kicked petulantly at the wood and dragged himself to the cabinet for a glass, resigned to the fact that angering Teach was a bad tack to follow.

'I apologise, Edward, for my outburst.' He poured himself a drink and clinked his glass against Teach's bottle. 'We are in this together, I know. I will get my secretary Tobias to issue your letters of ownership.' He drank fast, the instant warmth in his belly soothing and bracing him. 'You blockaded a town at great personal risk and I am sorry to have doubted you. Ignatius has fooled us. Rather, fooled me.' He poured another.

'The chest I was led to believe contained some letters. Letters that have whispered around the world for years. I felt they were in my grasp.' He eyed Teach over his glass. Threw him one card. 'Did Ignatius mention what the chest might have contained?'

Teach's beard rose, a smile presumably under the thicket of hair. 'Important enough matter I gather. I had to kidnap a councillor and his son to sway him, and only then when I promised to deliver their heads ashore. Two heads better than one!' He elbowed Eden's drinking arm, splashing his drink and bellowing out a laugh that rolled through the house.

Eden paused for the roar to subside, unable to join in himself. 'Quite. Now however, I must regroup.' He walked to his desk and sat with a sigh. How much did Teach need to know? How much did he know? He had known the villain a time. Violent, certainly; drunken, always. But no fool.

'Ignatius now knows I am after the letters. And I am probably not the only governor seeking the same.' He chanced a quick glance at the drawer to his right where a pistol waited. 'Did you know Black Sam Bellamy, Edward?'

Teach snorted. 'Aye. Knew of him plain enough. One of Hornigold's through and through.'

'No doubt. It was a pirate named Thomas that survived Bellamy's shipwreck. Did you know of him?'

Teach shook his head slowly, trying to recall, taking a swift swallow to aid his memory.

'No mind,' Eden went on. 'Young Thomas was acquitted for being a pirate. Mainly for his fascinating evidence, as it were. He told of the letters being on board and of the promise of a pardon for Bellamy and all of them if they took them north, up to Cape Cod. I assume to safety or to a buyer. Thomas swore that Bellamy and Palgrave decided to unload their precious cargo at Block Island, perhaps to haggle for more money, perhaps to take the letters for themselves, who knows?' He drank solemnly, listening to the slave gangs bringing in the evening with their songs lilting up from his plantation acres.

Teach's voice almost rolled along in the same tune as he spoke the inevitable. 'Or perhaps this man Thomas knew the letters were still aboard the *Whydah* when she went down. And took that acquittal, and your fifteen-hundred pounds, to fetch them his-self maybe?'

'That indeed occurs to me now, Edward. Either way he has vanished and the letters with him.' He drained his glass and beckoned for another. 'Or with God knows who else.' Teach came over with the decanter and poured slowly.

'My counsel,' Teach proffered, 'would be that if a pirate got a hold of such a prize he would make his way to a safe point. Somewhere he could conceal his luck from those that might enquire. Somewhere a pirate can hide and bide his time maybe, until he can capitalise on his good fortune.'

Eden nodded and could already feel his pockets getting lighter. 'Such a place as Providence, by any chance?'

'Aye,' Teach agreed as if the thought were not his own. 'That would be such a place as good as any, aye.'

Eden sat back. 'And if I afforded you, perhaps, the necessary to take a trip to Providence, on my behalf, you would
not be too disinclined?'

'Well now, Governor. Times have changed. Providence
now be the King's Island. Propriety has switched quite a bit
now I gathers. Be an awful risk for a pirate to sail within five
leagues of such a place, what with all the wood and lobsters
patrolling her. Take an awfully big purse to persuade a
gentleman of fortune to take a risk like that.'

'And what would it take to persuade *you*, Edward?'

Teach straightened up, pausing for a breath as he thought
on the matter. 'I suppose I could manage such a task for the
promise of some land. Land to do with what I pleased with
no objections. That might persuade me.' He turned away.

Eden was genuinely impressed. The only thing he could
think to ask was where and why would Teach require land,
except to conceal corpses perhaps. Teach walked through the
remnants of the chest, crunching the mahogany beneath his
boots as he pondered, then slowly turned round again.

'I have a sailcloth base at Ocracock. I want a fort there.
My own stone fort to protect my interests. And I want no-
one to stop me building it.' He pointed his face hard at Eden.

Eden could not comprehend the consequences of Teach
having a fort on the point of his colony. The entertaining of
such a scheme, to turn Carolina into another Providence or
Tortuga, would condemn even the men who carried the stone.
It would never happen. Could never happen.

Like a father promising a begging child he tried to appease,
confident that Teach's tomorrow was a long way off.

'I believe we can come to some arrangement, Edward. Yes.
If that is what you want. How soon could you get under way?'

Teach strode to the oak desk to snatch at the decanter.

'Tomorrow. I can leave when your Tobias brings me my Admiralty notes.' He swigged and slammed it down. 'You'd best find him tonight. I ain't patient when I'm waiting.'

Eden concurred. The thought of how much Teach really knew, how much he had gleant from Ignatius or fathomed in his own mind, would grow within him as a cancer, but for now he glowed at the concept that he had Blackbeard himself preparing to rain down upon Providence.

It was not by theory, Eden surmised, that Teach had suggested the place. He knew something. And by design Charles Eden would always profit, as did all advantageous men, from the knowledge of others. But Teach's knowledge would not come cheap.

If Eden had to dig into the town's taxes to bid against Ignatius, a day that would surely come, he would give as graciously as he could.

Teach idled on the gravel outside, waiting for Eden's cob to carry him back to his ship. As he watched the dusty cloud of insects floating over the fields in the dusk, following the slow bobbing of the black heads of slaves, he wondered only about the Chinese gun Ignatius had told him of, and that Eden had never mentioned. The gun that Palgrave Williams had taken to Providence and hidden therein.

He had Eden now promising land and legitimacy. Ignatius promising even more. All for a Chinese gun hiding some priest's letters that meant nothing to him. Teach's losses after the dust settled would be as light as his conscience.

In England he would be vilified and hung. Here, he was a landowner and a personage of promise. The opportunities that this New World offered were limitless to a shrewd man of means. He tapped the lump of wax hidden beneath his shirt. The chance to remind Devlin of his affront would be a suitable final act to the life he was planning to leave behind, a final pirate glory to warm him in his days of fireside and grandchildren to come. That thought pleasured him all the way back to the shore.

Chapter Twenty

*T*he *Talefan* caught the trade winds. A week coursing east-southeast on a broad reach; sailing fairer than a ship has a right to. Devlin stood on the larboard gunwale, hanging off the shrouds and watching the streaking grey dolphins effortlessly match the *Talefan*'s nine knots and even take the time to leap from the water, stitching the ocean as they plunged again and again.

Devlin glanced aft to the man at the tiller who waved as his captain stuck out his right arm across the deck, pointing west. The helmsman heaved on his iron staff and the gunwale began to rise beneath Devlin's boots. The aproned larboard guns rolled back one turn of their trucks, squealing with delight.

The hull heeled away from the grey streaks. The spars started to creak and labour with the turn and Devlin watched the sun sweeping to the stern, then hanging behind them. The helmsman steadied his tiller when the binnacle by his right knee read 'W.S.W.'

Devlin swung off the gunwale and looked over the bow, watching the bowsprit rise and fall before the horizon, now scattered with islands, glowing almost white.

For three days and nights they had sailed to keep the Bahamas far to starboard, passing almost two hundred miles east from New Providence, shouldering Abaco, Eleuthera and at dawn, Cat Island. The *Talefan* ploughed steadily south, invisible to all patrols but the petrels, the albacore and dolphin. To sail from Charles Town straight to New Providence was risky. The northern waters were full of hunters. It was best to keep Providence over the western horizon, then run down to the 24th parallel and turn back, as they did now, to reach the shallows, the white waters where the men-of-war could not go.

Come up through the cays, through the soundings by the threes – perfect for the *Talefan*'s keel. It meant many miles added to their journey but a safer course. And besides, Devlin had one more stop to make before the game could begin.

Dandon stepped up to his friend and captain on the flush deck of the fo'c'sle, observing him in thought or calculation as he stared at the hazy protrusions in the distance. The ship leant to leeward in her course, the stays protesting, and Dandon weaved in his walk as the deck angled against him. He swung himself beneath the halyards and steadied himself on Devlin's shoulder.

'Are you sure this is a wise course, Patrick?' he asked through the light rain thrown up by the dipping bow.

'I can show you again, Dandon,' Devlin made a triangle with the sweep of his hand. 'Once we reach Dead Man it'll be shallow all the way north back up to Providence. We'll mark up along the Exumas. Be able to pluck the fish up from the jolly-boat. And no warship can find us. Lay to that.'

'Oh that I grant, Captain. It is the other course I was after referring to. Dead Man itself.'

Devlin looked ahead, contemplative again. The warm soft wind plucked at his black hair, unhindered by bow or bag.

'We have fifteen men from this ship who do not belong. I

don't want them coming into Providence with us. We have enemies enough.'

'But to leave them there? And us down to fifteen souls then ourselves? That leaves us awful weak, Patrick.'

'The *Shadow* will pick them up. Bill was to make for Dead Man and meet us there.'

Dandon looked suddenly healthy and pink. 'To join up with? Oh, grand joy, *mon capitaine aventurier*! Praise be!'

'No,' Devlin looked out again. 'We will have no time to wait for the *Shadow*. I've given enough time to divert on this course and keep our hides out of sight. Besides . . .' He turned to look along the deck. Beneath the bulwarks men dozed or carved their own fancies into the wood, or played cards on Indian rugs stretched across the hatch.

'It's been almost two months without a sniff for our lads. These *Talefan* men have not signed. They're not us. Not one of us. I couldn't trust them to stand.'

He looked up at a couple of *Talefans* languishing barefoot in the rigging, grabbing some breeze and shade from the fore topsails.

'And what of us?' Dandon drawled, and waved an arm towards the six-pounders on deck, always loaded and ready, and now corked with tompions to prevent the sea slipping into their mouths. 'Am I to be privy to some greater plan other than sailing into a naval fleet with only fifteen men and these eight pea-shooters?'

Devlin slapped his friend's arm and called for a fiddle to the deck behind him. '*Now* you're thinking true, old friend! That's the tale of it! Fifteen men and eight little ladies against the whole of Providence! We haven't a hope in any of it!' He checked himself. 'Make it two fiddles!' he demanded. 'And lively now, Hugh!'

Hugh Harris sprang up from the aft companionway, already plucking on his fiddle. He was joined a moment later by Sam Fletcher's wailing scrape. A guitar appeared uninvited and, where men a moment before were lolling and masticating idly, a Saturday night in Boston now jigged upon the deck scattered with rugs and bottles.

> *'They call me hanging Johnnie,*
> *Away, boys, away!*
> *They call me hanging Johnnie,*
> *Hang, boys, hang.*
>
> *They say I hang for money,*
> *Away, boys, away!*
> *But saying so is funny;*
> *Hang, boys, hang.*
>
> *I'd hang the highway robber,*
> *Away, boys, away!*
> *I'd hang the burglar jobber;*
> *Hang, boys, hang.*
>
> *I'd hang a noted liar,*
> *Away, boys, away!*
> *I'd hang a bloated friar;*
> *Hang, boys, hang.*
>
> *Come hang, come haul together,*
> *Away, boys, away!*
> *Come hang for finer weather,*
> *Hang, boys, hang.'*

The petrels wheeled high above the little two-mast ship, cocking their heads to look upon the tiny dancing figures and screeching against the strange sounds that beset their fragile ears. Soon a whole cloud of birds circled and joined the dance, joined the song that for an hour of the glass was the only sound in the whole empty world.

Chapter Twenty-One

✗

'Captain' Seth Toombs

*H*owell Davis, a Milford man, was a good chief mate when he was a merchant sailor. Half a year ago he sailed with one Captain Skinner and had almost made it to Sierra Leone aboard the sweetest little snow that was ever Bristol-made, when a black flag brought a blight to their harvest.

Captain Skinner, rest his soul, shared the unfortunate fate of every man who forgets that the Lord had informed him when he was a boy that he shall reap what he sows.

He found himself taken aboard the great pirate Captain England's ship, and Skinner hoped to strike a bargain to save some portion of his lading, and a good deal of his blood.

Once there he met a smattering of acquaintances who recognised old Captain Skinner as the very same who had denied them any wage on a cruise a year before, then sold them into service on a King's ship where conditions were hard and hungry even compared to the near slavery of the merchant trade.

Justice, to Skinner, was not kind. His wife would be spared the detail of it, for anyone who has ever had the chance to deliver a blow to a man who has wronged him can affirm just how sweet a lick of his blood can taste.

Tied by his neck to the windlass, Skinner was bloodied by the crushing of broken bottles into his naked form or having bottles broken upon him, empty or otherwise.

Then he endured several circuits stumbling around the deck, being whipped on and on should he falter or slip in his own blood to the boards.

After a time, whilst he still retained the power of speech, he entreated through a foaming mouth to his former crewmates for an easy death.

His old mates obliged with several shots to his face, then went about their trade upon his snow.

That was how Howell Davis met and took the measure of a sang-froid pirate captain.

Captain England, a generous man according to all who put pen to paper about him, gave Davis the snow, *Cadogan*, and set him on his way. Davis sailed to Barbados, with what scant cargo still remained for the merchants that owned the lading.

The merchants and the magistrates did not believe the barefooted sailor when he told them of the tale, preferring the more obvious occurrence that Davis and his crew had turned pirate themselves for the best part of their goods and done away with the brave, resolute Captain Skinner.

Assured that evidence would be forthcoming, Davis passed three months in the vision of hell that only an eighteenth-century prison can imprint on an innocent man.

Someone may have apologised to him when he finally emerged like a ghost from his dungeon, but history affords us no such record, and a single extant yellow page only relates that after Davis was freed he thought long on his future and on those that had imprisoned him – and on the truth that one may as well be hung for a sheep as a lamb.

This was the story he relayed to Seth Toombs the second

night out on their errand to Hispaniola aboard the *Mumvil*, for Davis had made his way to Providence to become a pirate only to find that he had arrived too late. But not too late for Toombs.

Woodes Rogers had decided to send two sloops to trade with the Spanish, an illegal act for the navy but craftily avoided if the ships were privately manned. Unfortunately Rogers' only available crew had their own ideas of what was and what was not illegal.

And so it was that when Captain Finch found himself gently woken in his cot at midnight by the tapping of the cold blade of Toombs's gully upon his forehead, it was Davis that stood by in the dark, aiming the captain's own pistol into Finch's bleary eyes.

Toombs shushed Finch like an infant before he had a chance to blather some objection.

'Whist now, Cap'n,' he said and put a finger to his lips. 'It's time.'

Finch looked about him in panic as more figures weaved in the dark behind the two men, monstrous in size as the single candle on his writing desk danced and warped their shadows.

He heard the stifled pleadings of surgeon Murray in the darkness and the nervous giggling of the treacherous rats restraining him.

Toombs, almost mournfully, patted Finch's chest and sighed. He turned to address his men.

'Davis and I are in command, lads. What say you all?'

The howled agreement grew from the cabin and went through to the weather-deck and climbed up the masts to the top-men until even those on watch aboard the *Buck*, two cable lengths away, over twelve-hundred feet to windward, strained an ear and looked slowly to each other.

The ships were anchored for the night but the two-man watch on the *Buck* could see the deck of the *Mumvil* buzzing with heads all over, and for them the distant cheer chilled the warm Caribbean midnight.

The two men met at the larboard gangway, seeking comfort from the tell-tale sights abroad of them.

More than half of both forty-man crews were reformed pirates, the rest being legitimate sailors and colonists, striving to improve their lot in the New World.

Rogers had mistakenly believed his own ideals, that all men require is a bit of land, a little home, a little future and a lot of Government and they *will* be happy.

Some however, like the dog that chooses to wander the streets and alleyways, like the horse that kicks in his stable and gnaws at his saddle, some men stand out in the rain, walk through the trees rather than along the path and believe that hearths are only for taverns.

Captain Finch knew this and had always known this. He had traded on the *Mumvil* for five years and had seen them all. He kept quiet as the court around him now convened and each man grabbed a small part to play.

He had read of the fates of those that resisted during such a night and had taken Toombs's scarred face and swivelling eye as a man who knew a mood or two.

He watched without recrimination as Toombs sawed free the bell and threw it as his feet with a dulled clang drowned out by a roar of approval.

He was silent when he was lowered with the gig and the eight others who chose to remain part of the larger world. They picked up their wood and rowed to the *Buck* with jeers and bottles flying through the air all around them.

Toombs had spared them, in part not wishing to be a

monster to his new crew and in part using his wealth of experience that told him how survivors of a pirate will enlarge his terrible reputation until he becomes a giant gorging on islands as he strides across the seas with men's livers running down his chin. And all to season their own cowardice in the affair with whole handfuls of salt.

By the time the *Mumvil* was under way in the night, Finch would be a hero who could do no more than liberate the eight others from the cannibal rites he had witnessed aboard.

Toombs watched the gig slop across the expanse between the two freeboards. There was only curiosity along the *Buck*'s larboard gunwale. No attempt to make sail. No busying at the guns.

Mumvil's cable was slipped. The forecourse cracked in and out as it fell, belly filling, spraying salt water in all eyes foolish enough to watch her drop. Toombs swelled his chest at the hum of the reevings through the blocks, his heart enraptured by the eagerness of the young men running around him.

His men's eyes were blinkered from the gallows, and they worked not for fear of the 'captain's daughter' or a belting from the master, but in anticipation of the gold and drunken concupiscence that Toombs had promised them.

He strode fore, shouting as he came. 'Larboard tack 'til we're away, boys! Get those jibs running!'

She was fifty-two feet long and eighteen feet across the beam, the bowsprit almost as long as the ship. Only ten four-pounders were mounted but there were more in the hold, brought for trade.

He had a ship again. A sloop. Half the woman that his precious *Lucy* was, but it was a start. It would do.

He had sighed with a heavy heart when the young Porto had gesticulated wildly through his stilted English that the

Lucy had been blown to firewood and that Devlin now commanded the *Shadow*.

The men had all mourned for Toombs's loss as he showed them the white wound on his cheek from the bullet gifted him from Valentim Mendes. It was only the luck that always followed him, so he told them, that the shot angled to travel out of his mouth, burning his lips. The blow that came after caused him more discomfort.

He awoke hours later, he told them, to find that he had been betrayed by his new navigator. A former servant to an English captain that he had rescued himself from his indenture had repaid that favour by abandoning him alone on St Nick when his plans to kidnap Valentim had ended with the deaths of trusted men. One traitor was still alive. Devlin was still alive.

How Devlin must have laughed to hear how the enraged Valentim, delirious from finding the will to hack off his own hand, ordered Toombs to endure the agony of having a sail needle twisted in his cheek, embellishing what would have been a faint memory into a four-inch scar that dragged up his face into a permanent sneer.

It had taken half an hour for Valentim to determine that Seth Toombs did not know where Devlin would sail. By then both of their wounds had stopped bleeding and Toombs had to think fast if he was to survive and sail again.

Toombs bartered for his life with the most valuable information he had and hoped that Valentim could see the worth of it, as he had just weeks before when he spared one of Bellamy's old crew who had not sailed but who knew and revealed Bellamy's latest plans.

So Toombs told him of the letter. The secret of the making of porcelain, stolen and lost but now found and free again to tantalise the world. He withheld sufficient information to buy him a fishing boat and an escort to row alongside him.

When he had rowed half a league he raised his mast and tossed his companions a bamboo tube. Inside was a rolled-up sheet on which he had written the name *Whydah* and her destination, the tale of the gun that held the letters and the name of the man in Charles Town that had sent them north with Bellamy. It was a name Valentim knew well enough to mark Seth Toombs as a veracious man.

Now Toombs was back. Back amongst the silver waters where the gold flowed like wine. It had taken him almost a year to get here. He had heard of Devlin's gold, had heard of the legend that should have been his.

It was only a matter of time before he would have both.

'Run out the log, Howell!' he yelled aft to his new quartermaster. 'No more than eight knots, boys! Trim all but the jibs!'

They were on the Bahama Bank: three hundred miles of sandbank and north of the 22nd parallel with Cuba at their bow and Crooked Island to their stern.

For now they would raid the stores and drink their fill as he had promised. Once the *Buck* was far behind they would rest up and wait for noon. He would consult Finch's charts with Davis and reckon their next course. It was his limit of the 'art'.

But tonight he would fill himself with rum and picture the expression on Rogers' face when he learnt the fate of his illegal sloop-trading.

He looked about his world. The endless ocean was still filled with hiding places where good men dare not go. Satisfied, he walked to the taffrail, slapping the back of the young man at the tiller and staring over the sloop's wake, the *Buck* already just a twinkling buoy far behind.

He spat on the rail and rubbed his spittle hard into her wood.

'Good girl,' he whispered lovingly, drawing a raised eyebrow from the timoneer. 'Good girl.'

Devlin could not drown an uneasy feeling; not with rum, nor with song and fellowship. He dragged his feet out of the cabin where a late supper had stretched into midnight, leaving a small company of his men to lap at their rum and poke at the chicken laid out for them.

A funereal dolour had come over him. His humour of late often grew dark when the lamps were lit and his second bottle was half sunk. His eyes glazed in the lamplight. He was thinking too much on the year gone.

His men were in good spirits for the most part. The year had gone well for them. They had pirated a few sloops here and there, mostly Spanish and Dutch trading between the lesser Antilles from Maracaibo to Antigua, and then sailed on to the charms of Madagascar, taking a few Porto merchants trading back from the Indies on their way. It had been a good drunken year. But something of it felt like a clock winding down, its key misplaced withal. The world was still wide enough but the pardon would end in September. Hundreds had taken it already, some had taken it and become hunters of men themselves, a course without honour amongst thieves. What then after September? What course then to set? The price of freedom seemed to grow more expensive with each rising sun.

Then there was the task to come. An adventure to free Peter Sam, a return to the Caribbean, to the heart of the world, rather than hiding like rats in the still heat and fat of Madagascar. Devlin had a chance to redeem himself in the eyes of the man who had come to save him on The Island. A settling of debts. An adventure.

But others sought payments of debts too. Debts that a captain's servant did not have to face a year ago. The Porto governor, Valentim, was out for revenge, and rightly so. Coxon too, represented a score unresolved and was sitting in Providence awaiting him with a man-of-war. Then there was Ignatius, a black-suited spider picking at the carcasses of flies such as Devlin and Blackbeard, as the world closed in around them.

He needed a plan. He had to seek some advantage over them all. If his clock was winding down and the key was lost he would have to fashion a new one.

What had Dandon said about Ignatius? *He is like all the well-born and wealthy, believing ignorance to be the common man's contribution to the world.*

'He knows our history,' he had also said. 'But he does not know *us*.'

Devlin stared out over the stern to the still horizon and drank slowly from his cup. Then grimaced at the liquid as though it were poison and tossed it into the sea. Drink would not help. His head had to be as strong as his limbs.

The morning would bring them to Dead Man's Chest. Then on to Providence, the north and danger. There was blood in his future.

The light wind whispered through the shrouds, purring to him, the laughter from the cabin below assuring him of nothing. He stroked his neck as a chill came upon it.

He went for his pipe to spend ten minutes lost in the Brazilian tobacco. His face flashed in the dark from the three strikes from his tinder box. Devlin had spent his last peaceful day in the world, of this he was sure, and his peace would end with the final draw of his pipe.

From the morrow, it would be the beginning of the end.

Chapter Twenty-Two

✗

Dead Man

Somewhere, some would say nowhere, between Exuma and Crooked Island, amongst the three-hundred mile string of pearls that spanned north from the Caicos, lay a nine-acre cay of sand and trees almost invisible to spyglass until it came up and bit your keel.

Favoured by fishermen and their dories as a place to rest a night during extended cruises, it boasted a long wooden smoke-house yards from the beach and nothing more.

The hut itself told no-one who built it, and even the descendants of the Indians and the old French filibusters and buccaneers with all their shuddering tales could not spin a yarn long enough to reach the origins of the empty hut.

For the pirates it was an ample landing to careen a small vessel far from curious eyes and, to them, the name was enough to justify their presence.

Dead Man's Chest.

But Devlin did not come to careen. He brought in all fifteen *Talefans* in both boats, along with five of his own men, and landed on the green and yellow smudge that appeared along the centre fold of a page in his waggoner.

The men of the *Talefan* did not welcome the plan of waiting on the island for Bill and the *Shadow* to float by. But neither were they too willing to sail into Providence on a pirate ship after such recent changes in government.

They would take their chances with the firkin of small-beer and the barrel of beef and sauerkraut, all afforded them from Charles Town, and wait for the *Shadow*. A peaceful few days of fishing and eyelids closed.

John Watson issued two firearms to them, the 'snaps' removed until Devlin's men were away. The guns were muskets, not for hunting, unless they felt good enough to target sea-birds; more for chance encounters with birds of darker plumage.

He also left a belly-box of cartridges, a powder flask for fire, and sailcloth and bamboo for tents should the ghosts of the smoke-house not allow them to stay beneath their roof.

Devlin gave each a single Louis for their time aboard and his signature for another from Black Bill in the instruction they were to give to him.

They would not wait long, he swore. Devlin, when the course was plotted on the day Peter Sam had gone from them, shook hands across the chart with Bill to meet on the deso-late spit of land, the first arrival to wait for the other.

Here, however, Bill would not find Devlin but fifteen men he had never met holding Devlin's signature.

This place, this desert in the ocean, was to have been a fond reunion for them all. They were to consort here, drinking to their brotherhood, before sailing on to Providence to gather up more of their gold from Sarah's chambers that she guarded far better than she had her maidenhead.

Instead, Bill would read the cold words of his captain and ruminate on their implication, stroking his beard and tight-ening his fist around his hanger as he gleant the fate of them all should he fail. He would fold and pocket the parchment carefully. In it Devlin marked him as a friend and Black Bill Vernon had never before counted a man as such. He would keep that note, keep it for the rest of his days and show anyone who disbelieved that he had once known the pirate Devlin and that he had signed his name as a friend. Aye, that would be worth a glass or two. More so if the letter's prophetic tone came to pass.

The day began well enough. Three hands spent the dawn, whilst *Talefan* was at anchor, sitting out an hour or two in the jolly-boat, fishing for albacore and relishing the cool of the morning as well as the time alone and away from the redolence of below-deck.

Proudly they sang themselves back aboard with their seven silver rewards. The skeleton crew awoke to the aroma of eggs, rice and the glorious fish, their flavours made finer still by the boiling black coffee and sweet rum that rinsed the bones from their teeth. Before noon, before Devlin would take his latitude, the fifteen remaining crew were assigned their quarters for the day.

Eight men were on gun duty, should any play commence. The larboard four cannons were loaded with chain for heading north with the trade winds behind, the larboard would be the lee and where Devlin would place a ship to receive a shattering and steal her wind.

The starboard sakers were fed partridge shot, bags of small grape that would scythe across the deck and make men tough as oak howl like newborns.

Talefan ran for the most under topsails and courses. Her beauty came, like a butterfly unfolding for the first time, in the running of her lateen fore and aft staysails when she could sail head into the wind and turn on a pebble beneath her keel.

From any Christian shore such a sight could warm the heart of the most land-locked old soul and provoke the lament, as he watched the gliding white swan with her gleaming triangular sails running from fore to aft, that it was now too late for your old frame to go to sea.

With such a short crew the sails were tied loose, brailed to be dropped from the deck. It would take two men two minutes to get a fighting sail underway; fine for a calm Caribbean sea but disastrous in anything heavier.

Devlin, who had worked on fishing sloops around Brittany, sailed with the Marine Royale out of St Malo and spent years under John Coxon's able gaze, knew a good ship when he felt one. For all the *Shadow*'s power and miles of rigging she ploughed through the water like a lame ox compared to the ballet that the *Talefan* performed.

She would be the one that back-boned his rambling sea-dog tales beside the fire-sides of old age, that much he was sure of. It was always the little ship that stayed.

He was wrenched from his daydreaming by the sudden bellow of the straw-hatted pirate sixty feet up the main-mast.

'*Sailho! Sail-ho!*' Then, without a prompt, '*Two points off larboard beam!*'

All heads turned to the sea across the gunwale between the shrouds. Two leagues away to larboard, bearing east-north-east, appeared the white sails and boiling foam of a sloop powering along, quartering large.

Dandon appeared from out of the small arched door of the cabin. He stretched from slumber and slapped the salt off his hat, looked first at the crowd of arched necks by the bulwark then instinctively up and behind to the quarterdeck where Devlin, in a billowing white shirt, held out his spyglass like a musket aimed straight for the strange sail.

He was silent and rigid in that odd pose of study. Dandon stepped up to the deck, quietly, so as not to disturb his captain in his surmise of the small ship bearing on a course to meet their own. He waited until the telescope was lowered.

'What is it, Patrick?' he asked.

'A sloop. Ten minions. Two more than us any rate.'

The *Talefan* was reaching, the wind to her starboard quarter, flying along under staysails, heading north-northwest on a direct bearing to the stranger. Devlin had only minutes to ponder how the next hour was to play out.

He looked at the stanchion beside him along the rail. There was a breech-loading falconet for a swivel, but it was the only thing they had if it came to a close.

'Then we should hold up?' Dandon queried. 'Let her pass?'

'She's a trader. We could close for news.' His voice was curt. His mood sullen. He turned to John Watson at the tiller. 'What make you, John? She's coming right for our bow.'

Watson pulled out his pipe and stared one-eyed into the bowl as if to scry an answer from the leaf within. The quarterdeck had filled with more bodies all wishing to hear the order spoken, their minds already set.

Watson looked out to the ship. 'No colours, Cap'n. Then neither have we.'

There was nothing unusual in that. Most ships apart from men-of-war sailed silent until one closed for news or bartering. 'If she's laden she's moving fast. Probably has no more men than we.'

Devlin grew warm with the press of bodies around him waiting for the word. The decision was no longer his: the fate of a pirate captain was to be bolder than his men, and love was earned with blood.

But Devlin had a destination – a destination that would

need a healthy crew and ship. Then again, if it were a trader, she would most likely buckle at the first shot and the sight of their grinning flag.

The faces of his men said the rest of it. They had been almost two months without a 'vapour'. Like Greek warriors without a battle. Bottled up hornets scratching at their glass tomb. They sweated on his quarterdeck like gasping drunks and waited for their captain. He swept his rakish grin at them all.

Then a hoarse declaration from above plucked all responsibility from his shoulders.

'*Red flag! Blood from her bow! Blood from her bow!*'

All heads swung to the sloop. Hurriedly hung from the bowsprit, the barefooted soul who pulled it still inching his way back to the deck, fluttered the square red flag. The flag of no quarter. No mercy. And, to underline the intention, a single salvo of powder from the first starboard minion wafted on the wind.

Devlin gripped the rail, looked to the ship, an uncommon blood rising over his judgement.

'Dandon. Fetch me my hat, my coat. And a bottle.'

Dandon moved to comply as a roar broke and feet beat to their stations without another word. Devlin called after them, pushing them forward.

'This one's for Peter Sam, boys! We're plucking a crow before we get to Providence! Show the King the blood on our linen!'

The uneasy feeling that had prickled on the back of his neck was wiped away as the cheer echoed back. The sea seemed faster, coursing along, keeping pace with the blood thumping in his veins. The deck was empty again save for John Watson, the cooper turned quartermaster. Devlin slapped his shoulder.

'Fill a hawser coil with shot, John. Canisters on deck. Take a man to bring up a tub from the scuttle. Linstocks are yours. Don't let me down now, John.'

Watson tapped his forehead and chuckled away down the steps. Devlin was riled at the arrogance of the red flag. If it were a pirate or a chancing privateer he would soon know the error of his ways. He too had a flag, darker than the blood to be.

'Fletcher!' he yelled fore to the skinny navy deserter. 'Take *it* to the bowsprit, Sam! Show them who we are! Open the weapons! Six men in the rigging with musket! Riddle their deck and send them to quarters! They'll be sorry their fathers met their mothers, by God!'

The coat and hat of a despondent Dandon appeared.

'This is folly, Patrick. There is the gold to consider and the letters that will save Peter. You should think on.'

Devlin shrugged on his twill coat and planted his tricorne. 'There are men's hearts to consider, Dandon. You can aspire to be my conscience but I *am* theirs. If I am to carry these men into Providence, better they be lean than tallow fat. I can spare an hour.'

'Only an hour?' Dandon passed Devlin the bottle after sloshing a swig himself. He made a distance from his captain watching the closing of the other ship. He disliked carrying any weapon save for the tongue in his head. This was a day in August. A year and more since he had tucked a pistol in his belt. He begrudged the weight upon his body and his soul.

'The tribulations I endure for drink,' he sighed and trudged to the weapons locker by the coop.

'Dandon!' Devlin called and Dandon looked back. Devlin was recalling the conversation in Ignatius's study when

Dandon's past had almost come into the light. 'Just what is your real name, *mon frère*?'

Dandon fingered his moustache and showed his gold capped teeth. 'I will graciously let you know in an hour, *mon Capitaine*.'

Devlin grinned and tossed back the bottle.

Chapter Twenty-three

✗

*H*owell Davis passed the glass to Seth Toombs across the quarterdeck. 'A brig,' he noted to his captain. 'Rigged square and lateen. Fast as rain if she wants. Eight guns. I count about a dozen men. We be across her bows in half a glass.'

Seth took the spyglass and whisked it along the sleek brig.

'Five hundred yards for blank range,' Toombs pointed out the limit of their guns. 'She's still coming. Even after we showed our colours. Bold bastard. She should be furled by now.'

'Maybe she thinks she can outrun us,' Howell offered.

'She could try. If she gets ahead we'll cross her stern. Rake her arse. Larboard guns with double shot. We'll cross her at two-hundred yards.'

'Mind, Seth, we've only the muskets we were to sell to the Spanish. No pistols at all other than Finch's two. And one cutlass to two men.'

'Howell,' Toombs blinked at the ignorance of his new mate. 'We take this merchant sot and have the makings of a convoy. A consort. Tender. Men. That's what it's about. Trust in me. Every man has his own gully to put to a throat. We've axes too and pikes and pins aplenty. That's the way of it!' He elbowed Howell merrily before the coldness of his eye was drawn to the black square off the bowsprit aside them.

He raised the spyglass to the black ensign at the bow. Perhaps he had been hasty in his action. Perhaps this was a brother. A consort to a larger brethren. A path to follow rather than lead, or turn tiller against and sail on.

He gave study to the black flag and felt his heartbeat slow. Through the mist of the glass he saw the skull above the crossed pistols and recognised the handiwork of the widow on Providence, plain and morose. A blank soul of a death's head set in a crude compass rose with two bony pistols beneath.

Even without the glass, Howell Davis could see the black cloth.

'She's a pirate!' he yelled. All the crew turned to his voice, then to the brig and each other.

Sighting through the glass, Seth agreed. Although he had never travelled so himself, and knew no good fortune to come of it, there was something to be said in joining up for a short time with a fellow pirate. He almost snapped the scope in the frustration that the first damn ship that crossed his bow would be a pirate, of all the hundreds that streamed these waters as prolific as the cod in his old Newfoundland home.

'Don't reckon on his flag,' was all he could vent himself to say but already he had resigned to simply hailing the ship and drinking well into the night with a fellow captain if it had not been for the young Porto sailor fairly bouncing out of his skin to grab Toombs's attention.

'What be ailing you, Porto? Be gone, man! *Capitao* busy. Can't you see me vexation, Dago? Leave me be.'

He shrugged the grasping hand aside to study the ship more. The young man pressed on with his scant but highly effective English.

'*Devlin!*' he cried to Seth's ear from a few feet below. Toombs lowered the scope and swivelled to the young Porto, now crossing his arms and using his fingers as pistols. Sucking in his cheeks for a comical skull rendition.

'Devlin!' he repeated, stabbing to the flag across the waves. 'Devlin's *Sombra*, Capitao. Si.'

Toombs looked hard into the young dark face. 'You sure, Porto? That be Devlin's flag?'

The youth again repeated his skull-face, rolling his eyes upward with his crossed pistol fingers. Holding the pose until Seth slapped him out of it.

'Well, that changes the whole party somewhat . . .' he trailed off, bringing the scope up again to spy along the deck of the opposing ship. 'Changes it quite a bit I dare say.'

Howell Davis looked to the rising and diving brig, now a pirate champion in his eyes.

'Ain't it wrong Seth, to go against one of our own?' Howell queried, unsure of the rules, only sure of his own ambition and the clarity of his destiny when he held a pistol to Captain Finch's face.

Toombs glared round to his new quartermaster. 'Is it wrong, Howell, to have *this* done for me?' He accentuated his snarl and his white wound. 'To pay for a woman all me life?' He struck a hand out to the bucking brig.

'Be that consort or the man himself, he took my face as sure as eggs is eggs and my crew along with it! That ain't no brother, Howell, that's a cow's son who ain't got no brother along the coast. And don't forget the tale of the gold that should have been mine – and now yours, I ain't forgot. That ship is the key to the lock and we've lucked upon it with all the luck that I sang about!' He spun away from Howell Davis and leered to the lads below.

'The luck I been telling has come to you, my boys! Miles of salt and we comes across the man who scarred your lucky captain! And took a king's fortune from the French that should have been mine!'

He pulled his pistol, Finch's pistol, and fired overboard. '*Your* gold now, lads! As it should have been by rights, for you're all mine now and shares in me luck likes I promised!'

They cheered, rapped each other's chests. Most of them had sailed with Toombs from England and had slept with the tale in their ears, but now it was true. For there was the pirate traitor himself. The gold within their round-shot's range. Seth had spoken true. His was the luck.

Seth leapt down from the quarterdeck and kicked the nearest gun to him. 'Load *that* and three with bar. The rest double-shotted. Never mind the larboard, I aims not to need it. Six men aloft with musket. Thirty rounds apiece and I'll be counting them as they fly, mind. Any man still carrying will answer for it!'

He ran to the hatch between the masts, centre of the ship, all eyes upon him, the hatch raising him inches above them all.

'Somebody make me some fireworks! Bottles and jars! Anything that will crack and burn, boys!' He slapped the remaining jolly-boat between the masts. 'Get this away over the side or it'll cut you to ribbons else when the shot flies!'

He slung his empty pistol to the young Porto. 'Load it. And keep it coming. I'll not ask again.' Then, loud as he could, deafening the bowing Porto, 'And bring me a cutlass, boy! I'm a-cleaving to glory!'

He held out his arms to all, twisting on his heels as the ship roared and roared to his twirling form, now almost a jig, with Howell looking on between the bulging chest of Seth Toombs and the black flag ever closing yonder.

Chapter Twenty-Four

✗

*D*andon sighed to the scarfed head that handed him a short overcoat pistol and examined the lock minutely, holding its action to his ear, nodding at the satisfying clicks.

'*In rebus asperis et tenui spe fortissima quæque consillia tutissima sunt*,' he uttered to the lurching pirate, who queried instantly to a mate at his shoulder:

'What did he call me?'

Dandon winked. 'In grave difficulties and with little hope, the boldest measures are the safest.' He patted the pirate's bare shoulder, tucked the weapon into his silk belt and removed himself from the energy all around the deck.

The aprons were plucked from the gun's vents with the wad of tallow that kept the touch-hole dry. Tompion plugs were removed, drawing yawns of relief from the mouths of the guns.

Buckets came from below filled with grenadoes and clay fire-pots to throw onto the enemy's deck and placed amid-ships where all hands could get to them. The barrel of water with the already smoking linstocks rattling in its notches was planted between the guns. Watson ordered the forelocks of the hatches closed, sealing off below-deck to any man whose courage fled.

Boarding pikes were stowed beneath the bulwarks along with one sponge, worm and rammer for each pair of guns.

Devlin yelled from the quarterdeck, 'Sling the fore and main yards! Puddings and chain! Set fighting sail!'

He watched the bosun and mate scamper to the halyards with their chains and caps to hold the rigging should it be shot away, and only then did he notice the little ship with fifteen lonely men.

Four men now at the larboard guns, no eight to spare, with Watson as gunner captain. Six men in the tops with muskets and slung bags of fireworks and crow's feet iron spikes. The bosun and mate to handle the foresails. The final pair to wear the hats of carpenter, fire-crew, and powder-monkey as well as marksmen firing over the gunwale. Devlin took a moment to name them all silently upon his lips, promising himself to say all their names again tomorrow when he called them for their share.

He lashed the *Talefan's* tiller straight. She would be steered by the fore braces for the remain of the hour. Devlin could spare no hand without a weapon in it.

Dandon let his coat drop to the deck and peeled off his waistcoat. His chest of medicines was in the cabin. Laudanum and rum were all that would matter. He was no surgeon, but there was a saw below.

He passed a look up to Devlin on the quarterdeck. Devlin caught it, winked his lopsided grin in return then called for grape for the falconet beside him and looked to leeward and the growing ship that planed over the sea to cut across his bow less than a quarter-league now.

He brought up his scope to the sloop, the misty image rocking. He swung it to the rigging and watched the clambering backs climbing ratlines, muskets slung. If he could he would keep from musket range, for that could be the end of it.

His eye fell to the fo'c'sle to meet the dazzle of his rival's scope following his sweep.

The blinding flash seared both their eyes and the scopes were brought down with a curse. For a blink of an eye each saw half of the other's face.

Devlin slammed the scope back in its becket. He paused, looking at its brass body rattling in its clasps, a lingering memory rattling in his head along with it. His hand slowly stretched out for the spyglass again as he turned his head back to the familiar body at the fo'c'sle only to be snapped to the deck and away from his thoughts by the sudden shout from Watson.

'Cap'n!' he bawled and Devlin stretched to the rail, half looking to the sloop, half to his gunner captain. Watson finished his cry with his primer in his hand, 'She be at three. Full range. We could try her?'

Devlin stepped down the five short planks to the deck and clapped his gunner-captain's back.

'Don't try, John. *Do.*'

Watson affirmed grimly and sent his primer down the vent to pierce the sack of powder. He walked the line and stabbed the other three guns.

The quoins were out. Muzzles high, staring up to the white sails of the sloop waiting for the sweet kiss of the smoking slow-match. The trucks squealed in anticipation as the deck rolled.

Without the need for the order the bosun, John Lawson, hauled hard to brace the topsails to yaw up and the guns saluted the sky and arced across the *Mumvil*'s sails as Watson swept to the touch-hole of the foremost gun.

There came the hiss of the small powder trail and men bit their lips like shy children. Watson leant to the next gun and stroked it with the linstock as the first report roared and the grey cloud veiled the deck.

The guns shrieked back like hogs at killing time then were clapped tight by their breeches and quickly soothed by the cool wet lambskin sponge shoved down their throats – just as their brothers slammed their wad and chain at the wood eight hundred yards beyond.

The wave of spent powder caked the *Talefans'* nostrils like boiling tar, they could taste it on their tongues as fine as rare beef and Devlin strained through the smoke to study the first meal of his six-pounders.

Their enemy's yards creaked, sails shivered and quaked. Some sheets waved free and a top spar fell and hung in the rigging along with two limp corpses rolling and hanging off the ratlines. A slow start but a good one.

Without celebration, other than a pat to a gun, every man hunched as he went to his work with canister and bar, expecting vengeance from the stranger's minions at any instant.

Dandon sat on the deck under the starboard bulwark. He could see the final feet of the twin masts of the enemy rolling past from where he sat, not knowing what chaos had rained down upon their deck. His brothers seemed happy enough as they reloaded and he took that as all being well.

He shuffled to the quarter that met the cabin and waited for the return, then heard the twin soft cracks echoing from afar and the spanker exploded above him, crashed to the deck in thunderous fury and draped itself over the rail in a cloud of sawdust and salt spray.

The spent chain and bar from the *Mumvil'*s guns flopped to the deck out of the spanker's yards, steaming like dumplings, as the last three of her guns fired high and shot hummed over the quarterdeck and away, taking nothing with it but prayers.

Dandon looked up. Nobody hung from the rigging. The spanker and her sail covered the door to the cabin and John Lawson flew in front of him with a marlin spike to pluck her loose sheets from the mast, swearing like a cheated whore.

Dandon pulled himself up. Both ships had a minute's silence due to them before their loads rammed home again and he took the time to look abroad as the crew heaved at the guns and Devlin shouted them on.

The enemy was ahead, pivoting to the *Talefan*'s bow. She seemed far away, beyond shouting, but now puffs issued from her rigging as the first musket fire spouted from her men amongst the ratlines – too eager, for the effort fell short, bringing up spouts of water like tossed pebbles in a pond.

The *Talefan*'s own sharpshooters responded with licks to their thumbs as they drew their dogheads back and blew their load to rap uselessly against the *Mumvil*'s freeboard, chipping her black paint white.

The six snaps brought confidence if nothing else. Two of them grinned down at Dandon, punching their fists at him as they bit off their second cartridge.

Devlin fell back to the larboard quarter bulwark, opposite Dandon, his face lost in the white smoke drifting to the stern. He knew the loss of the spanker had come too soon. Still, its death did not show upon his captain or in the limbs that had now readied the guns again.

It was clear that they had chanced upon no ordinary prize nor a fellow to share a truce with. They would share splinters and stab fire for a while before their hulls would scrape for onslaught.

Dandon would not know Devlin now. His crooked back, his creased brow, did not belong to Dandon's world of pleasant drink and long evenings of gaming. He had become the pirate again and Dandon kept his quarter from him and his bloody work.

Watson needed no orders. He checked once with the bosun who drew the guns up again with a heave upon the braces then brushed his faint crushed powder trail and fired again as his gun crew jumped aside.

The guns had been levered right, hard against their port holes, to grab an angle to the ship almost across them now. They fired, three seconds apart, and the *Talefan* bucked against her reins and keeled a point windward with the recoil.

This time the whistling chains chomped their way through their foe's rigging. After the tirade had faded and heads were raised again the yards hung at angles and cleat lines flapped free. Seth Toombs lifted himself from beneath the bulwark as he felt his ship slow.

They were closing fast now at less than six hundred yards, the sails, the breadth of his enemy, stealing his wind as he fell into Devlin's lee, the bulk of Devlin's ship sucking the breath from Seth's sail.

Those aloft began to buckle as hanging wood nudged against their shoulders but the snarl upwards from the scarred face on the deck stayed their hands. They bit at the cartridges and reloaded, living now only in the brass pimple sight of their muskets and the planting of their feet in the ratlines, the whole deck of the brig before them.

They picked their target heads and fired.

Devlin ducked beneath the gunwale as the four shots hailed over the guns. The lead rattled off the iron, sparked and spat into the mast. A couple poked forever into the gangway, but no flesh was torn or head caved.

Devlin snaked up to eye his enemy's guns. Still in, still reloading. He had a minute, maybe less. He looked up to the falconet on the quarterdeck. Watson slapped his men to action. Quoins were jammed back under the gun barrels to aim the mouths down. The hawser coil of chain gone, they loaded swiftly with shot. With a six-pound ball of iron, double-shotted, Watson would have four rounds from the pile inside the coil, enough to grind the *Mumvil*'s walls.

Devlin flew to the quarterdeck, leaping up the stair and shouting for Dandon to follow. Grabbing hold of the falconet he swung it to the deck opposite as Dandon appeared crouching at his side.

The quarterdeck was the most unshielded area. He was safe from the guns which would have to be levered round to front him but the marksmen had already spotted the hat and coat of a captain and were shifting their feet.

'Dandon! Free the tiller. Hard to larboard when Watson fires. We're bringing her round!' He took hold of the cord to fire the flintlock falconet, raising the brass barrel to the four men entwined in the rigging who were shouldering their muskets.

'I've never helmed a boat in my life, Patrick,' Dandon appealed.

'Just put your fat into it and push towards me!' He yanked the cord and the gun fired its grape, flaming wad and bag into the air like fireflies, giving Dandon cover as he unhooked the tiller and freezing the horrified marksmen as they watched the dark cloud hurtling towards them.

Watson stroked his guns. Eight seconds later, as the last ball sang out, Devlin yelled to Dandon, who leant hard into the iron rod so that the *Talefan* instantly began to lurch to larboard. Her bow slowly swung to face the bastard as if to charge.

Seth had forgotten what hell was like. He covered himself under the starboard bulwark as the shots hammered into his world, shaking the ship like a storm wave. He looked at the black spreading stain on his right boot and the spatters around it. His foot moved fine and as he glanced skyward a splat of blood from above burnt his eye, dripping from something lost in the swathes of the main topsail.

He cursed it out of his eye, smearing his face, pulling himself up to survey his ship.

A man named Johnson, his gunner-captain, was shaking his crew up to man the minions.

The mainmast had splintered. A jagged smile cut at head height. Some yards had fell over the hatch, sheets and clew lines lay about and the stench of pitch and brimstone poisoned the air.

He yelled for Howell and ignored the volley of musket shots that picked at the deck around him. He looked to Devlin's ship, her bowsprit now turning to face him, her yards bracing her round as if she were a spinning coin.

Howell bounded up to Seth's side. 'She's coming about, Seth!'

'Aye,' Seth checked his pistol lock was waxed and dry. 'He aims to cross our stern.' Seth spoke as if he were somewhere else to where Howell stood. 'Fetch me some water will you, Howell. And how's the powder?'

'One barrel of white,' Howell gasped. 'Ten bags ready. Grape and shot. Don't reckon there's any bar left.' Howell wiped his brow and grabbed a bag of water from the loops around the mast. The *Mumvil* had not sailed for a running battle. Her magazine would provide a good defence but she would be down to spitting glass and nails if the day went on.

Toombs drank long of the stale warm water. Wetting his

shirt cuff he washed off the streak of blood, calling to Johnson to hold his fire and not waste it on the bow of his enemy.

The *Mumvil* was heading away. Crawling though she was, they had put near five hundred yards between their stern and the wheeling *Talefan* incrementally bringing her starboard guns to bear.

A little distance would recover Seth's men. If Devlin were to cross his stern, up close, he might as well blow his own brains out to save him the trouble.

Somehow Devlin had fired three rounds to his pitiful one. The *Mumvil* had one more gun to bear over the *Talefan* but he clearly had a rabble for a crew.

Devlin had Black Bill and Peter Sam who could spit cannon faster than they could eat. *His* men. Surely his men still if they could but see him.

He stomped to the flush fo'c'sle, scanning the white waters for sandbars, cautious not to run aground.

Howell traipsed after, looking up at the cracking sails and torn rigging. Three dead in the tops, that was all. It was the ships that were taking the pain, not the men.

'What will we do, Seth?' Howell glanced over his shoulder at Devlin now at their starboard quarter, racing to cut their stern.

Seth turned from the fo'c'sle, a face as charming as his sneer allowed.

'Load the larboard guns. Double-shot. Helm to lee. Get our stern away and turn around. We're going back at her. Run straight at her.' He winked his final promise, 'I'm going to show you something you can put on your gravestone, Howell Davis.' Then he was moving aft, brushing ropes away from him like willow branches.

Chapter Twenty-Five

*H*aving had the temerity to unbatten the aft hatch and go below, Hugh Harris brought up his fiddle. He plucked and stamped to the rhythm of the sea, moving along the line of the gunners and winking at them all on every downstroke of his bow-arm.

Devlin watched the *Mumvil* creeping away northwards. Was she fleeing? No matter. His starboard guns were primed and they would be on her stern in four more risings of the bow. The deck of the *Talefan* became a jolly place and the gun-crew waited for their guns to float across the three windows of the stern cabin. But the wind seemed to chill Devlin's neck as he thought on the brown coat and the burgundy hat of the man with the spyglass that commanded the sloop running from his range.

He stepped away from the bulwark and stopped Hugh in his music. 'Are your pistols readied, Hugh?'

Hugh lowered his bow and looked left and right at the pair of duelling pistols stuck in his belt, tied to a linen sling around his neck. 'Aye, Cap'n. Always.' And he went back to his fiddle. Dandon was at Devlin's side, drawn by the hard look on his captain's face. He had seen the look a year ago, in the stockade on The Island, before Coxon had appeared and the *Shadow* had not arrived and all seemed lost. Then, Devlin had slashed into a table with a sword in rising frus-

tration, the frustration of an intelligent man thwarted. Before
he could question his captain's mood Devlin turned to him.

'Take down the time, Dandon.' Devlin's eyes had a guilty
look about them and he paused, glancing away and then back
again as the sun caught the *Mumvil*'s sails like a glinting
shield. He watched her as she began to heel around to larboard,
turning over, showing fresh strakes shining as the sea ran off
and her keel leant with bracing yards.

Needlessly some voice yelled out, 'She's coming about!'
and all of them watched the *Mumvil* turn.

Watson was ready but now the prize's stern spun away from
him, and his guns had yet to bear. 'She's coming back in!'
He checked his hawser coils. There were rounds enough.
'Warm her bow, lads if we can't have her stern!'

'Aim them high!' Devlin yelled at Watson. 'Her bow's no
use to me. Take her wind.'

Watson and his gunners tugged out the quoins and the
muzzles rose. Eight hundred yards between the wooden
worlds. The *Mumvil* wheeled around; the sea boiled white
and angry beneath her as she struggled against the waves, her
bowsprit pointing towards them now, her powder-scorched
sails facing and full. Whoever the captain was he was racing
his ship to face a broadside that would surely take at least
his jibs and forecourse and with luck the mast as well. It was
foolish, desperate even, and Devlin stood back to let Watson
to his work and wondered what he would have planned if he
were standing on the sloop flying towards him.

Five hundred yards and Toombs's bowsprit began to cross
the path of Devlin's starboard guns. The *Mumvil* turned fully.
Surely not to ram? Coming like a bull, but towards loaded
guns? Pride perhaps? A final glory of a dead ship?

The bosun yelled to his mate and they heaved the forecourse up to slow the *Talefan* just enough to let Watson's guns have a measured passage across the *Mumvil*'s draft and eat her bow like chopping wood.

Hugh Harris stopped his tune and the tiny sound of Watson dribbling his powder trail across the touch-holes of his guns and the hiss of the slow-match drew every man's eye.

Dandon sidled up to Devlin again, his own confidence wavering amid the sight of the ship ploughing towards their guns. 'Surely this is suicide for them, Patrick? Does he intend to ram us?'

Devlin did not turn from watching the bowsprit ducking and stabbing ever forward. 'Maybe,' he said. 'It's a bad angle to board anyways.'

Watson danced across all four of the guns with his linstock and the powder flared into life.

Dandon weaved away from Devlin's imminent fury as he spoke. 'Surely he knows we're about to empty our guns at him?'

And that was it. To empty the guns. *Surely he knows we're about to empty our guns at him?*

'He's going to club-haul at us!' he hollared to all as it came to him. 'He's to drop anchor at us! He'll swing round to bear!' Devlin sprang forward to a swab bucket on the deck plucking the rope handle as he yelled.

'Dowse them, John! He *wants* us to fire!' He tossed the water at the breech of number one just as she roared and hurtled back, shattering the bucket in Devlin's hands.

Watson and the rest covered their ears as the guns rolled one by one in four drumbeats that tore through the *Mumvil*'s forecourse and the whole ship vanished in the white smoke, the sound of whipping cleatlines and stays whistling through the air.

'Cap'n?' Watson shouted back as his senses returned.

Devlin bellowed for all hands to reload. The cloud began to drift fore just as they heard the unmistakable splash of an anchor from the *Mumvil*.

The veil of the cannon's breath lifted away to reveal Toombs's broadside swinging towards them. The reloading froze on the *Talefan* as they stared over at all ten of Toombs's minion guns aiming above the gunwale only a pistol shot away. The hiss of their touch-holes wafted like mocking laughter.

'*Down*!' Devlin bellowed and threw himself to the deck.

With two men lighting the touch-holes it took ten seconds to fire ten guns and Seth Toombs was the only man not clamping his hands to his ears but idly checking again the lock and leather-clasped flint of his pistol. He stood and watched the eighty pounds of double-shotted iron and chain explode away from his deck.

He winked at Howell, cowering behind the foremast, as the last gun echoed in the sails. If Devlin had been a better captain, thought Toombs, he would have noticed the fast heeling of the *Mumvil* as a sign of all the guns being shifted over to larboard, weighing her over. He would have noticed her leaning to her lee as she went at the *Talefan* under full forecourse.

His gunners had removed the quoins and the trucks of the five guns at the ports and dragged them back to angle over the gunwale. The starboard guns had been freed from their tackles and wheeled round to stand between and behind their brothers. Jury-rigged tackles reeved through the deck's fair-leads amidships. It was risky, a gamble. A pirate's chance. All ten guns peered over the gunwale. One round – an avalanche of iron that would turn a weak sloop into a man-of-war for one murderous broadside.

Seth had bellowed for the starboard quarter anchor to be dropped just as the shot from the *Talefan* hazed his bow, jibs and forestays. As the anchor bit it would club-haul the ship round to bear.

The fluke had dug into the coral, the sudden reining of the hawser bucking the ship and heaving her round, just as the timoneer did the same. The effect was like braking a carriage at full pelt in a harness race, to make the corner or kill the driver, except that ships did not risk toppling over. Instead they turn, and turn fast. The scream of the ship as her seams resist is the only similarity.

When the smoke cleared from the *Talefan*'s broadside they were beam to beam, the caps of their spars fencing playfully. Seth's guns stared ready at the powerless *Talefan*, an axe about to fall.

'*Fire!*' cried Seth, and snapped his own pistol at one of the grey shapes moving through the fog at the same instant his ten guns detonated at Devlin's masts.

The *Mumvil* writhed with the recoil, the deck quaking in her seams. It was ten seconds of nothing but pounding guns and smoking wood. Had they been anything larger than four-pounders they may have snapped away, killing or maiming as they flew from their breeches. As it happened, each man eagerly picked up a loaded musket with a cheer, for not even an eyebrow was singed.

Seth climbed up the larboard shrouds to fire down onto Devlin's deck, his smoke-filled eyes searching through the haze for the head of the Irish traitor. The ship opposite rolled in pain at each fresh fiery stab into her side.

It had been ten murderous seconds for Devlin and his men. After each new pounding from the guns beyond, Devlin had inched along the scuppers towards the cabin, aiming himself away from the splinters flying at his eyes and limbs.

A ton of yards and sail crashed to the deck all about. By the fourth shattering of wood his path was blocked by a cobweb of sheets and ratlines taller than a man and he looked over to the mainyards and maincourse shrouding the bodies of his men amidships.

The seconds dragged on and the rage continued. Three more and the topmasts came down like stone columns to the deck, crushing legs and skulls. Cries were cut short as men who had worked with wood and rope all their lives were suddenly spliced and hammered themselves.

The canvas and cordage had been a living thing only an hour before, its duty a world of tension and stays; now the iron had cleaved it free and four miles of rope and wood plummeted howling to the backs of the tiny men below.

Three more seconds passed and a storm of sawdust and choking smoke that tasted of paint and tar swirled around the deck. Devlin crawled away from the sight of bare bloody feet poking out of fallen sails and his hand lighted on a broken fiddle, its neck snapped, its strings splayed out like whiskers. He shoved it away for fear of what it might represent, then dived beneath the larboard bulwark to protect himself from the final storm of topsails and stays falling in defeat.

Slowly silence began to ripple through the air and the whisper of the sea and the creaking of the deck resumed as the world rolled on. Devlin's ears then began to absorb the other sounds: the roars from the other ship and the coughing and groans of the dying.

Devlin knew what would come well enough and he crept from his cover of the cannons and the bulwark and pulled his pistol, shouting for hands, as bold as if an army were waiting below for his call.

He stood and looked about for those who could still stand. A face riven with gore stepped to his side, the stark whites of its eyes gleaming from the mask of blood running from the black wound across his scalp.

Devlin did not recognise the ghoul until the matched pair of duelling pistols clicked into life with a snap of his wrists. Then he warmed to the power of Hugh Harris by his shoulder.

'I thought you lost, Hugh. I saw your fiddle broke.'

The red face spat a mouthful of blood. 'They broke my fiddle?' He kissed his pistols in turn. 'I'll eat the bastards when I'm done!'

More heads struggled from their stupor, blowing dust from the locks of their musketoons and pistols, before ducking from a volley of whistling musket balls splintering the deck. Then the risen men found the nerve to mock their opponents' lamentable aim, vowing as one to show them how it should be done, before joining their captain's side.

Only stumps of mast remained so there would be no climbing to the tops to hurl grenadoes or crow's feet caltrops. It would be a fire-fight now, cutlass and shot. Lead and steel, and blood.

Devlin saw Watson, linstock still in hand, lying dead by his guns as he counted the men still with him. Lawson, the bosun, locked his musketoon and crouched ready. Others checked their pistols and wound lighted fuses around their wrists for the grenadoes stuffed within their shirts.

Six, Devlin counted. Six, and him, still fighting, and he called all their names as he strode to the starboard gunwale to await the grappling hooks, plucking a boarding axe from the remains of the mainmast and passing it to one of his brethren to hack at the ropes as they landed.

He stepped into something wet amongst a mess of cloth and rope and looked down to his boot in the writhing guts of Sam Fletcher. Fletcher belched a torrent of watery blood and looked up at Devlin with a gasp.

Devlin lifted his foot, foolishly apologising, and lowered his pistol to Fletcher's head.

Fletcher whispered to his captain, his hands trying to tuck his insides back into place, his voice too rasping to hear.

Devlin clicked his lock. 'What you say, Sam?'

'My mother, Pat. Don't tell me mother about me.'

'You didn't hang, Sam,' and he winked at the boy for the last time.

'Nor you, mate,' Fletcher coughed a hot dribble of blood. His eyes closed to the sight of Devlin emptying his pistol into his forehead.

Devlin moved on, reloading as he went, using the clicks and snaps of his weapon to shake the memory before it formed. Then he heard his name, like a curse, bellowed in a Bristol accent from the ship opposite and he raised his pistol to the man astride the gunwale, hanging off the shrouds, aiming at him with a snarling grin.

Chapter Twenty-Six

W oodes Rogers paused, holding the bottle of Red Sack Madeira over the two tall-stemmed glasses and looking up in surprise at Coxon's explanation for missing their luncheon appointment.

'You had a funeral? A funeral for a diseased whore?' He resumed pouring, his shock dissipating with the gentle trickle of the limed wine that kept so well in the smothering heat of the Bahama Islands.

'I knew her.' Coxon took the glass held out by Rogers under raised eyebrows and offered his explanation. 'She was one of the women with Devlin on the island, Governor.'

Rogers purred his understanding, 'Ah, you had a connection with the strumpet. You thought you might give her a noble burial. For old times, eh?' Rogers winked.

'She recalled more of me than I did of her, Governor.' Coxon sipped his warm Madeira. 'I remembered only that she had hair a colour off of red.'

'You favour the auburn then, John?'

Coxon disliked the turn of the conversation. 'I only know of it from the church windows and paintings of my youth: when Eve is shown before the apple she is golden-haired. After the fall, she is always painted red.'

'I have never noticed, John. That is most interesting. Come, take a sit with me, I have a matter to discuss but first tell me how the fever goes.' Rogers retired to his desk, peeling off his waistcoat to relax in linen and cuffs against the warmth of the afternoon, the sounds of hammering and squeaking pulleys beyond through the broken-paned windows, as the fortifications and repairs dragged on.

Coxon scraped a chair across the room as he spoke. 'The death of the girl is an unpleasant fact. Very few of the old residents are ill, no more than one might expect in these climes. I had her room smoked and all her effects burned and I suggest that should be common practice.'

Rogers put a pen to his log and studied Coxon carefully. 'All her effects? I had heard that you buried some with her? You had eight of your men attend to the hole with a carriage of goods, did you not?'

Coxon never hesitated. 'Some of her larger furniture I had buried rather. There are some of medicine that suggest that fevers may carry in fumes. I would also suggest that large funeral pyres are to be avoided, Governor, in what is mostly a wooden town unless it is to be upon the beach. I burnt her clothes and bed linen in a brazier, broke up her bed and closet and buried it with her in the hills.' Coxon sniffed as if the memory disgusted him. He placed down his empty glass on the desk and wiped one hand with the other.

Rogers made a note, scratching rapidly, then leant back and toyed with the fletch as he resumed his habit of continuing a conversation he had already started in another room.

'The two captains have returned from our trading mission. Finch and Arnot.'

'So soon?' Coxon counted the days in his head.

'So soon that they managed to lose one of the ships in their haste.'

'I don't understand, Governor?'

'Pirates, John. They turned pirate. Thirty-two of them took the *Mumvil Trader*. The *Buck* returned this morning whilst you were in the hills with your whore. The news is probably the talk of the taverns, and my head the target for their jibes.' He tossed down his quill in dudgeon.

Coxon could not help raising a corner of his mouth in mirth and scorn. Although Finch and Arnot were Bahama traders the scheme of crewing the ships with former sea-dogs was clearly sailing towards disaster.

Rogers spied the edge of the smile. 'Seems the leader of them was one of your men, John, as were the ones that followed. A man named Toombs. Did you know of him?'

Coxon shifted and scratched his forehead irritably. 'He came on in Bristol before we met the fleet. Rum sort indeed, look of the lash about him. At least we have not lost both ships.'

Rogers' throat rumbled in disagreement. 'It'd have been better by far if we had. I know these fellows from back in Madagascar. Part of their power is to let men go, allowing talk of the horror over a noggin and how fortunate they were to have escaped with their lives. The most successful pirates spread more legends than sailcloth.'

Coxon heard German shouts from the scaffolding outside. An abundance of foreign capital had been invested in manual work since the pirates had refused to take up the hammer to rebuild the fort. One Teuton was abusing the other for his ineptitude. Coxon listened in amusement at the German curses volleying back and forth.

'What do you suggest we do, Governor?' He smoothed his short hair forward nervously.

Rogers sat up. 'We can *fight*! I have sworn to rid these

islands of pirates and that is exactly what I intend to do. This is my last chance, John,' he looked morosely into his wine. 'Not even forty and this my last chance to make something of my life.'

Coxon leant forward. 'You have done more than most men, Captain Rogers, and now you're governor of all the Bahamas.'

Rogers dropped his head. 'Aye. Ten years I've been at sea. At the cost of my family. My wife. My brother. Not a bean to show for it whilst those who have yet to leave the teat of England grow fat on what we bring them back.'

'Nobody ever got rich from adventure, Governor. It is the ones that follow that reap the rewards.'

Rogers nodded into his glass as he drained it then wiped his lips as his eyes bored into the future.

'Hornigold is out a-hunting south of here. He may find these bastards who have taken the *Mumvil* and bring them back. All I have is this place, John. My mark on it will be the eradication of pirates from her waters. I have a fort, a hundred men, and warships to defend her.' He stood up and crossed to the window to look down over Nassau. 'It can be done. This disease will clear if we can survive the summer.' He turned to Coxon's back. 'And I'll not allow these pirates the chance to encourage others with their success. No-one will enjoy the tale, I'll make sure of that.'

Coxon twisted round in his seat, 'Governor?' he queried, already fearing the response.

'We have a proper gallows in the square. Before these scum take measure of my failure I want you to hang nine more of the pirates. And reward the loyal men of the *Buck* with an extra acre of land as an example of the rewards for loyalty to the King.'

Coxon shot up. 'To the King or to Woodes Rogers, Governor? I have not come here to hang men.' He kept his voice peaceful as if to a friend making a terrible mistake.

Rogers' eyes stopped dreaming of the future and he stepped closer. '*Men*? My soldiers are men. *We* are men. These are *pirates*, John. You should know them by now.'

'These are pirates who have taken the King's proclamation. They are colonists now. *Your* colonists. They need food not fewer mouths to feed, Governor, and I will not hang subjects just to prevent a few tall tales slurring around a tavern.'

'Those tall tales, as you put them, could amount to insurrection if left to fester, Captain, and I will not have it! Not on my island!' He brushed past Coxon to grab for the Madeira again. 'No! I will not have it, *sir*! Men will hang before I have it!'

Coxon ignored the brimming glass held out to him. 'I'll not hang them, Governor,' he flapped his hat, shaking off the dust of the morning funeral. 'I'll hang the ones Hornigold brings back, if any, and I'll hang any pirate past September who hasn't taken the proclamation.' He squared his hat and touched it in salute. 'And that is all I'll do. Find another captain for your meat hooks. Good day, sir.' He dipped his head and made for the door.

'And your pirate Devlin, John?' Rogers sang out as he put the glass to his lips. 'Would you not hang him even if he turned up and took the proclamation? Or do you judge every pirate as entitled to a peaceful life?'

Coxon did not stop, uttered no comment he might rue, but only clicked the door shut gently behind him, catching Rogers' faint chuckle as he walked away. There was no need for the governor to know that Devlin was returning to Providence soon enough for his gold – the very gold that had now returned to the earth, still guarded by the same girl to whom Devlin had entrusted his valuable secret. Only now she had taken the secret to her grave.

Chapter Twenty-Seven

*T*he uproll of the ship spoilt Seth's aim and the gravity of the wooden worlds drawing together created a well of waves smashing between the freeboards. Fish slammed against the strakes, flipping up and away to escape the crushing swell.

The shot rang off a ringbolt beside Devlin's head but he resisted flinching and continued to count the bodies on the other ship as the survivors ducked to grab for their grappling hooks.

Hugh Harris wiped a sleeve across his dripping face and turned to Devlin. 'That's Seth! That's Seth Toombs, Pat!'

Devlin looked hard across to the man swinging in the shrouds. 'Aye,' he said. 'It surely is,' and he climbed to the gunwale ignoring the muskets levelled at him to shout to his opposing captain, the man who had pressed him to be his navigator one spring, a year gone now.

'Ho, Seth!' he yelled. 'We've come a long ways now ain't we, Captain? What say we talk awhile?'

Seth rolled up and down as the spars above clasped each other, chaining the ships for the final conflict. His leer widened then shrunk to a grimace as he bellowed to his men: 'Grenadoes!' and a barrage of bottles, catapulted from unseen hands, smashed to the *Talefan*'s deck.

Devlin's paltry crew danced around the shattered glass that

exploded from the dozen rag-lit bottles loaded with powder, shot and nails – the only 'fireworks' that Seth had the means to muster but effective enough, spitting at men's legs and turning the fallen canvas into kindling. Flames began to trickle up from the *Talefan*'s deck. Devlin set his eye to the grinning face a shot away from his own and leapt from the wood towards the six pairs of eyes waiting expectantly for some word.

'Throw 'em.'

Their turn.

Devlin's men pulled out grenadoes and matches coiled around their wrists and carefully picked the small smouldering wicks from the brass tubes in their waistcoats or pockets.

Good grenadoes, well prepared, unlike Seth's jury-rigged and cobbled affairs. The eggs full of brimstone, powder and slugs of lead in a mould of tar-pitched halved musket balls that could rip off men's faces as they detonated falling through the air.

The black missiles sailed over the gunwale as Seth slammed his boots on the deck and gave his last order, the only order of the day that mattered.

'Sling your hooks, boys! Boarding parties away!'

Grapnels flew over, Devlin's grenadoes streaking past them simultaneously, annihilating a couple of the hooks' bearers as they exploded at chest height with their half-second fuse. Teeth and eyes spattered the men pulling the ships together, and they found themselves spitting out the blood of their mates.

Devlin felt his deck camber away from him as half the hooks bit into the gunwale and the remainder landed amongst the shrouds. More than twenty snarling men pulled on the *Talefan* like a reluctant bull and only then did Devlin notice the absence of the yellow-coated Dandon and his air of despondent whimsy. He had no time to query his men as they raised pistols and musket stocks to the scarfed heads dragging them in.

Devlin looked down at the dead Sam Fletcher, the young face already grey. He lifted his head back to the ship and aimed his pistol at the burgundy hat bobbing along the backs of the enemy sailors. He climbed the gunwale with his aim held to it like a line so he could fire his pistol below the leather cross sealing the cocks of the tricorne.

The waft of his gunsmoke shielded the swinging boarding parties as the hulls collided and Devlin's six survivors fired up at the dozen men flying into the *Talefan*'s rigging.

A shot ploughed into a chest and Seth watched the screaming body slam into the conjoined hulls, the cries split by the silent shatter of the man's skull like a watermelon between the scraping wood.

'Davis!' he called to Howell. 'With me!' He scrambled to the gunwale, pushing back the shoulder of the young Porto sailor clambering to join him. 'You stay here with a musket, lad. Don't want you forgetting who your captain is now.'

He leapt to the *Talefan*, cutlass in hand, eyes locked onto the prize of the Irishman kneeling and reloading by the mainmast.

He landed squarely, elbowing a face beside him and Howell followed the blow with a cutlass thrust and kicked the body from his blade and stuck to Seth's back as he barged through the mass of men.

Hugh Harris had taken two boarders with his pistols, the flintlocks hanging around his neck. Now he had a sweeping cutlass in one hand, a parrying poniard in the other and three more dead lay around him as his bloodied face and clothes, his wild screams, weakened the spirits of his foes and he laughed as they backed away from his terrifying form.

Lawson had unloaded his partridge shot from his musketoon into three more and swung the club of it through the jaw of one of them, then put them down with his pistols that cracked one by one as he stepped away from the men still coming over the side. His third pistol snapped its shot and his back stopped at the larboard quarter and he could retreat no further. He checked once over the gunwale to the alluring waves then unsheathed his falchion sword and dagger, declaring loudly that the four men rushing towards him were most definitely in trouble now that he was cornered.

Devlin kicked groins and swung his hanger, and blood and flesh arced before his eyes. In his left hand he beat with his pistol at cutlasses and pikes stabbing gingerly towards him. His pistol was still loaded for the taking of Seth Toombs when the moment came.

There were too many of them, despite the better arms borne by his men. Three of Toombs's crew had remained on the ship. Three were dead from the grenadoes. Twenty-two had swung or leapt across. Nine lay dead or dying but still it could not be done with six – no, another stilted scream, five now – against the horde. Devlin felt the gunwale against his own back now as the tide came forwards and he too glanced to the sea behind. Then the tide slowly parted before him.

'*Back!*' Seth yelled above the riot and a moment later the only sound on the *Talefan* was the faint crackling of the flames chewing its way through the tarred, hanging rigging and the creaking of broken spars above the two captains' heads.

Seth moved cautiously, the cutlass in his right hand bouncing playfully, the gully blade in his left dripping blood.

'Well, well, Cap'n Devlin. As you said: We've come a long ways to be sure.'

'You've come as far as you're going to, my man!' Dandon's shout from the quarterdeck spun the heads of everyone aft to the mouth of the swivel gun aimed to the crowd of *Mumvils.* Dandon behind it. His eye ready to fire. 'Toombs is it?' he continued. 'I vaguely recall you now that I see you.' Dandon held up the cord that would snap the flintlock to its charge for everyone to acknowledge. 'You'll drop your arms if you please, else you have stepped your last.'

Devlin looked proudly to the man at the falconet and raised himself taller as his remaining men pushed back their assailants with contempt and curses.

Seth, one look to Devlin, stepped towards the swivel gun for its eye to cover him more than his men. His cutlass twitched.

'Dandelion, ain't it? Reckons I knows you from Haggins's knocking shop on Providence. A pox doctor. Not one for a fight as I recollects.'

Dandon bowed his head. 'Which is why I favour the spread of grape from my friend here,' he tapped the gun affection- ately. 'He affords me the position not to fight at such close quarter.'

Seth paced closer and the gun followed, the range enough for him to absorb every lead seed and shatter him like glass. Dandon tensed the cord and Seth stopped pacing. 'That'll do fellow. Lay down and you'll yet live.'

Seth dragged his curled lip upwards. 'Then fire, Dandelion. Fire if you can. I'm right here. Fire at Seth Toombs. He *needs* it.'

Howell Davis barked from the huddle of men, 'No, Seth!' He came out of the crowd. 'No need for this. The ship is sunk soon enough. We can sail on.'

Seth kept his eye on Dandon as he cocked his head back. 'I sail on with a heavier ship, Howell. Always do.' He ran his thumbnail up his cutlass blade. 'See, Howell, I ain't no fool. I don't walk towards loaded guns, mark my word. Now to my mind I reckon that gun be empty. I reckon that, because if I had such a loaded gun I'd have fired it as we boarded.' He turned his neck to Devlin. 'I wouldn't have waited until all was lost would I, Cap'n?'

Devlin, still by the larboard gunwale, heart steady, breath back to a more restful pace, held Seth's hateful gaze. He looked up to Dandon's hand at the cord of the falconet and tensed his own hand on his pistol, thumb gently resting on the doghead as soft as a spider's leg.

'Cut him down, Dandon,' he almost whispered and even the flames hushed as all eyes went back to the quarterdeck.

Dandon leant away from the forthcoming explosion, one eye closed, the cord ready to snap, as Seth opened his arms for the impact that he was sure was not there.

Every man that lived that day would retell the tale, again and again, from father to son, from uncle to nephew, and on from tutting widow to orphaned bastard: The day the yellow-coated Dandon fired an empty gun at Seth Toombs with a pitiful spark and the pirate Devlin clicked his left-locked gun into life and walked it into Seth's nape with the words:

'Lay them down, Seth. I ain't empty, and you'll die else.'

Seth turned his head, heedful of the cold barrel kissing his collar, and hissed over his shoulder, 'I've been dead once already, Judas. I'll not be bitten twice.' And Devlin caught the clockwork sound of a pistol near his head and the young man's face in the corner of his eye.

'My name is Davis, Cap'n Devlin. Howell Davis. Pleased

to meet you. Twitch a finger, blink an eye, and I'll send that head of yours to the sea.'

Seth turned. A cold grin dragged across his face painfully. 'Ain't no Peter Sam here I see, Devlin. No Black Bill. Just a mess of you against more than twice as many.' He brought up his gully blade to gently ease the barrel of Devlin's pistol aside. 'It be over, Patrick. Come to my ship with me and we'll talk. There'll be lots we can mull over.'

Devlin looked over Seth's shoulder to Lawson with cutlass poised, staring back. To his right, across the ship, the blood-black face of Hugh Harris glared above white bared teeth.

He glanced over to the others. Young John Rice. Adam Cowrie. Pirates to a man, Devlin read fear and bloodlust in their looks and his arm faltered with the weight of the pistol still outstretched to Seth's head. Lastly he met Dandon's face, and Dandon removed his hat, held it to his front over the small-barrelled pistol lifted from his silk belt and winked as Devlin recalled their exchange of less than an hour ago.

This is folly, Patrick, Dandon had said. *There is the gold to consider and the letters that will save Peter. You should think on.*

And he remembered his own reply about conscience, about men's hearts, and he winked back to Dandon.

'Fuck it!' Devlin spat and fired his pistol shot into Seth Toombs's yellowed sneer.

Chapter Twenty-Eight

A long the stone-walled harbour of Charles Town, below
the bastions long-abandoned after the last of the con-
flicts with hostile natives, several arched storm holes ran
around the sloping wall of the bay; each hole stood no more
than five feet tall, no two more than twenty feet apart.

To an approaching ship the arches would give the appearance that she were facing the many windows of a drowning
medieval castle. The aged stonework gave the burgeoning city
a façade of nobility that even the slaves on Sullivan's island
respected, perhaps relieved that they appeared to have landed
in an empire of kings and civilisation.

The night was coming on. Along the flowered streets
husbands with their wives perambulated before supper and
tipped hats to ladies and raised canes to gentlemen whilst
their black maids scrubbed their children like apples.

The working poor clung to the tables of the taverns like
limpets at low tide, lubricating their tired muscles with unreg-
ulated liquor whilst the even poorer workers in the slave quarters soothed and warmed away the day with horse emollient
and prepared for their seven hours rest from the rice fields
that provided the body of Charles Town's income.

The Angelus of ship's bells rang out the watch across the
bay. Sidelights and lanterns were lit and the smell of beef and

cabbage drifting on the air was only mildly weaker than the stench of pitch, kelp and damp wood.

Within one of the alcoves of the storm drains Ignatius sat upon a cobbler's stool, sifting through a book of Dryden, his interest fading as the light dwindled for his lantern was a poor substitute.

He would sit until the bells rang out twice more, an hour to add to the hour he had already waited and two more to add to the dozens of others he had spent over the weeks, his only comfort being the poet, the stool, and the coin for his trouble.

He lifted his head to the splash of a boat being lowered and listened, head cocked like a blind-man, to the path of the oars as they rowed onwards. From the narrow window of the arch he could see a square of the horizon and the bowsprit of some unknown vessel that had kept him company for several days on his nightly vigil.

His ears pricked up and his book slapped shut as the sound of the oars came closer to the sanctity of his storm drain rather than diverting towards the promise of the welcoming harbour.

He brushed off the hour of damp and salt and scraped his fingers through his greying hair as he rose from the stool and brought his light to the mouth of his cave and the cold of the night.

With a sweep of the lantern he lowered a rope ladder and grasped the gloved hand that reached out to him. The purple brocade doublet brushed past the black figure of Ignatius without a word and crouched in the tunnel awaiting his entourage.

The giant struggled up next and Ignatius was almost dragged to the sea by the lump of a hand that steadied itself around his forearm, and the tunnel seemed to shrink as his bulk huddled with them in the dark.

The light from the lantern rose with the breaths of the giant and lit the final face rising past the edge of the storm drain. Ignatius looked down at the pale drawn features with the silver and red beard and dragged the sagging six-foot-plus frame into the drain like a catch of fish.

'Can he walk?' Ignatius whispered to the dark, hearing the grey body gasping and sucking at the damp air.

'He can crawl,' Valentim Mendes replied and took to his feet along the low tunnel. Ignatius plucked up the lantern and slapped past the grey face paying it no more mind. Hib folded himself like a concertina and hauled the sunken shoulders into the blackness.

Ignatius kicked back the rug over the hatch that led to the harbour. The night was without. Good men had returned to their hearths while the bad plotted in taverns and Ignatius withdrew to his maple commode for liquid comfort before the rattle of manacles drew him back to the party within his study. A sound unwelcome. An iron chink that unsettled the comfort of his sanctum.

'Are those chains absolutely necessary, Governor Mendes?' He poured three guildive rums. 'That sound belongs to the slave quarter.'

Valentim took a seat, lifting his scabbard through the arm and resting his porcelain and gloved hand on the pommel.

'He feels better that way. Trust me on that.'

Ignatius turned and passed him a goblet. A wet sniff from the putrid head of Peter Sam spoilt the vapours of Ignatius' crystal glass. 'I have a room for him, bar-locked and secure.

Perhaps it is better for him to retire than listen to our conversation.'

'Perhaps.' Valentim raised a hand to Hib Gow without a word and the Scotsman took his eyes from the glass still waiting on the commode to tug at the chain between Peter Sam's wrists.

Ignatius's young servant tried not to look at Peter Sam's eyes as he held open the passage door, but his eyes alighted on the chains as they rattled past and he bowed and followed, closing the door as softly as he could.

'So, Ignatius,' Valentim sipped his rum with a grimace. 'We are alone. Tell me how we progress? What of my revenge?'

Ignatius moved to his desk. 'You mean what of the letters? The arcanum of porcelain, Governor?'

Valentim shrugged and angled his glass, his eyes lowered to watch the swirling of the cane spirit.

Ignatius sat and bided his time. 'How do you find Hib's company, governor? He is quite a find is he not?'

'He is an animal,' Valentim said. 'Even for an executioner. Where did you locate such a foul creature?'

'One of Tyburn's best I assure you. Unfortunately he lost favour some years ago. The English were mad for Jacobites, and a Presbyterian Scotsman was not to be trusted. It was most opportune that I could take him off their hands.' He swallowed his drink. 'My good fortune. Not so fortunate for some of London that met with the humour of a man used to killing men every day.'

'If you say it is thus, Señor. I myself believe him to be mad. And a madman does not make a good companion. I have spent months with him. He has a definite ability to break the will of a man. It is a gift. But he takes pleasure in it beyond simple duty.' He leant forward and placed his rum on the desk. 'He appals me even more than this slave *tafia* you choose to serve me. Now,' he sat back, 'I have had a tiresome voyage on that barge of a sloop of yours, Ignatius, so tell me only of the pirate.'

Ignatius leafed through his diary letting the pages of the last weeks pile a wall of tension between him and Valentim as they fell one by one.

'The pace has picked up, Governor,' he said at last. 'The pirate Devlin has been dispatched to New Providence to attempt to liberate the letters of Father d'Entrecolles. If he fails he will most likely be hung. If he succeeds he will be back here within the month.' He looked up to Valentim. 'And the pair of you can renew your acquaintance.'

Valentim tapped gently on the arm of his chair with his artificial hand. Even through the velvet glove Ignatius could detect the minuscule chime of the porcelain palm.

'I will look forward to his coming,' he said, his voice distant. 'I very much wish him to succeed.'

Ignatius cleared his throat. 'Much has happened in your absence, Governor, that makes for a very interesting prospect for our plans. Have you heard of "Blackbeard", Governor? Captain Edward Teach?'

The lifeless face that looked back heralded to Ignatius that he had not.

'He has enjoyed great infamy along our coastal colonies this last year as a privateer. Although perhaps "privateer" is a mite generous of me,' he corrected himself with a fleeting smile. 'He is a pirate with the worst of them.'

Valentim looked idly around the study, his eyes drifting momentarily over the porcelain display upon the commode. 'What is this to me, Ignatius?'

'Teach – Blackbeard – blockaded this town recently. Held

our Council to ransom. His ransom being the very letters that we seek. His partner was wrongly under the impression that I already had them, hidden in a chest that Palgrave Williams, one of Bellamy's captains, had brought ashore before the sinking of the *Whydah*. I admit I thought so too at one point. That perhaps Palgrave had conspired with Bellamy to remove the letters from the Chinese gun in some plan of blackmail against me. I wish you had come to me sooner, Governor, to save me months of hunting for that chest. But now of course I am aware that there are others who will take great risks to possess them.'

Valentim's interest flicked back. '*You* seek the letters. I have informed you of where they lie. Bringing the pirate to me is what I have engaged you for, Ignatius.'

'Of course, Governor. But should Devlin fail I will still not have my letters. Grateful as I am for knowing where they finally are, their acquisition remains of the highest importance. It seems that Blackbeard has cultivated close relationships with several governors, who see no harm in allowing some freebooting within their colonies. But the fact that he knew about the letters was most enlightening as to just how entwined he has become with powerful men.'

'What have this to do with our interests, Ignatius?'

'A little,' Ignatius said warmly. 'I have since engaged Blackbeard to assist *me* as well as his own gentleman retainer. I will have those letters one way or another. By any means necessary.'

Valentim rose slightly, his black eyes blazing. 'If this *Blackbeard* interferes with *my* plans Ignatius, you will pay dearly for his transgressions I assure you.'

Ignatius waved away Valentim's words like bothersome insects. 'No, no, Governor. Not at all. If Blackbeard should encounter Devlin he is instructed to bring him here to face you. I am a man of my word as my reputation attests. It is my intention merely to keep you fully informed, as you requested, on our progress.' He closed his diary and stood to look out onto his twilight garden. 'Now that they are truly real, and so near, these letters are provoking an interest that makes my position here potentially . . . uncomfortable.' Ignatius's final word was punctuated by the solid clump of Hib returning to the room and bowing awkwardly before sloping over to the waiting glass on the commode.

Ignatius sniffed and carried on. 'Normally in such a situation it would be advisable to distance myself from the matter, but that is not possible: I must remain here until it is settled, for this house is where they will come. What I can do, most certainly, is to control the number of people who know about the letters.'

Valentim yawned. 'And how do you propose to do that?'

Ignatius faced him. 'Oh, I have already set events in motion and relayed appropriate correspondence to ensure the end of Blackbeard and his liaisons with the governors. Our pirate Devlin is well taken care of, one way or the other.' He held out a respectful hand to Valentim and then swept it to the huge Scotsman across the room. 'And Mister Gow . . .'

Hib straightened at the mention of his name and, wiping some of the rum from the corner of his mouth, placed his glass down gently and looked across obediently at Ignatius.

'Mister Gow can be trusted as if his blade were my own arm. And I need only to glance at a man,' Ignatius turned his eyes back to the seated Valentim. 'And he be . . . *gone.*'

The commode shook with Hib's sudden movement. In two strides he was at Valentim's chair. It took one heartbeat to clamp him down with the slab of a hand that bit into Valentim's shoulder and to angle the cold blade of the polished Estilete at his throat.

Valentim felt the pulse in his neck racing against the gentle pressure of the razor edge and his eyes stared wildly back at Ignatius.

'What madness is this!' Valentim's voice slithered out above the blade. 'I am the *Regulador* of Sao Nicolau! An ambassador!'

'And by your own account, Governor, no soul knows that you are here. Except my men that you have sailed with, Hib, and myself.'

'You swore I was to have Devlin!' For the next five minutes of his life concern for his neck was less important than facing the pirate again. 'You betray me, Ignatius!' Valentim tried to rise but an enormous weight pressed him down with the merest force.

Ignatius pulled open a drawer of his desk, lifting out a pistol and balancing it in his fist. 'I have done nothing, Governor, save secure the privacy of the arcanum for those who can afford its secrets.' He gestured to Hib with the pistol to lever Valentim from his chair. 'And I will honour my word. You will see Devlin again. My reputation insists upon it. Providing of course he succeeds in bringing the letters to me. Providing, that is, he is not hanging from some yardarm by now.'

Valentim cursed as Hib stripped away his weapons like undressing an infant and pulled him from the room away from the smiling Ignatius. Valentim howled around the house as he was dragged up the wooden stair – howled that all English, all the world, were *pirata* and betrayers and only the *Português* had honour and how he prayed for the day that the *Espanhol* would drink their English blood. A minute later his anger could no longer be heard. The good remained at their hearths; the bad still jostled in the taverns and Ignatius returned to his maple commode to pour another drink.

He thought on his audience with Lt Governor Spotswood and Governor Cranston, the Bauta-masked gentlemen who had first called upon him after word of the letters had spread from China to their own shores.

It was always at night, Ignatius thought as he smirked into his drink. Conspirators meet like moths around a candle-flame. During the day they play with their children, flatter their wives and write to Whitehall like good white-wigged citizens. At night they don masks and cloaks, and gather to plot like witches in a coven.

The idea was as old as democracy: You can have no king, for the consequence of kings is war. Spain and inevitably France will always be your enemies as long as you hold to a crown. And one cannot trade with the enemy. Then again, one cannot get rich in times of peace.

Spotswood he trusted. Should Blackbeard survive, Spotswood would be the one to fund a private assault against the pirate. Chalk Blackbeard off of the list of those who knew. Cranston was different. Cranston was governor of Rhode Island. Palgrave Williams's father had been Attorney General of the Rhode Island plantations. Ignatius did not live by ignoring coincidence. Palgrave Williams had left the *Whydah* and came ashore at the colony before she sank. Then he had vanished and become the most wanted man in the Americas after the ship went down.

Cranston may know more than he purports to, thought Ignatius, tapping his lips. A question mark beside his name. If Devlin succeeded, returned, then Valentim could have at him. Chalk off one or the other. His calculations were interrupted by the movement of Hib Gow's return. He saluted his giant with the glass. And chalk off the other one as well, he thought. All achieved without a smirch of blood on Ignatius's hands. Just the taste of it in the air around him.

Hanging. As concise and definite in meaning to the eighteenth-century mind as crucifixion to a first-century Palestinian. A choking. The hempen jig before the perfection of the snap. Drowning on the end of a rope like a hare struggling overnight against the snare.

A man could escape the punishment of piracy in England by signing up to be a good colonist in the Americas. Better a chance against the savages and diseases than the man in the black hood who reserved the swift plunge for the blue blood but strangled your poor wrong-born throat with a hemp knot that grated like glass. Sometimes they would honour you by allowing you to tie your own knot. They taught it you like a new trade the night before and you cursed at the scuffing of your palms from the rough rope and your mind lingered over the same effect against your more tender throat.

Your trembling hand signed for the Americas in the morning.

But if you were already there, already confined to the promise of the Americas, and chanced your arm against the world? What then for you, my boy? Where do you go when you have already gone to the end of the world? Where do you go?

One place to go. Down. Only the rope and a short hard stop from a sudden drop.

John Coxon drank fast as he heard the slap on the horse's flanks and the intake of breath from the crowd – mostly made up of women and children.

There was the faint thrashing of heels and the solemn roll

of the cart's wheels but thankfully he could not see the sight in the square from his table beside the stair of the Cat and Fiddle. He sat alone and poured from a crock bottle of rum and lime into a leather mug furred by years of use and listened to the nine necks choking away in the square beyond the stone walls.

A sickness swam within him, caused he considered by the unnatural sweetness of the drink, and he raised his arm and voice for bread and cheese to offer a sour antidote to the sugar coursing through his head.

The pewter plate came. The bread was fresh, the cheese hard, but he swallowed it all the same and thought on his position as he chewed.

July and August were harsh. The fever spread unabated, although the pirates still dwelling there seemed immune, blessed by the devil. Two of the warships, the *Shark* and the *Rose*, had sailed on to New York, having no further orders to stay and Rogers having no further power to hold them.

He ripped at the bread. Still the *Delicia* remained with her forty guns, and his own command, the *Milford*. Over seventy guns and three hundred men between them. Enough to hold the island in check. Perhaps. Enough to warrant an afternoon's drinking whilst Rogers enthusiastically conducted his duty outside.

Mrs Haggins turned her bulbous eyes away from him as she drifted down the stair. The sickening waft of what passed as her perfume made the cheese even more unpalatable.

Sitting at his octagonal table on a raised stage behind a rail, Coxon grabbed the remnants of huddled conversation from the mosaic of tables below him. He overheard talk of Blackbeard spied sailing to Bermuda. Of friendly governors in the Carolinas that welcomed free trade. Whispers of Vane and dozens more still holding out, seeking their own independence. Indian attacks weakening the colonies like a plague.

Coxon grinned between gulps of rum. If a pirate could win the Indians to him, he thought with a drunk's philosophising, he could rule this country. The Indians, he recalled from his luncheons with the ragged captains that had survived a landing, only wanted to kill fathers and sons, to crush the seed that might poison their land. They were few, and they would die. Fuck them. He drank, drowning out the last slap on the horse's hide from the courtyard and the cheer and gasp that rang out at the spectacle of another fallen pirate. You can't beat the fall of coin. This world belongs to mad kings and the companies under them. He looked down at the black cup. *I am just building a bed to die in*, he consoled himself.

The face appeared before him silently, peering anxiously through the rails of the stage for quite a while before Coxon noticed it and pulled his coat tight and hacked the stale air from his throat and brushed the crumbs from his lips.

The marine slapped his chest and snapped to attention when Coxon finally acknowledged him.

'What is it lad?' Coxon said and pushed the rum aside.

The marine kept his voice low against the forest of eyes and ears that had followed his path through the mess of tables.

'Captain Coxon, sir,' his voice was hushed. 'You are required at the beach. To come with me if you will, Captain.'

Coxon drizzled small coin onto the table and staggered up. 'What occurs, sailor?' He straightened himself, ran a palm over his face and was sober in an instant.

The marine tipped back his tricorne at the prospect of the next half hour of his life. 'It's the *Mumvil Trader*, Captain.

She's back in the bay. A man called Davis brought her in. Escaped from the pirates so he says.'

Coxon stepped down to the sawdust floor. 'Does Rogers know of this?'

'Not yet sir. Davis, their captain now, asked for you only. I checked here last, Captain.'

'You found me last, lad,' he dragged the man to the door. 'I'll bring the governor from his hanging and join you on the beach.'

The marine stayed Coxon's hand. 'You best come first, Captain,' he said. 'Especially.'

Coxon fixed the man with his eye and waited for the soldier to continue.

'He has a prisoner, Captain,' the man began to grin and relished the rising of Coxon's eyebrows. 'He has the pirate Devlin with him. Chained. And his men also.'

Coxon's arm gripped the sailor and the man pulled against the clasp. 'I say, he has the pirate Devlin on the beach, Captain. Calling for the King's Act so he is. Captain Davis is calling for you especially.'

Coxon pulled the marine close. 'Are his hands tied?'

'Captain?'

'Are his hands tied, man? Devlin's hands *tied*!'

'He is manacled, Captain. Safe as houses so he is.'

Coxon walked on, pulling the red-coated innocent with him. 'I fell for *that* before.' And the hot bright world was before them as the door of the Cat and Fiddle swung out onto New Providence and John Coxon made his way down to the beach to meet Patrick Devlin again; the star-shaped scar on his forearm itching beneath his shirt.

Chapter Twenty-Nine

It was always the Portuguese. Wherever and whenever a man first licked his thumb and placed it on the edge of a map and questioned what lay beyond he did it upon the rocking deck of a carrack out of Lisbon. So it was that in the early sixteenth century the first of many dropped their anchors in Guangzhou harbour and began there also to drop silver, returning with the first batches of the mysterious Chinese hard-paste porcelain for the royal tabletops of Europe.

One hundred years later the Dutch discovered the fabled route, but rather than trade with the Chinese they preferred to pirate the Portuguese vessels to such an extent that even James I and Henry IV travelled to Holland to bid for the stolen wares.

Once the Portuguese route was known to all, the Dutch and English East India companies began to ship as much porcelain as the factories could produce and the Hongs would allow. It was only a matter of time, and greed, before Europe demanded the secret for themselves. Black Sam Bellamy's *Whydah* carried the letters of the priest, the wad of papers corked in a bamboo tube and sealed within the bronze cannon, the same cannon that Captain William Guinneys had purchased for the purpose of smuggling the letters out of China under the noses of the Hongs and all the East India companies.

The cannon was carried to Charles Town and to Ignatius, then ferried north by Bellamy for safety, once word went abroad following Guinneys' wake. Then the gun drowned along with Bellamy and his pirate crew in April 1717. Thus the arcanum was lost to the West again.

The ship had capsized in shallow waters off Cape Cod, making the hold tantalisingly accessible, and the wreck brought treasure hunters from as far as the Bahamas. The salvagers had found negresses particularly adept at the art of diving, their body fat a better insulator in the deeper, colder water – as the Spanish had discovered after they had exhausted their supplies of the local Caribs and Lucayans in scavenging sunken wrecks.

The teredo worm had feasted well on the *Whydah*'s keel and she was punched in easily by the slaves' fists, which opened a hole large enough to swim through.

Hours were spent plumbing the depths, with respite for the women found in the caulked wooden diving-bells floating around the wreck like giant jellyfish. There, some hot air could be gasped and the divers could fill the leather bags hanging inside with gold and silver coins salvaged from the *Whydah*'s hold.

Randomly their masters would slit open the belly of one of the returning women to check for precious stones and coins and deter the other divers from stealing.

For the local council the looting of the *Whydah* had become a circus. Locals and 'moon-cussers' set up stalls along the shore, gleefully selling rings still sitting on swollen fingers cut from the washed-up bodies that piled along the shoreline with each dawn.

In light of this, William Tailer, the governor of Massachusetts, commissioned the revered cartographer and captain, Cyprian

Southack, to officially salvage the pirate ship on the crown's behalf. Southack sailed back to Boston a week later with nothing more than: '*two anchors, some junk . . . and two great guns.*'

Much of the gold and silver, the ivory, even the bulk of the indigo blocks had been already liberated. Captain Southack's official haul was auctioned within the month. The crown remarked little on the paltry tribute. The only significant sale was the one of the guns, a curious anonymous purchase of fourteen hundred pounds for an antique minion, a small bore Chinese gun, its barrel blocked by crustaceans and clay. Its only possible value was as bronze scrap for smelting.

Palgrave Williams's wagon drove the gun out of Heston's auction house in May 1717 and Palgrave vanished from the earth. He had been Black Sam Bellamy's partner and had left his wife and children, also his business as a goldsmith, and had blackened the good name of his father to become a pirate. Five warships now cruised the New England coast seeking him. Warrants were posted even to the natives for the apprehension of the pirate who had become the Americas' most wanted man. And he had sat with his hands crossed upon his lap in the front row of Heston's auction and waited for his moment.

He had bid for and bought the gun, then hidden it in plain sight in the abandoned Spanish fort on Providence until the world had forgotten him and he could come back and claim his pension. But the King had reclaimed Providence, New Providence now deemed, and it was no longer safe to return. It was now a year after the sinking of the *Whydah* and the crown had still not laid a hand upon him. Only the Devil could find Palgrave Williams now for surely only the Devil would know where to look.

*

For Palgrave Williams in his current predicament, hell could threaten little more. Roped tight within the bowels of the sloop *Adventure*, half his body lay soaking in the well of the bilge and his arms were chained above his head keeping him from drowning. Rats scampered across his lap, nibbled at his leather belt and boots. The cool of the water accomplished nothing against the stale, hot air below the waterline.

It had been days now, feeling the pressure of water above his head outside the keel and the Bermudan tide swaying in the stagnant well all about him.

He had found sanctuary in Bermuda, in St George's Town, biding his time until the English gave up on saving New Providence and he could return to collect the gun.

Perhaps it had been a mistake to make his way to Bermuda. His reasoning had been that the English island had defended itself well from pirates over the years yet was just a couple of days' sail back to Providence and only six hundred miles from the Carolinas. He could keep his fingers in the pie but be far enough removed from the squadrons on land and sea that hunted for him daily.

But pirates did haunt Bermuda. Not as boldly or as veraciously as the string of islands to the southwest perhaps (a pinch of slave smuggling now and then around Rum Cay was Governor Bennett's most bothersome infraction), but come they did and it would have been in droves if it were not for the shallow shoals keeping their keels at bay.

Local fishermen, for a price, would guide pirate sloops through the rocks and Charles Vane, since fleeing from Providence, had fully taken advantage of their cupidity. Vane's boldness had caused a stir around the islands and Palgrave began to feel the need to move on.

He did not know the sloop, *Adventure*, that the swarthy

quartermaster claimed to be a part of when he paid a coin to be introduced one evening in the Angel inn but he liked the offer of free passage back to the Americas providing he could haul a sail. Palgrave had assured the man, Israel Hands, that his current formal dress was not to be taken as a measure of his worth. Had he not been a commander of one of Black Sam Bellamy's ships himself? Had he not spliced and reefed with the best of them? Israel Hands was not to worry about Palgrave Williams or his stout belly and advanced years. He would not slow them down.

Now Palgrave found himself wallowing in the bilge amidst the lead ballast of the *Adventure* waiting for the Devil to appear, as Israel Hands had promised, laughing all the while as he tied Palgrave like a hog and cast the darkness upon him with the closing of the hatchway.

Days passed, foetid days of starvation to lower his will, days spent counting over the last years of his life and charting his mistakes. The third time he stirred awake, startled by a noise above and disgusted at the tiny bubbles of his own urine floating over his breeches, he presumed it to be night by the movement of a lamp along the deck of the hold over his head.

The golden light sliced through the beams above as someone moved with a crab-like scuttling, too tall to just lower his head and creep along judging by the laboured breath and cursing.

The hatch door creaked open, the sound and descending light sending the rats swimming and jumping away from Palgrave's body, shrieking to their wives and children to hide themselves.

Palgrave recognised the rattle and clink of a man brimming with steel.

The lantern swung over, momentarily blinding Palgrave. A rum-laden chuckle aimed itself straight at him and the man stepped closer, swinging the lamp and throwing his monstrous shadow around the walls of the bilge.

'Well, well,' Blackbeard growled. 'I be pleased to meet you, Palgrave. You be a man well sought for. I've a mind to let you keep your freedom and as to that I have a proposition for you. I knows about the gun. I knows where it lies. But I don't aims on setting foot on Providence to gets it. But you, Palgrave. You have a use to old Blackbeard, so you do.'

Chapter Thirty

✕

*T*he beach seemed somehow brighter to Coxon. Perhaps it was just the clearing-up that had gone on over the past few weeks, the removal of the cattle carcasses and sweeping away of years of accumulated rubbish and bottles. Or perhaps it was the sight of chained men under guard of sailors from the *Mumvil* that met Coxon's gaze as he stepped down over the final dunes to the shore that made everything seem to shine and glow. At last here was his opportunity to reacquaint himself with the pirate who had once slept on his floor as a trusted servant. It had been a long year and now it was time to see what time had wrought.

'Should we not fetch more men, Captain?' the soldier by Coxon's side spoke anxiously as he counted the heads of at least thirty dishevelled and armed men jostling each other on the sands.

Coxon had already spied the tall form of Patrick Devlin, in waistcoat and shirt, indeed chained but still with his head held high and catching Coxon's eye with a smirk. 'No need,' Coxon said. 'This will not take long.'

He made his path to the men carrying the most weapons, those he supposed were the crew of the returned *Mumvil*.

'Which one of you is Howell Davis?' he barked authoritatively, hoping that the whiff of rum did not carry as far as his voice.

'I am, Cap'n.' A short scrag of a sailor, although with a handsome young face, stepped apart from the others. 'I be Howell Davis.'

Coxon walked towards him. 'I understand you are responsible for bringing the *Mumvil* home again, Davis. You are to be commended, man.' Coxon greeted him warmly.

Davis looked sideways to his men and the dark face of Devlin. 'Aye, Cap'n. Quite a tale it is, sir.'

'I will hear it, Davis. You will be a hero home in England.'

Davis tapped his skull. 'Thank you, sir. Wasn't easy.'

Coxon moved to the group that surrounded the chained pirates. 'And you good men who resisted the pirate way, you shall all be rewarded by your grateful governor! I will insist upon it.' Coxon did not listen to their cheer to his good name for he had stopped to face Devlin and ran his hands over his manacles, jury rigged from fairleads and chain.

'You are secure, Patrick,' he said. 'I am almost disappointed. I suspected some ruse of sorts. Like the last time.' He looked over to the horizon. 'And that frigate of yours? Is it not about now that she appears? Some rescue you have planned no doubt?'

Devlin said nothing, but he held Coxon's eye with his own and Coxon stepped back with a small flash of a smile. 'I would very much hate that to be the case.' He turned to Davis again. 'Mister Davis? Your men to my right side if you please, I wish to see the prisoners separate.'

Howell's men, the *Mumvil*'s original remaining crew, shuffled to Coxon's side, their muskets, cutlasses and belaying pins still in their hands, ready to strike. The six prisoners stood small and lonely before them all and the parting of the crowd revealed a mess of bundled bodies behind them.

'Howell?' Coxon queried of the more than a dozen corpses dragged onto the beach like turtles.

'That's the ones that ain't so fortunate, Cap'n. Some of Devlin's. Some of the pirates that took the ship.' He lowered his voice almost respectfully. 'Seth Toombs amongst them. He took the *Mumvil*. Forced us into it. Cap'n Finch will testify. We were all pressed into his mutiny.' Howell vaguely crossed himself, penitent for his sins.

Coxon wandered over to the bodies, drawn by the familiar brown coat and the red tricorne. Seth Toombs's body lay on the bellies and the shoulders of several of the others. The wind played the straw-blond hair across the face as Coxon looked down at the grey mask. The mouth and chin were a black chasm, the leer wiped forever clear, eyes dry and glassy staring over Coxon's shoulder. Coxon noted that despite the baked permanence of his wound someone had found it necessary to tie Seth's wrists together.

'Knew I'd see you again, sailor,' Coxon patted the brown coat and moved back up the beach. ''Tis a small world for evil men,' he aimed his words at Devlin alone as he came alongside him. 'You are quiet, Patrick. I am not used to this.' He clasped his hands behind him and inspected the rest of his prisoners, immediately recognising the yellow justacorps of the man at Devlin's shoulder. 'Ah,' he said. 'It is the French surgeon is it not? You know, I do believe that I hold you almost wholly responsible for the losses of the *Starling* that day. It'll be a cold day for you, sir, soon enough.' Dandon shrank before him, his eyes to the sand.

'And you, pirate?' Coxon stopped at the still bloodied face of Hugh Harris. 'You are also familiar. Are you glad to have stayed by your captain's side this past year?'

'Aye,' Hugh snarled. 'And I be the one who's carried your guns all this time. Shoot fine they did, with lead or shot. Parted many. I'll be happy to carry them again for you, Cap'n.'

Coxon spun round to Howell. 'My pistols! This man had a pair of duelling pistols that belong to me. Where are they now?'

Howell looked from side to side amongst his men. 'Reckon they be here somewheres, Cap'n. We took all the weapons from them.' A faint grin. 'He took your pistols, Cap'n?'

A slow laugh rippled through the prisoners and Howell's men. The soldier lowered his head respectfully but the crown of his hat trembled as laughter infected him.

Coxon looked back to Devlin's grin. 'A small world for evil men, Patrick. There is a hanging party going on in the square. We may still have time to join it.' He swung away. 'Howell. Private. Bring them to the square.'

The afternoon had clouded over, great grey sheets more akin to a London sky than the normally vibrant blue of the Bahama islands. The dead now lay flaccid on the hand-cart, the chill of the day no longer their concern. Eight were dead, one more to come, still kicking his heels at the end of a hemp rope beneath the 'Tyburn Tree', the triangular scaffold twice as tall as the victim, just high enough for the drop to grant a macabre dance for the audience; only now they turned their heads to the small parade advancing up the sandy path from the beach and missed the final faint twitch of the nineteen-year-old boy who had once dared to be a pirate but now had been unjustly rewarded for taking the King's pardon.

Woodes Rogers followed the heads of the crowd and stepped down from the box which he had upturned to stand above his subjects. He closed his Psalm book and left his German clerk and the push of soldier's muskets to dismiss the towns-folk.

'What goes on, John?' he looked past Coxon to the six chained men.

'We have a gift, Governor. Those that we thought completely lost have returned. The *Mumvil* has come back with these good men and they have brought us a gift.'

Howell took his cue and pushed Devlin to trip in the dust before Rogers. Devlin shrugged himself tall and passed his gaze around the crowd now whispering his name.

Coxon grabbed him by the shirt, pulling him like a child to Rogers' judgement.

'The pirate Devlin, Governor. Patrick Devlin.' Coxon offered nothing in the words, he spoke as if Devlin was an item on a list now marked clear. 'If you want a pirate to hang to make a point we could do no better today I'm sure.'

Rogers sniffed and wiped his mouth and took a step closer, aloof and careful, for the crowd was listening. 'The pirate Devlin, eh? Short of Blackbeard and Vane, sir, you are the most wanted head upon these seas. What do you have to say for yourself, my man?'

Devlin rubbed his wrists, the links of his chains already scraping a slave tattoo. 'You have me, Governor Rogers, and owe this man, Davis, for the fact. I would be honoured to take the King's pardon for your will and my men also.' He lowered his head. 'I surrender myself to you, sir, and your jurisdiction.'

Rogers raised his chin high above Devlin's lowered brow. 'You wish to claim the King's pardon, pirate? Yet you arrive in chains? Clearly you have come to us in guilt rather than sorrow for your crimes.' Rogers moved to reveal the hanging corpse revolving slowly behind his shoulder. 'It may be too late for you to repent, sir.'

'I ask nothing except an hour to discourse how I came to

this point. To talk of Seth Toombs, my lost ship, to sign Howell's statement as to how he came to end my days, and of what became of my gold,' his eyes held Roger's like a rope. '*All* my gold, Governor. And where it lies.'

Rogers checked his watch, the words of the pirate of little interest it seemed. Coxon pulled Devlin aside, dragging his body away from Rogers' view. He placed his face closer to the governor's than he had ever previously dared.

'It would be my opinion, Governor, to hang this man whilst we have a rope afforded. He cannot be trusted to respite. He is uncommonly gifted for escape.'

'Do you think he can outwit me, John? As well as you? Is that what you think? It is now after three. My clerk always takes my council at four for the order of the day. I can spare this pirate a few minutes, for what it's worth. It has been a most trying afternoon. Take what measures you will, John. I will hear this man and Mister Davis, as well as whatever light Captain Finch can throw on the subject. The *Mumvil* after all was his originally to command.' The governor had already begun to make for the stone fort, brushing the sordid afternoon from his coat sleeves.

Coxon pushed away Devlin's chains, ignoring his grin. He barked at the private still attached to him from the beach: 'Separate these men. A cell each if you can,' and pointed significantly at Dandon. 'You to watch *this* one, private. Him most of all. Mister Davis, you are to accompany me to the governor's office.' He clicked his fingers to the rest of the soldiers. 'Clear the square. Cut that man down,' he pointed to the swinging body now crowned with flies and the hand-cart with the repulsive burden. 'Build a funeral pyre on the beach tomorrow and burn those pirate corpses. Have their ashes brushed into the sea.' He came back to Devlin, the grin galling him now as it had done a year before, only now Coxon had the means to wipe it off his arrogant face.

'Don't expect the pardon, Patrick. No matter what you think you can offer the governor.' Again he checked the chains that bound the man. 'I buried the woman, Sarah, last week.' He savoured the look that came back at him. 'She died of the fever. I buried her and all that she owned. *All* that she owned.'

Devlin and Dandon's chains chimed as they pulled tight against their fists.

Coxon smiled, a rare thing since Providence became his home. 'By this evening I will scour the horizon for that frigate of yours. You will not catch me twice. This governor does not know you, but *I* do. Whatever you have planned, whatever you think you are doing . . .' He pushed Devlin away, up towards the fort.

Devlin shrugged off Coxon's hand and whispered in close. 'And did you tell the governor about Sarah, John? Or have you kept that to yourself?'

Coxon said nothing and shoved the pirate's shoulder harder.

The square emptied with enough tattle to carry through the night. The six pirates trudged up the hill, the afternoon heavy on their shoulders, now free of steel and iron other than that wrapped around their wrists. Faith in the tall man at their head was all that they had, and they were questioning that now, the sight of the Tyburn Tree having shrivelled all their hearts. '*A short life and a merry one*,' a motto to drink to, not one to wish for, not now, as their path left the sea behind.

Chapter Thirty-One

'O bury me not in the deep, deep sea,
The words came low and mournfully
From the paled lips of a youth who lay
On his cabin couch at the close of day.
He had wasted and pined till o'er his brow,
Death's shade had slowly passed, and now
Where the land and his fond loved home were nigh
They had gathered around him to see him die.'

The slow lament from the Spanish guitar and the low fife drifting from the open windows and doors of the Porker's End reached even the windows of Rogers' office where Devlin stood alone amidst a throng of enemies casting judgement. Chained still, a soldier to each side, standing before Rogers' oak desk like a schoolboy summoned, Devlin listened to the end of the song and the words from the desk that finally drowned it out.

Rogers, Coxon, Howell Davis and Captain Finch were all present and all seated except Coxon who stood a pace away from Devlin with an eye trained on him while Rogers raked over Devlin's past.

'As I understand from your crimes of piracy, Mister Devlin, it began with the theft of a Porto man of war from out of the Verdes. Is that a true assumption?'

'It has a manner of truth about it, Governor,' Devlin said.

'Well, is it true or not, man?' Rogers snapped.

'I was escaping with my life, Governor. A lot of death that night.'

'I have faith in that I'm sure.' Rogers lifted the paper from the desk, squinting as he studied the print. 'Then there is the matter of a Dutch ship, pirated mid-Atlantic, another enemy gathered against you. Another ally of your King you chose to defile.'

'She was a slaver, Governor,' Devlin interjected calmly. 'She was defiled enough.'

Rogers ignored the remark, not even lifting a glance from the vellum page. 'Then of course there is the theft of the French gold. Your most audacious crime. Fortunately we have a survivor with us in this very room who can enlighten us more as to the nature of that one.'

Nobody needed Rogers to indicate Coxon. Devlin spoke before Coxon could open his mouth.

'Am I on trial here, Governor?' he asked. 'I thought the Act of Pardon precluded such, Your Worship.'

Rogers blinked at the chained pirate. His features remained unperturbed but a vein had begun to pulse against his cravat. 'The pardon, *pirate*, is for those who give up their lawless ways voluntarily. Not for those that are captured and brought to justice.'

Devlin leapt on Rogers' words. 'Ah, then we merely have a difference of opinion, for I was on my way back to Providence for that very reason when the *Mumvil* attacked my ship. In defending myself and my men I was brought here. The means may be different but the ending is the same. I have come to take the pardon offered by my King. An acre I believe? Something with a sea aspect will suit me fine, Your Worship.'

Rogers looked at one of the soldiers shadowing Devlin and nodded curtly. The man stabbed his musket butt into the back of Devlin's knee causing the rest of the room, except Rogers and Coxon, to wince in their seats.

Devlin fell forward on his knee with a crack to the cap upon the stone floor. He twisted painfully against the soldier's thigh as he sucked up the pain. He lifted his head, eyes now facing the corner of the room as Rogers continued, but he was no longer listening to him.

His eye had fallen on the junk nestling in the corner and his pain had vanished when a red sparkling eye looked back at him enticingly. Rogers droned on but Devlin only noticed the Spanish guitar and the pirate songs lilting up from the town below as a contented expression flitted briefly across his face.

He looked up at the man who had assaulted him, checking for any empathy due a decent soldier simply following harsh orders. Instead he found the grimace of a man who enjoys the kicking of his dog or beating a horse beyond its labours. That would do. He spoke softly enough just for the soldier to hear.

'Touch me once more and I'll kill you.'

The soldier smiled at first, thinking of the manacles, his own weapon, his fellow beside him and the support of the room all around him against the man at his knees. His smile faded as Devlin rose slowly to his feet. He stood close to the soldier's side so the man could feel the elbow against his forearm and a solid shoulder close to his cheek as the pirate racked up to his full height and even leant his boot against the soldier's, touching it as if resting on a cobbler's shelf. The closeness felt cold to the redcoat, as if the man beside him had already delegated him dead and gone. His eyes shifted to his feet and he inched away just enough to stop any part of the pirate touching him.

'Captain Finch,' Rogers addressed the ex-commander of the *Mumvil Trader.* 'I must say I am a little confused.'

'How so, sir?' Finch asked.

'You said that your ship was taken in the night by at least half your crew. You indicated that a man, Seth Toombs, was the chief conspirator and that Mister Davis here was most certainly involved.'

'That he was, sir,' Finch confirmed.

Rogers lifted his head to Howell Davis. 'So how is it, Mister Davis, that you came to the point of bringing Devlin in? Tell us what happened after the night where you appeared to be one of the ringleaders of this mutiny.' He studied Howell carefully, watching his reactions. 'Is there something else going on here that I should perhaps be aware of?'

Howell, sitting beneath the window overlooking the square, looked nervously at Finch from across the room. He had been listening to the songs from the Porker's End and wishing he had been part of that gathering and not this ill-matched game of cards.

'Seth Toombs led the mutiny, sir. We were all pressed into it so to speak. Fear of our own throats, Governor. After a couple of days however, once we'd all sobered up that is, we saw the error of our ways and took back the ship from Toombs. He didn't take kindly to that but bowed to our numbers like,' he paused as Devlin threw a brief glance over his shoulder. All eyes were on Howell and only Coxon caught the look and felt his body tense.

'Anyways,' Howell carried on. 'We were attacked by the pirate Devlin here on our way back, so. He showed his flag but we won the day. We brought his ship in, Governor. The

Talefan. She be latched to mine in the harbour. All the men that live are with you now.'

'And what of the *Shadow*?' Coxon asked Howell. 'Where was she?' He kept his eyes on Devlin's.

Howell leant forward to hear again. 'What *Shadow*, sir?'

'The frigate. His warship.' Coxon moved in front of Devlin, blocking Rogers' sight. 'Where did this *Talefan* spring from, Patrick?'

'I took her in Madagascar. Left the *Shadow* with the bulk of my men. My quartermaster with her. I came here with but a handful.'

'And why did you come *here*, Patrick?' pressed his former master. 'Why Providence? If it was to take the pardon you could have done that at any colony. Why here at all?'

'Enough, John!' Rogers declared, his voice pulling Coxon back away from Devlin. 'I take it, pirate, that your ship still has some of this stolen French gold upon it?'

'It has some of it, Your Worship, enough to show my allegiance to yourself and my King,' Devlin gave a side look to Coxon. 'The bulk of it is in other hands now.'

'Wasted on women and drink I shouldn't wonder,' Rogers snorted.

'Hardly wasted, Your Worship,' Devlin grinned.

'Well, never mind,' Rogers sat back. 'John, you will escort Mister Davis back to the *Mumvil* and this *Talefan* and retrieve the gold,' he raised his voice to catch Howell's attention. 'Mister Davis, you are to be rewarded for your loyalty.'

Howell stood, hat in hand.

'You are to be given command of the *Buck*. A fairer sloop, that sailed with me from England and isn't so sullied with this pirate mess. It sailed back the first time at least. You have done well, sir. I should like you to continue the original mission and fetch supplies from Hispaniola and then onto Martinique to do the same for we are now in desperate need.' He had already begun to scratch the order into his log.

Coxon stepped forward and spoke as peacefully as he could. 'With respect, Governor, perhaps Howell is not quite the man to take such a voyage. Given his recent experiences.'

Rogers did not look up from his penmanship. 'He has captured a pirate, overturned a mutiny and returned with a hold of gold. Should I throw him in a cell perhaps, John?'

Coxon started a little and stabbed a finger at Devlin, his voice rising, 'I know *this* man, sir, and I would ask you not to measure him by the state of his clothes or the accent of his voice or the company he keeps but more . . .' he began to flush, feeling the focus of the whole room upon him. Rogers looked up.

'How should I estimate him, John?'

Coxon leant on the desk over Rogers' writing hand. 'By the moment when you first saw him and the hair stood up on the back of your neck.' He straightened. 'I would appreciate it, Governor, if you would register for the record that I recommended the hanging of this man.'

'I will note it, John,' Rogers continued to write. 'However, it is my duty here to reinforce the King's Act and in my considered opinion it would benefit that act if a man like Devlin were to bow to it. It may encourage others equally notable to do the same. To see value in its peace. I wouldn't be surprised to see even Blackbeard follow him to these shores after such an announcement.'

Devlin bowed, 'We can only hope, Your Worship.'

'In the meantime, take him to a cell below. Increase your patrols of the shores if you wish. Mount yourself upon my battlements with spyglass all day and keep an eye out for his ship. Do whatever you feel is appropriate, with my full warrant.' He put back his pen and stood. 'Gentlemen, that is all. I am retiring for dinner. The pirate Devlin will sign the proclamation in the morning. I will have my clerk convene the town for the occasion.' He moved away from his desk and tipped a hand to Howell. 'Congratulations, *Captain* Davis, I will have your papers drawn up also. That is all gentlemen, that is all.'

Howell bowed until Rogers left the room then ducked his way out, avoiding everyone's looks, Captain Finch's most of all, and made for the stairs and the relief of the outside.

Finch followed, watching Howell's heels kicking down the stone spiral steps. Coxon, Devlin and the two soldiers were alone.

Coxon wiped his brow of sweat, and replaced his hat. 'Bring him to the cells,' he ordered. 'And watch him.' He swept out of the room.

Devlin resumed his close position to the soldier at his right. Elbow, shoulder and foot touching to an uncomfortable closeness. The soldier stepped back.

'You take him down, Jim,' the soldier's voice a tremor to his mate. 'I'll watch his back.' He snapped up his musket at half-cock taking care not to touch any part of the pirate with his weapon, then followed carefully, his musket at the pirate's spine, and listened to Devlin talking about ghosts and dead men all the way down the stairs to the gaol.

Chapter Thirty-Two

'I've known worse,' Dandon remarked, wiping the mould from his coat after he had foolishly leant against the cool walls of his cell. He removed the garment and folded it carefully on the bench that would also be his bed. He tended to his wrists where the chains had chafed and listened to the collection of footsteps echoing from the stairs without.

There were six cells in the base of the tower, below the level of the town yet still high above the harbour, but with no grill to enjoy the view. The cells circled the walls.

In an alcove at what should have been one corner spiralled the stone steps to the upper storeys, and through Dandon's wrought-iron door he observed them for any descending sound or flickering lantern.

The soldier who had shoved him into his new home informed him that he should be honoured to be gaoled so. Most other drunken locals were interred in the wooden barracks. The cells were for the condemned of old, and that odour was the last reminder of the fort's Spanish past. Dandon was alone in his; Hugh Harris and John Lawson shared a cell; and the other two, Ben Rice and Adam Cowrie, younger hands no more than forty years between them, shared another.

They had scraped their way through the battle on the *Talefan* and now sobriety exhibited to them the clarity of their fate. The scratchings on the walls from men long dead prophesied too late to mend their ways and left them sitting silent and still, not caring for the yells of the others, as their captain entered the dark confinement with his armed company.

'Ho! Patrick!' Dandon yelled through the iron weave of his door. 'Could they not find a rope big enough for your head there, Captain?'

Hugh Harris chimed in. 'I've saved you a room next to mine, Cap'n. Hoping you didn't tell them you could walk through walls!'

In the centre of the stone quarters a square table and chair formed the station of the guard, who could see all the cells from his chair, and likewise the prisoners could watch him like an actor upon a stage. He was a skinny man, like every lobster Devlin had ever seen, not like the puffed up swollen marines who could blow you over. These were slivers of men, chipped off London's walls.

'Take out your pockets,' the wretch rasped as Devlin's escort brought him to the edge of the table. Awkwardly, with the chains, the waistcoat was emptied: a meerschaum pipe, hinged brass tobacco box, tinder box with lens. No coin, patches or cartridges. No knife, either. Devlin had not been without a knife since he was nine. Now he had not even a gully blade to eat with. He was less than a boy now. They ran hands over his belt and sash for the bulge of something, anything.

'Take off your boots,' the voice rasped again and Devlin did so, shaking them upside down to reveal no hidden weapons. With a nod to the right, leaving him nothing but his boots in his hands, he was walked to his cell.

Dandon and Hugh could not see each other, their cells sharing a wall, only the fists of the other as they hung onto their cell doors and waited. Their captain would do something. Any moment now.

The cell was unlocked. The soldiers tightened their grip on their muskets as the guard took Devlin's chains and slowly removed the makeshift manacles.

'Thanks,' Devlin said, his arms lighter with freedom, and he stepped in under the stone lintel.

Confidence and cruelty flooded back to the one who had struck Devlin before. He raised his musket again and rammed Devlin's shoulder, tripping him into his cell as the door slammed with a throw and the three padlocks were clicked shut in seconds by a well-practised hand.

The lobster stood in front of the door, judging the distance for a hand grab from the man within. 'I thought you were going to kill me if I touched you again, dog?' he sneered and spat at Devlin's feet.

Devlin rubbed his wrists and rolled his shoulder through the pain. He looked past the soldier, as if he could see to the ocean beyond the walls.

'I *have* killed you,' he said flatly. 'Spend all your coin tonight. Find a woman.'

There came the click of the musket's dog-head pulled back and Dandon and Hugh shook at their iron doors with cries for quarter.

'*Enough!*' The bellow from John Coxon at the steps made the soldiers jump away from the cell. Dandon and Hugh held their breath as they watched him approach. 'Get away from him!' Coxon scowled. 'Back to your posts!' He strode forward and was on them in three steps. 'Away with you. Wherever you should be. This man will be under my command.' The two lobsters beat away, back up the stairs; the guard saluted and returned to his table. Coxon looked briefly into the cell and called back the guard, his voice too low for Dandon and the others to hear. 'Get some supper.'

He pressed a reale into the man's clammy hand. 'I'll watch them.'

The guard passed an eye over Coxon's pistol in his belt and the hilt of his sword. The captain breathed over him. 'Two minutes,' he whispered.

'Aye, sir,' and the man ducked away to the mess upstairs, where a mug of small beer and a plate of cheese awaited him.

Coxon looked at the pirates hanging off the doors opposite, pacing in front of them as he spoke. 'Without your steel and pistols you seem much smaller, gentlemen. Almost like good citizens.'

'Come closer and I'll show you how good I am, Cap'n,' Hugh Harris growled.

Dandon raised a finger through a square of his door, 'And I tend to carry neither, Captain Coxon, as is my wont. I prefer much subtler methods if you recall.'

'Of course you do, surgeon.' He whipped back to Devlin's cell, close to the door where Devlin joined him, both leaning in to whisper as if merely partners at cards.

'I promise you Sarah died of the fever, Patrick. And before she did, she entrusted me with your secret. I reckon two thousand pounds' worth, what say you?'

'About that I'd say, John.' Devlin gripped the iron door, bringing his mouth closer. 'And what are you to do with it?'

'The rest of it is aboard the *Talefan*?'

'Perhaps,' Devlin cocked his head, judging Coxon's voice, which held a different tone from that he recalled of his old master. It was the tone of gold rattling in a pocket.

'Or perhaps a large portion with that Howell Davis? I have sent him and his men to bring your load in. But I might order the *Mumvil* to be searched also. Just in case. And whatever he might carry to the *Buck*.'

'What are you after suggesting, John?' Devlin leant back, his voice louder.

'I *suggest*,' Coxon moved closer in, almost biting the bars with his bitter words, 'that Howell Davis is not the valiant hero that he is sketched to be. I suggest that you were coming back for your gold and that Davis did not capture you. He is *with* you. I know it. And a day will tell it I'm sure. But there is something I am missing. I have taken your gold, but I can feel my own skin crawling and telling me that there is something afoot here, Patrick.'

Devlin let go the bars, falling back, cocksure as if the future were only his to know. 'And what of you, John, this past year? I sent you back in shame to your masters yet you turn up here under Woodes Rogers, no less. And all the pirates pardoned, and Providence a colony as bright and English as Bermuda, although covered in shit and salt. And me but one of the flies upon it. Shall we not tell Rogers about the gold now? Together like the good friends that we are?'

Devlin's rising smile stopped as the walnut butt and brass cap of Coxon's pistol rattled through the crossed bars of the cell. A small pistol, but its presence felt like a battering ram through the bars.

'Take it,' Coxon said coolly. 'Take it now. I offer it. I'll say you wrestled it from me. You've done that before, remember? The guard will be back soon and you can free yourself. And your men.'

The others had seen the pistol lift and twist between the bars, but the words were dim and they strained against the iron to hear. Devlin looked down at the beckoning weapon – as sure a key to his cell as if he had forged it himself.

'What goes on, John? Do you think I am hard enough to kill my own men and a dozen more just to get here under some ruse? Pretend to be brought to justice? Can you not imagine that I am simply caught by a crew that bested me? Or does it rile you that a fool like Davis bested me when you could not?'

'Take the pistol. It's a simple test. I give you the chance to escape. On my own head.'

'But why, John? I am caught and barred. What harm am I to you, now?'

'You won't take it?' Coxon edged the weapon further in, its steel scraping over the ironwork. Devlin backed away more, his face now in shadow, his palms up in retreat.

'As I thought,' Coxon dragged the weapon clear. 'There is more to come.' He brought the weapon up, twisted it in one casual movement, and aimed through the mesh of iron to the trapped man in the cell. 'If I can't hang you for the sake of others in their ignorance . . .' He thumbed back the hammer suddenly, held his breath and fired before Devlin could move.

The head flashed into the pan with the spark of an empty charge. A candle snuff of smoke between them and nothing more. No bullet. No death. Just answer enough for Coxon to finish his sentence grimly.

'Now I know it. I can prepare.'

He looked no longer into the cell and buried the pistol back in his belt, ignoring the jeers to his left and barging past the guard returning with his pewter mug and muslin-covered plate.

The *Milford* and the *Delicia*. Enough. More than a match. The night was coming in. And it would soon be dark enough for shadows to be upon the waters.

Chapter Thirty-Three

Eleven of the Clock

*I*srael Hands helmed the skiff. The small single-masted boat towed behind Blackbeard's *Adventure* was now free. She was fast and nimble enough to carry him and Palgrave Williams around the north shore of Providence and into Nassau harbour. The *Adventure* with Blackbeard still aboard lay anchored at Goulding Cay at the island's most western point, and would wait the night out until the skiff returned, with or without Palgrave, depending on how well he had played his part, or how much Israel believed he had.

Palgrave studied the young man with the handlebar moustache and bare chest. Israel lounged against the tiller, his eyes fixed on the horizon and looking straight through Palgrave, occasionally checking the sail as she luffed under the slight wind but leaning back lazily for the most part, his left hand tapping out a rhythm against his belt, never far from the pull of his pistol or his knife should Palgrave have a mind to dance.

Palgrave settled back and watched the black coastline crawling by, belying the swift weaving of the boat. Dark now, past eleven at least, the sky a blue-black under a quarter-moon, the island darker still, her palm trees towering over the beaches silhouetted against the night.

Palgrave had no weapons and carried only the leather satchel he had first set out with three years ago with Sam Bellamy and their dreams of treasure hunting amongst the sunken wrecks of the Spanish Main. That seemed a time ago now. He wondered if his wife had remarried and if he might ever return to the Rhode Island colony – if he might ever return alive anywhere – as he took in the dark man at the stern of the boat.

There are those who might also wonder why a forty-year-old man, a respectable goldsmith with a dutiful wife and two young children, would suddenly throw in all he had and follow the life of a pirate and rover, having never before trod upon the ocean.

To Palgrave and thousands more it had always been simple: I might be a millionaire today or dead tomorrow. *Hoy por mi, mañana por ti.* Today me, tomorrow thee. The beating of his heart beneath his chest was enough, even with the fear that charged the air around him this night.

An hour later and Israel had brought the skiff around Long and Silver Cays and through the sleeve between the harbour and Hog Island, the four-mile stretch of land that kept the warships out. The courting cries of the *cochons-marron* howled out over the bay from the forested island, breaking the cold silence between the two men, and the soft pulse and bounce of the thimble jellyfish eerily lighted their way into shore.

Palgrave was encouraged by their degree of cooperation in mooring the boat to the jetty; Israel had even put out a friendly hand to assist Palgrave as he disembarked.

I am not old, he thought. *I am not dead. I was a pirate with Black Sam Bellamy. I am the most wanted man in America. Who will remember the name* Israel Hands *when he is dead?*

His confidence shrivelled as Hands pricked Palgrave's potbelly with his dagger's tip. 'Remember I'm here, Palgrave, waiting for you.' He nodded down the wooden jetty to the beach and the burning brazier with two soldiers shuffling around it. 'You mind that.'

Palgrave tipped his hat and clopped off across the planks, leaving the smell of the pirate behind with the skiff.

The brazier's glare destroyed what little night vision the soldiers guarding the beach might have enjoyed. A whale could have beached and they would not have seen it; thus they jumped as Palgrave stepped out from behind a curtain of black and swept off his hat.

'Whence came you?' one of them squeaked, his musket rattling.

Suddenly breathless, Palgrave gave his speech to the private.

'My name is Palgrave Williams. I am late of Black Sam Bellamy's crew. One of his commanders. I come to give myself up to Governor Rogers. I come to take the pardon of my King.'

Chapter Thirty-Four

*T*he guard's charges were quiet. The cells were for the condemned, and the condemned of the colonies had nothing left to sign to gain their freedom. They were always quiet.

It had been hours since Coxon had quit the cells but would be at least another two before the man was relieved. He sat at his table, his cheese and beer long gone, and smoked his third pipe of the evening, all from Devlin's tobacco. It was smoother than the Bermuda sweepings he could normally afford.

'Hey!' Hugh Harris hung his arms through his cell and whistled. 'If there ain't no belly timber for us, lobster, how's about some tobacco? Just a bowl or two for me and Lawson here, eh?'

'Quiet, filth,' the guard leant back on his chair. 'Bad enough I'm in here with you, I don't have to hear you an' all.'

'Aye,' Hugh snapped back. 'Reckon it's probably only a magistrate's mistake that you ain't in here too, mate. What happened? Too scared to hang?'

'Not stupid that's all, filth.' He grinned through his pipe over his shoulder to Hugh.

'Aye, you are. All lobsters are. That's why you're lobsters. Can't tie knots.'

'Least I ain't the one waiting to hang. Now quiet down, filth.' But in truth he enjoyed the exchange and the baiting.

Adam Cowrie was now at his bars, a face not yet twenty, younger even than the lobster. 'Why would they hang us? We're taking the pardon ain't we?' Despite the warmth of their prison his voice had a chill, a cold breath.

The guard looked at the boy. He knew the look behind the eyes and remembered it on himself more than once. He raised his voice wickedly for them all. 'Oh, your cap'n be taking the pardon, sonny. Ain't no use in the rest of you. I reckon "Old Rusty Guts" is up to about twenty of you hanged already. And *they* had taken the pardon. How do you favour he feels about them's just arrived all covered in blood?'

'Reckon he fears us,' Harris laughed.

Dandon's voice whispered from his door. 'Did you say you were not stupid, soldier?'

'Aye, ponce. I ain't as stupid as you lot anyways.'

'*Comprenez-vous le francais*?' Dandon asked.

The soldier swung his head to Dandon, the pipe hanging off his lip.

'*J'ai pensé autant*,' Dandon said, 'I thought as much.' He shouted in French across the gaol to Devlin in his cell. 'So, Patrick,' he winked at the soldier and then aimed his voice over him. 'Does all go well? Are we ahead yet?'

Devlin came to his door. 'All goes well enough, my friend,' he yelled back, even affording a Brittany accent.

'What occurred above?'

'It is here, Dandon. In Rogers' chambers. The Chinese gun.'

'Ho,' Dandon clucked scornfully. 'Then all we need to do is walk out of here, carry it out from under the governor's nose and swim with it upon our backs to Charles Town.' Dandon waved a hand to the direction of the stairs. 'After you, Captain.'

The soldier looked back and forth between them, unsure whether this exchange meant trouble or not. Being unable to follow the conversation afforded him some consternation. Devlin, unused to Dandon's sarcasm, shot him a dark look back across the room.

'I got us here. The *Shadow* is coming. Bill is to look for the *Talefan*. He may even be here by now.'

'And then? I see tomorrow as uncertain for us even though Howell will do well with our gold and Coxon with the rest of it.' He kicked his feet as cockroaches as large as eggs scuttled across his shoes.

'Do you not trust me, Dandon? I thought you wanted the game, as I recall, back in that tavern in Charles Town?'

'I prefer it when the cards are more in my favour, Captain.' He slunk back into his cell.

Devlin spoke in English for all to hear, 'I did what I had to do. To save our six lives.'

He resumed his French for Dandon, no longer visible to him, recounting how he had bargained with Howell to save any further whittling of both crews. That Howell could take their gold to bring them into Providence. Howell to be his own captain. Have his own ship and theirs. But warned that the *Shadow* was behind them over the horizon and would not take kindly to any other course if Howell did not comply.

Coxon would at least not find all the gold but just enough to appease Rogers. Howell had his anchor cable and buoys hung 'apeake', straight down and tight to the hull, with the gold beneath the *Mumvil*'s keel.

Dandon reappeared, his French now coarse and bitter. 'And just what of the *Shadow*, Patrick? Two warships stand off without. A garrison of soldiers is here within and us all lost as much as Peter Sam.' The others looked up at the sound of the quartermaster's name.

The soldier had heard enough. He sprung up, his musket at his hip and pointing into Dandon's cell. 'That'll do! No more dago talk, the lot of you, so help me!'

Dandon lifted his palms apologetically. Devlin carried on, in English. 'Trust Black Bill like you do me, lads, and Coxon to give us a hand. He's to take one of the ships out on patrol. He told me himself. Bill will see the *Delicia*'s petticoats long before they see him. He has his orders, long agreed.'

He thought back to the last time he had shaken hands with Bill, aboard the *Shadow*, climbing down into the boat to row to the *Talefan*. Bill had confessed to him how he and Peter Sam had almost changed course a year ago at The Island. Almost left Devlin and the others to their fate. The words almost whispered themselves off his lips but he held them in: *But you came back, Bill. And you would again.*

'Don't fret, lads. This is an English cell with fine Englishmen to look after us. What more could an Irishman want?'

The soldier listened and took in carefully the words of the pirate who ignored the loaded musket just yards from him. 'That's better,' he said, and returned to his seat and waited for the end of his watch.

John Coxon had paused. Just for a moment he queried the reason and sense of removing the *Milford* to trawl the coast, but in passing the *Delicia* at rest two miles west from Dick's Point, blocking the entrance to the harbour, watchful and serene, his resolve became certain. He thought on the *Shadow*. Her three hundred tons would keep her out of the harbour and her broadside was no threat to the twenty eighteen-pounders per side boasted by the *Delicia*.

Coxon sent one boat to the *Delicia*, a sail-cloth packet accompanying her, informing Captain Gale, now commanding Rogers' guardship, of the need to test the eyes of his starbolins that watch for sight of the pirate.

A cable length away, south of *Delicia*'s lee, Coxon rowed the six hundred feet to the *Milford*. Urgently, on arrival, almost before the whistle had stopped piping him aboard, he began poring over his map of Providence and the islands. He began to imagine what he would do, where he would creep ashore in the middle of the night.

The soundings gave limited service to a large ship. It was too dangerous to come in from the south. The only landable shore lay on the west coast but between it and Nassau was nothing but almost sixteen miles of jungle and swamp with a massive lake in its centre.

He placed a finger on the map. He was alone and took conference only with his own intelligence and the spectre of Devlin plotting over his shoulder.

So, a ship could anchor west at Goulding Cay and row in but the jungle would make a heavy passage. His heart beat faster as he ran his divider along the points and cays of the north shore.

There were beaches aplenty north and enough low ground for a landing party to march perhaps four or five miles to come in behind the town. He poured a draught of Madeira sack. He would point his bow west and follow the shore, at least two miles out to be certain of missing the reefs and beds, making sure to sound all the way. His pencil scraped in his shaking fingers.

He would patrol past Goulding's Cay and Northwest Point, and maybe find them there or carry on further north to North Cay and then back again. And again, and again, until they came.

He swallowed his wine and twirled his divider over the map, stepping along the shore, adding the distance and already picturing the best sail to set.

Thirty-two miles would bring him to North Cay. It would have to be four knots at night for safety and the lowest profile. He snapped open his watch: it was after eleven already. By six bells, seven o'clock in the morning, he would have made his first pass of North Cay. He clapped the watch shut.

At worst, thought Coxon, he was overreacting to the presence of his old servant. The land was protected by a hundred soldiers and twice as many militia. The island had lost the *Rose* and the *Shark* but the *Milford* and *Delicia*, both fifth rates, could hold fast. At best he was providing much needed extra duty for the idlers his *Milfords* had inevitably become over the past months.

He stepped briskly out onto the night-deck, almost into the back of Sailing Master Halesworth, and began snapping orders to his lieutenants who, fresh from their cots, were still pulling on their coats and patting down their hair.

Whistles blew and brails shook free from cleats and pins – the deck alive, a street-market of shouts and tramping feet. Coxon walked up to the quarterdeck and waited for the capstan's bars below to wind them away and free.

There was no harm in a little patrol. Perhaps it would prove a waste of time but perhaps not. It would be just enough exercise to shake the land from his coat anyways. But Devlin had arrived. Again on a smaller ship, as before. He and that doctor, and the *Shadow* nowhere in sight. All as before. As on The Island where Devlin had trumped him before. Never again.

The *Milford* sighed reluctantly as she lurched out of a dream and more shouts came from the fore, but Coxon was now looking out over the stern back to the dim light of the round fort sitting above the town, north of the harbour.

He was sailing away. Away from Devlin and the gold that he had still not settled on. He was leaving the governor of New Providence, Eleuthera, Harbour Island and Abaco alone with the pirate Devlin. But with one hundred soldiers, two hundred militia and two warships with two hundred and fifty men.

Nevertheless, alone with the pirate Devlin.

He sipped the coffee that his valet, Oscar Hodge, passed into his hand. He had missed something, he was sure of it. Something in Devlin's grin as always told him so. But he could not just sit and wait for the other shoe to drop. The *Shadow* would be somewhere. He stared on at the old Spanish tower as it withdrew slowly, until the light from her windows merged into one brilliant red, sparkling jewelled eye watching him leave.

Woodes Rogers leant back in his chair. 'I am intrigued, Mister Williams. Go on with your proposal.' Despite the hour Rogers had not retired for the evening, his hours of sleep engaged instead with the letters from merchants who were reporting an increase in Spanish and French activity around the islands – dangerous reports and uncomfortable reading now that the new war was spreading and any admiral worth his salt could see Providence as a watch-tower for Florida and the supply route to the Mediterranean. The only good news from his own island was that the pineapple they had brought with them was prospering. Conversely, the new populace was wilting with the humours of the fever. This Palgrave Williams had offered a welcome distraction when Rogers' secretary had brought the stranger into his office.

Palgrave swallowed hard, relieved that he had made it thus far without being removed. 'As I said, sir, I can put up papers of ownership that will confirm that the gun belongs to me, but in light of my past endeavours I am willing to forego that ownership, which as you see by the receipt I have furnished, is worth a substantial sum, if you will allow me to retrieve the letters that are inside.'

Rogers peered dubiously at the receipt from Heston's auction house. 'This could all be forged of course. You are infamous in the colonies for being one of Bellamy's commanders. Suppose this is all some trick that is not apparent to me now, but for which I will suffer later? And what is Blackbeard's interest in all of this?'

Palgrave stepped forward nervously. 'No trick, Your Worship.' He drew from his satchel a square folded packet. 'I have here a letter signed by Captain Teach himself in which he swears to give himself up to the council in Charles Town, to where he will sail immediately if I afford him the letters forthwith.' He flopped the packet down before Rogers who unfolded it carefully.

'And you are to remain here? Once these letters are passed over?'

Palgrave confirmed that he was to take the Act of Grace and willingly put himself to the mercy of Rogers' governorship.

'And what do I stand . . . what does the *Crown* stand to gain from allowing such an odd transaction?'

Palgrave's eyes had wandered to the Chinese gun lying innocently beneath the sacks and discarded articles in the darkest corner of the room. 'You, sir, stand to gain an ornamental object of great historical value. An object that Heston's sold to me for fourteen hundred pounds that I will sign over to you. You gain the fact that myself, who has eluded the best of the King's men, chose to surrender to your grace above all others. And that the scourge of Blackbeard will come to an end also, as that paper testifies, for the same reason: your great stature among these islands.'

Rogers hummed thoughtfully over the hand of Blackbeard on the paper before him. 'These "letters" that you prize have some value to yourself and Teach that I am not to be a party to?'

'They are letters of property from my father, he who was Attorney-General for the Rhode Island Plantation. I bargained with Teach that they would be his if he gave me passage to your protection. Teach too has seen that there is no long future to be had in piracy. He wishes to take the pardon as well as I.'

'And Teach? Can he not surrender to me directly?' Rogers began to bloom under the thought of having Devlin, Teach and Williams all take the Act of Grace in one day. His image of the mass of raised eyebrows in Whitehall caused his crooked jaw to drool.

'Teach fears that not all his men will take kindly to . . . surrender. He does not wish to bring any untoward danger to the island, especially as it has such a history with his men. He also has his . . . wives to consider. Better to take care of them on the mainland.'

'Ah yes,' Rogers had just come to that very line. 'Pity. I should like to have laid eyes on the man.'

He stood, the receipt for the gun and Blackbeard's affidavit in his hands. 'Your offer is a sound one, Mister Williams.' He strode around his desk and to the broken windows to look out over the slumbering town. 'Sound but not strictly fair.'

Palgrave followed Rogers' back. 'Sir?' he asked tentatively.

'My own thoughts are that I already have this gun as part of my lawful and appointed estate. *And* your letters within it. I also have you, Williams, within my jurisdiction, without the need for bargaining, for a hanging awaits those who do not voluntarily take the Act of Grace.' He turned from the window and looked at the Chinese gun, wiping his jaw with his lace cuff as he meandered to his desk. 'It seems the only thing I do not have is Teach. And if he truly wishes to "settle down" as you say, I'm sure I will have even him soon enough.' Rogers plucked up a small bell from the desk, dropping the papers as he did so.

The bell rang, tolling for Palgrave Williams. Rogers sat and waited for the guards to come, emoting a determined speech. 'I have sailed the world several times, Mister Williams, captured treasure galleons, sacked the city of Guayaquil. Had my jaw shot out, and part of my foot, in battle. Seen my younger brother killed before me in the same. I am here for a reason, Mister Williams. And I do not bargain with pirates.'

The door flew open and with a wave of Rogers' hand Palgrave was clasped hard between two boulders of men. 'Take him down with the others to the cells. He can sign in the morning with Devlin. And send four men to the harbour. This man had a boat waiting for him.'

Palgrave looked at the soldiers holding him. Such a long time coming but one day expected. This was the day. He appealed with a logic that would have stayed most men's hands.

'But, Your Worship, if I do not return Teach will know! He will come!'

Rogers was unmoved. 'Then he will come. It is known that he no longer commands four hundred men. Nor his French Guineaman bastardised with cannon. I think we can manage if Teach's feelings are hurt.'

The door closed, smothering Palgrave's protesting cries. Rogers flicked idly at the promise from Blackbeard and at Heston's receipt as the cries echoed away. It would be quite a feather in his cap for Devlin and Palgrave Williams to sign the act. The others could hang whilst Coxon was on his wild goose chase hunting for Devlin's frigate.

He dabbed away the spittle from his chin and rose to take a more curious look at the Chinese cannon in the corner. The red eye of the dragon seemed to be beckoning him closer. A bell in the square below rang out twelve times and the hollow bawl of the Charley announced that all was well. For an hour past at least.

Rogers surveyed the heap of nonsense piled around the gun, weighing the effort against the hour with a yawn. He settled for the morning to closer study the clay seal for there was time enough yet. The day had been long and there was the prospect of Devlin, Palgrave, and maybe even Blackbeard on the morrow. Aye, a long day well ended. All was very much well.

Chapter Thirty-Five

Quarter of the Hour of Midnight

'What's this?' The guard held up between pinched fingers the small vial of orange liquid that he had plucked from Palgrave's satchel.

'It is an elixir, sir. A compound for my own use. Particular problem of mine.' Palgrave watched the guard remove the glass stopper and reel from the fume with his eyes smarting. 'A potent bowel discharger, sir. But most foul in nature.'

'You can keep it, mate,' the guard gave it back to him and rifled his way through the rest of the satchel as Palgrave observed the eyes looking upon him from the cells circling the scene around the table.

Palgrave gripped the vial in his hand and paid no attention to the words from the guard as he fired a trio of questions to the soldiers accompanying him.

'What's he doing down here anyways? Why ain't he in the barracks? Ain't I got enough to bother me?'

'Governor says so,' the grimier of the two escorts declared. 'He's to sign in the morning with that Devlin. Something queer going on, I says.'

The guard snorted in agreement as he returned to the bag. 'No weapons. No knife even. An apple, pencil, compass, leather gloves, pennyworth of paper.' The guard dropped the satchel to the table scornfully. 'No purse. Travel light don't you?' Silence. The other soldiers by Palgrave's side elbowed him.

'I came to surrender to the governor, nothing more.'

The guard shoved the satchel back at him and picked up a pen. 'What's your name, patroon?'

'Williams. Palgrave Williams.' To his left he saw one of the inmates suddenly jerk at the mention of his name. The guard scribbled the name as best he could, his hand pausing slightly as some remembrance of it flitted across his mind, its importance lost as he concentrated on his spelling.

The trio ushered Palgrave to the cells, away from Devlin's corner. The guard glanced once into Dandon's cell, dismissed the gold-capped smile as undeserving of company and wheeled Palgrave away to join the young and quieter prisoners, Rice and Cowrie. The guard whistled the soldiers away to their duty.

'You'll do better than this lot, patroon, anyways.' He slammed the door and began the neat securing of the locks as he continued. 'You'll be free tomorrow with that Devlin over there,' he cocked his head behind him to the man who had visibly recognised his name. 'This lot will hang. It'll be a silver oar for them in the morning!' The gaoler's reference to the traditional procession of a pirate to his gallows carrying a mock silver oar brought a wicked laugh from his fellows.

He strutted to his desk shouting for all to hear. 'The *great* pirate Devlin!' he mocked. 'Brought to me with a broken ship, five men and nothing else!' He sat down and helped himself to more of Devlin's tobacco. 'I heard you had a frigate and a hundred men. Richer than the pope you were. Pirated your way from Maracaibo to China. Where's it all now then eh, Paddy?' He chortled into his pipe as he puffed it into life. 'Bloody bog-trotter,' he smirked, then snapped upright to the sound of a coin chiming in Devlin's cell as it chinked against the wall.

The pipe drooped as he looked at Devlin sitting on his bench rolling a gold coin between his fingers and looking to the wall where he had tossed the other. The second coin flew from his fingers and rang around the cell as he tried to land it closer to the wall, the guard's eyes followed its flight. His chair scraped as he rose, mesmerised, but he still remembered to take up his musket.

From across the way Hugh Harris tapped Lawson's arm and grinned. 'Here we go, mate,' he whispered as the pair watched the guard walk over to Devlin's cell.

'Where did you get that?' he demanded, sure that Devlin had emptied every pocket of his clothes.

'King Louis,' Devlin replied as a third coin joined the two others.

Dandon looked over and thought of his own six coins snug in a leather strap sewn inside the rear seam of his waistcoat. He had settled on it being used as a bribe for some breakfast wine but Devlin clearly had other notions.

The guard began to grind his teeth as he blinked at the gold. 'Let me see one of them coins,' he demanded.

Devlin stopped his game. 'You can have one, soldier, if you would bring my lads some beer and bread. Been hours since they ate. Ain't too fair to hang a man on an empty belly.'

The soldier ran his tongue around his mouth. 'Reckon I could manage that, patroon. Give me the coin and I'll make it so.' He lowered his musket to have an open hand towards the bars, not foolish enough to put his palm through. 'Toss it me.'

Devlin closed his fist around the coin, its glint snuffed out. 'Food first. You know the game.'

The soldier stepped back, musket up to his hip, thumb across the dog-head. 'I could come in there and take them all, pirate.'

Devlin stood up slowly, a few good inches taller than even the soldier's hat. 'You could try,' he breathed.

The soldier gripped his musket tighter. 'Reckon I could drop you from here, pirate. Reckon you'd hit the wall like a dead pig from here.'

Dandon hung his arms out of the cell and yelled across helpfully. 'I shouldn't wonder that Governor Rogers would be most pleased with your decision to cancel his famed signing of the pardon in such a manner. Do you not think so, sir?'

The soldier lowered his gun, staring at Dandon for a moment. 'Aye,' he conceded, 'I'll get your plate. My watch is almost done anyhow. No skin of mine.' Without waiting for a word from the cell he made for the stairs, settling in his head that almost three weeks' wages for some bread and beer was more than enough for a bit of his time.

Devlin did not care whether the gaoler was still within earshot and began calling for Palgrave even before the footsteps had echoed away. 'You! Palgrave Williams! I know you. You were one of Bellamy's captains were you not?'

Palgrave came to his door, leaving behind the dour silence of his cell-mates. 'I was, sir. And I gather you are the pirate Devlin, from that gentleman's address?'

'I'm Patrick Devlin,' he rushed out the name, not bothering with any exchange of pleasantries for it would only be minutes before the guard returned and he wanted to waste none of them. 'You're here for the Chinese gun. Who are you with?'

Palgrave reeled a little at the knowledge vouchsafed from across the room. He stammered as he spoke back. 'I . . . I am alone. Why should I not be?'

'You're a pirate, Palgrave. I says you are here with Blackbeard. I knows all about the gun. Knows all about the letters. I'm here for the same and you be sharing a cell with my men.'

Palgrave turned back to the men in the cell with him who winked merrily as Devlin continued.

'You've found yourself in good company, Palgrave, even if it be in a cell. I ask you only this: you know Teach and so do I. Put yourself in my undertakings and know that your throat be safe with me. Or trust Teach, knowing the manner of him.'

Palgrave listened. Confused as he was there was only one fact that the man across the way seemed oblivious to. 'We are both in a cell, sir. We will be free tomorrow to be sure but Rogers knows about the gun, if not its true nature. Granted my future may be safer with you rather than Captain Teach but I am inclined to let the Devil have the matter, sir. I will take the pardon and settle my days here. The destiny I thought I may have had with the gun is too noisy for my temperament.'

Dandon coughed, placed his left cheek against the bars and yelled along the row to Palgrave. 'And how do you suppose that Captain Teach will take the news that you have decided to nestle down under Rogers' breast and not return to his patronage?' He waited a moment for the words to filter across. 'Sometimes the devil you know is not always the prudent choice. I have wagered so myself, sir.'

Palgrave touched his lip and thought on. Aye, he would be free tomorrow but his neck would still ache, even without the prospect of the gallows, from the days he would spend looking over his shoulder and waiting for the slow knock upon his door. The soldiers would have reached Israel Hands and his boat by now. And even if Israel had got away, got back to Blackbeard, then Palgrave would be a lonely man for the last days of his life.

'I will bide with you, Captain Devlin,' he called out. 'If you can grant me some security.' He looked at his companions. 'Besides, I'm sure your men would have it no other way. Tomorrow then, when we are both free, we shall talk on.'

Devlin could hear the footsteps returning. 'My men will be hanged tomorrow. I know men like Rogers. They believe that necks speed men's signatures.'

'And so what else do you suggest, Captain Devlin? What are the letters to you, anyways?'

'I can take care of the guards. I need the letters of the priest to free my quartermaster. No coin in it for me. If you can aid in that I'll be indebted to you. And that ain't a bad credit to have. You came here alone and not to drag a cannon back to Blackbeard. I reckon that bottle of yours discharges more than bowels. What does it do on porcelain?'

Palgrave's voice became lower as the guard tapped back into the room. 'About the same as it does on metal, Captain Devlin.' And all of them stepped back from the bars as the soldier looked at them one by one, placing down the wooden jug and bread, and feeling the unpleasant shiver of silence all around him.

Chapter Thirty-Six

*D*espite what governments and navies hoped was true and represented to their courts, pirates were not the simple opportunists and lucky misanthropes that chanced upon poorly-defended cities and ships at slumber. Apart from gold and whatever pleasures a town offered, the pirates craved and prized one thing above all else to secure their future:

Intelligence.

It was not how many guns and men you had that was important but to know how many guns and men your enemy had. *That* would favour the odds to a successful 'surprisal' at sea or a deadly raid upon a shore.

Days, even weeks, would be spent journeying onto land under cover of night, mapping fortifications, calculating the numbers and watches of soldiers, often kidnapping the odd local fisherman or two and 'questioning' them most thoroughly as to the strengths and weaknesses of their target, until piece by piece a plan became history and the pirates moved on to the next target along the coast, leaving whole countries to lick their wounds.

Time and again the governors of the Americas would question Whitehall as to how, with the vast numbers of patrols, the pirates avoided capture, eluded the largest floating contingent of men ever seen, and managed almost to strangle trade between the North American coast and the motherland; and how the pirates, on the other hand, appeared to suffer no difficulty in finding the merchants, regardless of what latitude they took.

The answer lay in the bottom of the boat paddling its way back to the *Shadow* that night, still paddling even though they were now more than a mile away from their study of the *Delicia*. Oars out of the thole pins of the boat for silent running and the salt-raker at their feet gagged with his own nether-hose to muffle his cries.

The jolly-boat bumped home, the rope was belayed, and the pirates dragged their haul up the ladder to Black Bill waiting by the entry port. They presented the salt-raker as if he were the governor himself, and the terrified man's eyes weaved all about the deck, widening at each dark face that leered back at him. Bill ignored him, pushed him behind for the others to drag him below for preparations, and asked the two kidnappers of what they had seen.

Time enough wasted, Bill decided as he stood over the map of Providence across the table, a soothing pipe steadying his thoughts. It was past one now, four and some hours before dawn, and the night was all he had if the *Shadow* were to remain as her name declared. No lanterns had been lit and dead-lights to the windows shielded Bill's lamp. They lay silent and dark three miles south of the *Delica*'s starbolin watch.

The reconnaissance had provided much vital intelligence. The jolly-boat, its oars paddling in perfect time with the lap of the tide against the *Delica*'s hull, had sallied leisurely past the frigate barely a spit away. The *Delica*'s lanterns around her masts and stern ensured the watch enough night-blind-ness to see nothing but the blanket of darkness wrapped around the gunwale.

The salt-raker, a foot to his throat in the bottom of the boat, had looked up at the giant wall of the freeboard towering above the little boat. Around her closed ports as they drifted beneath seeped out a faint trim of amber light from her lanterns within, and the occasional hacking cough or powerful snore made her appear as a sleeping giant. It would only take one man to open a port for a breath of air or to sneak a pipe and they would be seen but the pirates showed no sign of such worry as they idled past and gathered all they needed to know.

The captured salt-raker confirmed that Devlin's *Talefan* was in the harbour, as much tinder as ship, and that the pirate Devlin had been paraded in the square that very afternoon and was now in the fort's basement gaol along with five of his men.

The jolly-boat had witnessed Coxon's *Milford* sail west and away. If anything were to be done, it had best be now, while the *Delicia* was alone. The *Delicia*, two miles from the harbour to the south, had forty guns. Guns the *Shadow* did not want to see.

Bill listened to Dan Teague report that the *Delicia* would have one hundred and twenty to one hundred and fifty men. They were out-gunned and out-manned. Bill shrugged at this. Had that ever mattered before? Besides, it was not the ship that they wanted.

A little 'woolding' had measured the salt-raker's conviction of his new companions' intentions. Woolding was a favoured pirate torture. The term coined from the act of winding rope around masts and yards to bind them. The hemp rope twisted over his eyes and knotted tighter and tighter to his skull had given the salt-raker bright recollections of a garrison of one hundred men, plus local militia of another two hundred odd ex-pirates and new settlers. The other ships had sailed weeks ago. Only the *Milford* under Captain Coxon and the *Delicia* under Captain Gale remained.

Bill breathed deep on his pipe. He penned a cross where the *Delicia* lay, two miles west of Dick's Point and almost as close as she could get without scraping the shoals. He inked the path of the *Milford*, left two hours ago now according to the men of the jolly-boat, and he estimated her almost at Cay Point. Far west. Out of harm's way. He slipped his divider across the map from their own point and past the *Delicia* to the harbour.

Dan Teague watched him scribbling at the edge of the map but had long given up trying to fathom the depths of the numbers that meant so much to Devlin and Bill. He simply waited for his orders. Eventually Bill's head lifted.

'Why, Dan, do you suppose the *Milford* and Coxon have sailed off west at such an hour?'

Dan shook his head and waited to be enlightened as he knew he would be.

'See, I'm picturing,' Bill's voice rose as his eyes turned misty and he feigned mystical knowledge, 'a conversing with our captain and Coxon. A converse that led Coxon to believe that the *Shadow* was on her way. Now,' he tapped his divider on the map, drawing Dan's eye, 'if you looks at the soundings around the island, and terrible they are too, we all know that the *Shadow* can't sail straight into the harbour. But around the north shore she gets deeper and we could land there.' Dan looked at the wavering lines and numbers that indicated more than shoals. Bill blew smoke over the island like a fog. 'And like Coxon I would have noticed that the west of the island is nothing but jungle and this great lake right in the middle. Take two days to get across to Nassau from the west.

Cap'n Coxon, just as I myself, would see that our girl would have to come in from the north to rescue Devlin. She's no other choice. The *Delicia* guards the harbour from assault from the south.' He dropped the divider with satisfaction and ran his eyes over the map.

Dan looked up, his brow creased. 'But we've come in from the south, Bill.'

'Aye,' Bill seemed pleased with Dan's summation. 'For the moment.'

Dan looked back, still waiting for the order, understanding nothing Bill had said. Bill gripped his shoulder. 'Nassau is on the north-east corner. Why lay a town there, Dan?'

Dully, Dan just stared back. Sometime an order would come. He just had to stand on his patience.

Bill slapped his back. 'The harbour is too narrow and shallow for anything but little'uns! And what makes the harbour so shallow and narrow, Dan?' He did not wait for a reply. 'Hog Island, Dan!' He tapped the sliver of land that sat off of Nassau. 'We can make there! Come in from the east. Harbour behind her and use her like a stepping-stone! Boat around her! I'll be damned if some Spaniard hasn't thought of that before! Sail nor'east away of the *Delicia* protecting the south and old Coxon gallivanting around the north!'

Dan chewed his tongue and seemed to understand. Bill handed him Devlin's letter.

'The note Devlin left us on Dead Man with them *Talefans* is short enough,' he handed it to Dan from his waistcoat. 'Make what you want of it.'

Dan unfolded the paper that had been handed to them at landing on the island among the Exumas. They had expected to find their brethren there. Instead they found only the fifteen men who had welcomed them like old friends, running into the surf to drag in the longboat, and had now signed on willingly. The week on the island had obviously brought on some fine bonding and speculation on the sweet trade. Devlin had a glamour about him after all. But the note was not so welcoming.

We are to make for Providence. Now under king's government. Take these men and give a Louis to each.

Peter Sam is held until I can return to Charles Town.

I intend to surrender to King's Act in order to get aboard Providence. I will need you to get me out again. Look for the Talefan to shore. Make your way into Nassau. Any way that is best suited to the day you find me. Woodes Rogers is governor. I aims to be as close to him as I can, for Peter Sam's freedom lies within the fort where he resides.

You will be expected, as Coxon is also on Providence.

Note only this and plan accordingly:

Peter Sam will be lost if I do not return.

Our gold is in jeopardy now Providence is lost.

Coxon will be looking for the Shadow.

Valentim Mendes waits for me in Charles Town.

Blackbeard is also against.

May the Lord and Saints preserve you, friend Bill.

D.

Dan folded the paper and passed it back, hoping an order would be given in return. When none came he edged towards an opinion.

'I make, Bill, that we would not be welcome in Providence no more.'

'Perfect, Dan,' Bill slapped him hard and rolled up his map. 'Pirates are not welcome in Providence and Coxon is out looking for us and our girl.'

Dan opened his mouth to speak but could find nothing to say. Bill tapped his finger to his head. 'You have to think like the captain, Dan. I'm starting to get the measure of it myself. Come, we've little time to us,' and he pulled Dan out of the cabin with him to summon the men, a fresh drama itching over his skin and coursing through him. The notion of it drew him up like a rope as he barked his orders and men cheered back at him.

In all his years pirating the round, chance had never occasioned Bill to take a whole island before.

Chapter Thirty-Seven

✗

Two of the Morning

*I*t had taken Israel Hands almost an hour to race the skiff back to the *Adventure* and relate his tale. Sitting in the boat, waiting for Palgrave to return, he had seen the rocking lanterns rush towards the jetty and heard the rattle of lobsters' belts and buckles pound across the sand. He sculled the skiff away until he could make a sail and left the soldiers staring after his stern as it vanished in the dark.

Teach looked his panting quartermaster up and down. His eye looked at the thin knee that he had shot a knuckle's worth off some months before when the mood had taken him. Israel dared not lie.

'So, we are betrayed!' Teach bellowed. 'Palgrave saved his own hide rather than take me offer of peace at Ocracock. Bellamy would shiver in his grave. If he had one to own.' He turned to his men, all forty of them waiting for his word, the narrow deck of the sloop bulging with bodies. 'It's two in the morning, lads. Nassau will be sleeping. If Palgrave does not wish to join us with the letters, we'll take them ourselves!' He barged his way along the deck and plucked a dark bottle from the hand of one of the men. 'We'll show good Governor Rogers what we thinks of his pardon! Make all sail! Course north along the shore!'

324

A chorus of cries echoed over the ship as Teach emptied the bottle and threw it at the head of the furthest man. 'Make to, you dogs! An hour will tell all!' He leapt to the fo'c'sle, pulling his cutlass and whacking the back of any sloven not shifting fast enough.

Aqua Regia or 'King's Water' was a goldsmith's tool for thinning and etching in use since the Middle Ages, its discovery encouraging alchemists in the pursuit of the fabled philosopher's stone. It was a substance as common to the goldsmith as his loupe and scales.

Palgrave Williams was a goldsmith before he sailed and he explained all of this to his cell-mates Adam Cowrie and John Rice as he held out the small vial of orange liquid which would kill a man in seconds if he could bear to drink it past the fumes. They looked at the squat portly fellow with new eyes as it dawned on them that the frosted bottle held more power to free them from their current unemployment than either cannon or key.

'My intent was to dissolve the clays that stop the mouth of the Chinese gun but these here locks will fare as well.' He whispered the words, not wishing to catch the ear of the new watch, the unfortunate soldier who had courted Devlin's displeasure and now sat with his back to his cell, whistling softly to himself to show his indifference to the pirate captain's cold stare.

It was two o'clock in the morning, an hour before the 'witching', the three of the clock that mocked the three of the afternoon when Christ breathed his last. This was the hour when men awake doubt the world around them and every sound that shuffles and scrapes is magnified to crick the bones of the neck of him that hears it.

Dandon rested his arms through the lattice of his bars and balefully recited to his gaoler, *''Tis now the very witching time of night, When churchyards yawn and hell itself breathes out Contagion to this world: now could I drink hot blood, And do such bitter business as the day Would quake to look on.'*

'What shite are you raking now, you fuckster?' the soldier bowled back.

'That be Shakespeare, my man. Or as close as I can muster to it. Can you not feel the night around you? These are the last placings of dead men that you guard. Does that not cause you unease?'

The soldier rocked in his chair and fumbled for his tobacco. 'Not as much as you, pirate,' his voice rising gleefully. 'I'm only sorry that I'll be sleeping when you hang.'

The voice rang out behind him. '*I'll* be alive when you wake, soldier.'

The soldier twisted round, his tobacco forgotten. He looked at the man leaning against his cell door. More shadow than form. He thought of a dozen words to throw at the shadow but turned back to fill his pipe in silence. It had only been half an hour since his watch began and the time already dragged.

'Did you find yourself a woman in the time that we've been parted, lobster?' the voice continued.

The soldier ignored him and put his boots up on the table while humming through his pipe. He slammed his feet back to the floor when Hugh Harris banged the wooden jug against the bars.

'Hoy! More beer there, man! Rum if you can! Dying men here!'

'Where'd you get that?' the soldier demanded as he strode to the cell. 'Ain't no beer for prisoners. Where'd you get that jug?' He grabbed the jug and sniffed at it in his investigations.

Devlin tapped a coin against his bars, the sound of gold more distinctive than the closing of a whore's bedroom door. 'I bought it, lobster,' he sang out.

The soldier was drawn to the coin, the jug at his side.

Devlin spoke warmly as he approached, 'Gave your mate one for some beer and bread for my men. The same to you for a bottle of wine or noggin of rum, lobster.'

The soldier slammed the jug on the table and wiped his mouth. 'Let me see that coin, patroon.'

Devlin closed his palm and the gold winked away. 'No spirit, no gold, lobster.'

The soldier grinned. 'Fair play, patroon. I'll sees what I can scurry.' Picking up his musket and keys he jangled his way to the stairs, pausing to call back before he ascended. 'Anything for the great pirate Devlin and his men.' And he chortled his way upwards.

Dandon watched him depart and called across the room. 'Are we in a hurry now, Patrick?'

'Time and tide, Dandon,' Devlin replied. 'Time and tide.'

Half past two. The guards on the beach checked their brazier, sifting embers with their bayonets and sending sparks high into the night to stimulate their spirits a while longer. They had shared tales of the local whores, shared the woes of their tawdry pockets and the foul and venal paths that had brought them to the Caribbean rather than Flanders: a wheel of cheese here, a bit of paid protection there, a transfer hither.

They lay back on the comfortable sands and listened to the surf, waiting for the end of their watch and a few hours of sleep before they could slake their thirst in the taverns again.

They both raised themselves on their elbows at the sound of the surf breaking against wood, then sat up as voices carried from the dark beach. They stood up with their muskets at the sound of boots running towards them and oars being thrown into boats and squinted through the light of the brazier that shortened their vision until a dozen faces blazed into their lit circle of sand.

'Whence came you?' the sentries shouted in automatic response as they fumbled at their muskets.

'Men from the *Milford* and *Delicia*,' someone panted. 'Need to see Governor Rogers.' The man stepped forward and they saw he sported a sailor's black beard, soiled slops and Monmouth cap.

'Cap'n Coxon and Cap'n Gale sends us back to warn the governor.' The sailor pulled off his cap and ushered his men forward. The soldiers took relief in the familiar wide slops and rags of seamen and lowered their muskets.

'What goes on?' one of the sentries asked, seeing more men stumbling forward from the dark. Perhaps twenty now stood in front of him, two boats' worth. 'Coxon and Gale, you say? Warn of what?'

'Aye,' the bearded one mopped his brow. 'Pirates are afoot. Devlin's ship is along the north shore,' he announced, ignoring the shared look between the two soldiers. 'We're to aid in holding the fort. Ten from *Milford*, ten from *Delicia*. My name is William Vernon, bosun's mate. We be yours to command, Corporal.'

'Private Woolcott, mate,' the guard corrected Bill and straightened. 'You say Devlin? From where? From when? Devlin is in the fort. Below in the gaol. Seen him taken there myself.'

Black Bill took the soldier's arm. 'Aye. Reckon his ship has come for rescue. Coxon is giving chase in the *Milford*, as you know. Take us to the fort. An hour or less and they could be on the north beach.'

Woolcott looked around at the belts of the men bulging with cutlass, dagger, belaying pin and pistol. He moved along reluctantly with Bill, protesting that Rogers would be asleep at this hour.

Bill did not stop, half dragging the arm of Woolcott up the beach. 'Your captain will wake him for the word I'm sure, Private. Cap'n Coxon insists. Let us go.' And twenty armed men escorted by two soldiers marched towards the fort.

The lobster returned to the cells, his musket slung. He held a fat green bottle of rum in one hand and in the other some hardtack wrapped in a cheesecloth packet. He dumped his load on the table and ignored the whining from the pirates about the time it had taken him to scrounge such a feast. A stench met him, a fug of urine strong enough to make him pinch his nose closed. 'Jesus lads!' he moaned. 'Piss down the grates why don't you. Stinking in here it is.'

'Just the rum, lobster,' Devlin called out. 'No need for any lip.'

The lobster unfolded the cheesecloth to reveal the biscuits. 'Aye. Rum. For a gold coin I believe we accorded.' He left the table and swung his musket from his shoulder. 'Reckon that the price be higher though,' he stepped closer and lowered the musket to Devlin. 'I'll take any coin you have, Devlin,' then added magnanimously with levelled gun, 'I'll take all you've got to save you paying later.'

Dandon pointed out with exaggerated decorum, as he had to their previous attendant, that shooting the governor's pride and joy before he had a chance to sign the Act would not be received so favourably upstairs.

The lobster spoke slowly. 'Oh, I knows that patroon. But

I reckon "Old Rusty Guts" won't be too fussed about losing one of you lot so much.' He swept the gun round to Dandon, cocking the head back with his left palm. 'Reckon *you* might care though, Cap'n Devlin, if I send this yellow scum to hell early.'

Hugh and the others, Palgrave even, cried out against their latticed doors. Dandon stepped back, finding that his narrow cell gave no shelter from the barrel's eye.

The guard grinned and turned back to Devlin. 'All your coin now, Cap'n, 'fore I drop this mate of yours,' then yelled at the rest to simmer down lest he spoil his shot, his voice just loud enough to cover the dragging scrape of the cell opening behind him.

He rolled his head back to launch into more mockery but his grin disappeared at the sight of Devlin stood outside his cell. The lobster stared into the empty space beyond, as if Devlin would surely still be there.

He brought the gun back, fast he thought, trigger trembling, but still the barrel was grabbed and twisted and plucked like a blind-man's cane from his hands.

The question, '*How?*' almost slipped out but the powerful hand at his throat strangled the word to a gurgle.

He felt his feet leave the floor under the grip as the freed man spoke gibberish at him in his madness.

'*There can be slain,*' Devlin hissed, pulling the guard's face towards him, '*No sacrifice to God more acceptable Than an unjust and wicked king!*'

Dandon cried out from his cell. 'Damn, Patrick! I only gave you that Milton a month!'

Devlin could not hear. His pulse deafened him as he slammed the lobster down on the table, crushing the biscuits beneath his back and puncturing the scrawny neck with the man's own bayonet grabbed from its sheath. As a butcher's boy he had stuck pigs with the same stiff wrist and swift stab that came from the shoulder blade not the end of the knife, and he closed his eyes against the narrow spurt of blood as the red meat burst within.

He pushed the body from the table and took up the rum and drank until his heart begged for a break from the neck of the bottle. The rum sat cold in his empty belly and his drinking arm shook. Devlin watched his hands tremble. He had promised himself less of the rum so to keep strong in mind and body for all their sakes. But some things men cannot drain with water. He raised the bottle again, his eyes on Palgrave standing in front of him, free from his own cell with John Rice and Adam Cowrie, their liberty owed to the timely application of Aqua Regia to the padlocks.

First Palgrave had freed himself when the lobster had mounted the stairs, the acid excreting a noisome redolence not unlike the odour noticed by the late lobster. He had then run across the gaol and burnt through Devlin's locks before returning to his cell just as the footsteps began to echo down the stairs. It had taken less than ten minutes to change their fortunes.

Palgrave looked down at the lobster with the bayonet saluting straight up from his throat. 'Seems I have made a good choice in who is best to secure my future, Captain Devlin.'

Devlin said nothing. He wiped his mouth and picked up the keys from the table and tossed them to Cowrie. 'Get the others out.' Then he picked up the musket and bent to the corpse to pluck the cartouche from its belt.

'Your liquid works well, Palgrave,' he said as he checked the primer on the gun. 'Do you have enough left for the Chinese cannon?'

'Aye, Captain,' Palgrave tapped his satchel affectionately.

'Then we shall go.' Devlin rounded on Dandon. 'Will you be joining us *mon frère*?' he asked sardonically, alluding to Dandon's comments when the doors had first closed. 'Are the cards in your favour yet?'

The sound of jangling keys and falling padlocks rang around the room. Hugh Harris's and Lawson's boots scuffled to their captain's side.

Dandon gave his most effacing gold-capped grin as his shackles were lifted away.

'I would have it no other way, Patrick,' and he stepped to join them.

'Weapons, Hugh,' Devlin slapped Hugh Harris into action. 'Some rope maybe. Make a couple of monkey fists?'

'Aye, Cap'n.' Hugh rushed to the fallen lobster, dragged the bayonet from the throat without a wince at the sucking noise it made and stuffed it in his belt. He flipped the table like a turtle and began wrenching out the legs. 'Reckon these will do better though.' The first leg snapped free and he tossed it to Lawson. Devlin and Dandon left him to it and walked to the base of the stairs. They inched their heads around the corner to check the coast was clear and then followed the spiral steps upwards.

'Seems a longer way up than it was down,' said Devlin.

'Aye, Patrick,' Dandon agreed. 'It always is.' The final sound of wood breaking heralded the others trailing behind them, armed with a hefty wooden club apiece, Palgrave last in the pack with just his stubby fists at the ready.

Sixty worn Spanish steps led to the floor above. They crept close to the curving wall, ducking beneath the lanterns circling the stairwell, Devlin at the front with the musket sniffing ahead.

The arch at the top of the stair loomed suddenly and Devlin's head appeared in an empty corridor. To his left was the windowed passage leading to Roger's rooms, the black door of his office visible forty yards away. Veering away to his right was the passage that looked out to sea and led to the barracks and mess. From above, the petrel's-eye view, the small fort was laid in a scalene triangle. Two round towers hung over the sea with embrasures and fat hungry guns staring out forever, waiting patiently for Drake or Morgan to return. The third tower, square, sitting over the town like a throne and hidden in bamboo scaffolding was the one that the left-hand passage led to – where Rogers' office lay, but more importantly where the Chinese gun lay, and the stairs to the town and the harbour. That was their way out now.

Devlin fell back to his men. 'No guard,' he whispered, the only words the others wanted to hear. From now on they wished every word to be a comforting one. Night and sleep were their stoutest allies: including the militia, there were over three hundred armed men about the town.

'We take the letters then get out of here best we can.'

Palgrave's heart had weakened. Freedom tasted sweeter than danger. 'Hang the letters. Just get us out of here!' He pushed past them all. Devlin pulled him back into place with a snarl.

'Those letters save the life of a man worth more than what they promise, Williams. I don't need you to make the acid work.' He allowed the grinning faces of his men to make his point, and his eyes went back to checking the passage.

'Rogers' bed chamber is also in that tower,' Dandon obliged. 'That would be guarded. As would our exit I'm sure.'

'Aye,' Devlin agreed. 'I wasn't planning on venturing through the barracks neither.' He waved them on and loped into the corridor towards the door, never looking behind. They would follow.

John Hamlin was born in Bath Town in 1696. His father was a tanner and his mother a housemaid. At sixteen John Hamlin had stolen a carter's wheel for a dare and now wore a red coat as punishment. He had not seen his father for six years but had visited seven islands in the Caribbean and had slept with twenty-two women, which to him was more important. He earned fifteen pounds a year but owed twenty-five to the King over the last ten years of his service. In the last month of his night-watch he had succumbed to temptation, lifting a little piece of smoked pork and cheese and a small measure of rum from the mess and keeping it about him, for John Hamlin was a hungry man. The breakfast coffee, biscuits and bread and the cabbage soup for supper were not enough to keep such an ardent man full of lead. So rather than pay for sustenance from the taverns, which would make no hole in his debt, he would sit under the shade of a tree and nibble through his pilfered rations admiring his own cleverness in saving himself a shilling in the right quarter of his life.

The wrong quarter now it appeared, justified or not. Hamlin turned the corner to the passage and fell into a party of seven pirates. He opened his mouth and raised his musket.

And then Hugh was pinching the hair and skull fragments off his makeshift club and wiping his hand on his breeches, the sounds of violence still echoing around the passage as everyone looked down at the breath of the hot blood steaming from John Hamlin's head. Lawson picked up the musket and belly-box of cartridges.

They gathered around the door of Rogers' office, heads

swivelling on the lookout for other wandering souls. Devlin tried the ringbolt lock without success.

'Open it, Palgrave.'

Palgrave nodded and reached into his satchel. Then Devlin suddenly stopped his hand. 'Wait!'

Palgrave watched the plotting behind the eyes. 'Can you ruin the lock as well as burn it through?' asked Devlin.

Palgrave attested that he could, that melting the lock to nothing would be even easier but noted that they would also be locked out of the room as there would be nothing to pull back the lock from its mortice.

Devlin went to the leaded windows, pushed one open and looked out at the scaffolding all around the walls. Planks of wood below the sill formed a walkway that stretched around the fort. To his left he could see Rogers' open office windows. His head came back in. 'No,' he corrected Palgrave, 'we'd be locked in. To it. Burn that lock. We go in by the windows.' Palgrave understood immediately, and pulled on his leather gloves.

Chapter Thirty-Eight

Quarter of Three in the Morning

*T*en minutes from the beach to the fort. Bill Vernon again wiped the sweat from his brow and beard with his woollen cap.

'Wait here, sailor.' The guard held a hand out to the troop. 'I'll fetch Captain Tolliver. He can wake the governor, not I.'

Bill replaced his Monmouth and tapped his forehead. The soldier trotted up the steps to the ground floor barracks. Bill steadied his men who already showed blood in their eyes. One by one he whispered to them, pointing out the tower that the salt-raker had told them was Devlin's gaol, the scaffolding that could be scaled easily and the faint light from Rogers' rooms. They calmed as Bill's patient voice and a twist of tobacco went round the group and he bade everyone follow his lead. Devlin was here and they would get him back even if they had to kidnap Rogers to do so.

Hard jaws bit into the tobacco and deft hands checked the pans of their locks as the captain of the watch stepped out of the fort to meet them, suspicion contemptuously dragging down the corners of his mouth as he looked them over. Bill opened his watch as he moved to meet the captain. A quarter to three. All Godly men were asleep under prayers, Bill consoled himself, his left hand on the hilt of his cutlass. The watch captain must be no saint to land such a duty. Only the wicked trod the earth at such an hour. That would make their work easier.

Two muskets. Four table-leg clubs. One bloodied bayonet. One room. For the second time in his life Devlin controlled a room. The first had been a year ago, on The Island, in the stockade, just himself and Dandon, and John Coxon at the door. He was holding onto a tiny corner of the world and waiting for the door to be stoved in. Waiting for the fire and the blood. He turned from the window where he could see the group of men huddled below. He did not share the view with his companions.

Dandon and Palgrave had the cannon upended. A smidgeon of acid had been poured and was eating through the white mass of porcelain and oysters sealing its mouth. All the pirates except Hugh, who licked his lips anxiously under his blood-caked face, held cuffs and linen to their noses against the stench of rotten sea-life and ammonia that fogged the room, their eyes darting to one another as the cannon mouth hissed.

'How's it coming?' Devlin asked, closing the window despite the foetid atmosphere.

Palgrave nodded as the porcelain and shell cracked and fell into the barrel. Dandon raised his eyes to heaven trying to hold the gun steady.

'Christ! Put it down!' Devlin ordered, suddenly picturing the caustic mix eating through the bamboo tube inside. The whole daring escapade would be ruined in a moment and Peter Sam's throat as good as cut.

Carefully they lowered the gun to the rug floor. Rogers' clock ticked on his mantel. Quarter to three. No time to die. Certainly not sober. Discovery of the dead lobster was still more than an hour away, the end of his watch being at four, but the soldier in the passage with the leaking skull merely waited to be stumbled upon.

The Chinese gun vomited onto the rug, which burnt instantly with the spew. Palgrave tugged his gloves on tighter and gingerly lifted the rear of the gun. Until that point, even to him, the letters of Father Entrecolles had been but a legend, the gun he had taken with Sam Bellamy the previous April just an old silent scrap of bronze, the crouching dragon atop a portent, a promise.

Dandon grabbed some parchment from Rogers' desk and placed it beneath the lip of the mouth. With Palgrave struggling two of the others helped him drag and shake the gun until, like a tongue, the fat bamboo tube slid out onto the paper. Six inches in diameter, a foot in length. Still green and fresh, sealed tight as it was for at least five years in the gun by anybody's reckoning, the tube further sealed by a hardened cork stopper.

Devlin reached for it, was first to hold it. He recalled Coxon telling him how Dampier's memoirs were discovered just so, sealed by cork in a bamboo tube. The mariner and navigator had been well aware that the end of his life would likely be occasioned by the sea, but at least his writings would remain dry.

'Peter's freedom, lads,' he shook the tube in front of him. 'Come from Madagascar to here. For this.' Their answering grins stayed thoughts of the danger ahead. They had done what was required and found a back door from failure. There was always a way out, always a way to stay dry. Even the dead they had lost along the way were now smiling down on them – these last survivors of the *Talefan*, their brothers from the *Shadow* still there, still alive. And Devlin was now holding the secret of porcelain in his hands. King George himself had no more.

'Hugh. Dandon. Look here,' Devlin took them to the window and whispered to the rest to douse the lamp that lit the room. The lamp thus snuffed, Devlin creaked open the window and they peered down onto the scene below.

A bearded giant in Monmouth and blue was conversing with a lobster of white trim. The blink of the light had caused the bearded man to look up through the scaffolding, whereupon Hugh praised the Lord that the face of Black Bill Vernon was below them.

'Aye,' Devlin whispered. 'Maybe two dozen of us at least, I reckon. How does that fill your balls, Hugh?'

'Like sand, Cap'n. Sure if I hadn't thought I'd ever see the dawn!'

Devlin slapped Hugh's back. 'Ways to go, mate. Yet our hour.'

Eamon Tolliver, captain of the watch, followed Bill's glance up at the scaffolding but saw only darkness. He had listened to the tale of Captain Coxon and Captain Gale sending two boats of men ashore and now he looked over the motley group of sailors armed to the hilt. They looked like seamen and it was possible that the pirate Devlin's ship was attacking from the north. Rogers would have to be stirred, much as he regretted it, and men would have to be roused from their beds to man a defence. Somehow he still had his doubts, however.

Perhaps it was the long black beard. Perhaps it was the untidy hair and scarfed heads of the sailors. Something itched in him but then was scratched by the big man insisting that a signal be fired to the *Delicia* that they had arrived and were ready.

Tolliver begged to hear the question again.

'Fire a gun to the *Delicia*, Cap'n. Let Cap'n Gale know all is well.'

Tolliver was appeased. Legitimacy would indeed ask for such. A single salvo from the embrasure. Captain Gale would be looking for a salute from his men.

Tolliver looked up to the towers. 'The signal gun is on the far side. I'll order some men over to it. Mister Vernon, your men should stay here. I'll rally a squad and we'll head for the north shore. Coxon will engage I hope?'

Bill pulled out a square of paper and angled it beneath the torchlight of the tower, unfolding it and squaring his shoulder with Tolliver who sidled in to see. It was a map – further proof of legitimacy. Conspiracy did not show you its maps.

'Coxon is here,' Bill tapped to Northwest Point. 'The pirate vessel is at North Cay and will make the beach at any moment, if not already. They'll be in at the north of the town.' This was the first time Tolliver had ever seen a map of the island. To him it resembled the Isle of Wight and he was much surprised at the small size of his new home. Bill carried on. 'The *Delicia* is here, facing south. She'll turn and head north at our signal. Coxon will engage with the pirate ship.' He folded back the paper. 'Whatever you see fit to command, Cap'n. We be your men.'

Tolliver rallied his thoughts. Some men to fire the gun. Twenty more to accompany the sailors. Five more men to guard the cells. Summon the militia. He suddenly had a dry mouth at the thought that the moment had come to wake Rogers. Then he heard the window open high above and swung round to the sight of the legs coming through and seeking out the wooden walkway of the scaffolding.

A brown boot was followed by a dark trouser-leg and then

joined by a white shirt. Then a man with a musket looked down at him with the face of the pirate Devlin, not in his cell.

'Punk me mother! They're free!' Tolliver yelled. He pushed Bill to respond. 'Shoot him! Shoot that man! That's the pirate Devlin!' He watched Devlin swing along the scaffolding to the ladder and other bodies followed through the window, more weapons in their hands.

'Shoot! *Guards*!'

Tolliver's pair of soldiers swung off their muskets and aimed high only to feel their heads pushed over by pistols at their temples and they quickly rested their hands.

Tolliver heard a dozen pistols shake into life around him but his eyes were stuck to the scaffolding, and he stood back from the oncoming barrage as he watched the pirates above swinging between the poles.

'*Fire*!' he commanded, and immediately regretted his words as at least six pistols hovered exclusively at his face.

'Begging your pardon, Cap'n,' Black Bill explained apologetically over the pistol barrel levelled at Tolliver's eye. 'He be with us.'

Tolliver took in all the grins and hungry looks and raised his arms. Bill lowered his pistol. 'Good man,' he winked.

'Who be you then?' Devlin stepped down from the ladder and walked straight to Tolliver, briefly nodding to Bill. The bamboo tube was passed back to Dandon.

Tolliver brought down his arms and introduced himself warily.

'Then you should take better care of your prisoners, Captain. I haven't eaten for hours. No wonder I was inclined to leave.' Devlin reached in and pulled Tolliver's sword from his belt. 'You'd best tell Rogers of our departure. Tell him I took your sword. Nothing you could do.'

Tolliver almost thanked him. The soldier's muskets were plucked from their hands and they huddled next to their captain, all three of them forgotten, worthless, as the pirates welcomed Devlin back into their brood, although respectfully quiet considering the hour of the morning.

Devlin caught Bill's eye. 'Where away, Bill? We have a plan?'

'Some,' Bill said. 'Boat's on the shore. Wasn't expecting to see you so soon, Cap'n. Thought we'd have to break you out. Should've known better.' He looked at Devlin's six companions. 'Is this all that remains?'

Devlin did not answer but moved through the crowd towards the path, pulling the rest with him like a magnet. Dandon tugged at Palgrave's sleeve to accompany them but Palgrave pulled back.

'If I may, sir, I should prefer to stay. Take the pardon as it were,' he bowed in gratitude.

Dandon looked to Tolliver then back to Palgrave, 'They may kill you, sir.'

Palgrave sucked on his lip. 'I'll say I was forced. My remaining should benefit me greatly in that.' Shyly he held his voice lower for only Dandon to hear. 'I have had enough of that Chinese bad luck and a belly full of adventure, sir. Teach waits out there for you as well as the English ship. I'll take my chances here for now.'

Dandon turned away to follow the others. Lamps had begun to be lit in some of the windows of the town. Sleepers awoken by Tolliver's shouts and the stamp of men's feet began to bob their heads out of doors.

Palgrave called out once more to Dandon's back. 'That is not to say, sir, that at some other time I would not be pleased to re-acquaint. Good luck to you in finding your friend!' Dandon showed no sign of hearing him. Palgrave sighed and walked slowly to Tolliver who was already pushing his men up the steps to wake Rogers.

'Captain Tolliver, sir, I should . . .' But Tolliver was running up the steps towards the barracks, his blank white scabbard flapping like a tail, and Palgrave was left alone.

This sight provoked in him an assessment of his lot. He thought about Black Sam Bellamy and Blackbeard, about Devlin, and lastly about himself and the family he had left behind to pursue this mad life.

Hoy por mi, mañana por ti. Today me, tomorrow thee.

His solitude was broken by the approach of the cloaked Charley to his designated plot beneath the fort, his great bowl of a bell held silently in his hand. Three o'clock had come. The Charley looked at Palgrave's grey face, the open doors of the fort and the odd number of townsfolk who had begun to gather around it.

'All's well?' his voice croaked to Palgrave.

'I don't think so, mate.' Palgrave looked at the path where Devlin and his men had vanished into the night. 'I most definitely do not think so.'

Woodes Rogers' bedroom door flew open at the words and he appeared dressed in his cambric nightshirt, his cropped hair betraying a restless night. The soldier jumped at the sudden sight.

'What do you mean the pirates have escaped? How?'

The guard stuck to the doorframe as Rogers reached for his coat and keys. 'Don't know, sir. Captain Tolliver is getting the barracks together to give chase.'

Rogers swept into the corridor and headed for the stairs and the yard outside where Tolliver would gather his men. 'Give chase? The barracks? For six men?'

'No, sir,' the soldier tipped his hat back. 'Others came to the fort. Least twenty of them. We led them up here from the beach. All his, sir. All Devlin's.'

Rogers stopped and glared back, needing to hear no more. The idiocy of the army. Marlborough had clearly been a miracle. 'Palgrave too? Has he gone?' He resumed his stomping to the stair.

'Don't know, sir,' the soldier dogged Rogers' heels. 'Don't know why Devlin should want to escape: he'd be free this morning.'

Rogers froze at the words, then changed his course instantly to bolt for his office.

The corner turned, they were confronted by the corpse of John Hamlin and its caved-in bloody skull. Rogers flew to his door and took the key from his coat, his hands shaking as he rattled the lock again and again with no effect. He shot a look at the soldier and received a shrug in reply.

Rogers removed the key and knelt to press his eye to the metal plate. The room beyond lay in darkness but Rogers only needed to see one thing. His vision rolled to the floor, and in answer two sparks of red glinted back. He sprang up at the sounds of Tolliver's men's cantering outside beginning to fill the morning. His voice spoke to no-one.

'He came for the gun. Devlin. For the papers. Just for the papers.' His words trailed too feebly for the soldier to hear, but his next ones were louder as he stormed to join Tolliver, wiping a sliver of frothing drool from his sunken mouth.

Chapter Thirty-Nine

✗

Escape

To the beach. To the boats and oars. A chink of dawn showed on their left, the night still their greatest aid against the law that would grind them into the earth. To the law they were a band of cut-throats, devils in lead and steel, spitting powder. The reek of death seeped from them, drunk and rapacious, these villains of blood – as long as night remained.

Daylight would shatter them, remove the hooded cloak, reveal barefoot sailors ingrained with grease and pitch, clothed in dirty slops and harlequin waistcoats, drunkenly slurring with dull eyes above, the scrapings of the sea. Daylight was for knights in glinting armour not for alley dogs who were wolves in the darkness but pitiful rats at noon.

But their weapons shone like jewels. Pistols were waxed and oiled, the screws tight as nuns. Muskets stayed dry, their priming pans gleaming like virgins and treated with just as much tenderness. One shot fired, one man dead. They would show nothing of the clumsiness of the mutton-handed soldiers bearing down upon them, blinking as they shot, muskets rising high with the lurch of the trigger. Pirates milked their triggers and fired with their shoulders not their hands. They marked men like sewing needles, their bullets threaded through their enemies' eyes. As long as the night remained. As long as the legend stood.

Five of Devlin's men sheltered among the trees, a rear guard checking the approach from the town, shuffling back to the next tree like hunchbacks, scuttling through the ferns and spreading out like a hand waiting for the herd of soldiers to come lumbering forth.

They sweated and heaved, out of breath, but their barrels remained steady as if separate from the tired, anxious forms, the pimple of a gunsight waiting for a pale English face to appear through the gloom.

Silence.

Nothing.

They move back again to the next tree downhill, then wait again for five more breaths, knowing that their brothers are creeping back with them, unseen, to the beach and the boats, beside them somewhere in the dark.

Then it came. A rumble of leather, brass, buckles and ammo boxes under thumping boots, and at once a crow's call echoed its way to Devlin and Bill whilst the five men of the rear guard pulled back the hammers of their guns and held their breath.

Devlin was on the beach now, beholden to Bill to lead. The white of the surf was welcoming, crashing around the two boats.

'They're coming.' Devlin cocked his musket, Dandon filtered in behind him, cradling the bamboo tube in his arms.

Bill spied the brazier on the sands, smouldering red and shrunken now but with white coals still waiting for food. An idea began to form in his mind, but it was shattered by the sound of the first shots from inland.

It was the smooth wafting crack of partridge shot from the

rear guard. Not one bullet but a weight of lead grain, a shotgun spread, inaccurate and short of range but murderous to a cluster of bodies funnelled along a narrow path.

Ten lobsters dropped their guns and howled. Eyes were peppered, uniforms flayed and skin burnt. Checking for wounds their comrades buckled to their knees and fired blind into the dark whilst Tolliver ducked and counted his fallen men.

He had heard the crash of five shots, yet almost a dozen of his fifty men limped backwards. He went for his sword to beat them back, but his hand found only an empty scabbard. Devlin. In the end he pushed the wounded down to the beach with kicks and curses.

'We're to row to Hog Island, Cap'n,' Bill said as he dragged Devlin away from the snaps of gunfire. 'The *Shadow* is on the other side.' He pulled his captain along, Devlin's survival the honour of these last hours, but something would have to be done to stop them becoming fish in a barrel as they rowed away.

Bill yelled for those with canvas satchels of fireworks – bottles, iron grenadoes, anything loaded with scrap, powder and nails – to jump to his back. 'Dump your load around the brazier, boys!' Then he led them down to the shore as cracks of musket fire spat out from the dunes. Devlin watched as men threw their loads to the brazier and understood, but still he crouched and raised his musket to the path, Dandon at his shoulder. This had been the beach he had come upon that afternoon. The same beach where Rogers had landed over a month ago now. To his left he saw the pile of dead pirates due to be burned in the morning. Seth Toombs lay some-where within the stack.

'Should we not retire to the boats, Patrick?' Dandon ducked as the rear guard appeared and a spark above the beach sent a musket ball humming past his head.

'Just hold the letters, Dandon,' Devlin spoke over his shoulder. He fired back at the spark then stood and ran, biting into a fresh cartridge. Dandon huffed and fell in behind him again as Devlin knelt and fired like an archer into the white waistcoat of a lobster running down the path. Dandon began to slap him in approval but Devlin was already up again, falling back, and Dandon quickly followed behind.

At the boats men were already scrambling aboard. Oars rifled through thole pins.

'*Devlin*!' Bill yelled back, throwing himself into one of the boats. 'Come now, Captain!'

Redcoats began to pile from the path onto the sand, spreading left and right, going down on one knee, bringing up muskets to shoulders, but the glow of the brazier shielded the boats just enough. Devlin fired once more, his last act on Providence, and sloped to the surf before the powder cleared, Dandon running by his side, a storm of bullets following them.

They leapt aboard the boat just as the sea pulled them back into its bosom. But slow, too slow despite the power of the oars and now Tolliver was on the beach, looking up and down his line of thirty guns ready to fire.

'*Down*!' Devlin ordered but those pirates with loaded muskets still aimed their guns at the land.

'*Fire*!' Tolliver bellowed and his men slammed their dogheads home, mouths of fire tearing along the beach.

Wood splintered around the boats, lead sang off thole pins and musket barrels, thudded into oars and flicked the water like rain. The pirates stood and ignored it all. They shot at each other daily for sport; they grazed on lead. Tolliver heard them laugh as they fired back and saw five of his men topple to the sand.

'Shoot the fireworks, lads!' Bill roared but Devlin held up his hand to halt them, looking only to Hugh kneeling beside him in the boat, his musket already raised and loaded.

'Hugh,' he said slowly. No order. No expectation.

Hugh Harris nodded, kissed his thumb and leant into the shot. The brazier was his beacon, a green bottle glowing beneath it his target, the roll of the waves mere impetus. His cheek pressed against the stock of his musket and sweat dripped coldly on his arm; the brass sight was the extent of his world as he closed his left eye and fired.

The bottle exploded and old powder shivered into flame, glass and nails whistled and the powder hungered as the rest of the crock and glass bottles ignited.

The grenadoes of halved musket balls and twine, the iron- and powder-filled balls, gave in to the heat and the brazier itself burst into flame, sending a storm of ash and sand thirty feet into the air and a hail of glass, nails and shrapnel blazing towards pirates and soldiers both.

Tolliver raised himself from the back-turned crouch he had adopted when the brazier went up. He coughed through the cloud of powder, trying to wave it away but seeing only a wall of fire and smoke, the boats rowing away no longer visible.

He thought of Woodes Rogers, of facing him and explaining his failure, his lost sword, his lost prisoners. He screamed at his men to get down to the shore through the blinding fire and the choking sulphur. Instead they stood, turned their eyes from him and wandered back to the path with their muskets trailing: it would soon be breakfast and they had lost hours of sleep. Tolliver was just one captain of many and did not Rogers deal them out like cards? Perhaps another was already waiting in the wings. The men had done their duty.

Tolliver was left alone to meet the dawn and listen to the laughter rolling off the tide and echoing along the beach. He ran his hand along his empty scabbard. *Tell him I took your sword. Nothing you could do.* And Tolliver had almost thanked him. He began to walk back, then prised something from the hours past and stopped in his tracks.

Coxon. John Coxon.

Eleven o'clock Coxon had sailed, hours past now, and would be somewhere north of the island, this little Isle of Wight island, long gone now. But the fact was that Coxon was out there, patrolling. *His* duty was not done. All the way back to the fort Tolliver began to build in his mind the importance of the man he had only seen count the pineapple plants off the ships after they had first landed. The horizon began to glow white. A hot day in August was just beginning.

Fear no more the heat of the sun. Tolliver's recollection of Shakespeare vague and weak but relevant nonetheless. He tramped up the path behind his men. *'And fear no more the frown of the great.'*

Chapter Forty

✖

END GAME

Log entry of Captain John Coxon:

His Majesty's ship Milford under order of His Governor of New Providence, Eleuthera, Harbour Island and Abaco August 1718

Hauling round Goulding Cay in the morning. Light airs. Land trend away NWBW. Some places around the ship 3 or 4 fathom of water. In some places not quite so many feet. Got up main topmast and main yard. Got the sail ready for fothering the ship. Put it over under the starboard.

4 am. Following coast ascertaining threat to islands of possible pyrate landings. The known pyrate Devlin apprehended on Providence. Assume pyrates may attempt rescue. Full traverse of island by 10 am expected.

Sail sighted 1 league out of Simm's Point. Head NEBN to intercept.

Coxon handed the glass to his First, his head weary and eyesight blurred. 'What make you, Rosher? Sail there.'

Rosher put the telescope to his eye and saw the ethereal

light of the hour before dawn grow slowly in his view. They stood at the raised fo'c'sle of the *Milford* beneath the stays and rippling jibs, elbows and backs jostling around them, oblivious to their presence but still making sure not to brush the officers on the crowded deck.

Rosher swayed with the tide and waited for the murky image miles distant to steady itself. 'A sloop,' he said at last, confident in the sight of the lateen sails between the two masts and the flush deck beneath. 'She's hauling fast,' Rosher lowered the glass and looked at Coxon, then up to their fore- and mainsails at forty-five degrees, the deck lee-lurching to larboard beneath his feet as they tacked painfully north-east. 'Fast before the wind. Faster than us at any rate.'

Coxon looked down at his watch, waiting for more Rosher felt, or perhaps gauging the other ship's speed by invisible points along the gunwale.

'What else make you?' Coxon asked without looking up and Rosher breathed in and raised the glass again, taking the moment of re-sighting to consider what his captain might be looking for. The little sloop soon obliged as Rosher caught the forestay in his eyepiece and saw the black pennant playing on the wind.

Rosher's back snapped up straight and he stretched out to the sea.

'A pirate! A black flag from her forestay, Captain. A pattern upon it.'

Coxon clicked his watch shut. The speed made. He had been measuring the sloop against his *Milford*. Too fast. Too far. The *Milford* like a whale to a seal. 'What pattern do you see, Rosher?' he asked idly, already resigned to the chase, but never the capture. Maybe he could stab at her with the chasers to keep her from the shore.

'A red heart,' Rosher said beneath the scope. 'A tall skeleton pulling at it . . . no . . . I see blood dripping from the heart . . . he's piercing it . . . piercing it with some sort of spear I believe, Captain. Something in the skeleton's hand . . . Can't make it.'

Coxon shook his head. 'It's an hour-glass. It means our time is running out. Such vanity from such filthy coats.'

Rosher brought down the telescope and was back to the world of men in slops who rushed by, always busy, always dipping their heads at him. 'Should we not record the flag, Captain?' Rosher sounded rather too excited for Coxon's liking. ''Tis my first pirate sighting to be sure!'

A King's Letter boy, thought Coxon, the promising younger sons thrown aboard as minors. Six years at sea to be made lieutenant at no younger than twenty. He might just have seen the last edge of the war.

Coxon swung away from the young man and took two steps to the rail above the deck.

'Listen up, lads!' his hands gripped the rail as if trying to pull up the ship, and he raised his voice, commanding all to abide his words. 'Who amongst the pirates shows a skeleton stabbing a bleeding heart for his putrid black flag of colour? What say you now?'

The crew looked at each other, unsure what their answers might betray to their captain and also unsure what the lack of an answer might summon otherwise. A mop handle rested for a moment on a chest and an arm was raised gingerly.

Coxon's finger shot out towards the sailor, pointing like a priest's at a blasphemer. 'You, sailor! Tell us all and young Rosher here. Who sails under such a flag?'

The man looked about his mates, who ducked away from his silent pleas as if he were standing knee-deep in his grave.

He looked back to Coxon high above him and spoke louder than he thought he ever could. 'That be Blackbeard's colours, Cap'n. Blackbeard I believe, Cap'n.'

Coxon whisked his hand back. 'Bosun! Pint of rum to that man whenever he chooses to take it. Blackbeard it is.' He wheeled back to Rosher. 'No need to mark it, Rosher. That's a bold sod to wave his presence without a challenge. You have the watch. All sail to make him if you can.'

'Aye, Captain,' Rosher pulled the front cock of his hat, but paused before descending. 'But what of Devlin, Captain? Was it not his frigate we were expecting?'

Coxon leant on the gunwale and stared at the stern of the pirate turning her heels to him. 'Birds of a feather, Rosher. You can watch the tree and wait for the fruit to fall soon enough. Or you can take a bloody great stick and knock the shite out of it.' He heaved himself away from the spray as the ship turned and straightened his coat. 'We will set sail to chase. Send a boat back with my regards to Governor Rogers that I intend to do so. Send the Master to me, Mister Rosher.'

The young man tipped his hat again, his turn of shoulder stopped by Coxon. 'And Mister Rosher?'

'Aye, Captain?'

'Hoist the colours. Rabbits run from hounds' teeth.' He winked and turned to follow the horizon from westward over his shoulder to Blackbeard's sloop bobbing against the cap of the sun in the east. Unashamedly, to Coxon's senses, the sloop appeared quite beautiful under the faint amethyst sky of the dawn. Fine artists had painted less.

Devlin had not been seen. His *Shadow* remained elusive. Perhaps he had joined with Teach, with Blackbeard, for *there* was Blackbeard and Devlin had been taken on Providence only hours before. Coxon felt sure that the *Delicia* would keep Devlin's men from coming in south. If the *Shadow* were here, or were on her way, north would be her waters.

A glint flashed in the dawn before him and his imaginings were suddenly wiped away by the gleam of a gold band blinking at him across the leagues – the reflection of a telescope's brass ring off the morning light. He moved to the stair and left the watcher to his study of the *Delicia*'s coming on.

Hog Island was a swampy, boggy stretch of almost-land barely four miles long and not even half a mile wide, so that you could nearly see to its other shore through the palms and fronds upon it. A hundred years before, some Spanish or Porto traveller had marooned several *sanglier*, some wild chestnut pigs, letting them run free and breed, to rule the island alone, the only price of their freedom to submit to being hunted on occasion by the residents of Providence. Travellers well knew the spot and its mouth-watering indigenes. Now the lords of the island grunted and squealed away from the crash of the pirates passing through their home.

A panting mass of men was charging to the opposite shore, hacking at the gnarled branches that blocked them and cursing at the sucking ground at their feet.

Hog Island gave Providence its narrow harbour, the channel that stopped the men-of-war from coming close in. The channel had saved the pirates from many attempts to oust them and had allowed Charles Vane his avenue for escape a month before. Now it gave Devlin his as the day suddenly broke through the trees and he almost fell to his knees on the beach at the sight of the *Shadow* waiting in the cove.

Anchored fore and aft, restless at her cables and bucking like a foal desperate for the field, she tugged at her lines as if chomping at the bit and pleased to see her master. Bill had plotted the hands to sail from the *Delicia*'s starbolin watch through the dark while it still covered them. She had sailed north-east, keeping three miles at least from the East Indiaman's forty guns then turned and headed for Hog Island and the dawn. The *Delicia* was waking now, unaware that the pirate ship had crept past her in the night. Captain Gale was sitting in his nightshirt at his table sipping his first coffee of the morning.

Dandon stumbled to Devlin's side breathless from the run. Resting on his knees he gulped at the air and looked thankfully up at the black and red freeboard and the security of the three masts that promised strength and speed against anything that sailed to oppose them.

He looked to his captain grinning at the sight of his frigate, high in the water, blistered by barnacles on her pale lower strakes. The smell of Dog Leg Harry's peaberry coffee and egg-rice breakfast was already drawing them in: two boats lay on the shore waiting for them and cheers came from the deck as their brothers waved them on, hats tumbling and pistols firing into the sky.

Bill brushed past Devlin and Devlin grabbed the Scotsman's blue sleeve, turning to him.

'Thanks, Bill,' he said, acknowledging the slight blush above the beard and following the big man to the shore with Dandon, carrying the bamboo ransom, trailing behind.

'Can we abandon this place, Patrick?' Dandon panted, collapsing into the boat. 'I have grown tired of the world of ordinary men.'

'Aye. North to the lanes then to Peter Sam.' Then he darkened at the remembrance of Ignatius and the promise of Valentim Mendes's vengeance. At least the passage should be plain and smooth enough, if not the outcome. 'At least we have beaten Teach to be sure. His face will be a picture when he finds it is us who has the letters.'

Devlin permitted himself a smile.

Chapter Forty-One

*B*lackbeard brought down his scope and spat at the frigate toiling towards his wake.

'Cap'n?' Israel Hands followed his captain's glare, anxious if not afraid, for such an expression did not bode well with the man beside him.

'I reckon on that being the *Milford*. One of Rogers' own. Over thirty guns against our ten.' He raised the glass again. 'She be heading for our stern but she be a third slower,' he slammed the tube shut and spat again. 'But that means we can't make it to Providence. Not with him on our stern, Israel.'

'We should never have abandoned the fleet and the *Revenge*, Cap'n. We'd have had a fighting chance then.'

Teach reached down and lifted Israel like a pillow, his knees above the gunwale, Israel's face wincing down at him, and Israel was not a small man.

'I'm for the greater good, Israel! Eden wanted as few as possible to know about this cruise!' He slung his quartermaster to the deck. 'Question me, Israel, and the Devil will listen.' He went back to his survey and spoke gruffly. 'Get the plugs out of the guns and get me a speed: I want to know what an hour will do between me and this fool.'

'Aye, aye, Cap'n.' Israel scrambled to his bare feet and scuttled away but his footsteps halted with a skid at the cry from the topmast.

'*Sail! Sail! Deck there!*'

Blackbeard stomped to the shadow of the mainsail and called straight up the wood to the man's feet. 'Another one? Where away?'

The man bent to the deck, hand cupped to his mouth. 'Two points off head to starboard!' He watched Teach almost leap to the starboard gunwale and arrow the scope over the water.

A new sail. Bowsprit and jibs snaking out from the edges of North and Long Cays, then fully visible and showing her grey sails against the rising sun and the black and red paint of her freeboard. Another man-of-war, another frigate in the dawn, and Blackbeard the meat between the bread.

'Who the devil?' Teach counted the guns as his brain raced.

Israel bounced to his side, squinting at the ship in full sail skating along the glass surface of the white water. He tapped his captain's shoulder and pointed to the black flag at the bowsprit. 'Friend, Cap'n! A pirate for us!'

Teach strained his eye to the dancing cloth, expecting little. Vane he trusted, even liked. Hornigold, his former commander, had sold his soul and become hunter. These were dark days for pirate allies. The brethren of the coast had short memories in a world that no longer had need of them.

The flag billowed and waned. Teach clenched his jaw as the calico skull showed itself in all its grinning glory.

'A skull in a circle! A compass rose!' He yelled the description to those behind him and bodies stepped forward, necks craning over the side, watching the three masts. 'Two pistols crossed beneath the death's head.' He turned, momentarily taken aback at the size of the crowd. Then he scowled and demanded an answer. 'Who knows it?' he bellowed. 'Who knows that flag? Speak up now!'

Looks passed amongst the crew, then a few whispers, a few lowered heads. A bronzed hand waved above the crowd, from a broad Dutchman come aboard in Martinique almost a year ago.

'This is the flag of the *piraat* Devlin, *Kapitein*.' He bowed away as the black pistol eyes fired at him from the bulwark. His brothers nodded at the Dutchman respectfully, letting him shrink back into their midst.

Israel Hands noticed the swelling of his captain's chest, the beard rising above the brace of pistols strapped across him, and he watched as Teach reached inside his coat for the stump of a spermaceti candle – some significance unknown to Hands. The candle disappeared as quickly as it was revealed.

'So, Devlin is it?' Teach said. 'The pirate Devlin.' He raised his spyglass and turned back to the black frigate, and more to himself than to Israel he muttered under his breath. 'All the Caribbean and he has come to me. Off the very island I sent Palgrave. Off the very island where the letters lie.' He let down the scope. 'She's high in the water,' he yelled. 'She'll be fast. And where do you think she'll be heading, Mister Hands?'

Israel fiddled with his shirt hem and looked between the black ship and the black face of his captain. 'Maybe she be bound for the Americas, Cap'n. Maybe for Charles Town?'

Teach slammed his quartermaster in the chest, sending him flying back along the deck. 'Of course she's going to Charles Town!' He faced them all. 'As will we, boys! Devlin has saved us the task of surprising Rogers!' He pushed through them all, elbows out to scuff their brains as he yelled. 'Port the helm! Stand to and ride her lee! But slowly now boys. Stays at her larboard quarter, I don't want those guns to us. Stand to!'

Those too quick to have their heads knocked were already climbing to the top- and foresail or slipping the halyards from the belaying pins to haul up the main to half-sail, speeding their turn to shadow the *Shadow*, whilst Teach held onto the foremast stays, leaning against the falling-off and watching his bowsprit begin to sweep across the *Shadow*'s quarters half a league away.

A race now. A King's ship behind and Devlin to starboard, but the *Adventure* fastest of all. Teach almost regretted not having the *Queen Anne* and her forty guns but abandoning her and the bulk of his men had been part of the plan to side with Governor Eden. All the same such an act did not sit well with the chosen men aboard the *Adventure*, and only the rum and Teach's aptitude for swelling their account kept their heads bowed, their voices still. Now Devlin, his name rolling around the Caribbean since the year past, another one of the few not to take the pardon, and aboard a twenty-six gun frigate to boot, was leaving Providence hours after Palgrave had gone ashore, with Ignatius sitting on his bony arse in Charles Town waiting for someone to bring him his letters.

Teach rubbed the stump of the candle sitting in his vest against his chest and thought about a long year ago, on a hot evening in The Porker's End on Providence, and of how he had backed down when the smirking upstart had stopped him killing the yellow-coated pox-doctor. And Seth Toombs's old crew was now with the pirate Devlin . . .

But he had taken the candle stump to measure the last hour of Devlin's life when the time came for them to meet again. That prospect of burning away his final hour had now almost come to pass.

The sails backed, the bowsprit rose, the sloop gained and

a rare glow of joy came over Edward Teach that had nothing
to do with the cap of the sun growing on the horizon.

'Two ships upon us?' Devlin came from the Great Cabin at
Bill's urgent call and stepped up to the quarterdeck. 'Where
away?' but he had already seen the white sloop gleaming in
the rising sun, perhaps fifteen cables behind.

'That's Blackbeard's flag upon her,' Bill pointed to the
black square billowing off the forestay of the sloop. 'He be
after the letters you spoke of.'

'Aye,' Devlin said peacefully, as if the sight had been
expected.

In the half a glass it took them to sail away from Hog Island
and out amongst the cays Devlin had enlightened Bill as to
the man Ignatius, Valentim, and the letters that would free
Peter Sam.

Bill listened as Devlin changed, ate, loaded two fresh pistols
to replace his left-locked one and grew taller before his eyes
with a strange blend of anger and anticipation which, by the
end of the tale, made Bill feel he had known Devlin all his
life; his joys, his woes, forever mixed.

Bill looked beyond the sloop to the square sails and yards
of the man-of-war, still emerging out of the dawn mist like a
phantom. 'That I know is the *Milford*,' he said. 'I plotted her
thus.' He began the slow loading of his first and best pipe of
the day before speaking again to Devlin, standing silently
beside him. 'Cap'n Coxon be her master.'

'I know. He's got my pistol. Has buried what's left of our
coin. Teach will be heading to Charles Town. Coxon will be
at us.'

Bill shielded his eyes and watched the two ships. 'We
could destroy Teach with our girl. But heading him off will

bring Coxon to us all the quicker. To the maps, Cap'n, I say.'

Devlin agreed. 'I'm going up,' he looked up at the mainmast. 'I need to see my world.'

He stepped up to the gunwale and mounted the shrouds to ascend the mast, Bill watched him climb and others scattered around the deck followed their captain's walk to the lubber-hole circling the mainmast amongst the tops.

Across the waves the second cry to the deck from eighty feet above had shocked even Coxon. He looked up to the arm pointing over the bow and the man's speaking trumpet echoed down again. '*Ho yo*! Deck there! Another pirate! Three masts! Pirate two points off the head!'

Rosher went for the scope sat in its becket beside the binnacle but stopped when he saw Coxon speed from the deck to the mainmast and heard him call to the man aloft to describe the flag. Coxon, not waiting for the reply, had grabbed for the larboard shrouds and hauled himself up the rigging.

It had been a long time since John Coxon had taken the walk and his thighs burned after the first five steps while the sounds of the deck began to be whittled away by the wind about his head. The ghostly voice of the man at the maintop was more normal now as Coxon made the first forty feet and closed upon his loft.

'I make it a skull in a circle, Cap'n!' he yelled down from the topmast shrouds above the platform where he had moved to give his captain more room. 'Crossed pistols underneath I believes.'

Coxon shouted back. 'It's a compass not a circle!' The *Milford* rolled to leeward as the tide fell back against her and

Coxon gripped the uprights as the sea appeared beneath his heels from below, the deck gone and his whole body leaning over the water for a moment before she rolled back and the small men below came back into view.

His hands, now pale and tight, carefully moved higher again another five times, knee to elbow, knee to elbow, over the ratlines until the mast and the hole around it were beside his face and the sailor pulled him up to his cramped loft.

'I reckon you be right, Cap'n,' the man saluted, shouting above the whistling of the wind all around them. 'A skull in a compass rose so it is.'

Coxon thanked him for his hand and took the spyglass from him. He had to see for himself, so brushed past the fellow and put the hard vellum tube to his eye. The world swam before him for a moment, sky, sea and horizon all blurring together, then the picture cleared as if standing back from a painting and the black and red ship bucked before him; an inch to his left and there was the mocking cloth for an instant and then gone as the mainsail powered into view and then the mast and top, and a dark figure hanging off the futtocks just below it.

Coxon stiffened as a figure pulled himself to the top and stared back, only without a scope. Just the outline of a man leaning on the platform and staring back at him through the wind and the canvas. His eyes followed the ship, unable to look away from the dark figure.

Him. Coxon's thoughts howled within him as much as the wind beating on his eardrums, and he could feel the same word echoing back from the black ship. *Him.*

They had fought once, on The Island. Cutlass steel and a pistol shot to Coxon's arm whilst their ships had fought without them. Devlin had won the day. His damned grin belittling all of Coxon's experience. But this now was wood and iron, sail and wind – Coxon's world for two decades.

Not this time, he thought as he ground his teeth under the spyglass: Not this time. Both of us are now upon the sea, not in some landlocked stockade where you commanded and connived like a fox but the sea. My sea.

Not this time, Patrick. Not this time.

'Full sail!' he shouted below. He pushed away the speaking trumpet offered. 'To him!'

Chapter Forty-Two

Waiting

A basement for Peter Sam, drier than the cell in Madagascar but sharing a similar narrow grating of light from the street above, and him wearing the same filthy smock rag on his back.

There had been the weeks in the hold of the sloop, the comforting sounds of working men above his head, then the night passage to the tunnel, the drawing room of a wealthy man, Valentim Mendes somewhere, then the two weeks of this cell of straw and hard mud.

He had glimpsed the sun briefly in Madagascar during the journey from the harbour to the sloop, but other than that he had only seen its short sweep along the floor as it crept through the afternoon. He would roll into its rays, basking on his floor like a turtle, relishing the burn of it upon his closed eyelids, and fearing its withdrawal which would signal the approach of the Scotsman; all the time the Scotsman, and the loathsome wait for food tainted with a beating if the mood came upon him. It had now become normal to measure happiness, even affection, by the absence of pain and degradation. Guilt with it. Gratitude without.

The door at the top of the wooden stairs crashed open. Peter scrabbled at the sunlit straw, its warmth proving, assuring him, that the door opened too early, that someone had made a mistake, and he shrank from the sun and to his corner to panic about whatever it was he had done.

With a drawn-out step the Scotsman's buskins descended and met the straw. He threw a small smirk at the cowering bulk in the corner, then came a toss of the arm and a slap on the floor and Peter's old leather jerkin and breeches had landed at his feet.

Tentatively Peter poked a foot at the leather bundle, felt its familiarity but still sat frozen, wondering what he had done, what punishment the leather package signified. The Scotsman chuckled and moved closer.

'Them is your old clothes, Peter, my boy.' And he laughed again as Peter shook his head. 'You're to put them on.' He knelt, lowering his voice as he drew level with Peter's eyes, shielded by his hugging forearms. 'Time's almost up. Been nigh on two weeks now, my boy. Time for us to have our revenge on that old captain of yours. If he's coming.' Hib Gow stood up to his full height, hair brushing the beams as he began to pace and wring his hands.

'The things that captain of yours has forced me to do. Forced me to do for money to feed meself. And me an honest working man, Peter. The torments we have endured together for his vanity. The vanity of all men with power against us common hands.' He dropped to his knees again, a moistness around his eyes – eyes shrunk like a pig's against the broken and twisted horn of a nose. 'But soon it will end for both of us, Peter Sam. Soon, just a few more days, I'll make sure you get some meat and rum, and we'll both be free.'

Peter crept forward and ran a hand over his leather jerkin, fingering stitches of whale gut he had sewn himself, pockets where scrimshaw pipes and spare flints had nestled, and his sewing palm and whistle. All gone now, but the stitches were his. Startling Hib, he pulled it lovingly towards his face and breathed in the sea, the pitch and the smoke and with its aroma something flitted about his eyes that unsettled the Scotsman.

Perhaps it was too early to give him his old clothes back, but Ignatius had insisted, in order to make him appear normal for the men that came for him. They were to provoke no more ill feeling than was warranted. Sam had been fed three meals a day for the last fortnight, albeit rice and cabbage, with a little pork fat for supper. But Hib disliked the eyes. His head swivelled around the basement. A bald path through the straw from one wall to the other. A round patch where Peter Sam basked and maybe exercised some? Sunlight gave hope. Certainly, as Peter stripped off the smock, Hib noticed the return of shadowy muscle around the arms and chest where once was flaccid yellow flesh that had taken weeks to cultivate. Hib rolled his own muscles beneath his shirt and sniffed as Peter held out his arms to him to remove the chains from his wrists so he could put on his clothes.

'Help me, Mister Hib, sir,' the red and grey beard pleaded. 'Help old Peter, sir. Don't want to let you down, Mister Gow, sir.'

Hib absorbed Peter's words, the power of them, gravy to his meal. Sam's voice carried the same whimpering note as those fellows at Newgate who thanked him in the morning for the bacon rind and black bread before he swung them from the rope they had helped him make the night before.

'That's right, Peter,' Hib glowed kindly as he lifted his keys to the manacles. 'You don't want to let old Hib down now do you? Don't want to make Hib do anything he don't want to do now, mate?' Still his hands drifted to the shining dagger stuffed at his belt as he watched Peter Sam tug on his clothes as gladly as if they were a new suit. 'Remember I don't get paid if you misbehave, and then what would I have to do? God knows what I would have to do if you let me down.'

Peter stood, snapped his jerkin into place and rubbed the leather down. Met Hib's gaze. 'I won't let you down, Mister Gow,' he grinned back and Hib raised an eyebrow at something he wasn't sure of beneath Peter's words. 'I promise I won't let you down.'

'See that you don't, Peter,' he said and then whispered: 'I'm minding you. And we'll kill that treacherous captain of yours for what he's done to you when he gets here won't we? Together, man.'

Peter Sam sniffed again at his leather. 'Aye. Kill him that has done this thing to old Peter Sam.'

A room for Valentim Mendes. *Regulador* of Sao Nicolau, the Verde island of the blessed Portuguese. Chained by his wrists and ankles to ringbolts sunk eight inches into the red flock walls of a window-shuttered room. One wrist, the left, was also tied with rope to the chains, the weakness of the porcelain appendage at its join giving some concern to his captors. Valentim had indeed struggled for some hours, pulling down at the screws riveting his flesh to the lifeless hard-paste hand ordered from the Vienna factory of Claudis Du Paquier – the factory built on the stolen secrets of Meissen, secrets that now threatened to flood the world once the letters of the Jesuit Father became widely known. Gold, saffron, diamonds, they were all the scrapings of the earth picked up by beggars. But this was industry like the ships, the iron, the guns, the sugar and the slaves before it. Factories would spring up all over Europe. Saxony would lose its monopoly, China its mystery.

Villages that had toiled to make bread for the hamlets that surrounded them would now fight to make genteel cups and tapered pots for coffee and chocolate for gentlemen who knew nothing but the craving of admiration for the best service at afternoon coffee, the most exquisite silk, the choicest lace finally available now the wars were over and kings could be kings again.

And Valentim, noble by birth, but not noble in the right world, his faith a little too papist to be entirely Christian, would be chained and starved until such a moment when he would be worthy to be addressed.

The door opposite swung open and there Ignatius stood, holding orange-scented linen to his face at the mess around Valentim's black riding boots.

'Could you not have held on, Governor, until the hour I give you?' Ignatius choked behind the kerchief. 'For the sake of others can you not restrain to be a gentleman?'

Valentim lifted his head. 'You give me cabbage water and cider vinegar. My suit must now be burnt because of you, Ignatius, and my father will turn in his grave.' He pulled against his chains and spat his words. 'And you will *die* because of your insolence! Your throat will be cut at the hour of my freedom!' Valentim spoke louder: 'I am the governor of his majesty's island of Sao Nicolau and you will—'

'Enough!' Ignatius waved dismissively and closed the door behind him. 'I grow tired of your bleating, Valentim.' He moved across the room, bare of furniture save for a chair and a perfunctory table for Valentim to eat his meagre rations; a lamp upon it lightened the gloom behind the shuttered windows. 'I have suffered you no physical harm,' Ignatius remonstrated. 'I have taken care of you as well as I would expect you to take care of me should the situation ever be reversed. Do unto others, Valentim. Do unto others.' He paced in front of him. 'Besides, the worst is over. If I were to expect Devlin or Teach to return it would be imminently, and if they do not . . . then I will definitely need to think of some . . . new arrangement.'

Valentim straightened at the mention of Devlin. 'I could not allow you to live once I am free, Ignatius, and if you kill me—'

'*Please,* Valentim! No soul knows you are here. I do not make mistakes. I have been at this game a long time, Valentim. I am a study of Walsingham and a master of *espionnage*, which in this age has less to do with people like *you*,' he pointed a mocking finger, 'and more and more to do with companies, investors, thieves . . . and pirates. I have grown wealthy by knowing what others will pay to know. I am not a monster, Valentim. It has become my responsibility to have as little of the world as possible know about these letters. The last time I had them the world beat a path to my door. I sent them north for safety with Bellamy and even that was not enough. Once I have them again all of those who know of them will be eradicated until I can use them to their full value. I would wager that if I informed even *your* court that I had the arcanum of the true *porcelana* for their approval, but that it would cost them your life for them to receive it, not an eyelid would blink at the thought.'

Valentim weighed the words, unable to prevent his eyes growing wide at the notion. Ignatius watched with pleasure and laughed through his words. 'Do not fear, Valentim. I am sure that will not occur.'

'I do not *fear*,' Valentim hissed. 'I fear nothing from an English *porco filho de um whore*!'

'I would save your tongue for the pirate when he arrives.'

Valentim's eyes gleamed, not unseen by Ignatius. 'I promised you the opportunity for revenge. You may fight to the death the man who maimed you.' Ignatius placed his hand on his breast. 'My word as a gentleman. But for my records I must barter with you once more for such a duel.'

'What else is there that you do not have?' Valentim hung limp in his chains, for noble spines bend as any other.

Ignatius strolled around the room, casually examining the bars and shutters of the two windows. 'A year ago, when we began our correspondence, you knew what I did not. You knew where the letters lay after Bellamy's ship went down. That you knew of the letters at all from that rock you call home was intriguing enough, but I would like to know how you found that which I could not?' Ignatius paused and waited for the reply.

Valentim rolled his eyes to focus on Ignatius. 'Pirates,' he said. 'A pirate named Toombs told me of the letters in exchange for his life. I knew of you through the court, the agency of conspiracy. This "porcelain mystery" had value. But *I* did not value it.' Hate breathed through him. 'I have higher ideals that you cannot understand. But *you* could find Devlin.'

'But the cannon on Providence?'

Valentim sighed wearily. 'I told you, English: *pirates*. It will always be pirates. Palgrave Williams had to take the gun somewhere. It would be a pirate that took him. And pirates will talk . . . eventually. I know pirates well.'

'Ah,' Ignatius made to leave. 'For a moment I thought you had a grasp of facts that may have been of further use to me. Pity. I had not counted on the energy of hate, although I rely on it often. However, I will stand by my word.' He opened the door, revealing Hib Gow filling the frame, the keys to Valentim's chains hanging from his fist and the black servant dwarfed beside him with a tray of bread and soup. Every mealtime was the same. Ignatius bowed his leave. 'If the pirate Devlin returns successfully you may have your play at him, Valentim. It will doubtlessly save me the trouble of what to do with at least one of you.'

Chapter Forty-Three

✖

Three to Charles Town

*T*hree cabins and the same scene played out three times
within. Three captains hunched over tables, the tools of
their art before them: brass-hinged sector rule, dividers, compass card, loupe, pencil and log all dancing across charts of the
Bahamas and south-eastern shores of the Americas, all working under the intense application of their magicians and the
stifling heat of the noon.

The *Adventure* . . .

Edward Teach – Blackbeard – was shadowed by Israel
Hands and Black Caesar as he crossed a pencil along the
soundings. He knew the waters well but still the threes and
fours beneath his plotting reassured him that the two frigates
could not follow his path. The two men at his shoulders
watched the lines draw out, the miles pencilled in effortlessly,
excluding the shifting of lateen sails and hard reeving that
would make them.

Aft through the slanting stern windows, a mile off his
larboard-quarter swelled the ivory squares of the *Milford* under
full sail, heeling to leeward from the easterly airs, the island
of New Providence just a white and blue smear on the horizon
far behind.

Israel Hands looked uneasily to the rippled glass and the

three masts inching across the window frame. Teach saw the glance and slammed the desk to bring his quartermaster back to the chart. 'Pay attention, damn you, man! Those sails will still be there else! We're shaking him loose!'

'Aye, Cap'n.' Hands turned back, contrite, and stared down at Teach's runes upon the chart. 'We're to traverse through Abaco and the Grand? Lose the *Milford* in the shallows?'

'Aye, that be it,' Teach growled and returned to the chart.

The *Milford* and Coxon drew too much water to follow through the white shallows of the passage between the two islands, now in sight already before their bow; and Blackbeard's *Adventure*, built for speed, although with a quarter of the canvas could make the passage before the *Milford*'s sails had dried in the wind. Consequently she would follow Devlin, Teach affirmed.

Teach's own passage, from this noon, would be sixty-nine miles nor'west until the 27th parallel and Hobe Sound then course up the coast, no colours, for another four hundred-odd miles to Charles Town. That meant nearly five hundred miles still to roll beneath their keel.

Teach dragged his log across the map, his calculations pencilled into the margins with his concentrated delicate hand. The *Adventure* could make seven knots off and on all the way and be in Charles Town in three days, or four with drinking and sleep. At best estimation, a pirate's odds, his contemporaries upon the sea could make it in five days at full sail if they could wet four knots.

Teach sat back and let Caesar and Hands congratulate him. The *Queen Anne's Revenge*, run aground weeks before, could not have helped them in such a task with her four hundred tons, and they slapped their captain's back with the measure of it and his wisdom to trade down, sink his lot into one of his smaller tenders, which had trebled their account and would now safely take them back to the inlets and points of the Carolinas.

Never mind the white crisp sails, diminishing even now from their stern, nor the grey ones of the *Shadow* to their starboard beam, the *Adventure* would reach Charles Town and Ignatius first. Without the letters, true, but reaching him first alive far superior in choice than first dead if he chose to stand.

The *Milford* . . .

John Coxon threw the dividers to the table. His sailing master and Rosher flinched at the outburst.

'Four knots! *Four knots*! That sloop, Mister Halesworth, Blackbeard's sloop, is making seven! Devlin is almost ten cables from our bow and you offer me four knots!'

Halesworth stood his ground, 'I cannot force the wind, Captain. The *Milford* has not been cleant since she came from England and these waters are as ugly as a parson's widow.'

'Then turn her into a brigantine, Mister Halesworth!' Coxon went back to the chart, his knuckles digging into the table. 'Rig staysails between the masts, get some boom-irons on and studding sails out. Good hands and carpentry should have it done in three hours.' He picked up the dividers again and tapped urgently at the chart's surface as the others looked on. 'Devlin can't make it through Abaco and Grand Bahama. It's forty miles wide but barely knee deep to him and to me. To *us*. We shall make north-east by north to Eleuthera now, before he turns. Then we'll see where he runs. By the time you have your new sails we may have the speed to catch the *Shadow*.'

'That will put the wind to our starboard quarter, Captain,' Halesworth sighed.

'All the more reason for you to make up staysails between. What we lose to leeward we'll gain abaft.'

Halesworth pulled out his book and licked his inch of a pencil, the shake of his head barely perceptible. 'Aye, aye, Captain.'

Rosher mopped his brow, leaving beads of greasy sweat smeared across his linen. 'What of Blackbeard's sloop, Captain? Are we not to chase him in preference perhaps?'

The dark look from his captain shrivelled his voice like salt on a slug. 'Is he not more notorious, I mean . . . more worthy . . . to some that is . . . to others that is?' He smiled uneasily.

Coxon went back to his chart. 'Devlin is already far ahead of him. This Blackbeard is conning for the shallows north, away from us both. They may be cohorts. They may not. They may join up somewhere later, which we will establish once we are further into the Atlantic and in a better position to determine. For the now, and this is not personal, Mister Rosher, the *Milford* is better suited, both for speed and for power, to chase after the rated ship rather than the sloop, would you not agree?' Coxon looked calm again and waited for the young man to answer.

Rosher seized the opportunity to reaffirm his loyalty. 'Absolutely, Captain. I would advocate no other path.' He bowed smartly.

'Good,' Coxon nodded. 'Then make it so Mister Rosher, Mister Halesworth. Dismissed and about your business.' Their salutes were disturbed by the sailor in straw hat and slops who lurched breathless into the doorway, remembering just before he spoke to rap urgently on the door.

''Tis the sloop, Cap'n!' he blurted. 'She's making north! Toward the islands!' He backed out of the shadow of the cabin to make way for Rosher and Halesworth as they hurried deckwards to confirm his words.

On paper the islands of the Bahamas were scattered like Dandelion seeds blown from the Gulf of Florida. Skinny strips of land almost too numerous to list. Most sailed round them, their sand bars and shallows too treacherous to navigate. These were grand pirate waters for sloops and xebecs but hazardous to the men in heavier ships that hunted them. Their treacherous and shallow draft was perfect for Teach's keel to forge ahead. The others would have to make for the deep blue Atlantic.

At the starboard gunwale they descried the larboard beam of the sloop slowly moving across their bow through their forward rigging and they ducked to maintain the view when the foot of the courses blocked the sight as the bow rolled down.

Halesworth nodded approvingly. 'She's going for the shallows to be sure. Box-hauling. Running away from us.'

'So the captain is right,' Rosher looked above to the sails on a hard reach. 'We should stand on. Make for Devlin's ship as best we can.'

Halesworth tipped his chin to the dark cabin, the door still open and Coxon still within, for he had no need to follow them in looking after the route of Blackbeard. 'I don't think there was ever going to be any other way, Mister Rosher.' He tapped his hat. 'I am to my sails. This watch will be a busy one.' He turned away, leaving Rosher to stare out at the black pirate frigate now maybe eight cable lengths distant, a nautical mile, and alone before them. He wondered, swallowing drily beneath his necktie, at what the pirates made of them at their tail.

*

The *Shadow* . . .

'I see it, Bill,' Devlin said, declining the offer of the scope to watch Blackbeard's sloop cutting away. They stood out on the larboard quarter gallery, where the black-pitched shrouds met the hull at the channels some feet out, giving them an observation platform. The wind played an evil howl through the dead eyes as Devlin leant through the ropes, resting his forearms on the ratlines, and contemplated the *Milford*'s square courses and gallants shining brightly in the distance, steadfastly encroaching as if the *Shadow*'s capstan was winding her in.

'Blackbeard will make to course between the islands and to the Americas, whereas we can only go by way of Eleuthera and the sea. If we can make five knots we'll be to him in as many days.'

'Aye, with Coxon at our hawser hole all the way,' Bill noted. 'And him with you always in mind.'

Devlin agreed. 'And he came to me in the gaol in Providence. Offered me a pistol which I didn't take. Knowing I had something else brewing. I think it was purely the man's instincts that must've kept him alive through the war.'

'Aye. Whether he catches us now or catches us in Charles Town we'll find out soon enough. Either way we've caught us a Tartar.' The pirate's reference hearkened back to the savage Asiatics, and meant through ill-luck or bad judgment to come up against a foe that could not be taken nor would quit.

Again Devlin agreed but now turned his head back to the cabin and to the table where he had plotted the five-hundred-and-fifty-mile course up the coast of America; and to the pile of yellowing parchments that curiosity could not withstand examining – the letters that the whole world seemed to seek, made up of the intricate writings and diagrams of Father d'Entrecolles. Devlin thought again on Dandon's words concerning the limit of Ignatius's knowledge.

He knows our history. But he does not know us.

Devlin's customary, almost childish grin began to form again, and Bill saw the warming of the game in his captain's eyes.

'Make your sails, Bill. Keep Coxon at our quarter. I'll grab Dandon from out of a bottle and confer with him a while.' He ducked back into the cabin, leaving Bill alone to sample the sight of the first of the staysails appearing between the masts of the *Milford*.

Chapter Forty-Four

✗

*N*ight and the Atlantic, the darker blue, the wide rolling waves instead of the ticklish crystal lap of the Bahamas. Two ships laboured beneath the first planets of the evening and Venus and Mars had seen it all before. Abaco and Eleuthera far behind them, both ships were trimmed by the head and bows down as they ploughed through the deeper waters. Some time before the first dogwatch the *Shadow* had set north-west by north, and the *Milford* had followed and closed to less than a mile. But the darkness had fallen too soon for Coxon.

'Too late to engage her tonight,' he concluded, looking about the stars above his sails. 'We'll keep to this course and hope she is still there in the morning.'

Such a comment drew a querying word from Halesworth. 'Surely she is not apt to vanish in the night, Captain?'

Coxon nodded towards the stern of the ship to their fore. 'She is vanishing even now, Halesworth.'

Halesworth looked out, noticing only then that in the swift blackness that was drawing itself about them the pirate ship ran without stern or sidelights. She was a black blot on the horizon at best, but soon even that shape would be indistinguishable against the night and the *Shadow*'s presence would only be marked by the brief snuffing out of a star as her sails and masts rolled by.

Coxon patted his sailing master's shoulder. '*Shadow* by

name and nature, Halesworth. Never mind: thanks to your sails we are gaining. I shall have him on the morrow. Bring him back to Providence.'

'*If* Devlin is on the ship, Captain.' Halesworth checked his log as the bosun's mate yelled out the speed from the drogue. 'This could just be a ruse to draw us from Providence. A goose chase with nothing to show for it whilst Devlin is cutting Rogers' throat as we slumber.'

Coxon laughed. It was the first time Halesworth had heard such a sound and he baulked as if punched by the man beside him. 'Oh, Mister Halesworth!' Coxon patted his shoulder again. 'What sport! It could be a fine ending for the world whatever side the dice come up! But a man without a feeling in his gut is a curious thing. We should have you stuffed by and by!' Coxon moved to the fo'c'sle, leaving Halesworth shaken by the sudden bout of joviality he had just witnessed, his pencil and the speed forgotten.

'This is a trick not known to me, Cap'n.' Black Bill spat to the deck for luck.

'For me also, Bill. But it should work. I'm all for engaging Coxon after we get Peter Sam, but beforehand don't seem quite as fair. I just needs to gain an edge. Put some space between us and keep on to Teach.'

Bill demonstrated his compliance by loading his pipe in silence and looking over the taffrail with Devlin to the *Shadow*'s cutter and jolly-boat sent out behind them under the conspiracy of the night. The ship had been brought-to, her sails braced aback to give her the barest movement, slowed to luffing so as the lads sent out in the boats could swim back and grab the man-ropes laid alongside and be hauled to the Jacob's ladder once their job were done.

Devlin and Bill heard the sea swallow the anchors but could see nothing; then came the sound of the ten men assigned to the task swimming back to the ship.

'Get them in and get us out!' Devlin's voice was urgent, conscious of the ten minutes lost and mindful of the ten minutes it would take to get up a speed again, but Bill was already at the helm, waiting until the last man was pulled aboard so he could yell at those straining at their braces and waiting for the word.

Devlin stared hard at the dim horizon and there he saw, at the limit of his sight, the soft twinkle of the *Milford*'s sidelights along her rigging jigging up and down under a trio of stars. He held out his thumb, one eye closed, and she disappeared in front of it. 'Stay to that course, John,' he whispered along the line of his outstretched arm. 'Just for an hour more, if you please. Stay right behind me.'

Then Bill was shouting, and men, rope and canvas worked together as the *Shadow* let go and moved on, obediently, willingly, as much a member of the crew as any of them. She'd sprout wings if her captain only asked it of her.

She was built for war and painted black for subterfuge with swords and guns for ballast. A death's head for her colours and crewed by miscreants and thieves, the *Shadow* was a pirate ship. Freedom was her only country. What could indentured men do to her?

'I hold, Captain, that we can only follow Devlin's ship.' Halesworth sipped at his port, his cheeks already flushed at half a glass. It was past twelve and had been a late indigestible supper if it were not for the port, blessedly warm. Halesworth leant in from his seat over the table. 'We do not know where he is going. Whether he is tied to Blackbeard or not. What he intends to do.'

'He intends,' Coxon refilled Halesworth's glass, 'to be a pirate.' He sat back, fulfilled by his statement. 'And, may I remind you, Mister Halesworth, of the object of your commission as part of the King's proclamation.' Coxon stretched to his desk, the paper to hand, snapped it straight up and read from it in an affected German accent but with an added French lisp: '"*And we do hereby strictly charge and command all our Admirals, Captains and other officers at sea, and all our Governors . . .*" and so on and so on ". . . *to seize and take such of the pyrates who shall refuse or neglect to surrender themselves accordingly.*"' He leant back in his chair and returned the paper to the desk. 'So there it is, Mister Halesworth. Devlin forsook his chance for surrender. Who cares where he is going? I'll ask him when I catch him. All I know is that we are gaining on her, even in her dark cloak. But she can't hide in the light of day.'

'Well I just hope we have the men for it, that's all.' Halesworth tipped back his glass. 'They say you can only stomach to fight a pirate once.'

Coxon smiled. 'Let me tell you about the pirate, Mister Halesworth. First,' he held up his hand and began to count off his fingers, 'they have what they call, "the vapours",' he swallowed a belch. 'This involves a cauldron of green or black smoke, shielding the ship, terrifying the other crew into thinking they are something mystical or fanciful.' He plucked his second finger. 'Then they have music. Drums, pipes, whatever. Makes them sound indifferent, makes it seem like their victory is so assured that they can play a song whilst your men are wetting themselves.' A third finger. 'Then there is their "fireworks". Grenadoes, bottles, anything they can throw. Smoke and mirrors, nothing more.' A fourth finger was pulled, Coxon amused now by Halesworth's interest. 'Then there is the—'

His sentence was choked off by the sudden jerking pitch of the ship that jammed the table into his guts and sent both men flying onto their backs, lucky not to be hit by the crash of breaking plates and bottles landing around them.

Panicked shouts ensued without and the rushing of feet came through the overhead from the quarterdeck as Coxon scrambled to his feet and checked that no fire had spilled from the swinging lanterns.

'We have run aground!' Halesworth pulled himself up and made for the coach and the deck with Coxon.

'Impossible,' Coxon snapped back, reaching for his hat just as Rosher heaved in the outer door.

'We have hit something, Captain!' Rosher exclaimed. 'Bosun is pulling in sail lest we break the rigging.'

Halesworth mumbled to Coxon's back as they crept onto the creaking, protesting deck. 'Perhaps a ship-wreck. We are in the Florida trade routes. They say these are haunted waters between here and Bermuda.'

Coxon pretended not to hear and made for the fo'c'sle, shouting to every man he barged past, his stride confident, hands clasped behind him and hat snapped low, all mannerisms designed to show the panicked men that he and not the faithless sea was in command.

'What goes on here? Why have we been brought to?' He had reached the bow and the huddle of men leaning over the cathead looking down at the hull.

'A hawser is on our keel, Cap'n.' One of them held a lantern over the cathead for their captain to see for himself. 'It'd have been slack. Else we'd have just broke through. Like as not floated up by barrels. Caught us like a net. Must be maybe four shackles long I reckon to drag us to, Cap'n.'

Coxon looked down at the cable stretched along the strakes, creaking and straining to hold the ship that still had some momentum but was now tending to leeward as the stern came about and the cable held. Coxon looked aft, out into the darkness, and imagined the cable perhaps threaded through the thole pins of ship's boats then down into the depths to be anchored at least five times the depth of the sounding, for that is what he himself would have done, and then repeated on the other side. Similar to the anchor chains that would be laid across harbours such as at Maracaibo or Cadiz to prevent men-of-war from entering.

A slow drag. Four shackles. Three hundred feet of rope across the water. Aye, no doubt floated with empty barrels like a reef marker. Devlin had counted on his, on Coxon's, accuracy of sail not to waver from the *Shadow*'s stern.

The *Milford* was caught fore, by the gripe between the keel and the cutwater. Devlin was lucky that the trapping anchors held as the ship pulled against them and lucky, too, that the thole pins did not wrench from the gunwales of the boats set against them. And finally he was lucky that the *Milford* stayed her course and fell into the rope. Just lucky. Not clever at all.

'Lower a man and cut us free,' he said calmly to the hands around him. 'All's well, boys. The pirate has cost us a few minutes, nothing more. Cost him two anchors and two boats and all his cable no doubt.' He pushed away from the cathead to the uninspired face of Mister Halesworth.

'We have broken brails and earrings, Captain. Ripped free from the sudden stop. Some gaskets to be replaced also. It'll maybe be an hour before we can make sail again, what with the dark and all.'

Coxon brushed past the sailors and pushed Halesworth

gently along with his shoulder away from the fo'c'sle. 'An hour will cost me the *Shadow*, Mister Halesworth. We would be giving Devlin five miles whilst you give me bare poles!' His voice had lost the comforting assurance from mere minutes ago within the cabin, where front buttons were undone and neckties loosed.

Halesworth's defence did nothing to remove the rigid animosity from his captain's face. 'It is not my error, Captain. It is your orders to maintain full sail throughout the night!' He sighed and wiped his face then offered as much as he could. 'The main and fore courses are fine, I believe. Perhaps warp us along some as well. I could make two knots before full repairs, Captain.'

Coxon touched Halesworth's forearm and thanked him warmly, which unsettled Halesworth even more. 'So it will not be an engagement as soon as I had hoped. You were correct after all, Mister Halesworth: we are to follow him and nothing more.' He looked about the deck absently. 'He has bested me again. Without a shot. The pirate does not wish to engage, which means he is nearing his goal. He is heading for the Americas. We shall follow his wake.' Coxon sniffed the air, looking about the ship. He nodded, agreeing something within himself before resuming his past conversation. 'I was telling you of the fourth thing, Mister Halesworth, before we were abruptly interrupted, was I not?'

Halesworth looked at the hand still on his forearm then up into the eager eyes boring into his own. 'Indeed. After the fireworks, you said. A fourth aspect about the pirates . . .'

Coxon let go the arm. 'They *love* each other. That is the thing about them. They love each other like brothers. It is their greatest weakness beside drunkenness.' He turned away, vanishing around the foremast, moving amidships, shouting encouragement at every busy back he saw, his voice like a giant's above the urgent clatter and clamour of repair.

Chapter Forty-Five

✖

Taken from the Navigation Acts.
Pertinent to England and her colonies
with regards to foreign trade.

For the increase of the shipping and encouragement of the navigation of this nation wherein, under the good providence and protection of God, the wealth, safety, and strength of this Kingdom is so much concerned. Be it enacted by the King's most Excellent Majesty, and by the Lords and Commons in this present Parliament assembled, and by the authority thereof, that from and after the first Day of December, 1660, and from thence forward, no goods or commodities whatsoever shall be imported into or exported out of any lands, islands, plantations, or territories to His Majesty belonging or in His possession of His Majesty, His heirs, and successors, in Asia, Africa, or America, in any other ship or ships, vessel or vessels whatsoever, but in such ships or vessels as do truly and without fraud belong only to the people of England or Ireland, dominion of Wales or town of Berwick upon Tweed . . .

. . . And be it enacted, that no alien or person not born within the allegiance of our Sovereign Lord the King, His heirs and successors, shall from and after the first day of

February 1661, exercise the trade or occupation of a
Merchant or Factor in any the said places.

Blackbeard snorted through his rum and tossed the paper back to Ignatius. 'Aye. That's what pirates are for. I've grown wealthy on the fact. America trades only with England. Piracy would be gone overnight if it were otherwise.'

Ignatius folded away the transcript with a smile to his ignorant companion. 'It is true. A gentleman here must pay three times the price for a hat than he would in London. For he can buy it from no other place. It is almost a public service that you and your kind perform, Teach.' He saluted him with his glass.

They were in Ignatius's study, alone, waiting both for the clock on the mantle to chime for luncheon and for the call from the harbour that the *Shadow* was at anchor.

Ignatius eased back in his leather chair, taking in the tall crimson-coated pirate that had governors at his hand. 'Do you not see however, Teach, that these colonists must grow tired, frustrated, at shipping everything they produce through England? They have no free will to create a trade with any other European nation. They must purchase everything from the motherland. And sell their produce only to the motherland at a price set by a King they have never seen.'

Teach shrugged. 'I have never seen the King. I trades with who I please and he stays out of my pockets.'

'But the motherland produces what? Cheese and cloth,' he scoffed. 'Yet it suckles from this land some of the most valuable commodities in this world: rice, coffee, sugar, even cotton soon enough if it takes. And by the time it comes back, the man who sowed it gets one third to call his own.'

Teach dragged a chair from the wall to sit on. For two days

now he had endured Ignatius's conversation, that never meandered to women or to cards, the libation as dry as caked mud and feathers.

'I care not for Parliament's botherings, Ignatius. Just for me own neck and those of me men.'

'Ah, but if just one governor of just one colony could have the secret of the production of true porcelain things could change. Not a thing that must be grown and reaped, not a ship built from the oak of her land. A *product*. Unique and respected. Craved throughout the world. More valuable than gold. Things would change.' He sighed. Some fulfilment was lost on Teach beaming proudly across him. 'But it is no matter: you, Teach, do not have the letters.'

Teach licked at the last of the rum on his lips and looked back to the bottle on the commode. 'Aye, but as I said, Devlin surely does. And he comes for his man. I believe that in securing Palgrave when none could I had the best bargaining. But that Irish patroon had beat me to it.'

Ignatius said nothing on the matter. Blackbeard's eyes revealed sufficiently that such a compliment to Devlin's ability wounded the pirate's ill-earned pride.

'It was fortunate for me that I had put both of you to the task. Although in truth I did not suppose that the pirate Devlin could outdo the great and terrible Blackbeard.' His gentle insult was softened by his hand gesturing to the green bottle for Teach to help himself.

Teach rose and strode across the room. 'But I came to you, Ignatius,' he poured four fingers' worth from the bottle. 'In deference. My relations with Governor Eden hold me in good stead for best price for your letters,' he raised his glass respectfully. 'And for the dispatching of Devlin if you wills it. No blood on your hands as it were.'

Ignatius did not return the raising of glass. 'I do not need your assistance in either matter, Teach.' He looked out the window to his secluded high-walled garden, indifferent to the murderer within his walls. 'You may think that you are in a room in a colonial house in the council of Charles Town, a town that is sworn to kill you, and that you have friends in valued positions on your side.' He swung his grey eyes back to Edward Teach. 'But you are in *my* world, and you are waiting for me to let you remain alive within it.'

Teach sank his rum, his eyes staring over the rim of the glass to the man at the desk beyond. The blood pulsed behind his eyes and his fingers gripped white against the rummer as Ignatius looked back at him in sympathy for his ineptitude.

The silent commune between them broke off as Ignatius's office door burst open and his servant gasped an apology for not knocking. 'Begging your pardon, Mister Ignatius sir, Mister Teach, but the pirate ship you described, Mister Teach, is in the harbour, sir. A boat is coming to the wharf!'

Chapter Forty-Six

✖

*O*n a hot afternoon near the end of August the people of Charles Town went about their business. Rice was sacked and carted to the customs house for its long journey back to England. Beer was supped warmly in the taverns by those who had earned its comfort and swallowed bitterly by those who had not, and who rued their days.

Roughly pasted above the stone fireplaces of the inns and on the wooden walls of the customs house were the general notices and by-laws that the council deemed imperative to inform its visitors and denizens of.

Amongst the fines for unescorted slaves and failure to prove ownership of a vessel were the waxed and dog-eared black-rimmed warnings that served to dissuade any of the populace from pursuing a life a-roving on the sea. They were the faded 'Wanted' posters for the pirates known to ravage the Carolinas now that the Bahamas no longer welcomed them.

Blackbeard, Vane, Bonnet: all had hit Charles Town and hit it hard and Charles Town would show them no mercy if they returned. But for now, that afternoon, a small black youth in white wig, bright red coat and gold epaulettes walked two strangers from the harbour and through the dogwood trees lining the streets.

Only one of them had his name printed on the bills on the

walls. It had been there over a year now and lay beneath the fresher names of younger men inspired to follow, now dead and gibbeted or rotting beneath three tides waiting to be so.

A short life and a merry one had been perhaps too inspiring a motto.

The strangers paused when they reached the inn, where ages ago it seemed they had bade goodnight to the girl, Lucy, and where they now looked about them for some inkling of a trap, ignoring the impatience of the youth waving them to follow him to the powder-blue house opposite.

The taller of the two drew dark looks from the passers-by, not just from his stillness amongst their urgency or for his bow-less black hair straggling over his shoulders, but for the deadly cutlass hanging across his body, over his black coat, which hinted at a man more accustomed to pulling out the steel than pulling off the coat. The more observant noted the pommels of twinned pistols nudging the coat aside and ducked their eyes away from him.

The other wore a dirty Dandelion-coloured justacorps and matching wide-brimmed hat, but appeared harmless because he carried no weapons, only a thick bamboo tube, and bowed and dipped to every passing unescorted woman, who grimaced at his gold-capped teeth. He paid no mind to their disgust, using as he was every bow to check every corner and doorway for any observer beyond the naturally curious – the ones that might harbour darker thoughts and cling to the shadows. Some sign of satisfaction was exchanged, a look between the two with no word spoken, and they followed the pristine servant across the street.

It was Ignatius himself who opened the door before they had taken the final step to the threshold. He appeared to them clad in his pious pilgrim black and raised white collar, just as they left him, as if he had sat waiting for them frozen and inanimate whilst Devlin wore the weeks upon his clothes and unshaven face.

'Captain Devlin,' Ignatius looked at the pirate fondly, snubbing Dandon on the step behind. 'I am so glad that you have returned safely. I trust your journey was a pleasant one. Please, do come in.' He stood aside and gestured down the long red passage. 'I have a guest who has been dying to see you again.' He halted Devlin with an arm. 'However, I must insist that you hand over your pistols to my servant boy.' Then added generously, 'You may keep your sword.'

Devlin said nothing and slipped out the pistols to lay heavy in the boy's crossed arms like firewood. Ignatius's attention fell to Dandon. 'Your man, Captain, can wait outside.'

Devlin looked back at Dandon. 'He is unarmed. He has the letters only.'

Ignatius reached for the bamboo. 'May I?' his voice purred beguilingly under his malevolent eyes.

Dandon tossed the tube to Devlin and flourished his hat. 'No need, sir.' He smiled, front teeth shining. 'Captain, I will take no offence by not being permitted to enter. I can pass my time. I believe the Pink House worthy of my attention.' The famed whorehouse of Charles Town was not lost on Dandon in his researches.

'Back to the harbour, Dandon,' Devlin said, and looked coldly at Ignatius. 'Me and Peter Sam won't be long.'

Ignatius pushed closed the door.

'Then good day and good luck to you both!' Dandon called as the door swung to before his nose.

'Filthy fellow,' Ignatius shook his head and joined Devlin's side. 'Now, Captain, shall we begin with some refreshment after your journey?' He placed a soft palm to Devlin's back then flinched in shock as Devlin slapped it away and slammed him to the wall by his neck.

'Enough of your shite! Bring me Peter Sam!'

For forty-nine years Ignatius had led a life that had skirted death, a life that relied constantly on dangerous men, both to protect him and to be subjugated to him, yet it had never occasioned for anyone to stick their hands around his white lavender-powdered neck until their fingernails drew the first pink scrapings of blood.

It seemed so obvious to him now how differently his life could have been if, in the first days, someone had not bowed and done exactly as he said but had begun instead to choke the life out of him, their grip powered purely by hate. What a terrible wasted life that would have been.

How fortunate then that he did indeed lead a life that relied on dangerous men, and his eyes slid along the passage to where Hib Gow darkened the corridor.

Devlin loosed his grip as he followed Ignatius's eyes and understood, his hand creeping towards his blade, how it was Peter Sam had been taken from them.

Hib had maybe nine inches on Devlin, but Devlin had faced big men before. Yet something in the still frame bracing the walls, the solid assurance like the great oak door of a castle and the bony, sharp face with the gnarled giant nose that told of a thousand battles, declared to Devlin that the sword held no fear for the man.

Devlin checked the boy holding his pistols who instantly ran behind the giant and then devoted his hands to simply embracing the bamboo tube. It was perhaps his only defence, and even that growing weaker all the time.

Ignatius coughed and levered himself off the wall, soothing his neck with his hand. Straightening his clothes he made the introductions. 'Captain Devlin, this is Mister Hib Gow, my confidant and aide. He was once a hangman, you know? At Tyburn, no less. Who knows? You two might have met in the future if destiny had not sent you both to me.' He coughed again while the marks on his neck from Devlin's fingers still lingered. 'Shall we?' he said and waved Devlin down the corridor.

Hib glared down at the pirate as he passed by and followed faithfully at Ignatius's back with the gilded servant close behind.

'I trust that you have looked inside the tube that you have brought me, Captain? It would have been difficult I imagine to resist.' They turned one corner, approaching what Devlin supposed was the dining room of a gentleman by the double door ahead.

'Aye, I looked at them.'

'Of little use to you, no doubt, being as the entire volume is in French. Ignorance is often the best security.' The party stopped at the door and Ignatius lifted a key from a silk ribbon at his side.

'I will fetch your quartermaster for you. You may keep the letters until then. I wish you no harm, Captain, despite your violence upon me.' He unlocked the door and ushered Devlin in. 'Wait here, Captain. A few minutes at most, if you please. You can cool some of that blood that boils within you.'

Devlin stepped into the room, bright and cheery from the glass panelled doors that led to the garden standing at the far end. A figure sat at the head of the dining table in front of the doors, as if beatified in the afternoon Charles Town sun. The door was locked.

He had known what to expect. He had thought long on it during the voyage from New Providence and indeed ever since Ignatius had given him the packet with the white raven's feather, inside this very house. Still it came as some surprise to see the purple-doubleted and black-gloved form sitting at the long oak refectory table. The long smooth black hair and beard were not as well groomed as Devlin remembered but the eyes looked just as hate-filled as the last time.

Devlin took off his hat and slung it with the bamboo package on the table. He noted the bottle of wine in the centre that Valentim was already working through. 'Well met, Valentim,' Devlin grinned and held out his hand for a welcoming shake as if they were old friends, then pulled it back in jest and winked at Valentim's out-sized left hand. 'I almost forgot, Valentim: I must beg your pardon.'

Ignatius listened to the sound of crashing glass and the scrape of steel over the shouted Portuguese curses, then stepped away with Hib to leave the intimacy of the room to those that deserved it. He was a man of his word and had promised Valentim Mendes his moment with the pirate Devlin.

Chapter Forty-Seven

✗

Peter Sam

he first strike at Devlin's throat sliced across the white wall as Devlin fell back, the rapier permanently scoring the masonry, leaving later generations of owners to speculate on its origins.

Devlin gave a small laugh as he drew his shorter cutlass, perhaps out of excitement, perhaps at the absurdity of the snarling creature swinging away, kicking the chairs from the table as he edged towards him.

'Valentim!' Devlin's cutlass clanged against one of the swings of the other's blade and held it there, pulling Valentim close. The striking of the steel striking off Devlin's smile. 'This is not the time for us to fight!'

The pirate could fight, would always fight, but a man like Valentim had been educated to it, had been parrying at court probably before Devlin could read and would surely beat him if the play came down to skill alone. But he had probably also always fought like a gentleman. Devlin shot his left elbow in Valentim's eye and Valentim reeled back in shock.

Valentim shook the sting away to see Devlin pacing back, swigging from the wine bottle he had snatched from the table. He offered it to Valentim.

'You should die with wine on your lips.' It was a statement

not a promise. 'Come, Valentim: am I really your enemy this day?'

Valentim's sword whistled through the air, his back and thigh muscles set for his strike. Killing is not drawn in the arms. To the properly trained it is in the hips, the feet and the lungs. One breath, one second. Devlin drank again, his eyes watching over the bottle's neck as Valentim roared.

'I am the *Regulador* of Sao Nicolau, *pirate*! Do not use my name, dog! I have told you such before!'

He sprang forward, half the length he needed to, intending to bring Devlin to parry and open up for the rest of his thrust, but Devlin swept back as Valentim came on, raging. 'You killed my friend! Killed my men!' Their swords rattled and chimed again and again as Valentim backed Devlin towards the wall, spitting his anger at every clash. More than a year of waiting for this moment crying from him. 'You took my ship, and worst of all of these . . .' Devlin's back hit the wall as Valentim's rapier pricked his ribs and held him there. Blood spotted his shirt and Devlin looked down at the sight, something entirely new to him. The blood of others on him more common.

Valentim raised the dead thing at the end of his left arm. 'You took my hand! My body! *My body*!' He pulled back for his thrust, as if Devlin were just a straw-packed dummy in his fencing class, but this was an error against a man accustomed to fighting in the gutters, and Devlin used the gap that had briefly opened up to swing the wine bottle into Valentim's skull.

He had not seen it, and registered only the blackness filling his vision as he collapsed and the floor twisted under his feet. A burnt-in instinct made him fall to one knee and focus on his rapier held out before him, but then something swooped into him hard and he heard his sword falling away and over the flagstones as his head cracked against the same.

Then the voice was above him, whispering like a confession, one knee down on his chest, weighting him to the floor, the other on his sword arm, a cutlass across his throat.

'The bones we have against us may well be due, Valentim,' Devlin bored into Valentim's eyes, reading first one then the other, looking for signs of reason. 'But we are fighting for *him*, not ourselves.' Valentim struggled and began to lift the porcelain hand but had it pushed down and the blade pressed colder and deeper against his flesh. 'Maybe you kill me. Maybe we kill each other. But that's what he wants, don't you see? Less of us all. Together we could take down that carrion he keeps. I'm guessing from your looks you ain't been his guest.' The body beneath him softened. 'I'm here for my quartermaster. You're here for me. Not for him, Valentim. Don't give this to *him*. If you want me, try and take me, but what happens after?' He lifted the blade, a white stripe across Valentim's neck. 'What happens after one of us is dead?' Devlin stood, his sword low, and waited.

Valentim dragged himself to where his sword lay, crawling with added ignominy through the shards of glass and spilled wine. His black glove wrapped itself around the hilt and he used the strength of its blade to heave himself to his feet.

For a moment his back was presented openly for Devlin to run his cutlass through the spine, but the pirate let him rise. Valentim uncoiled upwards, bringing his sword to face his opponent, and he measured the pirate and his words.

'You are right, *pirate*,' he sneered. 'I will kill you . . . later.'

Devlin picked up the bamboo tube without his eye leaving the governor of Sao Nicolau. 'To the garden,' he nodded to the glass doors. 'More room to fight.'

*

Ignatius weighed Devlin's pistols in his hands. They were carbine-bore Dragoons with twelve-inch barrels and brass escutcheon plates screwed into the wrist to strengthen them. The plates announced they were by Barbar of London no less, and they would be worth maybe sixty or seventy pounds apiece. He marvelled at their handsomeness and tucked them into his belt. How easily the pirate had given them up, he thought. How easy it was to pluck a crow.

'They are in the garden. Together.' Hib's voice drifted over from the doors looking over the walled sanctuary of Magnolia and Azalea. 'Far corner.' His hand was already on the brass catch, waiting for Ignatius's response.

Ignatius swept to the window. 'What are they doing? They are not fighting?' His voice was lilting with surprise.

Hib looked out to the men, at the drawn swords, at the gap between them. 'Not now,' he said. 'Devlin has the letters at his feet.'

Ignatius confirmed the sight before them. 'They have joined. Interesting.' His eyes lit up as if he had hoped for and expected such an outcome. He put his hand on Hib's shoulder and faced the other two men in the office.

'Teach, I may have need of you.' He nodded to the chained Peter Sam haunting the room. 'Bring *that* to the garden.'

Blackbeard put down the rum bottle and looked at the figure of Peter Sam standing with his shoulders drawn down by the long chains hanging from his wrists. He had known Peter Sam. He did not know the eye of the man who now looked up at him. Edward Teach moved away and for the first time he thought of the men he had left behind at the grounding of the *Queen Anne's Revenge*. A shudder rippled across his back as he turned away from Peter Sam.

'I will not befoul my hand with such, Ignatius. Let his gaoler bring him. I wish to see Devlin for meself.'

Twelve feet high stone walls enclosed the garden, which was twenty feet across with fifty feet of paved walkways and trees, and an iron sundial in the centre that never caught the sun. Ignatius had chosen his property well. The garden could hold many secrets.

Valentim and Devlin watched the three men emerge from the house and the blades twitched in their hands. Devlin looked once at Peter Sam, smaller, paler, but still Peter Sam despite that, he was sure. Blackbeard wore the same crimson coat and the same look of arrogance and Devlin felt a vague crease of his brow at the recollection of the last time he had faced the scourge of the coast.

Valentim caught Devlin's look, counted the weapons facing them and leant to the man beside him. 'Do you have a plan, pirate?'

Devlin reached down and picked up the bamboo tube. 'In London I worked at an anchorsmith's with a man named Kennedy,' he announced, prompting a confused look from his companion. ''Til I was trained to it I forged cable-chain. I learnt never to mind about the link I had just made, or the link I was going to make, just the one I was working on. Get burnt else.' He winked to Valentim.

'I am allied with a madman.' Valentim balanced himself and held his breath.

Ignatius stood between Hib and Blackbeard, his confidence undiminished. 'My letters, Captain, if you please.' He stepped forward, a friendly hand outstretched.

'My man,' Devlin said. 'Bring me Peter Sam.'

Ignatius pointed to the waist-tall sundial in the middle of

the grove, circled by stone seats. 'There,' he said. 'We will talk, you and I.'

Ignatius walked calmly forwards, alone, and Devlin went to meet him, casting an eye to Valentim to watch the letters as he placed them back to the ground. He kept his cutlass low.

The sundial was between them, no shadow upon it, as the men faced each other. Ignatius began a speech long thought of, his hands resting sedately on the wrists of Devlin's pistols.

'A new war is here, Captain.' He spoke as if it were his own joyous creation. 'England and her allies are again at the throat of Spain. Perhaps before the end of the year the Ottoman empire will join also. It will be a good year to be a privateer. It will be a good year to be my acquaintance. Not my enemy.'

'I brought your letters. Bring me my man.'

Ignatius gently shook his head. 'Do you not know what those letters are, Captain? Surely you are not as much an Irish imbecile as you appear to be?'

'I understand what you have told me. The making of porcelain. Cups and pots for kings.'

'No, Captain. Much more than that. They are the secret of making *free* trade. A bargaining tool that could cut America loose from England's apron strings. Which one of your lives do you think is worth more to me than such a power? By the end of the last war I was a phenomenally wealthy man. By the end of this one I will be the mark of avarice itself, and you, Captain, have brought me the means. I may have use for a good privateer in the months to come.'

'You have Teach,' Devlin said.

Ignatius stiffened. 'No, Teach will be dead soon. He knows too much. And he failed to bring me the letters. You have succeeded. I may have a need for you to live.' He looked fondly at Devlin then remembered where they were. 'Go get your letters. You may take your man when I have them. I must check their validation first.'

'You do not trust me, Ignatius?' Devlin began to turn away.

'Do you trust me, Captain?'

They retired to their corners.

Valentim's eyes were now wide with fury. 'What is happening, pirate? What is said?'

Devlin picked up the tube, his back to the others. 'I'll go for the big man. You go for Ignatius.'

'What of Blackbeard? Who goes for him?'

'Teach will hold until he sees a coin land. I have the advantage that he may want me for himself.'

'So I am to go for the man who has two pistols against me? You pirates and your rules of war!'

Devlin grinned. 'You can trade if you want.'

Valentim silently declined the offer as he watched Hib glowering at them. 'What of your man? I disbelieve he will assist. He is broken, you understand?'

Devlin turned and considered Peter Sam. 'No. He won't help us. But with luck he may yet help himself. Wait until I move, Valentim.' Together they crossed the path.

Hib leant towards Peter Sam's ear. 'Here he comes,' he whispered, his voice as soft as a lamb's tongue. 'Here comes the man who has led you here to me, my boy. Here we are against him, my Peter Sam.'

Peter Sam lifted his head to the familiar face walking towards him.

How many months now? A different coat. Different hat. *Might not be him at all. No matter. Little to matter now*.

'Your letters, Ignatius,' Devlin held out the sleeve of bamboo. 'From Father d'Entrecolles, to a Father Orry, to Captain

William Guinneys, to you, to Black Sam Bellamy, and now me.'

Devlin placed the bamboo tube in Ignatius's arms and looked Hib's frame up and down, regretting he had not packed his ebony dagger. Ignatius unbound the cork and string to pull out the volume within.

Valentim Mendes saw only that Ignatius's hands were occupied. He saw that perhaps together, with this *porco* dead, himself and the pirate could fell the Scotsman. Perhaps just two strikes from the pair of them. The odds would be in the favour of the Portuguese and those of righteous birth.

He thrust his rapier exactly as he had been taught to.

Devlin shouted something but Valentim would never understand it. He saw Devlin's cutlass strike down at the Scotsman's arm as it stabbed towards him but the giant swatted away the pirate; and then Valentim was looking down at the hilt of the Estilete as it stuck out from under his chin and his doublet was soaked with blood.

He touched the warm flow as he stumbled back, mystified by its streaming. He staggered, dropped his sword and pulled out the spike rammed in his throat, a white piece of his spine stuck to its tip like a rough diamond. Valentim croaked a bloody grin at its ghastly beauty that seemed as strange as his exquisite porcelain hand.

He saw nothing else and Hib left him twitching on the grass. Then the Scotsman stomped over to where the pirate lay.

Devlin scrambled to his feet and tried to get away from Hib's approach. He looked around the garden. Valentim lay dead. Blackbeard was standing fast but his fists were pulling out pistols. Ignatius was white-faced and checking for wounds about him. Peter Sam did nothing. The Scotsman brought a cudgel from behind his back and grimaced happily as he approached Devlin's outstretched cutlass.

He looks like a farmer, Devlin thought absently. A poor worsted waistcoat and calico breeches and buskins like a Dutchman's, but a big bastard nonetheless. Go for the head. Slice something off. He'd stop at that.

He looked at the boulder-like hands closing in on him. If he gets inside the blade I'm dead. Think on that. Accept that. Know that in a fight you will get pain so wait for it. Move with that in mind.

Hib kept grinning. He made a playful lunge for Devlin's coat with his empty hand and the pirate swiped at his head with his curve of metal.

Hib leant away easily and wrapped his fist around Devlin's falling sword hand, crushing the blade loose. Holding him high and away like a struggling rat and revelling in the pain across the pirate's face as he hung from his arm, Hib felt Devlin's bones grind inside his monstrous fist.

The cudgel dove inside at the pirate with enough force to punch straight through his back, and then Hib batted Devlin away with another strike as he laughed at the splash of blood leaving his stick.

Devlin landed whimpering like a boy. Pain wept out of him. Then a boot like a paving stone lifted him clear across the garden.

He rolled painfully; tried to raise himself. Coughing, he searched desperately for his cutlass: *Always find your steel.* The sight of it gave him strength over his pain.

Devlin clutched his sides and staggered across the grass to where he had seen a glint of metal. The shadow of the Scotsman fell over him, his faint giggle the only sound in the garden.

Ignatius found his voice again, feeling secure rolling the

bamboo tube in his hands. Now he could save the pirate or let him live. The Irishman might even be grateful, for Hib could break him as easily as the other.

But Hib had cut once already and would need more. The *Regulador* of Sao Nicolau was stretched dead and open-eyed but that was not enough. One was never enough. The bowels of Newgate had vomited Hib into Ignatius's hands after the hangman had lost his position in the fallout of the Jacobite uprisings, but Hib had not lost his taste for murder with the loss of his employ and London had dribbled blood for months afterwards from alleyway to alleyway.

The giggle came again and Ignatius knew what it signified. The pirate was no real loss, after all.

'Finish him, Hib!' Ignatius cried. Devlin looked up as Hib's eyes upon him grew round and white, and Devlin called to the lowered head of his quartermaster.

'Peter Sam! Stand to!' Devlin choked out the words, gaining a moment's respite as Hib looked round at the chained man. Devlin dragged himself away and continued to call. 'To me, Peter Sam!' Still coughing he pulled himself to try and stand, finding his vision had cleared enough to see his cutlass a few feet from him. But he couldn't rise. Nothing worked. Everything wanted to sleep.

Hib twisted his cudgel in his hands, slitted eyes observing the big quartermaster. The head still hung down. The Scotsman switched back to Devlin. He was just flesh and bone like all the rest. He giggled once more as Devlin began to crawl towards his cutlass and still tried to speak to ghosts.

'Back for you, Peter Sam . . . Ship waiting for you.'

Hib's boot tipped him onto his back. He wanted to see Devlin's face before he died and still the stupid choking voice prattled on.

'Come back for you, Peter Sam . . . Come back for my brother.'

The voice came like a dog growling in the night. Hib's head whisked back to look at Peter Sam. Ignatius watched the chains pull tight as shoulders flexed and a back rose straight. He inched away as the growl whispered across the garden.

'Get your filthy Scottish arse away from him, you dog!' And Peter Sam began to move. Hib turned and smiled, slapping his bloody cudgel between his hands.

'Forget him, Gow!' Ignatius called. 'Kill Devlin!'

Obediently Hib spun back to the pirate Devlin who was pulling himself closer to his blade.

Ignatius backed to Teach's side. 'Teach! Kill this animal!'

But Blackbeard holstered his pistols. 'Do something yourself. I think you've spoken enough to pirates.' And he stepped into the shade as Peter Sam lumbered away from them.

Not enough, Peter Sam thought. Nothing in my arms except cabbage water and broth. Not enough strength in my limbs to stop him. His eyes sought for steel, any metal, even wood – and then he saw it.

But enough in my arms still to pick up an iron sundial.

His fists wrapped around its leg and with its heft of iron came the memory and the memory ran hotly through his arms. His strength had been gone but the feel of iron was as strong as meat.

Hib's prey inched away from him like a worm. He stamped a buskin on the hem of Devlin's coat. 'Where do you think you're going, little man?'

Devlin looked up at the beast and spat his own blood at the boots. He turned a bloodied smile on the Scotsman as the sun hit the garden for the first time. 'I'm getting out of the way, you fat fuck!'

'*Hib*!' Ignatius warned, cocking his pistol too late and fate-fully causing Hib to turn just as Peter Sam ploughed the sundial's flat edge across the broken, bent and twisted nose that defined his face.

A staggering flash of agony jolted through Hib and a ferrous odour seemed to explode in his head. For the first time, even after all the laughing boys of Greenock, the taverns and gutters of London and his own father's terrible fists – never forgotten – Hib Gow fell to his knees, and the great and masterful proboscis that set him apart from all others plopped onto the stone path before his eyes – eyes that were already beginning to swell and close as his body panicked to protect his sight.

Hib tried to mouth some plea to the suddenly monstrous man in leather but only the gurgle of his own black blood dribbled out. His jaw hung loose. He swayed, attempting to grab the man moving behind him, who now stood on his legs, who wrapped chains around his neck, who was pulling the life out of him, whose knees were pushing Hib's back away from the tightening iron garotte, whose wrists were straining rivulets of blood down the chains as the links coiled and choked him.

'*It's Hib!*' the hideous crones would cry. '*Hib's doing it!*' And the cheers would ring out all around the Tyburn tree because the black mask could not hide the proud ugly nose stretching the cloth sack to its furthest. '*Hib's doing it!*' the biddies cheered, and he always gave them a choking to remember. He had been good at that one thing all his life. Knew it now.

Peter Sam felt the last rattle shudder through his arms, and the last of his strength fell away with the huge body as he slumped alongside it in the grass and the gore. Only Peter

Sam's chest rose and fell with his gasped breaths. His arm lay against Hib's.

Ignatius had witnessed a man who seemed potent for another forty years slaughtered before him. Flies were already playing in Hib's blood; his protector was gone.

Ignatius's peaceful garden was now a butcher's drain hole. He raised the pistol like a man lost in the forest who hears the baying of wolves all around him and aimed at the pirate reaching for his cutlass as he struggled to his feet.

You hold too much faith in steel, pirate.

He laid his sight.

To kill you with your own gun and then your own man with your other gallant pistol. All that you deserve.

He fired.

He had underestimated the pirate. Plucked the wrong crow.

Ignatius let go the pistol, unable to hold it now his thumb and forefinger were no longer part of his hand.

Devlin had given up a pair of rich, fine London pistols, hard for a gentleman to resist, but Devlin had overloaded them with two fists' worth of powder and iron scrap and plugged them with hemp. On firing, the breech, plates and walnut stock had exploded in Ignatius's fist.

A laugh burst from Teach as he watched Ignatius buckle and wonder at his hand.

Ignatius dropped the bamboo tube as he grabbed at the blood and stumbled for his rooms. His shoes crunched on his own shattered fingers like the crushing of snails. He needed cloth for staunching, he needed water, he needed help. For the first time in all his years of dining with kings and princes he needed help.

Here be pirates.

Chapter Forty-Eight

Do you want to be a pirate?

He closed the door to them, biting back the shock seeping through him as he summoned his boy with a scream. Outside, Devlin stood over Peter Sam and gave him his hand, hauling him up like a fallen child.

Peter stumbled but stood. He touched Devlin's hand. 'I think I been lost, Captain . . .' his voice faded.

Devlin held him up and gave him his shoulder. 'You came back, Peter. Besides, I didn't have anything else to worry about.' They hobbled together to the house and Teach stepped out from the trees.

Peter Sam straightened as best he could, pulled his bloodied chains taut again and stepped in front of Devlin.

Devlin levelled his blade. 'Come on then,' his voice grating as ribs pinched inside him. 'Let's have you an' all.'

Edward Teach slowly reached into his waistcoat, past the pistols holstered about his chest, and brought out the stump of candle he had carried with him the past year.

'I am due to light this,' he said as placidly as his growling tones would allow. 'I need to light it to end your days, Captain Devlin.' He pulled down his broad hat to cover his eyes and tossed the candle to Devlin's feet. 'Too much wind here to light such a promise. We should go inside and finish that dog.

I've a ship to gets to and so has you.' Then Teach gave up his only secret, and he gave little to any man: 'He has a tunnel to the harbour.' Devlin said nothing and Teach lent an arm to Peter Sam and they walked to the house, only Devlin giving a backwards look to the blood-soaked body of Valentim Mendes staining the fallen Magnolia blossom. No-one cast an eye to the abandoned bamboo tube or the fleshy slab that had once been Hib Gow.

Inside, Ignatius's boy had helped him wrap his blackened hand and pulled back the rug to reveal the ringbolt door that led to the storm drain and the harbour. Tossing aside the other of Devlin's pistols, Ignatius took his own from his desk, awkwardly cocking it with one hand, accustomed as he was to palming back the dog-head. It clicked just in time to meet the crash of the doors from the garden and tremblingly played over all three men stepping into the room.

'Keep your distance!' Ignatius's voice rattled, the shot nearly let fly too soon.

'Do you not want the Jesuit's letters, Ignatius?' Devlin called. 'You left them in the garden there.' Devlin and Teach separated instinctively, the only defence against a single shot. Peter Sam attached himself to Devlin, the room crawling with memories around him.

Ignatius bade his boy open the hole and as the trap door slammed back it belched a breath of sea and moss.

'I am leaving for my ship, gentlemen. I will fire on you should you follow.' He moved around his desk to the hole, sparing an eye to check the ladder, convinced that he could climb down and still keep an armed hand upon the pirates. 'For now you may have the letters. That is the price I pay for my escape. Perhaps time may come to haunt you for what you have spoilt this day. I very much hope so. You could have been witnesses to the birth of a nation.' He took his first step down into the tunnel and neither Devlin nor Teach moved a muscle. 'For the moment you are free, but mark me, gentlemen, I am not one to be tried.'

The black youth suddenly realised he was to be abandoned to the mercy of cut-throats and skipped to the hole. 'Master?'

Ignatius swung the pistol at him. 'Stay, boy!' Then he vanished.

He ducked along the passage for only a few feet before he noticed that something blocked the shaft of light that should have been shining in from the sea.

One lightning-fast hand slapped his pistol loose while another whipped its own across Ignatius's jaw.

'Hullo, chum!' Hugh Harris chirped. 'Where you planning on going then?' he asked as he slipped his kidney dagger from his belt.

Ignatius scuttled back towards the light from above, his hand to his mouth, horrified by the taste of his own blood. He looked up at the bright square light above him just as it was blotted out by the silhouette of Peter Sam looming over the hole. Peter descended in silence and Devlin slammed the hatch behind him.

'What's your name, lad?' Devlin put his face close to the youth's, who had begun to shake tears from his wide eyes as the screams came wrenched and muffled from the cellar beneath them.

The boy looked deep into the pirate's eyes and wondered how the man could not hear the terrible sounds from below, the face so kindly looking upon him. 'Matthew, sir,' he caught a sob and pleaded. 'I is fifteen years old.'

'Well, Matthew,' the pirate squeezed his shoulder. 'I could do with some help getting back to sea. How do you fancy being a pirate, my boy?'

The cellar door rattled once, desperately, like a storm door, and then all became still. Only the dark eyes of the pirate remained, looking softly and questioningly into William's face as if nothing had happened to any of them.

'I think . . .' he stammered, 'I think I should not like it, thanking you kindly, Captain.'

Chapter Forty-Nine

✗

*T*he immutable law of the sea was the only faith that John Coxon knelt to in spite of his parson father's vigorous attempts to make a church-going Christian of him; and, in spite of Devlin's ingenious attempt to shake the *Milford* from his *Shadow*'s stern, to Charles Town Coxon inevitably came.

In London he could stumble out of The Grapes into Narrow Street after dark and not know east from west; but streets did not have tides, did not leave wakes, apart from the ebb and flow of vice and the morning roll of the brewer's dray. Ships he could follow. Seas he knew. And he had followed Devlin.

South-east of Charles Town harbour, far away from the acres of wood bustling along Cooper river trading indigo and rice, black backs and beaver laps, the *Milford* sat and waited. She had been cleared for action since dawn.

'A sail!' The cry echoed around her decks. It was a grey sail, above a black and red freeboard, sporting a ragged kingdom pennant trailing from her backstay but fooling no-one. She was making for the *Mer Du Nord*, hiding herself amid the merchants and Indiamen. But not hiding well enough.

'That's her,' Coxon grinned as he stood at the larboard chains with Rosher, who had not seen the *Shadow* this close before. There, threading through the forest of masts, against the tide, less than a mile away, he could count the red gunports facing them. Nine along the weatherboard and two quarter-deck guns, another at the fo'c'sle. Nine pounders. One broad-side, 216lbs, if double-shot. The *Milford* could hurl 312lbs in reply and Rosher tapped the gunwale proudly.

'Weigh anchor!' Halesworth yelled in response to Coxon's nod. 'Make fighting sail!'

'We'll meet her in less than an hour, Rosher,' said Coxon, checking his watch. 'Away from the lanes. Meet her in the Atlantic. Take her once and for all.' He noticed a tremor of concern pass across the young man's face and shooed it away. 'Come now, Rosher, you are to be congratulated! It is not every day we get the chance for a prize!'

'No, Captain,' he agreed. 'But I am glad for your presence also on such a day.'

Coxon sniffed away the compliment. 'Lay dead-lights to the cabin windows and prepare for closed-quarters, Mister Rosher, then to your gun-crew.' He looked over to the *Shadow* where some activity drew his eye and also Mister Halesworth to his elbow.

'Captain, it appears—'

'I see it, Mister Halesworth: they are raising arming cloths.'

Along the ship the pirates were stringing 'fights', red sheets trimmed in white that would both shield them from accurate targeting and hide their own actions and numbers. The reason for the choice of red was obvious enough and the sheets were pulled up even to the tops until the *Shadow* looked more like a costumed circus tent than a man-of-war.

'He knows we are on him. Stand to, Mister Halesworth. Putting up his fights shows he is troubled.'

Halesworth traced a finger out to the *Shadow*'s stern to the gig being lowered from the counter. Two figures were aboard. Coxon followed Halesworth's finger to the sight and watched the white flag shimmy up the *Shadow*'s mainmast from the cover of the arming cloths.

'Troubled indeed, Captain,' Halesworth raised his eyebrows at the unexpected behaviour of a man he had begun to fear, sure now that one of the dark figures rowing towards them was the pirate Devlin. 'He wishes a truce of some kind perhaps?' He looked carefully at his captain who seemed to be studying the boat stoically but whose hand was tight and pale against the gunwale.

'Stay your sails, Mister Halesworth. Let him come to me,' decided Coxon, then turned his back to Halesworth and walked aft to the Great Cabin. 'I'll kill any man who fires against him.'

Coxon spared one look over the water to the black and red ship. Whatever Devlin had planned to do, whatever fate Charles Town held for him, whatever trickery New Providence had provided, had come to an end. And he wanted to hear what picture the man who had once been his thrall had painted on the world this final time, before his inevitable end.

Chapter Fifty

Master and Servant

*T*he gig slammed between the wind and water of the *Milford* and was handsomely belayed despite the repute of the men below; there was even a shrill whistle to announce the boots of the tall rake standing on English boards.

He had not changed his clothes and had not shaved. He looked as worn as a Newfoundland whaler captain but nobody met his eye and judged him. He carried a book and a volume of tied paper beneath one arm. Perhaps he had come to preach to them?

Halesworth removed his hat, the action not reciprocated, and bid him welcome which greeting was also not returned.

Devlin spoke carefully, quietly, for Halesworth alone and not the thirty armed men and marines crowding the waist and main hatch, all shifting and vying for a view like bridesmaids craning their heads for a peek at the best man.

'My man, Hugh, will stay below,' he said and opened his coat to show his belt full of weapons. 'Would you take my arms?'

Halesworth searched for a threat in the almost sleepy eyes that he took for an inebriate's. He thanked him for the offer but declined to reach into the black coat and instead gestured to the cabin with a bow. 'Captain Coxon will receive you. On your honour, sir.'

The pirate lowered his head to hide his grin under the brow of his hat. 'I would like to see John very much,' he said and walked along the gangway with Halesworth following, shaking his head at the familiarity.

Coxon had removed his coat and the wax from a bottle of Madeira sack and was drinking a glass of it as the door from his coach opened with a timid knock. A half-cocked pistol rested beside the bottle. There was no need to conceal it; Devlin would expect no less.

Halesworth gave no introduction and hovered in the doorway as the pirate ducked beneath the overhead and removed his hat. Coxon waved Halesworth away without a word and the coach door clicked shut.

'John,' Devlin dropped his hat next to the pistol, 'I have brought you a gift under a flag of truce. A thanks for leaving me to escape from Providence and not hanging me as you saw me. Without you gone I am sure it would not have been so simplified.'

'I will hear of it all from Rogers when I return. No doubt some portion of blame will fall to my quarter. That is I take it, that Rogers still lives?'

Devlin sat down. 'He may regret it but I made no offence against him.' He put his package on the table. 'A book. From Miguel De Cervantes. I know your fondness for words and I thought you might be interested in the purpose that has brought us together again.' He rested his arm on the pile of papers and passed over Book II of *Don Quixote*.

Coxon took the book and placed it on the chair beside him without a glance. 'Your purpose is well known to me, Patrick. Whatever nobility you wish to attach to yourself . . .' he paused as a trio of yells resounded outside the door chiding slack hands, '. . . you are still only a pirate under the law.'

420

He poured more Madeira, two more, and offered Devlin a glass. 'And I out-gun you and out-man you I'm sure, since you hide behind those arming cloths, which is why you come to me under a white flag.'

'I do not come to surrender, John,' Devlin took the glass. 'And I hope you will not take advantage of the matter.'

'And you would not take advantage? If I were sat in your cabin?'

'That I cannot say. But I gambled that you were a better man than I.' He saluted Coxon with his glass and closed his eyes on the warm sweetness in his mouth more delicate than the harsh, brackish rum he had drunk a quart of that morning to steel himself for the meeting with his former master.

Whatever he had achieved, whatever he had become, John Coxon had been his master for four years. He had beaten him, fed him, owned him. You could never be equal to such a man, until that man were dead. Freedom began at the grave. Coxon undoubtedly knew the same.

'This conversation will end now, Patrick. What was your purpose on Providence?' He let his right hand lay beside the wrist of his pistol. 'If not simply for your gold?'

'A man named Ignatius told me that the world is again at war. Is that true, John?'

'It is so. Spain fancies Philip on the throne of France. War rages in Sicily as we speak.'

'So would not this folly in the Bahamas be at an end soon enough? Colonising hell-mouths that struggle to build even churches.'

'It might be ended at that. But it is not for me to say. Perhaps men like Rogers and his kind hold too much faith in this New World. They did not ask my kind for our opinion. Perhaps the answer is in the natives and yourselves. Company men have sent me for their own mercantilist motives. Warranted from the King no less. This age of your rover friends is ended. And I may have been forgotten enough to be asked to fight. My role now is to sweep you and your kind from the profit ledgers.'

'Aye, I reckon one day it will just come down to me and you swearing at each other from across the sea.'

'That could be today, Patrick.'

Devlin rubbed a weary hand down his face. 'I would hope not, Captain.'

Coxon laughed. 'Thank you, Patrick! Thank you indeed!'

'For what, Captain?'

'For giving me my title at last. I would flog Rosher for less.'

Coxon poured more Madeira and pulled the tale from Devlin. In spite of all he now was, in spite of the star-shaped white scar on his forearm Devlin was still the servant, still his man. The man that he had seen promise in and even liked, when time and duty had permitted; and in some misbegotten sense that would reflect like filth in Whitehall, there was even a feeling akin to pride in the brigand that Coxon himself did not fully understand and which no-one else would ever feel. Until the end, still to come.

For now Devlin told of the taking of his friend and quartermaster by an agent, perhaps of courts, perhaps of governments, perhaps of companies, but not a man of honour.

'Men of honour, John, talk of men such as you and I. And always will. Always. In the singular. They don't speak of armies and nations but of men's names. For sword points and lead all end singularly. Learned souls talk of maps and nations, forgetting that it all falls down to limbs and the dead. We sit at a table surrounded by two hundred singular men of honour. We can save some blood today for whatever purpose the others have for them tomorrow. We have virgins and whore-mongers. We have widows' sons, orphans and thieves. But they are ours, yours and mine. Not theirs yet. Not today. You have my gold on Providence. Buried with Sarah. I'll leave the end up to you.'

'And what of that fellow, Howell Davis, what did he get to conspire alongside you, Patrick? I surrendered only a thousand pounds of your account to Rogers after we searched the *Mumvil*.'

'He had some. Needed it to brush off Seth's bad luck. I bought my way into Providence. Lost my favoured gun because of it. I had to go in naked as I came into the world.'

Coxon stood, his movement prompting Devlin to hover over his pistol; a sideways look glinted from Coxon at the move but nothing more.

'I got back my own duelling pistols,' Coxon moved to his cot and turned to Devlin with a sailcloth packet of bulk and familiar shape. 'And I believe this is yours, Patrick. Left-handed lock. Ugly brute.' He tossed the packet, amused by Devlin's pleasure as he unwrapped and stroked the octagonal barrel of his old friend.

'I am indebted to you, Captain. I have missed her so.'

'I note the stock is damaged. You should have it sanded.'

Devlin secured the gun in his belt. 'That is the strike of a cutlass. From the man I have just rescued. He was attempting to kill me at the time.'

Coxon raised an eyebrow and changed the subject back to Howell Davis. 'He will be a pirate now. Howell, I mean. You spawn like frogs.'

'*Hostis humanis generis*, George has named us. An enemy to all mankind. The enemy being freedom, I do not doubt. But I have met more dangerous felons these last few months and even some that perhaps I should reconsider what they meant to me. And what I have done to them.' His hand moved to his glass as he thought of Valentim Mendes and he swallowed away something more than the Madeira sack, the wine now catching in his throat. He shook the thought away with a smile and slapped the pages of parchment he had brought with him. 'Anyways, Captain John, I have here a secret to bestow upon you. Boons to buy safe passage of my men to wherever we shall roam, and the same to your sons who might suffer else.'

Coxon resumed his seat and the pouring of wine. 'Are you sure you can offer me that, Patrick? I have seen the *Shadow* fight before. And the *Milford* is much more. Much more. I could break her before sunset.'

Devlin leant forward and Coxon saw again the dark face from the island the year before. 'But I will have a hundred pirates upon you before that. Not a running fight of cannon, Captain. Only cutlass and teeth. Can your men stand that? Your fine young men against cannibals and Sodom? I'll take odds against that judgement.'

Coxon pointed his glass to the papers, avoiding the wager. 'What are these?'

Devlin smiled, accepting the diversion. 'Death, Captain. Lives whipped away by a rush of falling paper. The arcanum of porcelain. The secret of its making. The reason I have come to you.'

Coxon sat. He looked at the smile of Devlin and then the hand resting on the papers. '*Porcelain*? The making of porcelain? Take me for a fool now, is it? How would you and your filthy rogues fall on such a secret? Saxony has Europe begging at his door for its exports.'

'Ah, and Saxony has only lucked on the recipe, so I am

told, through a decade of concentration, but even that does not compare to the true variety.' He tapped the pile of paper. 'The true kilns and clays, firings and fluxes, all the manner of it. All sitting here at my hand. All for easy reading.'

Devlin let the power of the yellow paper sink in and then pushed them across the table, picking up his Cervantes from the chair under the table and leafing through it as Coxon glanced through the letter.

'It is in French,' Coxon said and then understood. But still Devlin had much entertaining to do.

'Of course the man who sent me to take the papers did not suppose that a dribbling ignorant gallows dancer such as I could ever interpret his soul's desire. My ignorance was his security, apparently. Between me and Dandon, who reads better Frog than I, we had five days to Charles Town to make a good copy and provide him with the original, which is in Teach's hands now – our own bargain – and winds its way to some ill-inclined governors of His Majesty. With just a few alterations to the text of course, just enough to the mix to make it worthless.' Devlin picked up the Madeira bottle himself, putting down the book, and poured another measure. 'And I gives these letters unto you, Captain John. Price of passage if you will it. For my men and me to sail where we will.' He slapped a full glass in front of Coxon. 'What do you suppose King George will make of such a parcel, Captain?'

'And naturally you have not altered *this* copy in any manner. Entranced as you are by your King, I'll wager a wig.'

'That accusation will have to ride on my honour, Captain John.'

Coxon picked up the worn Cervantes and it fell open to the author's first page, the preface written after the loss of his left arm while serving in the Spanish navy, the thread of the spine almost broken where it had been read and re-read. He read the page aloud, knowing something in its lines must have weighed on Devlin for him to offer the book as a gift, so much they had shared over the years. His new comrades, for all their worth, were no good for that. Coxon guessed that something in Devlin missed his world, though obviously not enough:

If my wounds have no beauty to the beholder's eye, they are, at least, honourable in the estimation of those who know where they were received; for the soldier shows to greater advantage dead in battle than alive in flight.

'Rogers disdains novellas, you know. They are not for Englishmen. I did not know that Cervantes was one-handed. Lost his left arm. That is very interesting. An English copy no less. It must mean something to you, Patrick.' Coxon thumbed through the pages.

Devlin lost his politeness, drank high and slammed his empty glass upturned on the table, shaking it and causing Coxon's glass to spill a little. 'I have regretted the death of too many, Captain! I will have no more of it if you can find to grant me so. Not this day.'

Coxon leant back, still reading on, his eyes to the page. 'Then go, pirate. The price is enough for King George and Rogers I'm sure. Secretary Popple back in Whitehall will have palpitations when Rogers writes home with this. And you have nothing now. No gold, no friendly ports in these lands,' his eye flicked back up to Devlin's for an instant. 'Some guilt finally being assuaged perhaps?'

Devlin's face flashed venom for one eye-blink. Coxon knew nothing of Valentim Mendes but he recognised remorse when he saw it.

'Even your pirate lords have become your hunters. When I return to Providence I will be sent straight out after you again. I can give you this day, but what of tomorrow? What will you do then, Patrick?'

Devlin scraped back his seat, picked himself up and tipped his hat, then flashed the rakish grin that belonged to the crude, stained posters fading above the fireplaces of the inns of the world and warning of his presence.

'*Hoy por mi, manana por ti*. Today for me, Captain John, tomorrow for thee.' He pulled open the outer door to thirty pairs of eyes staring into the cabin and cocked his head back to the table. 'I'll see you tomorrow, Captain John.'

'Aye, Patrick,' he went back to the book, not granting Devlin a parting glance. 'That I reckon you will.'

Epilogue

Letter from Governor Woodes Rogers to the Council of
Trade and Plantations, Whitehall. (Extract)

Oct 1718.
Sirs,

*Pursuant to my Instructions I take leave to acquaint
your Lordships, I arrived in this port 26th July in company
with the men-of-war ordered to assist me. I met with little
opposition in coming in, but found a French ship burning
in the harbour, which we were told was set on fire to drive
out H.M.S. the* Rose, *by one Charles Vane who commands
the pirates, fled away in a sloop wearing the black flag,
and fired guns of defiance.*

*On the 27th I landed and took possession of the fort,
where I read H.M. Commission in the presence of my
officers, soldiers and about 300 of the people found here,
who received me under arms and readily surrendered,
showing then many tokens of joy for the re-introduction
of Government.*

*We have scarce half of those who have been pirates left,
for they soon became weary of living under restraint and
are either gone to several parts of North America, or engaged
themselves on services at sea, which I was willing to
promote, for they are not the people I ought to think will*

make any land improvements, and I wish they may be
faithful at sea.

What with the pyrates robbing us and the inclination
of many of our people to join them, and the Spaniards
threatening to attempt these Islands we are continually
obliged to keep on our guard. Above 100 men that accepted
H.M. Act of Grace in this place are now out pyrating again
and except effectual measures are taken the whole trade
of America must be soon ruined.

> *Woodes Rogers.*
> *Captain General and Governor in Chief*
> *New Providence, Eleuthera,*
> *Harbour Island and Abaco.*

They left Peter Sam to his own care and ablutions. He joined none at the head in the dawn, ate alone below behind a curtained wall of hemp close to the manger where the skinny goats and hogs tripped and swayed against the ever-growing swell and squealed and kicked through the night. He sought no company and they let him be. Only Dog-Leg Harry held the key to the hemp curtain. A tin of small beer and rum, stewed meat and potatoes and Salmagundi on a Sunday. The rule and article of everybody eating equal was waylaid for the time being.

'No rice for Peter Sam,' Dog-Leg would insist. 'He needs bones a-building, Virginia potatoes is the only way.' Devlin, still an Irishman at heart, agreed.

For ten days and nights the quartermaster was apart from the ship, a churchyard spectre haunting the lower decks like Jonah. The rest of them felt he had gone from them now, even more than during his actual absence.

Black Bill Vernon joined Devlin on the quarterdeck, standing at the breastwork rail, looking over the deck at rest, ten days east, heading back to the realm of the Malagasay.

'Stores be low, Cap'n. Need to keep the men hot.' He kept his voice low.

'Good morning to you too, Bill,' Devlin was more jolly than the brooding Sailing Master.

'And what of Peter Sam? Ship needs a quartermaster as well as a captain. If he's lost we should leave him lost and makes us another.'

Devlin rolled his back to the ship, his eyes now over the helm and the wake creaming along behind them. 'Aye. He's had the worst of it. But I saw him back in Charles Town. Saw what he did. Can't think what he might have been through to come to this.' He pushed back his hat and breathed in the salt and sun. 'Some things a man has to chew over a while, Bill.'

'Aye. But all that sailing. Men of ours dead and gone. And for nothing but an empty purse. Coxon with our gold won't lie well.'

Devlin grinned back at the big Scot, 'Sixteenth parallel, Bill. Trade route to the Indies and a war to boot. Back to Madagascar to pick up Will Magnes and the others. Start again. Don't count the days we have yet to live.'

As if in response, as if indeed designed for her captain's mood, the *Shadow* heeled as the scent of a sail caught her bows.

'*Sail! Deck there!*' A joyous cry erupted from the top as a white speck of promise and lading crept along the horizon fore. Devlin let others reach for scopes, he did not have to see her to bring her closer. 'As you said, Bill, purse be low. Have to keep them hot.'

The sound of the hatch opening below drew them both to look over the rail. Dandon appeared and swept off his broad hat to them both and wished them the best of the morning, then stepped aside to let Peter Sam's bald head follow him up.

'I found a man lost below,' Dandon beamed. 'Says he heard a sail, Captain.'

The leather-clad figure stepped onto the deck and men moved away as he touched and fingered stays and wood like beloved books in a library, a tender touch for each as they spoke back to him.

He turned and looked up at the two at the rail studying him, then lowered his head and made for the steps, pulling himself up with arms taut again as they once had been.

'Where away, Cap'n?' he said.

Devlin pointed to the head. 'There,' and he gave him room at the rail. 'The men are slack to move, Peter. They're looking at the sail and blushing like farmers' daughters.'

Peter Sam ran his eyes over the heads staring up at him from below and pushed back Bill and Devlin to fill the space over the deck.

'Are you not hungry, boys!' he bellowed. 'We're going back for old Will to be sure, but we needs timber and rum!' He aimed a fiendish eye at every merry look that shone back at him.

'Make sail, you *hijos de puta*! You sons of whores! All hands, you dogs! Get me down those gallants and God's pity if I see one hole in that canvas! By God I'll give you a hole in your back to match it!' His arm punched towards the white face of one of them. 'Cowrie! I be looking at you lad! Haul, you apes, and bring me some punch! By God I'll scrape the deck with the lot of you! Close up on that slut if you wants to drink tonight!'

A cheer rolled and the deck hammered with the sound of a hundred feet beating to their duty; and Dandon sensibly backed away to the Great Cabin, his swaying elegance in everyone's way.

The helm wheel spun, the yards began to turn. Black Bill gave the order to stand to their prey's forefoot, to cut her off from her path to the colonies. Chase to leeward.

The bow dives. Strakes lean up wet as the *Shadow* heels. Running by the head she cracks the tide sending great sheets of white water over the bowsprit and a song begins to weave along the deck as men bound to their stations.

Weapon lockers are loosed. Gun ports are opened and shot garlands carried to the deck.

Word is given.

A black and calico cloth is brought from below.

> *O'er the glad waters of the dark blue sea,*
> *Our thoughts as boundless, and our souls as free,*
> *Far as the breeze can bear, the billows foam,*
> *Survey our empire, and behold our home!*
> *These are our realms, no limits to their sway,—*
> *Our flag the sceptre all who meet obey.*
> *Ours the wild life in tumult still to range*
> *From toil to rest, and joy in every change.*

> Byron, The Corsair.
> A Tale.

Author's Note

This is the second adventure for Patrick Devlin and if it is your first I hope you have enjoyed it enough to read another. Whereas the first story was very much cut-and-thrust straight-forward pirate lore – treasure map, sword-fights, cannon-fire and lights, camera, action! – I wanted the second to be just as exciting but diverse enough so that it wasn't a mere repetition.

To me the underlying story will always be of the men themselves in a world where freedom was limited to those who could afford it. Perhaps the world hasn't changed all that much.

I have a pirate and he will be a pirate. I assure you at no point will Devlin see the error of his ways or fight the good fight. He will fight for his men, for his right to be free, and, of course, for fortune. If you are reading this book because you love pirates you'll understand. If you're reading it because you love adventure you'll understand. If you're reading it because you love intricate naval fiction and gentlemen pining over women and rising book by book through the ranks, your ship is over there. I'll take my berth on the *Shadow*.

And so on to this story. At first I think the hardest part was trying to say to people, 'It's a pirate story. It's about porcelain.'

Doesn't exactly stir the blood does it?! But to take it in

context you have to try and imagine a world without porcelain. Then try to imagine a world of glass, pottery, gold and pewter drinking vessels and even leather mugs, and then pour a boiling drink into them and hold it in your hand. I don't think it stretches credulity to say that pretty much every ceramics maker in Europe worked feverishly to discover why Chinese porcelain had such properties that their own products did not.

So imagine that you could turn up in that world with a cup that kept cool to the touch. And only you knew how to make it. There's a reason why it was called 'White Gold'.

Early European ceramic makers believed the secret was bone, human or otherwise, crushed and mixed with clay that produced the hardness. Consequently, Bone-China and porcelain are still confused.

The story of the letters of the priest is true, and they did disappear, although in reality when they reappeared the secret was known throughout Europe, and by 1750 European production even outstripped that of China, but the mystery of the letters and the hunger to obtain the secret was enough to fuel my imagination. It really was as valuable and mysterious as the Philosopher's Stone. It's a fascinating subject and I encourage anyone to look into it.

Now, the pirates. Chronologically this story takes place in real history. From the moment Woodes Rogers arrives in the Bahamas the story follows actual events. In fact, with the exception of Devlin and his men (Coxon, Seth and Ignatius etc.), every other major character is real. But I must clarify some details.

Firstly, Woodes Rogers. For purposes of drama I may have painted him to be a bit more ruthless than his biographers would like. He was a great man, but (and I'm sure pirate aficionados would agree) you don't sack cities, capture treasure-ships, get half your jaw blown off, whilst still giving orders holding your face together, without being a bit of a hard bastard. Challenge that if you want.

Rogers remained governor of New Providence until 1721 when he was imprisoned for debt after the insolvency of the company that sent him there. He was given back the office in 1728 after it was resolutely agreed he was the only man for the task. He died in Nassau in 1732. His statement back to Whitehall: 'Piracy expelled, commerce restored' remained the motto of the island until independence in 1973. His statue in Nassau is the only statue of an English governor of the colonies of England portrayed drawing a sword.

Howell Davis. A real pirate, and every pirate fan knows where he ends up and so, no, we haven't heard the last of him. But, my liberty as a writer, in order to work Seth Toombs into the story and to get Devlin to Nassau, was to tweak history and place him with Seth on the *Mumvil*.

In reality Howell turned pirate on the *Buck* when Rogers did actually send the two ships to sloop-trade with the Spanish and he never returned to Providence. I make good on this of course in that Howell leaves Nassau on the *Buck* and into his own future. That closes my circle and fully opens his. We will see Howell again.

Palgrave Williams. One of Sam Bellamy's captains. Yes, a goldsmith, yes, married with children and son of the Attorney General of Rhode Island who in middle-age decided to up-sticks and join Bellamy to become a pirate. He did get off at Block Island before the storm that sunk the *Whydah* and the official salvage of the ship produced exactly as quoted, the final line of which was '. . . and two great guns.' Enter Palgrave Williams to purchase the Chinese gun and get it to New Providence for me.

Palgrave did retire and even married again. A few years later returning to piracy before retiring again. Why would a successful business and family man keep returning to the sea again and again? Risking death by noose in middle-age for a life of adventure and swift reward? I can only assume, not having Palgrave's opinion on the matter, that it is for the same reason that some men today buy motorcycles or sports-cars or take up surfing past a certain age.

Blackbeard. I don't think I could have had a pirate story set in this period without having the most infamous pirate of the time strutting his stage; which is why I also put him in the first book in order to set him up for this one.

His involvement with Governor Eden and Eden's complicity is still a matter of debate and his deliberate or accidental grounding of the *Queen Anne's Revenge* still produces fist-fights amongst pirate historians. He did blockade Charleston and did ask for a chest of medicines for his ransom (he also raided a few ships and had a few thousand pounds' worth of coin) and he never came ashore, but I thought it more romantic and relevant to my story that the chest had purposes other than that his men were riddled with syphilis.

By November 1718, after this story ends, Blackbeard was dead. Hunted down by private purse courtesy of Governor Spotswood despite seemingly having immunity since he first arrived in the Carolinas.

Or then again perhaps he simply knew too much about a Chinese cannon and a bundle of letters. You can never tell with pirates.

Mark Keating. July 2010.